MURDERS OF CONVEYANCE

MURDERS OF CONVEYANCE

By
Jeanne Burrows-Johnson

A Natalie Seachrist Hawaiian Mystery

Artemesia Publishing
Albuquerque, New Mexico

Conveyance...The transference of property from one owner to another...

To Kevin Charles Horstman PhD, who loved and honored family, friends, and the earth that brings Life to all!

CAST OF CHARACTERS

Stan Carrington	Former colleague of Keoni Hewitt
Jason Chin	Honolulu radio personality
Veronica Ching	Restaurateur
Jesse & Jimmy Comacho	Murder victims; cousins
Leah Coombs	Fiancée of Bō Shēn
Esmeralda [Izzy] Cruz	Neighbor of Natalie Seachrist
John [JD] Dias	Lieutenant, Honolulu Police Department
Akira Duncan	Master Chef; owner of a restaurant and culinary school
James Durham	Honolulu Architect
Maria Espinoza	Tenant, Makiki Sunset Apartments
Bertram Fong	Owner of a Chinatown bookstore
Brianna Harriman	Granddaughter of Nathan Harriman; twin of Ariel Harriman who is deceased
Nathan Harriman	Twin brother of Natalie Seachrist; psychologist
Keoni Hewitt	Boyfriend of Natalie Seachrist; retired homicide detective
Alena Horita	Uniformed officer, Honolulu Police Department
Chu-Hua Lee	Amah of Pearl and Jade Wong
Harry Longhorn	Publisher and Chief Editor of *Winward O`ahu Journeys Magazine*
Cory Lowell	Son of a tenant, Makiki Sunset Apartments
Lori Mitchum	Intern at the State of Hawai`i Coroner's Office
Dan and Margie O'Hara	Friends of Natalie Seachrist
Makoa Pane	Contractor and furniture craftsman
Miss Una	Feline companion of Natalie Seachrist
Alec Salinas	Retired police detective; hotel security manager
Natalie Seachrist	Semi-retired journalist

Bàozhǐ Shēn	Granduncle of Bō Shēn; murder victim in 1953
Bō Shēn	Chinatown businessman
Chāng Shēn	Grandfather of Bō Shēn; now deceased
Toitoi Naiporo Shēn	Grandaunt of Bō Shēn; widow of Bàozhǐ Shēn
Martin Soli	Assistant Coroner, State of Hawai`i
Evelyn and Jim Souza	Nathan Harriman's neighbors
Linda Tan	Contestant, Aloha Scavenger Hunt
Samantha Turner	Neighbor of Natalie Seachrist
José Valdez	Assistant to James Durham
Joanne Walther	Neighbor of Natalie Seachrist
Pearl Wong	Co-owner and manager of the Makiki Sunset Apartments
Brian Yamaguchi	Boyfriend of Toitoi Shēn
Fù Hán Zhāng	Murder victim; Chinese linguist

Conveyers of
The Shēn Family Legacy
Beloved Sons and Their Wives

ınli Shēn *ɡreat truth*	*1882* **Marries**	**Lehua Yi** *beloved*
Xiǎochén Shēn *new morning*	*1902* **Marries**	**Lilíng Yang** *plum-tinkling of jade pendants*
Fēng Shēn *wind*	*1920* **Marries**	**Lani Wilcox** *heaven*
Chāng Shēn *prosperous*	*1949* **Marries**	**Zhīlán Ing** *iris orchid*
Bàozhǐ Shēn *full of wisdom*	*1951* **Marries**	**Toitoi Naiporo** *earth*
Kāng Shēn *well-being*	*1979* **Marries**	**Amber Huang** *she knows*
Bō Shēn *precious wave*	___ **Marries**	

PROLOGUE

I met murder on the way.
Percy Bysshe Shelley [1792 - 1822]

I look around at the metal cage surrounding me. Below my sandaled feet are scuffed tiles framing a Chinese logogram. With heavy vibration, the vintage elevator stops. The gate opens by an unseen hand and I walk out to the black and white scene of a film noir.

I face three sash windows, the center one being wider than those flanking it. Above them, is the beginning of three clerestory windows reaching toward the roofline. My view to the world beyond is dimmed by sheer curtains. I look down at a patterned carpet runner on a dark wood floor.

I am presented with an immediate choice. Which way shall I turn? With little hesitation, I move to the right and soon reach the end of the short hallway. I then turn to the left and stop as though halted by a glass panel. I am looking along a dim corridor lined with several numbered doors. Stretched diagonally across the carpeted floor is the still form of a man. I blink and check to see if this tableau is being observed by anyone other than me. No. I am alone.

I walk forward slowly until I stand above the man. He is definitely dead. He wears a white suit. Although he is lying on his stomach, I see the collar of an aloha shirt. Two-toned shoes stick out from his pant leg cuffs. Beyond his head, a fedora leans against the base of the wall.

A few inches to the left of the man's shoes, the door to room 312 stands ajar. The opening widens. I look within. A woman rises from inspecting the space below a single bed. Turned away from me, she examines each drawer of the room's dresser, desk, and nightstand. I suddenly find myself positioned directly behind her as she opens the door to a closet with dressing room. She is obviously practiced in her work. After going through the pockets of the few hanging garments on the left, she quickly searches each compartment of a suitcase sitting open on a luggage rack to the right.

Debating whether she is at the end of her task, she gazes steadily at a large mirror resting against the back wall. The glass is mottled with age and I cannot see her features. She walks to the mirror and pulls it toward her. She looks behind, and then with a disgusted sigh, pushes it back in place. Stepping backward, the woman again looks into the mirror and straightens her tailored skirt and jacket. Other than her dark upswept hair, the only characteristic I note about her is her height, because she is considerably taller than I am.

I watch numbly as the stately woman strides past me and into the bedroom. I turn to face her retreating figure. Shortly, I hear the elevator clang open and shut.

CHAPTER 1

Adventure is worthwhile.
Aristotle [384 BCE - 322 BCE]

An unrelenting yowl demanded my attention. I withdrew from my private showing of the film *noir* and sat up. "All right, I'm awake. What's the problem, girlfriend?" I asked my tortoiseshell companion. "I left you with a full bowl of dry food last night and your usual serving of canned. You can't have finished all of that," I said, dragging myself up to follow Miss Una to the kitchen. There I noted that every morsel had been licked from both plate and bowl.

"If you weren't spayed, I'd suspect you were pregnant."

As I laid down a fresh helping of her favorite salmon, she rushed to devour it. After changing her water and setting out her usual supply of dry food to nibble throughout the day, I pleaded for a return to our normal routine. "Now, that should keep you satisfied until tonight when you're going to have to make do with Izzy's scrumptious goodies."

With an adventure in the offing, I turned to my own needs. I was glad there was just enough coffee syrup to meet my desire for an intake of caffeine, and equally glad that I did not have to share it with my sweetheart Keoni who had spent the night at his home in Mānoa Valley. For Christmas he had given me a French coffee press. I have discovered that the resulting rich extract delivers the smoothest beverage—hot or cold. Since we were in what passes for winter in the Hawaiian Islands, I was ready for the heated variety.

Soon I was seated at my parents' old Formica table, where I

enjoyed a leisurely breakfast of fresh papaya from our neighbor Izzy, and the last piece of cake my grandniece Brianna brought us from the Oʻhana Hawaiian Café in Portland, Oregon, during her holiday break from college. People may laugh at my savoring an Island treat from the mainland, but Sandie's desserts are a special treat. She uses freshly roasted macadamia nuts in her pie crusts and on top of some of her cakes!

I checked my voicemail while sipping a second cup of coffee. The recording announced it was Friday the thirteenth of February—my lucky number. I took that as a sign of good fortune for our participation in the forthcoming First Annual Aloha Scavenger Hunt. Keoni and I would be staying in the heart of Honolulu with friends for the week-long event, so it was good I had no messages—especially from publishers with writing assignments for me.

Of course, it was possible that the hunt might yield a tale or two worth telling. I could not wait to partake of the *lūʻau*, Chinese New Year feast, and other meals planned for the event. The locales and their taste treats could be good material for my food and entertainment column in *Windward Oʻahu Journeys* magazine!

Glancing at a memo on the refrigerator, I was reminded of how thoughtful Keoni is—and almost as note-driven as I am. We have been together as a couple for over a year and have developed a routine that nurtures each of us in this new phase of life. We first met when he was a detective with the Honolulu Police Department. We became truly close when I experienced an unexpected tragedy a year and a half ago, shortly after I took early retirement from my career as a journalist and occasional television presenter for an international media corporation.

I had been enjoying the freedom of selecting my research and writing assignments and was delighted when he asked me to undertake a research project. Tragically, Brianna's twin sister Ariel was murdered the next day, and I do not know how I would have survived if I had not had his backing. During that experience, we became intimate on many levels. By Thanksgiving, we were a couple. We were living together a couple of months later when my Auntie Carrie died and I inherited White Sands Cottage in Lanikai.

I knew I should be preparing for our departure, but it felt so nice to savor the moment. I carried my cup of coffee into the living room and sat down on my mother's old *pūne`e*. The room had benefited from months of remodeling. The art I had acquired during my world travels and Keoni's distinctive *koa* furniture were ideal additions to my aunt's classic Hawaiian furnishings and paintings.

After moving to the cottage, we immediately became friends with our neighbors across the fence. The owner of Mokulua Hale was Miriam Didión, a retired human rights activist and psychologist. Her housemates were retired teacher Joanne Walther and Esmerelda [Izzy] Cruz, who had been the housekeeper of Miriam and her husband. When Miriam mentioned needing a live-in housekeeper since Izzy had developed rheumatoid arthritis, my twin brother Nathan offered to locate potential candidates as he is a psychologist and former director of Hale Malolo, a women's shelter. This was how Samantha Turner, a young woman in a failing marriage became the fourth person to join our neighbor's household.

Sadly, tragedy inserted itself into our lives again. Miriam was murdered just as we were adjusting to life in this welcoming beachside community. Dismayed by the dramatic loss of their friend, The Ladies, as we refer to Miriam's housemates, rallied to support one another. Both Keoni and I have experienced many sorrows in our lives; being together eased our acceptance of this tragedy.

The benefits of our new surroundings also fortified our adjustments to our new lifestyle. We celebrate the fruits of our years of labor with long soaks in the hot tub and daily walks along the nearby white sands beach. And, at the end of our varied daily activities, we frequently join with The Ladies for potluck meals. The delicious dishes Izzy prepares from the bounty of Joanne's garden are often paired with the wine and delicatessen treats we provide.

Despite being nominally retired, Keoni has expanded Hewitt

Investigations. Through liaison with a national security firm, he now accepts assignments to analyze security systems for small businesses. He maintains his bungalow in Mānoa for times he needs to meet clients in the evening—or for breaks during a stakeout. My own schedule is quite flexible since I am a free-lance writer. My latest project is a magazine article featuring a gourmet cooking school founded by Akira Duncan, a *hapa* Japanese-French chef noted for gastronomic delights of the Pacific Rim.

Inspired by what I learned from the man's biographical information, and the amazing food Izzy produces, I have decided to broaden my meager culinary abilities. It seems only fair to use the exquisite kitchen Keoni designed and helped construct. So, without letting anyone know my plans, I am going to check out Chef Duncan's school personally as well as professionally. I have already looked over the curriculum and am thinking of signing up for the course on cooking basics. Aside from tips on food shopping and kitchen organization, it will teach me the proper use of knives. You never know when a girl will need a skill like that.

The course does not start for a couple of weeks and I have some lead time until the deadline for my article. Therefore, Keoni and I are extending our celebration of St. Valentine's Day to embrace a full week of fun and romance by competing in the scavenger hunt which coincides with Chinese New Year. The hunt is sponsored by a conglomeration of non-profits aiding women and children, including Hale Malolo. A notable feature of the event is that contestants can designate which member organization will receive a percentage of their entry fees.

We can participate since Nathan is no longer serving on Hale Malolo's board. As winners of the early entry prize drawing, Keoni and I will be enjoying a week at the luxurious downtown hotel serving as the hunt's headquarters. Certain that the hunt would appeal to a variety of people, I emailed the promotional information to friends who have enjoyed holidays with me during my overseas assignments.

Most were recovering from the rush of the holidays. But

Margie and Dan O'Hara immediately replied that they would come. That pleased me specially, since they had last visited the Islands at the time of Keoni's birthday party and we did not get to socialize after Miriam's funeral. My friendship with the couple goes back to the short period in which Dan served with my husband Bill in the U.S. Navy. They have remained my lifeline in many ways since Bill's death from encephalitis during a six-month deployment to the Western Pacific.

I glanced at the clock and saw that I needed to stop my reminiscing and finish getting ready for our late afternoon departure. I realized I had not given The Ladies a key to the new lock on the back door. They would be watching over the cottage and Miss Una and I wanted to ensure they had everything they might need. Thankfully, Izzy was home when I called so I dashed through our back gates to deliver a key.

Although we would be driving against the flow of afternoon traffic, we needed to leave as soon as possible. So, by the time Keoni returned, I had tidied the house, taken out the trash, and shut my single suitcase. I greeted him with a kiss and a glass of strong sun tea with cinnamon, cloves, and orange peel. We chatted briefly while he downed his tea and an energy bar. He then showered, dressed, and completed his packing. As he wrapped a light shawl that had been my Auntie Carrie's across my shoulders, we looked down at his two suitcases, laptop and briefcase alongside my single suitcase and carryall.

"You haven't packed much. Do you have everything you'll need?"

"We're only going for a week, dear. Perhaps your other girlfriends were big on luggage, but with all my years on the road, I'm a minimalist when it comes to travel. One suitcase, a carryall, and one small handbag for evenings on the town. I think that covers it, don't you?"

"Well, that philosophy will certainly make international travel easy."

"I'm glad you approve, sir. Now let's hit the road."

"Final check: The Ladies have keys to the house, know the security system, and where I keep the keys to my truck?" Keoni asked with a smile.

"Yes," I nodded. "Most importantly, they know Miss Una's routine and where all her food and goodies are. I just hope the supply of food holds out. All of a sudden, that cat has more than doubled her intake," I noted.

"I don't think Izzy would allow anyone to go hungry—certainly not your precious baby."

"You're right about that. And as a second-generation cook-to-order chef, she's likely to create an entire line of cat cuisine delights while we're gone," I added.

Izzy is the only one of Miriam's Ladies who is from the Islands. I had thought she was of purely Filipina background, but recently I learned the diminutive woman's mother was Portuguese. At the time her parents married, there was much less mixing of ethnicities. Her maternal grandmother had not been pleased when her granddaughter married a short man with little education who worked his entire life as a fry cook in a diner. I, for one, benefited from the results of that union, since the delicacies created by Izzy greatly enrich my daily life.

Keoni grinned. "Who knows what Joanne might contribute from the garden—aside from the catnip I saw her planting the other day."

Joanne came to her love of all things horticultural late in life. She journeyed throughout the world before arriving in Hawai'i, but sometimes I hear a hint of the South in her voice. I recently learned that she comes from a poor Creole family in rural Louisiana. After escaping her limited prospects, she joined the Army and eventually used the benefits of the G.I. Bill to earn a bachelor's degree in education. Returning to government service, she became a teacher for military families. In addition to providing the neighborhood with luscious fruits and vegetables, she inspires our youth as a volunteer photography instructor.

At that point Keoni got a call. His Bluetooth system kicked in and I heard Samantha Turner's voice. While she clarified details of the work she would be performing for him during our absence, I thought about how we know her.

After being an abused wife of a man noted for sordid business dealings, Samantha had been delighted to join the loving circle of women that welcomed her to Mokulua Hale. And although she was not originally one of Miriam's Ladies, being present at the time of the psychologist's death also awarded her lifetime occupancy of their benefactor's home. Now, in addition to helping us with odds and ends that arise in our individual work, she is looking forward to a full-time career and is studying European languages and international business.

Within a few minutes we were pulling up at the front of our hotel. I dropped Keoni with our luggage and opted for self-parking, since the scavenger hunt might require access to rapid transportation. When I entered the lobby, I saw that Keoni had already checked us in. He was visiting with someone near a huge pot filled with blooming *ki* plants.

"Natalie, I'd like you to meet Alec Salinas. You could say we spent a lot of our misbegotten youth together. We both attended Queen Lili'uokalani Elementary, served as MPs in Nam, and entered the police academy together."

"Nice to meet another survivor of Keoni's working life," I said, extending my hand.

"The pleasure's mine," replied the scarecrow of a man.

The two men may be the same age, but it appeared that life had been less kind to Alec. Although his jacket fitted his body as though it had been tailored for him, he was completely white haired and hunched, as well as skinny. When he clasped my hand with his left, I realized he was missing a couple of fingers on his right hand.

"Those were the glory days, my friend. After that, I moved to the Big Island for a couple of decades of alternating rhythms. Between the slow pace of upcountry policing in Waimea and the hustle of tourist-driven Kailua-Kona, I had the ideal balance—until a little run in with a man piloting a plane-load of contraband ended life as I knew it."

"I don't think anyone would say you slept through any of your career," responded Keoni.

Alec shrugged and rolled his eyes. "I'd better get back to writing some reports. One nice thing about this gig is that I don't have to be dexterous. I can use voice recognition software for most of my paperwork. You two enjoy yourselves. Here's my card if you need anything."

In a moment, we were alone in the elevator. Keoni squeezed my waist and leaned into me for a kiss.

"Hey, where's the luggage?" I asked.

"Already taken care of. That's the beauty of a full-service hotel. I checked in and the bellman took everything away. By now it should all be in our suite."

We soon arrived at the door of our suite. Keoni popped in his entry card and passed a second one to me. I have not taken any trips since retiring and had never been in this hotel. But I could tell we were going to be comfortable in this suite featuring a coffee bar, five-strand cane furniture, and lithographs of classic paintings by Paul Gauguin and maps drawn by James Cook.

"Mm, there's even a kitchenette with a rice cooker. I think I could get used to this kind of compact living," I said gleefully.

Calling from the bathroom, Keoni added his acknowledgement of the value of our prize. "If you think you like the kitchen, wait until you see the Jacuzzi tub."

We then played house for a while, arranging our clothing and toiletries. "You may not have brought much clothing, but you certainly didn't stint on the bottles and jars," he laughed while fanning his hand across the bathroom counter.

"Well, this is our first getaway and I want to make the most of our rendezvous with romance. Especially tonight, since we're alone."

"Promises, promises. And now my dear, how about a little champagne to christen our week in the big city. If you'll look in the refrigerator, I believe you'll find a little something has been dropped off by Ben."

"That neighbor of yours really gets around," I commented, moving quickly to open the refrigerator. "Oh, my...Pierre Gimonnet Champagne Brut...Blanc De Blancs. And who made the choice of this fine wine?"

"I did. And I'll have you know I even did a bit of research. Balanced with floral and fruit notes and a crisp finish."

"Sounds like a heavenly assurance of the evening to come," I replied.

"That was the idea. One thing though, let's not get too comfortable. Alec suggested we check out the hotel's facilities, including the restaurant and lounge on the top floor."

"All right. Although I thought we might live it up and dial room service for dinner."

"Great minds think alike. Alec said the restaurant handles room service. They've got superb seafood. They even have Maine lobster flown in once a week. On Fridays. It's the one night the business crowd hangs around town after work. We may need to place our order before the kitchen runs out. Not that I mean to force you into eating lobster."

"You did say *Maine* lobster? I haven't had that for several years. Why don't we order our dinner at the restaurant during our tour?" I suggested, anticipating treats of many kinds.

While sharing a single glass of bubbly, we looked over the hotel's comprehensive album outlining their amenities. The only decision we had to make was whether to go upstairs or down. After slipping into our sandals and closing the door, we decided to check out the first-floor shops and spa prior to enjoying the lounge.

Keoni was patient as I salivated at high-end jewelry and handbags. I tried to be as kind while he contemplated aloha shirts and kangaroo leather hats. When we entered the doors of the spa, we were greeted by a team of one man and one woman—obviously wanting to ensure that each guest felt welcome. Upon learning we were locals on a tight schedule, they eased up on what I was sure was normally a prolonged pitch for the many services we could experience.

Back in the elevator, I announced the one spa service I would truly appreciate. That evening. Delivered not by the hands of a stranger, but those of the man I love.

"Happy to ease your stress, my dear," responded Keoni with a leer. "Will that be now, or do you want to complete the tour?"

"It's a difficult choice, but I guess as long as we're upright with shoes on, we might as well continue exploring our temporary home," I said with a sigh.

Never one to ignore an opportunity to assure me of his affection, Keoni pulled me to him and planted a kiss on my brow. He had just straightened up when the elevator doors opened on a crowd of business men and women who looked like they had been enjoying an early round of TGIF liquid delight.

Within a few moments, we were seated at a table overlooking the city and the ocean. Knowing we would be enjoying a private dinner in our room, I ignored the *pūpū* menu, and simply nibbled at the mix of nuts and dried fruit the waiter set in front of us.

"I don't usually play tourist, but I haven't had a Mai Tai in years. What kind of rum do you use?" I asked the young man serving us.

"As a *connoisseur,* I can say you'll be pleased with our signature Mai Tai which includes Coruba Jamaican rum, Amoretti Orgeat almond syrup, Giffard curaçao liqueur, and lime juice."

"That sounds divine," I said.

"The only catch is that I may end up having to finish the champagne by myself," observed Keoni with a sparkle in his beautiful blue eyes. "It's a good thing I'm going to stick with the classic iced tea served with a spear of pineapple for now."

Recognizing the potency of the drink I had ordered, I began eating the house nut mix in earnest. "This is really good."

"I'm glad you're getting a little protein to go with the liquor, but don't overdo the snacking if you want to appreciate your dinner."

"Yes, Daddy. I'll have you know that in anticipation of tonight, I restrained myself from eating much today. Besides, we've got a refrigerator for storing any leftovers."

"Good point, dear."

Soon we had consumed our drinks and eaten a full bowl of the nut mix. After settling our bill, we moved next door to look over the restaurant. As I glanced through the menu, I realized that the restaurant was owned by the chef who had opened the culinary school I would be writing about. Since it was Friday, there was no deliberating on what I would order for dinner.

Upon returning to our suite, we moved into the bathroom for one of our favorite pastimes—a long relaxing steamy shower for two. By the time dinner arrived an hour later, I was attired in one of the fluffiest bathrobes I had worn outside of a five-star hotel in Europe. With Keoni wearing swim trunks and a T-shirt, it seemed prudent to let him answer the door.

When I heard the waiter leave, I came out to find a lovely setting on the table in front of the sliders leading to the *lānai*. We began our feast with halves of artichoke stuffed with crab and then shared a Caesar salad. In addition to one entrée of lobster and another of grilled `ahi*, we relished a medley of wild rice and quinoa with slivers of Maui onion and asparagus.

"Well, honey, welcome to my world. At least the world I knew as a leisure journalist. I know it may not be the blast you and the guys have when you go deep sea fishing, but what do you think?" I inquired extending my glass for a refill.

"Now this is a form of R & R I could get used to—on a regular basis," said Keoni.

"I agree, sweetheart. With a potential trip to Japan on the horizon, I'm glad I've maintained my travel industry contacts. I'll see what I can come up with for a party of four—unless your old HPD buddy Stan Carrington and his girlfriend Tamiko have better connections in Sapporo. When's the last time you spoke to Stan?

"I haven't talked to him since my birthday party, but I think I would have heard if he and Tamiko had broken up. He's always been one for sharing the big moments in his life...not always just the good ones."

"Here's a toast to romantic relationships...and continuing journeys of interest," I said.

After that, we filled a couple of glasses with the sun tea we had brought from home and went out on the *lānai* to enjoy the twilight sky. Later we settled in for a private film festival.

"What are you in the mood for?" queried my sweetheart.

"I'm game for most anything. Last night I had a funny dream from an old black and white movie. I just can't remember which one."

"Sounds like fun, but don't look to me for titles. I've probably watched them all, but I never remember the details—except for a classic like *Casablanca,* which I think would be a bit of a downer tonight. What kind of plot did your mental movie have?"

"It was a whodunit: a dead guy in a hotel hall; a woman going through his belongings."

"Intriguing. I don't know how we could figure out what its title is, so we'll just pick something that looks interesting. If we're lucky, we'll see *your* film."

For several minutes, we clicked through the movie guide. "Here's a classic. How about we begin our evening with *The Maltese Falcon*?" offered Keoni, pulling me closer. Little did we realize the events that would flow from our night at the movies.

CHAPTER 2

The joys of meeting pay the pangs of absence...
Nicholas Rowe [1674 - 1718]

It may not sound like a romantic opening to St. Valentine's Day, but Keoni and I started our first morning in the hotel with a simple breakfast of Kona coffee and bagels with macadamia nut butter. While sitting on the *lānai*, we looked over our packet of information about the scavenger hunt. Like many events in the Islands, the entry fees we had paid were inclusive. Every evening we were to receive two cocktails and *pūpūs*. There would also be a *lū`au*, Chinese New Year dinner, and banquet to award the grand prize.

"I've never been on a scavenger hunt," I noted. "But I've found there's one common factor among the people who have. They're the same ones who like car rallies."

"I hear you. I knew one guy who was really into scavenger hunts. He fit the profile you've mentioned perfectly. Loved anything to do with cars...muscle cars, that is. He was thrilled any time he could bring out one of his vintage babies—at least until one hunt took him out to some old sugar cane fields and he got stuck in a ditch and scraped the body of his high-performance cobra jet Grand Torino. After that he steered clear of any events that weren't held on paved surfaces. The only other guy I knew who loved scavenger hunts went on one because it beat sitting around listening to his wife's parents talking about her old boyfriends on Thanksgiving."

"I think this scavenger hunt is going to be somewhat different than other ones I've heard about. It's not really timed, other than different tasks on each day; and there are numerous references to Hawaiian culture and history."

"I noticed that. I think it's good that I was born here and you're a wiz at research. I don't see how mainlanders like Margie and Dan O'Hara could compete in the hunt without local assistance," Keoni said.

"It may not be an even playing field for non-residents, but the organizers would be foolish to limit participation to locals. If they're smart, contestants from off-island will team up like we're doing—you know, based on their knowledge of the area and individual skill sets. I just hope everyone has such a good time that the event is successful and becomes an annual affair. It would be a great way to gain funding for those suffering from domestic violence...and the hunt will bring media attention to the cause."

"I'm sure everything will work out. Let's just enjoy the week. With our free lodgings, we're already winners," observed Keoni.

"You're right. Say, I was wondering, how many movies did we watch last night? I remember *The Maltese Falcon*, but after that my memory's a bit fuzzy."

"You made it through two films. The second one was *The Thin Man*. I stayed conscious halfway through a third. It was some Charlie Chan movie. I think it was set in Shànghǎi. It's nice that some of those old movies are so short."

After we enjoyed our usual morning shower, we took a walk through the bustling downtown area surrounding the hotel. We were then ready to host our out-of-town guests. Since Margie works part-time for a travel agency, she gets fabulous deals on transportation, hotels, and even entertainment. This time it looked like they would be getting full value for their trouble.

Riding up in the elevator to the hotel's top floor lounge, I thought about the many trips I have enjoyed with friends and family through my career in travel journalism. London and Paris may sound the most romantic to many people. But taking in New Year's Eve in New York, the Parade of Ships during Fleet Week in San Francisco, or Rose Festival Week in Portland, Oregon, were more likely to draw companions to my side. It was not just the difference in cost. Domestic events allow for short side trips with the ability to move freely without the hassle of passports.

"So, Natalie, how does it feel to be back on the leeward side of the island?"

Coming out of my reverie, I paused to think. "Well, it's not like downtown Honolulu was ever my home, so I probably won't be joining John Denver in singing 'It's good to be back home again'. But I think our plans for the week have the earmarks of a pleasurable getaway. We're together, sharing time with two of my oldest friends, and about to embark on an unpredictable adventure. Who could ask for more?"

Keoni quickly replied. "I agree with your sentiments. I'm looking forward to playing tourist for a few days. Who knows how much of O`ahu we'll be exploring. As to the perks of being in *this* neighborhood, if I have to check in with a client, I'm within walking distance of most of them."

"Don't even think of pulling that on me. Hewitt Investigations is on hold for a few days. You've always said you can take off whenever you want to go on a fishing trip."

"That was before my marriage to corporate America. Now I'm a very popular guy with the jacket-over-the-aloha-shirt set!"

"For this week, you're *my* very popular guy. Are you already forgetting that we told Stan Carrington we'll join him for that trip to Japan next year? How are we going to manage a trip to the Sapporo Snow Festival if you can't take a short holiday on O`ahu?"

"Point taken. I've finished hooking my clients into their new security systems, so unless they're hit by some nasty guys with evil intentions, we should be fine. I've got my tablet to monitor any minor problems."

"That all sounds great—as long as you don't end up wired to your electronics all week."

Lifting his glass of Weasel Boy Ale, he said, "I hereby pledge that I will be in the moment throughout the week, okay?"

"Okay."

I then looked up and saw Margie and Dan standing in the

doorway looking across the room.

"*E komo mai*," I called out as Keoni stood to welcome them.

Dan was wearing a pair of slacks and what looked like a vintage Tori Richards aloha shirt in a blue and white leaf pattern. Being about five feet ten inches, he was the ideal height for partnering with Margie's five foot seven inches on the dance floor. And being as slim as she is, she fits perfectly into his arms. On this day she was wearing a cool halter top sundress in tie-dyed purple cotton, with a pair of wedge sandals that did not look suited to fox trotting.

"At last! We're finally together for a bit of fun in Honolulu," she declared, with a broad smile lighting her freckled face.

After a round of hugging and kissing, we settled down for appetizers of blackened `ahi and fresh crackle bread with humus.

"I don't know about you two, but I could go for several rounds of delectable treats this evening. How about we head over to Chinatown?" proposed Dan.

"Funny you should mention that destination. It's only a couple of blocks from here. I'm sure we'll all be able to find something *delectable* at Duc's Bistro," suggested Keoni.

"That doesn't sound like a Chinese restaurant," observed Dan. "You know a good Chinese dinner is one of the few things I asked for this week."

"We haven't forgotten your request. But in honor of St. Valentine's Day, we're going to treat you to one of the best restaurants you'll find anywhere," I said. "For over twenty years it's offered classic Vietnamese as well as French cuisine in a romantic setting. You know it wouldn't have lasted that long if it wasn't satisfying to our Asian residents."

"Honey, I'm sure the appetizer menu will have dishes you'll recognize. We can share a couple of entrées, so you'll feel you've had some variety," consoled Margie.

Soon we were walking into the bistro. Early for our reservation, we sat at the central bar where we could view the two rooms of diners enjoying a variety of delicacies. The ambience was romantic. In honor of the day, red was the accent color in linens and flowers. There was just enough light to appreciate the shadows cast by vases of golden cypress branches from Vietnam and settings of sparkling china and glassware on crisp linens. The music at the grand piano featured show tunes from Broadway. I did not see Duc, but since we were eating during the early service, he was probably checking on his noteworthy pastries and other desserts.

Rather than having cocktails, we decided to share a bottle of Louis Jadot Pouilly-Fuisse with our prawns served with a shrimp *coulis*. With the flowing serenade of the piano, we were definitely under the spell of Cupid by the time we were seated at our table. To begin our meal, we had a second bottle of the Pouilly-Fuisse and a variety of appetizers. The four of us shared Kobe beef *tartare*, blue crab cakes in herbed thermidor sauce, escargot in Chablis wine sauce, and spring rolls, with minced veal and mushrooms.

"Do you remember our celebration of your fiftieth birthday?" I asked.

Margie smiled broadly. "What an adventure that was. Dan was on a fishing expedition to Alaska with some of his navy buddies and I decided to drag you along on a dream vacation to the Banff Summer Arts Festival in Alberta, Canada.

Keoni looked questioningly at Dan.

"Yeah, don't blame me for the timing. I would have cancelled the trip when I realized I'd miss your birthday—but you told me to go ahead since Jay had already paid for the excursion."

I picked up the story again. "It was a real girls' escape. We enjoyed high teas, tours of gardens, and visits to art museums and galleries with a local friend who had recently retired from a successful career in television. The weather was ideal, and the hotel's amenities were superb. Best of all, the work of the fine artists, musicians, and performers was everything that had been promised in the promotional literature.

"Margie, obviously you didn't miss me at all," Dan quipped. Holding up the expansive menu, he asked, "So, what shall we have next?"

While he and Margie chose tomato and lobster bisque, Keoni

had a salad of greens and apples dressed with balsamic vinegar, walnuts and goat cheese. Suspecting I would splurge on dessert, I had a simple salad of avocado and papaya with vinaigrette.

By this point, we might have been better off to share a couple of the exquisite entrées, but we were in such a festive mood that we considered every course available.

"The rest of you can enjoy whatever you want," announced Dan. "I've been looking forward to a grand Chinese meal, so I'm going to have the duck breast sauced with Grand Marnier, and topped with orange slices."

"I doubt that this will be end of the evening, so I'm going to have Mekong River bass sautéed in a lemon-butter sauce topped with Spanish capers."

Keoni turned to me. "Well, you know I'm going to have my usual, the rack of lamb with a Bordeaux laced *chivry* sauce.

"I hate to be equally predictable, but there's a reason why the *paella* is popular with our Island Portuguese population. I've seldom had any as delicious as Duc's recipe of shellfish and filet of fish simmered in a saffron broth."

There was little food on our plates when the waiter returned with the special St. Valentine's Day dessert menu. While we pondered our choices, we enjoyed a rich roast of decaffeinated Kona coffee and listened to the captivating voice of singer Rachel Gonzales. Known for her captivating renditions of jazz classics, her repertoire that evening offered soothing songs of love.

"I thought I was saving room for dessert, but I don't think I can eat any of this by myself. Why don't we share a few spoonfuls of crème brulée with splashes of an accompanying glass of crème de cassis," Margie suggested to Dan.

"I actually think we should follow suit," said Keoni "You pick whatever you want, my dear.

"Now there's a superb idea. And I know the perfect end to both of our meals—the pastry chef's tart with Maui strawberries drizzled with chocolate.

By the time we left the bistro, the men's wallets were lighter, but all of our spirits were soaring. Walking back to the hotel, I thought about how seldom people pay attention to the varied resources in their cities. I had spent several years as a child and much of my adult life as an on-again-off-again resident of Honolulu. That's why I was surprised to feel like a tourist in the center of the city. I have to admit that my usual interaction with the area has been limited to popping into Chinatown to pick up *leis* on Mauna Kea Street and hitting the open market for fresh vegetables, fruit and fish.

Margie's obvious pleasure with our surroundings reminded me of a friend who had recently gone to work on a cruise liner. During a break in her oceanic adventures, Penelope Jones and I had dashed from shop to shop in Chinatown. Although she had given up her apartment and was living aboard the ship, she enjoyed visually sampling the many collectibles of rosewood furnishings, china figurines and curios of varied materials. Her favorite stop was a jeweler's that offered new and vintage piec es. I wondered whether she still enjoyed the necklace she had purchased of carved serpentine and rose jade.

As we lingered behind the men to window shop, Margie broke into my thoughts. "Oh, Natalie, this is so exciting. I can't wait to do some shopping here in Chinatown later this week. I'm finally converting one of the kids' old rooms to a girl's oasis, and some of what I've seen here will really give my project a kick-start."

Apparently, while I had purged as many dust collectors as I could, before moving into Auntie Carrie's home, Margie has been gearing up for a new phase of acquisition.

"How does Dan view your little project?" I asked.

"After all the moves I made for him during his years in the Navy, and the fact that he always had to have an office of his own, he knows better than to question my special room. In fact, I think he's looking forward to having all my sewing, craft, and scrapbooking supplies out of his way."

"I guess that makes it a win-win. I've been lucky that Keoni and I have similarly eclectic tastes. And with his growing skills in remodeling, we've managed to bring everything into the twenty-first century, while remaining faithful to the cottage's origins. At the moment, we're working on some embellishments for the house's woodwork. You remember the horror of Miriam's murder last summer?"

"Yes. It was unbelievable that she was killed on the night we met her," responded Margie.

"Well, at the time her murderer was trying to correct his mistake, Keoni and his friend Makoa were nearby harvesting an *alahe'e* tree. Since then, the guys have joined up on several woodworking projects. Keoni has been shaping cornices and brackets for some of our craftsman cabinetry. Best of all, we got a really long and thick slab of wood for a new mantle in the living room and a top for the built-in credenza in the dining room. Unless I push for one of those endless swimming pools, I think we're at the end of playing house beautiful," I declared.

Dan sniggered. "Along with your PI business, it doesn't sound much like semi-retirement."

Margie talked right over him. "I'm so happy for you. We've been in the same house for over ten years. There's nothing historical about our ranch-style home, so there's nothing to preserve. In fact, I'm afraid it's almost time to refreshen everything."

"Let us know if you need any help. I can load a couple of suitcases with any curios you don't buy on this trip, and Keoni can pack his favorite tools."

The doorman greeted us with his usual *bonhomie* when the four of us returned to our hotel. Soon Keoni and I were standing on our *lānai* enjoying the lights of the city. It was the perfect end to a St. Valentine's Day celebration of love—both romantic and fraternal. I felt like Keoni and I were kids out on prom night thinking about the future. I was appreciative of the luxuriously ambiguous mix of security and abandon I felt with Keoni.

Snuggled in the arms of my beloved, I experienced no dreams that night and awoke in a very relaxed mood.

"Are you ready to take on the scavenger hunt?" Keoni asked, bringing cups of tea to the bedroom.

I yawned and thought about whether I really wanted to get up. "I guess so, but with the comfort of this suite and your attentiveness, it's a good thing we don't have to dash off on task one this morning," I replied.

We checked in with Margie and Dan mid-morning. This would be our last free day for a while, so we decided to venture into Waikīkī. I played chauffeur since I knew the layout of the area the best. Although we did not have reservations anywhere, Keoni called a friend and was able to book a table for brunch at the Moana Hotel's Veranda at the Beach House.

When we joined Margie and Dan in the lobby of our hotel, Keoni declared, "If we keep up the fine dining, I'll lose the edge I've gained in restricting my caloric intake the last couple of years."

"Don't worry. I think we're going to be burning a lot of those calories this week," I countered.

"And all that exercise actually begins today. Unlike a lot of downtown areas, the shops in Waikīkī will be open today," said Margie with expectation.

"Oh, swell, I can't wait to pay for excess baggage when we leave," groaned Dan.

"There's no reason to think about that. I'll just have any-thing I buy shipped home. It should all be waiting for us by the time we walk in the door," answered Margie.

Saving time and energy, I drove under the *porte cochère* at the Moana Hotel and turned the car over to the valet. We were soon seated along the veranda's railing overlooking the ocean. By the time we joined the line at the breakfast buffet, we were hungry and glad there was a variety of choice dishes. At the end, I treated my taste buds to an entire slice of the silky three-layer coconut cake, with *haupia* filling—no sharing for me that day.

As we fortified ourselves for our stroll through tourist land, I thought about how ideal the scavenger hunt was for a couples' holiday. There would be action-packed days, wining and dining during the moonlit hours, and just enough time for rest ...of one type or another. As I looked at the mass of people enjoying the beach, I noticed there were few surfers in the calm waters.

"I have a feeling the serious surfers are out at the Banzai Pipeline today," I said.

"I don't know where they get the energy for all that work," commented Dan. "My idea of a good vacation focuses on more sedentary activities."

"That's not how you felt when we were stationed in Perth, Australia. You couldn't wait for weekends and holidays to get in a bit of surfing," responded Margie.

"Ah youth, how sweet it was," summed up Keoni.

"I may not be young anymore, but I wouldn't want to go back in time for anything. I'm just glad that we're together now and ready for some fun," I added.

After zigzagging through the galleries and shops of the Hilton Hawaiian Village, we returned to the Moana Hotel and hopped in my car for the short ride back downtown. Keoni and I were tired by the time we returned to our hotel suite and decided to take a short siesta prior to the launch party for the scavenger hunt.

When we joined Margie and Dan that evening, the banquet room was crowded. We had to stand in a long line to get drinks from the open bars dotting the room. Considering the number of people attending the event, we were lucky to get seats together near the front of the room. Set for multiple presentations, the long banquet tables were angled to maximize visibility of a huge screen behind the podium.

"Aloha!" boomed the *basso* voice of Jason Chin, whom I recognized from local radio and television commercials. "If I may have your attention, it's time to open the First Annual Aloha Scavenger Hunt. Please refresh your drinks and help yourselves to the buffet tables on either side of the room. In about ten minutes, I'll explain how you can win one of the daily and grand prizes we'll be awarding."

We then filled our plates with *hors d`oeurvres* that outshone many dinner parties I have attended. After we were seated, Jason Chin took clear command of the stage. He described himself as one of the Hunt organizers and our host for the five-day event. He then introduced the CEOs of the participating nonprofits and donors of the numerous prizes that would be awarded. Most of the speakers had brought pictures or video to highlight their talks, so the program was interesting as well as informative. Unfortunately, to avoid compromising security, they could only show blurred images of kids at play and interior shots of the homes where at-risk women and their *keikis* are sheltered. Nevertheless, after learning of the goals and accomplishments of the organizations, I felt validated in my decision to enter the hunt.

"Now that you understand the underpinnings of our member organizations, I want to note that our scavenger hunt is designed differently than others you may have participated in. You see, our goal is to challenge both your mental acumen and your knowledge of O`ahu. If you will open the envelopes you received upon checking in, you can follow the key points of our contest.

"Each day there will be one or more tasks for you to accomplish. As promised, in addition to first-place awards for completing daily tasks, a grand prize will be awarded at the end of the hunt. Tomorrow morning, we will meet here for distribution of the first clues. Hawai`i is the Aloha State for many reasons. Foremost is the spirit of welcome our people extend to family, friends, and visitors. Accordingly, our first event encourages participants to join together in accomplishing the day's tasks. I assure you that no one will lose anything by this teamwork and the partnership does not have to remain permanent.

"As advertised, our challenges will draw on both your common sense and knowledge of Hawai`i's history and multi-ethnic culture. I must warn you that you may need to draw on your math skills to reach your goals. To kick off our event, we want to extend a special welcome to our off-island and out-of-state visitors. We again ask our local contestants to join with our guests for at least tomorrow's challenges.

"Let's adjourn officially and take some time to get acquainted. Before you leave, I encourage you to pick up one of the packets of promotional pamphlets, fliers, and brochures from the table at the back wall. The information contained within will introduce myriad aspects of our island to you. Please note that each of the clues in our hunt is related to one or more of the sites and venues referenced in these materials. In addition, the discounts and coupons should enhance your enjoyment of our island's food and entertainment venues.

"Please eat, drink, and enjoy yourselves this evening. I'll

see you all here at seven-thirty tomorrow morning for a brief continental breakfast, before we kick off our First Annual Aloha Scavenger Hunt."

It was not surprising that Keoni and Dan collected two copies of everything being offered. Clearly the promotional information would provide direct hints to scavenger hunt clues. Meanwhile, Margie and I spoke with Nathan and a couple of members of the Board of Hale Mahalo. It was good to see my twin smiling and chatting with Adriana Gonzalez, a beautiful Indian-Portuguese woman whom I knew was a consulting physician for the women's shelter. Since Ariel's death, there have been few times when I have seen my twin look this relaxed and happy.

Glancing across the room, it was easy to identify the tourists, as they were intently earmarking the numerous specials and coupons featured in the evening's handouts. After a brief consultation with Keoni, we decided to scope out the competition and chatted with as many contestants as we could, before departing for a dinner of salads and sandwiches in the hotel's restaurant.

CHAPTER 3

The Game is afoot.
Sir Arthur Conan Doyle [1859 - 1930]

D espite a peaceful and dreamless night, I awoke on Monday morning feeling exhausted from our weekend of fun, frolic, and rich food. It would have been nice to spend the day with prolonged horizontal rest, but that was not on the schedule. After quick separate showers, and minimal self-beautification, Keoni and I hurried to the ballroom for our promised continental breakfast and coffee that was *not* decaffeinated.

Arriving ahead of Margie and Dan, we made an effort to visit with several people we had glimpsed as they were departing from the ballroom the night before. First, we chatted with Hale Malolo board members who had volunteered to staff the check-in desk that morning. Moving on, we found Linda Tan, a travel agent who volunteers at Hale Malolo. Instead of her usual high heels and silky garments, she wore blue jeans and a tank top.

"Hi Natalie, Keoni. What do you think of this little event Nathan has gotten us into?" she asked cheerfully.

"Anything to help Island damsels-in-distress," replied Keoni. "It's better to be helping them *before* the pot boils over than *after.*"

"Amen to that," Linda responded. "Fortunately, I've never had to worry about how I would care for a couple of kids if I left someone." After a pause, she added, "I don't know about you two, but that coffee urn is looking very inviting," she said, waving farewell.

With a sideways nod of his head, Keoni followed Linda across the room to a table serving beverages. In a moment he was pouring two cups of coffee and visiting with a man whose haircut and demeanor screamed law enforcement or military.

While it might be logical to assume the earliest arrivals would be people staying in the hotel, one of the first contestants I recognized was Jim Souza. He and his wife Evelyn are retired restaurateurs who have lived next to Nathan for more than a decade. When Ariel died, they applied their skills and sensitivity to helping plan her memorial.

"So, what brings you two into Honolulu so early in the morning," I asked. "Are you contestants, or the loyal backers of a women's support organization?"

"Can't we be both?" Jim responded.

"Of course. But I'm surprised Nathan didn't tell me you were joining in the fun," I said.

"I think he was as surprised to see us walk in the door last night as you are this morning," commented Evelyn, approaching from behind me. "Frankly, I didn't want to commit us until I felt relatively sure my new hip would be up to the pressure of five days of physical activity."

"Well then, I'm all the happier to see you," I said with genuine empathy.

At that moment, Keoni arrived at my side. "Good morning, Evelyn. Here you are, Madam. Plenty of cream and two sugars."

"Heavenly," I said with gratitude. Looking at the now-crowded buffet, I suggested we select a table and enjoy our coffee until the O'Haras arrived. Since the majority of the morning's attendees were standing in line for food and beverages, we were able to get seating near the podium.

Soon after Keoni and I sat down, Margie and Dan entered the room. Keoni stood and caught Dan's eye.

"Good morning," said Margie, with a sigh. "I'm sorry we're a bit late. Not knowing what we might need today, I packed a few special items."

"You know that old joke about packing everything but the kitchen sink?" queried Dan. "Margie not only brought everything you ladies might need for renewing yourselves during the day, but she's got enough beverages and snacks to keep us going until tonight."

"The better to win, my dear," she replied, placing a large travel bag and backpack under the table.

"I'll drink to that," said Keoni, lifting his cup.

At that moment, the Souzas arrived with plates brimming with muffins and fruit. I introduced the two couples and asked. "How hungry *are* you, Jim? That must have been a long trip in from the country."

He grinned, slipping several small plates onto the table. "I thought maybe *you* would like something to nibble on while the buffet lines thin out."

"Once a food server, always a food server," observed Evelyn, setting down another plate with baby quiche Lorraine and savory sausages.

At that moment one of the hotel's wait staff arrived with pots of coffee and tea.

"May I serve you?" asked the young man.

"Right on cue," answered Dan, extending his cup.

"Aloha, ladies and gentlemen," boomed the voice of Jason Chin. "Are you ready to begin The First Annual Aloha Scavenger Hunt?"

"Yes," responded the audience half-heartedly.

"I couldn't hear you. Is that a *yes*?" asked Jason.

"YES" boomed a stronger chorus in reply.

"I've been looking over the last of the entry forms and it looks like we have a fair number of tourists in our midst, despite our lack of mainland promotion. Therefore, my first instruction of the day is for you to practice saying 'A-lo-ha'. Can you do that for me? You have until tonight to perfect your response. If you have any doubt about what I'm expecting, speak to any of our resident contestants, who will gladly coach you."

After scattered laughter, Jason continued his opening with a recitation of the day's weather report. He followed that with a cautionary note about the sun, advising everyone to use sunscreen, sunglasses and even umbrellas. "I wasn't joking last night when I said we are encouraging you to work in teams today. But before I go into our first clue, I need to cover some of the basics about our hunt. First, we ask that each of you take a pledge to observe our few rules. As noted in your entry form, our event is a bit different than other scavenger hunts. One of our goals is to enhance participants' awareness of Hawaiian geography, cultural history, and commercial enterprises. Also, while we know you have access to GPS and other software programs, we want you to rely on your personal knowledge and wits. I warn you that reliance on electronic devices, like GPS equipment, will not assure success in the challenges we are tasking you with. To ease your concern about hauling out Hawaiian history books, I can tell you that the promotional brochures, fliers, and pamphlets we provided last night contain solutions to each of the clues in this hunt. You just have to read between the lines and connect the pieces of information."

Jason was good at working his audience and managed to elicit alternating groans and laughter at regular intervals.

"To aid you in solving the puzzles of our game, each contestant has been issued an official notebook. Please use it however you wish, but we'd like you to turn it in at the end of the week, so we can see how our clues have inspired your actions. Your responses will help us in refining future events.

"Unlike television programs with which you may be familiar, there is no need for derring-do in order to solve the mysteries of our clues. You don't have to worry about needing to power lift, speed skate, or sky dive. Also, there will be no *speed bumps*, other than those provided by your failure to discern the answers to the clues.

"If you are registered as a team for today, or for the entire hunt, you must remain together and perform as a team throughout the task—with exceptions for emergencies and breaks from noon to one each afternoon. Should anyone have to resign from the hunt, we will deem your team officially reduced in number.

"The location of each solution will be visible from the street, or public passage nearest to it. A distinctive greeter will await you at each point of solution. They will note everyone who makes it to their location and present the next clue for the day, if there are any. If you are the first individual or team to arrive, you will be given a prize certificate. All prizes will be awarded during the course of the Aloha Scavenger Hunt. Certificates for services will be valid for redemption for one year from date of their award. Should a prize not be won on the day it is offered, that prize will be awarded via a drawing at the banquet on Friday night.

"And now, let's look at our week's schedule that is beside each of your place settings."

I looked at the colorful card displaying a map of O`ahu's geographic features and major roads that sat beside my cutlery.

First Annual Aloha Scavenger Hunt Schedule

Monday	7:30 a.m.	Continental Breakfast; First Daily Clue
	5:30 p.m.	Cocktail hour; Award of Daily Prizes
Tuesday	7:30 a.m.	Continental Breakfast; First Daily Clue
	5:30 p.m.	Cocktail hour; Award of Daily Prizes
Wednesday	7:30 a.m.	Continental Breakfast; First Daily Clue
	4:30 p.m.	Departure for *Lū`au*; Award of Daily Prizes
Thursday	7:30 a.m.	Continental Breakfast; First Daily Clue
	6:00 p.m.	Chinese New Year Feast; Award of Daily Prizes
Friday	7:30 a.m.	Continental Breakfast; First Daily Clue
	6:00 p.m.	Scavenger Hunt Banquet; Award of Daily and Grand Prizes

"You'll see that beyond our nightly cocktail parties and the banquet on Friday, there are a couple of special events scheduled this week. The first is Wednesday night's Hawaiian *lū`au*. Knowing that some of our non-resident guests may be concerned about whether they will enjoy eating *poi* and *kālua* pig, I want you to know there will be a variety of Island specialties to satiate your hunger. Thursday is the start of Chinese New Year. As you might imagine, it's a fairly popular holiday in the Islands, so we're treating you to a traditional Chinese New Year's feast.

"You should know that each day will present clues of varying number and complexity. Some days will include a time limit. Today we ask that you check in here at five-thirty for our cocktail party and declaration of the first day's winners.

"That's all for this morning. Please see one of the board members if you have any questions. And now, please open the first clue of the Aloha Scavenger Hunt."

Keoni slit the envelope with the tip of his pen and said, "I think we can take a few minutes to analyze the task, since I've already moved the car out to a side street."

"How did you manage that?" I asked.

"I did it when I got up to make tea this morning."

As most of the contestants were exiting the room, we huddled around the clue and all of the promotional brochures and fliers we had collected.

First Annual Aloha Scavenger Hunt
Day 1, Clue 1
Shortest distance to your destination: 6.5 miles
Rising nearly straight up from today's point of origin, a panorama of significance to the unifying Royal delights both guests and residents, who pay no heed to the keening thrall of four hundred warriors who plunged in free fall to their deaths more than two centuries ago.

"One nice thing about your being teamed with a retired cop is that I know this island pretty well," declared Keoni.

"Couple that with the research I've done for numerous articles I've written, and you've got a unified approach to such riddles," I added.

"So what is the solution to this clue?" asked Margie.

In near unison, Keoni and I announced, "The Pali Lookout."

As we rushed out to the car, Dan asked how we had figured out our solution.

"Well, before we read it, I was prepared to bring out my compass and draw a circle on that map of O'ahu on the back of the hunt brochure, even though that would yield a distance based on how a bird would fly, rather than roadway mileage. But with the hotel nearly at the water's edge and the opening phrase, I figured the location had to be *mauka*, toward the mountains. And once I saw the distance to the point of solution was six and a half miles, I couldn't think of another location that met the rest of the criteria."

"For me it was the phrase *unifying royal*," I noted. "Years ago, I wrote an article on King Kamehameha the First. He was the man who unified the Hawaiian Islands. The mention of *warriors* is significant because the deciding battle in unifying the Hawaiian nation was fought up in the area of the Lookout. After subduing the island of Hawai`i, King Kamehameha set out with about 12,000 men in 1,200 war canoes. After conquering the islands of Moloka`i and Maui, he invaded southeastern O`ahu. I remember being surprised that the mountainsides were crucial because of the use of cannon. Finally, at the end of the Battle of Nu'uanu, the last four hundred warriors of the forces of O`ahu either jumped or were pushed over the precipice of the Lookout."

In a short while, we had reached our destination. However, we were not the first to arrive. Ahead of us were a couple of students from Chaminade University and the Souzas, who were standing in front of Miss Hawai`i, the first greeter of the hunt.

Welcoming us with a shake of her head, Evelyn said, "We almost did it. But these young whippersnappers from the mainland have been here long enough to have hit all of the usual tourist spots, including this one."

"And being on motorcycles, they had little trouble getting out of the hotel parking lot or navigating downtown traffic this morning," added Jim.

"That's right," replied the shorter of the young men clothed in black leather. "We took a bus tour the first week we got here, and the guide told us all about the Battle of Nu`uanu."

"What did you win?" asked Dan.

The taller guy smiled broadly and said, "The same day-long tour we took six months ago. Do you think anything's changed?"

"Well at least it's a tour for four. This time we can take a couple of friends with us," added his companion.

In her beautiful contralto voice, Miss Hawai`i called for our attention as she reached into a round basket woven of plaited palm fronds. "Don't leave without your second clue of the day, and make sure you sign my log before you leave the Pali Lookout."

Glancing around, I saw more of our fellow contestants arriving. Since all of us had been to the Lookout before, we decided to depart as soon as we could. Stepping aside, our foursome huddled while Dan opened the second clue.

First Annual Aloha Scavenger Hunt
Day 1, Clue 2
Shortest distance to your destination: 8.3 miles
Between here and the bay of two seas, ancient royals (including She whose song is beloved) frolicked. Within this expanse that was once an inland sea, a site, sacred even to the legendary diminutive craftsmen, is commemorated in bronze upon a public land near a modern center of wellness.

With Dan and Margie staring at us, Keoni and I looked at each other. "The *bay of two seas* is Kailua Bay," said Keoni quietly, looking around in case anyone was listening.

"I thought it was either that or Kāne`ohe Bay," I offered. "The wellness center has to be Castle Hospital."

"That's enough information for us to get back on the road," declared Keoni.

With Keoni at the helm and Dan riding as navigator, Margie and I sat in the back seat, pouring over brochures for a public landmark that answered the final bits of the clue.

"I'm positive that *inland sea* refers to Kawai Nui Marsh," I said.

"Isn't that where you two caught Miriam's killer last summer?" asked Dan.

"Yes. And that…man…is still in a coma, while the legal eagles continue to argue about whether it's right to leave him on life support at the public's expense," grumbled Keoni.

"That's a difficult issue," commented Margie. "Law and religion aside, I know very few people who would opt to be connected to life support indefinitely."

"You're right. But I don't think the case will go on much longer," concluded Keoni.

Margie shrugged and looked at the clue once again. "So, what we're looking for is a public place with a marker of some kind."

"Mmhm. Small craftsmen must be the *menehune*, a people, real or mythological, who are believed to predate the arrival of Polynesians. They're associated with all of the area, so that clue doesn't narrow things much."

"How many 'sacred' sites are there around here?" asked Margie.

"Actually, quite a few," responded Keoni, keeping his eyes on the road.

"Are they all on public land?" asked Margie.

"With a bronze marker?" added Dan.

"That narrows it a bit," I answered. "What do you think Keoni?"

"Well, the organizers have got about sixty people to deal with. So it's got to be a place with room to accommodate quite a number of cars, and that means public parking."

"The clue says the place is between the Pali Lookout and the ocean. I think that rules out beach parks. Also, I remember that several of the sacred places Miriam's housemates and I saw on our tour were on private or protected land."

Dan had been going over one of the brochures that Margie had passed him. "How about one of the public parks that's not at a beach?" he asked.

"That's it! Ulupō Heiau," announced Keoni. "There's room for several vehicles to park and there's a plaque describing the temple's huge stone platform."

Within a few minutes we were parked and standing at the historic marker where the Souzas and several people I did not recognize were grouped around a man dressed as an ancient Hawaiian warrior.

"You're pretty good at this," observed Jim, turning to greet us.

"You're not so bad yourselves," countered Keoni.

"This is practically our back yard," said Evelyn. "I come here with a group of water colorists every month."

"Who won this round?" I asked.

"We did," announced a towheaded teenage girl, holding hands with a balding man whose eyes resembled hers. "We won a beautiful Hawaiian quilt. Here's a picture of it. It's the *loke lani* rose pattern. All the tiny stitches around the Maui rose appliqués represent ocean waves."

Smiling widely, the man nodded. "My daughter and I have been taking day trips ever since I arrived here as the new manager of the Hickam Main Exchange at Joint Base Pearl Harbor-Hickam."

By this point, the number of people was thinning out. Realizing we needed to hurry up, we accepted the third clue of the day and went back to the car to contemplate the next leg of our journey.

First Annual Aloha Scavenger Hunt
Day 1, Clue 3
Shortest distance to your destination: 8.3 miles

It's not red. It's not white. It's three decades and counting since its previous incarnation. Framed with rich greenery and sometimes rainbows above, this canal-side favorite still features crustaceans to die for.

"All right, master of the map of O`ahu," said Dan to Keoni. "What do you think this clue refers to?"

"I don't think it's the Ala Wai Canal. That would be more than eight miles back into town," I quipped.

"When it talks about *crustaceans to die for*, I don't think it's referring to a place to go crabbing," said Margie. "It's got to be a restaurant."

I looked over at Keoni, who was staring at a map. "I doubt

if there are any canals at the Marine Base over at Kāne'ohe Bay. Besides, these days no military installation is going to admit sixty-plus unknown civilians. Buzz's restaurant is near the water, but not on one of the canals in Kailua."

"Of course," I said. "It's Pinky's!"

"That fits. It's *not* red, and it's *not* white. The original Pinky's Broiler had the best crab on the island," agreed Keoni. "A few years ago, the brother of the Broiler's owner opened Pinky's Pūpū Bar and Grill near the site of the former restaurant on the Kalāheo Canal."

Quickly, we were back on the road. Traveling down Kailua Road toward the ocean, Keoni and I kept up a bantering dialogue highlighting the natural and commercial points of interest we were passing. Within minutes, we turned onto Kalāheo Avenue.

"If our destination is a restaurant, I hope they're serving food, because all this work has stimulated my appetite," said Dan.

"Oh, you're always hungry, dear," replied Margie. "Be grateful your metabolism is so good that you can handle the calories you pump into your system every day."

"I wish I were so lucky," I responded.

"I'll echo that—for myself, that is. However, I think we've done enough walking this morning to justify a good mid-day meal," said Keoni.

By the time we arrived at Pinky's, we had accomplished all three of the hunt's first tasks. Although the restaurant is not open for lunch on weekdays, they were prepared to welcome us. Following a small sign, we entered a meeting room at the side of the building. Like the rest of the grill, the room had been designed around art deco Hawaiiana themes, with tiki torches and canoe paddles set off by rattan, stone, and wood accents that framed a rich tropical view beyond wide windows.

We were each presented with a purple dendrobium orchid *lei* by a young couple dressed in traditional *hula* attire. Next, we received gift certificates for two free dinners from a Don Ho look-alike. Not only did he resemble the famous Hawaiian entertainer, but the man sported a silky white shirt and pants and multi-colored carnation *lei*—just like Ho's 1967 performance of *Tiny Bubbles* at the Hollywood Palace. After announcing we had completed our tasks for that day, our "Don Ho" invited us to enjoy the delicious buffet lunch awaiting us.

With no formal program, we spent time visiting with our fellow contestants and sampling an excellent menu that included chop-chop and seared `ahi salads, vegetable penne, *kalbi* ribs and coconut shrimp. Long tables decorated with open *maile leis* and candles in coconut shells added to the congenial atmosphere. We soon learned that the winner of our third task had been an assistant professor of European languages at the University of Hawai`i. Margie and Dan met a woman who worked as a trainer of dolphins at SeaWorld San Diego—a favorite attraction of the O'Hara's grandchildren. Keoni visited with a man who had served as an HPD reserve officer for many years. I was delighted to run into a television reporter who would be covering that evening's cocktail party for her cable network.

When we finished our lengthy luncheon, we realized it was too late to run home for a gathering with The Ladies. Instead, we chose to complete our visit to Windward O`ahu with a walk at Kailua Beach. The weather that afternoon was superb, neither too hot nor too windy. A large number of windsurfers dotted the waters beyond the swimmers and sunbathers hogging the shoreline. Best of all, the warm sand was a wonderful massage for our toes.

As parents with children arrived, we realized that school must be out for the day, and it was time to return to town. Although our four musketeers had not won any of the day's challenges, we were anticipating a dinner courtesy of Pinky's. On the way back to Honolulu, I placed a quick call to Joanne to check on the home front. I learned there had been no catastrophes and Miss Una was enjoying playtime with The Ladies in their garden. By the time we reached the hotel, there was not much of a slot in the schedule for rest. We did need to bathe again after our fast-paced day, and this time it was not for purely hygienic reasons.

CHAPTER 4

How easily murder is discovered!
William Shakespeare [1564 - 1616]

B y five twenty, we were walking toward the elevator, attired in casual aloha wear, sandals and the purple *leis* we had received at Pinky's. Even as a *kama`aina*, I enjoyed dressing up like a tourist for an evening on the town. Having been proficient at solving the clues that day, we had arrived at each scavenger hunt destination in time to note the winners. Now we were looking forward to ogling their prizes at the cocktail party.

As usual, Jason Chin opened his program with the warmth one expects in the Islands. "Good evening ladies and gentlemen. I hope you've enjoyed learning more about Hawai`i, especially the lovely town of Kailua on the windward side of the island. This morning, I gave you an assignment, in addition to your first clue for the scavenger hunt. So let's see how you and your coaches have done. A-lo-ha!"

A resounding response of *A-lo-ha* answered him.

"That's much better than this morning, but I need a bit more spirit from you. Let's try that again. A-lo-ha!"

This time there was a booming reply, as everyone, including the wait staff, returned the word with the oomph Jason sought. Introductions of special attendees followed, including the mayor, one of the co-producers of *Hawaii Five-O*, and Miss Hawai`i, our first greeter of the morning. Finally, we got to see the successful contestants receive their rewards.

The college boys who had won the tour of the island were

as great at one-liners from the podium as they were at the Pali Lookout. Despite being computer science majors, it sounded like they could have successful careers in standup comedy. The father-daughter duo that won the Hawaiian quilt were newcomers to Honolulu and the girl's comments about her deceased mother having been a quilter were moving. Finally, there was the University of Hawai`i professor who won a year's worth of dinners at Pinky's. I anticipated that Keoni and I were bound to meet him and his wife some evening, since the restaurant is not too far from our home.

With a blank agenda that night, our group decided to prowl through Waikīkī. Both Keoni and I were tired of playing host and quickly agreed to have Dan be the designated driver. Margie and I left the men to their conversations in the front seats of the rental car. While they discussed the finer points of scavenger hunts, we sat in the back gossiping about families of naval personnel we have known over the years—and the remodeling project that awaits her delicate touch upon her return home.

After our encounter with the Don Ho look-alike, we were in the mood for a vintage dinner show and decided to use some of our discounts for the Blue Hawai`i Elvis show. The venue was fine, and the buffet dinner was superior to many I have consumed through the years. Best of all, the act was enjoyable, even for those of us who were old enough to remember The Man himself. We talked about having a nightcap but anticipating our early morning commitment we decided to halt our partying.

When Dan dropped Keoni and me off at the front of the hotel, we hurried into the lobby anticipating a quick trip to dreamland. But that was not to be. Fortunately, the O'Haras were staying on a different floor, so they were uninvolved with what materialized. Upon exiting the elevator, hotel security chief Alec Salinas was standing with a uniformed policewoman, ready to forestall anyone turning to the right.

"Sorry," said officer Horita, beginning her short speech of redirection. "Oh, hello, again," she interrupted herself.

"Alena, I'm sure it will be OK," said Alec. "These are friends of the Lieutenant. In fact, Keoni here is John's old partner."

"Yes, I know. We met last year on a case in Lanikai," the young officer replied.

"So, what's up?" Keoni asked, nodding to the officer and shaking his former colleague's hand.

"Well, if something involves John, you know the theme. There's been a murder. Just down the hallway."

"I guess that means we won't be staying in our suite to-night," I speculated.

"That's right. I'm supposed to send anyone headed that way back to the lobby to be assigned a new room," Alec said.

"What about our things?" I inquired.

"I'm sorry, but you can't take anything out of the crime scene," declared Officer Horita.

"I tell you what, Alena, how about I stay here with Keoni and Natalie and you check in with the Lieutenant to see if we can work something out."

It only took a second for her to concur. While she was gone, we chatted with Alec, who revealed the barest of details about the crime that had occurred in the last couple of hours.

"I got a call from the head of the night housekeeping crew. One of her staff was in hysterics over finding a man lying in the hallway. When I got there, it was obvious he wasn't going to get up again on his own, so I put in a call to HPD. John's usually on days, but he had a case that ran late. As one of his colleagues had called in sick, John said he'd take the case since he was over at the Hilton Hawaiian Village."

"COD?" asked Keoni.

"Cause of Death was a single gunshot to the head," answered John Dias coming around the corner.

Signaling Alena Horita to remain with Alec at the elevators, he beckoned us to follow him.

"So, what brings you two into the land of the *touri*?" queried John. "Nothing murderous I trust."

Keoni put up his hands. "We're completely uninvolved with whatever case brought you here. Almost tourists ourselves this week."

"You've heard about the Aloha Scavenger Hunt," I said.

"Yeah. A couple of young guys from the night shift are participating in it."

"Well, Nathan still volunteers at Hale Malolo which is part of a conglomerate of several non-profits. He was telling us about the hunt benefitting local organizations that help women and children, and we decided to take part," I explained.

"It's lucky for us he's no longer on Hale Malolo's board of directors. That qualified us to enter a drawing for a week's stay here at the hotel—which I'm glad to announce we won," said Keoni.

"The accommodations are really nice, with kitchens and whirlpool baths. I invited Margie and Dan O`Hara to come over from San Diego for the event and we've been hitting a lot of tourist spots," I added.

Looking toward our suite, I could see that the victim's body had been removed. Aside from various police personnel, the most obvious indication of a major crime was the taped outline of a body lying diagonally across the floor—and a sizable pool of blood.

Seeing me staring at the crime scene, John quipped, "Haven't had any interesting visions lately, have you Natalie?"

"No," I replied. "I haven't had *any* visions for months. And, except for dreaming about Miss Una chasing baby bunnies in The Ladies garden, the only dream I recall is something out of a black and white classic movie."

"That's good. After our last case in your neighborhood, we agreed you'd try to make it a full year without murder and mayhem tripping you up. Speaking of which, how are Miriam's Ladies doing?"

"They're fine. They still miss Miriam, of course, but they've settled into a quiet routine in the cottage. Joanne still plays in the garden, under Miss Una's close supervision. Samantha's continuing with her classes in college. And, Izzy's having a great time with her family down the road."

John nodded and asked, "So, which is your suite?"

"It's the second one on the left," replied Keoni.

"That's convenient. It's not really in the crime scene. Why

don't you go clear your things while I get the front desk to prep another room for you?" offered John.

"Thanks," said Keoni. "I would appreciate being able to use my own toothbrush."

"Do you have any idea how many rooms in this corridor are occupied?" asked John.

"Only a couple, since a high school sports team departed this morning. They're the reason why we couldn't get a suite for the O'Haras near ours," I noted.

I inserted my key card, sighing at the thought of having to change suites. Considering the possibility of one of John's bosses showing up and questioning our presence near the crime scene, Keoni suggested we hurry. We began stuffing our belongings into our bags. But despite the small number of items I had brought, they seemed to have increased in volume.

"Uh, honey, do you think you could put my slippers and nightgown in one of your bags?" I asked.

"What?" he replied, putting the last of his toiletries into his shaving kit. "*Miss I-travel-light* can't get the genie back in the bottle?"

As we re-entered the hall, I saw that the CSI team and their equipment had departed. John Dias was conversing with a woman who must have been a hotel guest since she was standing beside a single suitcase that looked as though it had been in storage for decades. Glancing toward the wall, I noticed a sun hat to the left of the stark outline of the victim's head.

"Do you want to wait here while I get the bellman, or at least his luggage trolley?" asked Keoni.

"Sure, dear," I answered, drifting off in thought.

Within a minute, the Lieutenant and the hotel guest had terminated their conversation. After picking up her small bag and hat, the woman in the deep red suit and white blouse straightened her posture. Instantaneously, a realization hit me: Everything I saw before me looked familiar. In fact, it mimicked the image of the black and white movie I had dreamed of more than once recently. The first time was last Thursday night. The next was Friday, when we were watching classic movies here. There was, however, one major difference between my dream and this crime. The images I saw were of an earlier era.

As John glanced over at me, I tried to gather energy for the conversation that was to come.

"So, are you two all set?" he asked, stopping beside me as the woman moved toward the elevator.

"Yes. We've packed and Keoni's gone to arrange for everything to be moved."

"That's good. I've spoken with the organizers of the scavenger hunt and they're going to proceed with the event."

"I'm glad of that. You can imagine how much the contestants will appreciate it—especially people like Margie and Dan who've come so far."

"That's certainly true," said the Lieutenant with a snort. "After what happened during their last couple of visits to the Islands, I hope you can finally have some fun with them."

He looked ready to leave. I had to say something.

"Uh, John...before you go, I think there's something I have to mention."

Twisting my hands like a school girl, I sighed and looked him in the eye.

"Oh, no, not again. I thought you said you hadn't had any visions lately."

"Well, I didn't think I had...until I got a clear look at your crime scene ...without all the people blocking my view."

"Uh-huh," he said encouraging me to continue.

"Well, mmm. Until I saw that lady's hat, I thought what I said was true. But, before we came to Honolulu for the scavenger hunt, I had a dream in black and white—like an old movie."

Recognizing the waters we were about to tread, John let out a sigh and pulled out his notepad. "All right. Go on."

"Then, like I said before, Keoni and I watched a couple of movies after dinner on Friday night. I fell asleep part way through our film festival and experienced the same dream I'd had the night before at home. We often watch old movies and I thought my dream was a replay of scenes from one I've watched before.

"But then—I mean, now—seeing that woman's hat set against the wall, near the head of the outline of a body angled diagonally, well, it just came together. Your crime scene really looks like my dream—except that what I saw in my dream dates from about sixty years ago."

The Lieutenant halted his note taking. "What do you mean?"

"Well, first of all my dream wasn't set in this hotel. It was an old hotel. It was a dark interior, with narrow hallways and scarred wood flooring with a runner down the middle for carpeting. And, there was a metal cage for a single old-fashioned elevator car."

Just then, a bell announced the arrival of an elevator on our floor. I heard Keoni talking to Alena and Alec. A moment later he came around the corner pulling a luggage trolley.

"With your moving so many people out of their rooms JD, the bellman was jammed so I just grabbed this cart. We'll be out of your way in just a minute."

"Actually, there's been a slight change in my plans. Go ahead and move your belongings to your new suite. Natalie will be staying with me until some of the CSI team returns. Once they've taken over, Natalie and I will join you, so I can finish a little, ah... research. Right, Natalie?"

"Yes, John," I affirmed.

"Uh, is there something you two aren't telling me?" Keoni asked, looking back and forth between John and me.

"You know those black and white dreams I've been having from an old murder mystery?" I began.

"Yes. We saw *The Maltese Falcon*, a Charlie Chan movie, and something else the night we arrived here," Keoni replied.

"Did I mention I'd had the same dream the night before we left home," I asked him.

"Oh. I see," responded my sweetheart with a slow nod.

"Well, *I'm* just hearing the story. I'm afraid tonight's festivities are going to be a bit longer than you may have intended," said John.

"Well then, I guess a little coffee is in order. I'll get some started as soon as I get in the new suite. We're up one floor, down the left corridor at the end," explained Keoni. After announcing the room number and handing me an entry card, he went to collect our bags.

"So, Natalie. I think we need to come up with a working title for you. How about *Special Consultant to the HPD Criminal Investigation Division*?" suggested John.

"You know I'm always happy to help you. But I don't think there's going to be very much that I can offer you this time. I just saw the man lying there on the floor. Except, well, it was a different floor. And a different hotel."

"Okay. Keep going," he said, writing in his usual small blue notebook.

"The hall in front of the old-fashioned elevator ran left and right. As you got out of the elevator cage, there were two levels of windows. The bottom three windows were covered by sheer curtains framed by dark drapes. Above those windows were three that were curved to form an arch."

"Hmm. I think you mean clerestory windows."

"Yes. That's right. I turned to the right after leaving the elevator. After a few steps, there was a hallway that T'd off in two directions, I went to the left. And there he was: a man, lying face down, diagonally across the runner, near the end of the hallway. The man in *my* vision was dressed in a white suit and an aloha shirt. He had on two-toned wing tip shoes. And there was a fedora on the floor, on its edge against the right side of the hall."

"You said he was wearing a white suit? You mean like an old-fashioned leisure suit?" questioned John.

"Yes, I guess that's what it would be called," I verified. "I think they've been making them for decades, with varying lapel widths and numbers of buttons."

"What you saw was something like this?" he asked, pulling out his cell phone to click on an image.

And there it was. Or should I say, *he* was—lying face down diagonally on the floor of our hotel corridor. Tonight's victim was wearing a vanilla ice cream colored suit. Except for the collar of his aloha shirt being wider than that in my vision, the scene was the same—down to a straw fedora leaning on its side against the wall, beyond the man's head.

I inhaled deeply. "Yes, that's him. I mean that except for the shirt, your victim and crime scene parallel my vision."

"Can you describe the man? Did you see his face?"

"No, like your picture, his head was turned the other way. And he'd been shot in the head. I, well, I didn't look too closely."

"I'm sorry to put you through this, Natalie. But do you think if I show you his face, you might be able to tell me something about him?"

I did not want to look at the face of a man who had just been shot in the head, but I knew I had to help in any way I could. "I guess I can try."

"It's not too bad, the side of the face I'm going to show you," John said, trying to reassure me.

He then touched his smart phone's screen and began scrolling through some pictures. When he had selected an image, he handed me the phone. At that moment, Keoni entered the hallway with the luggage trolley fully loaded.

Looking down, I cringed as I recognized the man. "It's the old linguistics professor from China. He was on that tour of Kawai Nui Marsh last summer with the Chinese medical students who were visiting the University of Hawai`i. He loves everything about the Islands and has helped with planning the scavenger hunt."

"Well, that will make some things easier," acknowledged the Lieutenant.

"I don't think he had a suite on this floor," Keoni interjected before departing for our new suite.

"He didn't have any ID on him. Now that we know his identity, we'll be able to run that info past the front desk," said John. "You're sure the vision you experienced wasn't in this hotel?"

"Definitely not."

Listening to movement and conversation coming toward us, John gestured for us to discontinue our conversation. In a moment, the CSI team came around the corner. After giving them some instructions, John nodded to me and we went to join Keoni.

When I opened the door to our new suite, I could smell the

aroma of fresh coffee. "I made an executive decision. The coffee is strong and fully loaded with caffeine," announced Keoni.

"That's good, because the evening isn't getting any shorter. But I'm not complaining, Natalie. Your little *dreams*, as you call them, have always proven invaluable," said our guest.

Once we were settled with coffee and an open box of white chocolate covered macadamia nuts, John pulled out his notebook again. "All, right, let me see where we were. You were saying that the layout of the body and the hat were like those in my crime scene. But *your vision* was set in an *old* hotel."

I looked around the suite we were sitting in. "This hotel is bright, wide, streamlined and modern. The rooms are large and have attached bathrooms. What I saw in my vision was from when I was a little girl—mid-twentieth century. The room behind the victim was small and dark. It had heavy wood furniture: a single bed; dresser; small desk with chair; one-night stand; two old brass lamps; and a closet with dressing room. No bathroom. There were a few clothes on hangers and an open suitcase on an old-style wooden rack. It had curved legs and wooden rods...not at all like the ones they use today with aluminum tubing. The woman was sorting through some things inside the suitcase, but I couldn't see what she was looking at."

"The woman? What woman?" asked John, looking up attentively.

I shifted in my seat and Keoni put his arm across my shoulders to reassure me. "There was a woman with her back to me. First, she was in the bedroom, crouched down looking under the bed. Then she went through all the drawers in the room. Wherever she went, she faced away from me, or was bent over at angles that prevented my seeing her face. When she finished searching the bedroom, she entered the closet. Suddenly I was standing behind her, but the space was dark and I couldn't see much."

"Tell me everything you can remember about the woman," requested John.

"I don't know what I can tell you. I couldn't identify colors, just shades—whether something was white, gray, or maybe black. And everything seemed slightly blurred—like an old homemade movie.

"I can say the woman was tall and slim. Her legs were muscular, like those of a dancer or athlete. She walked with determination and I felt she was fairly young. She wore high heels, but they weren't like today's. They were thicker and not as high. They weren't platforms; the soles looked like plain leather when she walked away from me. Her hair was very dark, maybe black. She wore it in an elegant French twist. She had no hat. No purse. Nothing in her hands.

"She was wearing a fairly dark suit. It wasn't as dark as black or navy blue. The jacket flared from her waist over her hips. It had a single row of buttons down the middle and I remember thinking the collar was rather wide. I could see the cuffs of a white blouse under her jacket at her wrists. I think the skirt had a kick pleat in the back because she moved very easily, even though the skirt was long and straight."

"As always, Natalie, that's a good description," John said looking at me and then Keoni. "The only catch is that the woman you saw is probably dead, or in a nursing home by now. Can you tell me anything about her face?"

"Not really. Her back was to me the whole time. She seemed to know what she was doing—methodical, fast, smooth, like she'd done that kind of thing before. At the back of the closet's dressing room was a large mirror, but I couldn't see her face because it was all speckled—you know—dirty and old, like the silver is coming off the back."

"Anything else come to mind? What about her skin color? Light, dark?" questioned John.

"Like I said, I don't know. There was contrast against the dark shade of the jacket, so I guess she wasn't African. She could have been Caucasian, Asian or *hapa* anything."

"I don't suppose you saw any tattoos, scars or birthmarks?"

I shook my head in reply.

"Nails? Watch? Jewelry?" he asked, reaching for any kind of distinctive feature.

"Well, she was wearing a dark fingernail polish. With the

clothes looking mid-twentieth century, I guess that would mean dark red. I saw the flash of a ring, but I don't remember which hand it was on. And since the scene was in black and white, I don't know if it was in gold or silver. With the long sleeves of the suit, I couldn't tell if there was a watch or bracelet."

"Hmm. She may have been engaged or married. Okay, Natalie. I think we've done as much as we can right now. You and I will talk later. I'll see if I can figure out some way to tap into your vision—like we did with those photos of the room where Miriam died. Of course, give me a call if you remember anything else.

"As always, except for Keoni, please don't discuss the case with anyone. I know it may be hard to avoid with Margie and Dan being teamed with you. But the fewer people who know the details of the Professor's case and your vision, the better off we'll be. Having said that, I'll happily accept any details you might recall from this or any other of your visions. And keep your eyes open. You never know what you two might observe on this hunt of yours. I guess that's it for tonight. Try not to have too much fun, kiddies," said John with a broad smile.

After he left, Keoni and I speculated on the amount of information regarding the murder that would have been released by morning. We could always check in with John to determine the limits of what we can mention in public.

I did know one thing with certainty. Last summer I had experienced another vision resembling an old movie. As then, I lamented the fact that things had not turned out well for the star of my private preview.

CHAPTER 5

All changes...have their melancholy...
Anatole France [1844 - 1924]

When we reached the ballroom in the morning, there was a pall over emcee Jason Chin and the other members of the Aloha Scavenger Hunt's board of directors. Having been told to keep *our* silence by Lieutenant John Dias, Keoni and I pretended we did not know about the Professor's murder. Since John was not present, Keoni felt his former partner might appreciate any observations he could contribute to the official investigation. However, we did not speak to anyone other than our teammates Dan and Margie and my twin Nathan, who was observing as a non-participant. We quietly filled our plates at the buffet and sat at the back of the room watching the interaction of hotel staff, hunt organizers, and participants.

Hearing the captain's bell ring from the podium, everyone turned toward the front of the room. Jason Chin began the morning's program with a somber look on his face.

"Most of you will have heard that a catastrophe occurred last night. Professor Fù Hán Zhāng, a man who traveled from Shànghǎi to volunteer in the operation of the First Aloha Scavenger Hunt, died from unknown causes. As his death does not appear related to the hunt, we have been told we can proceed as scheduled. After careful consideration, our Board has decided that despite the sorrow we feel for the passing of our colleague, we will indeed continue with our plans, while cooperating with the authorities in every way we can.

"Although he kept a low profile, Fù Hán was a moving force behind our event. He had visited here on a collegiate tour last year and had remained in touch with some of the University of Hawai`i personnel he met on that trip. He was so delighted when he learned of our hunt, that he volunteered to assist. That's why we scheduled our activities during Chinese New Year.

"Before we start our day, I ask everyone to join me in a moment of silence to honor a man whose enthusiasm about the idea of a scavenger hunt in Hawai`i has been essential in shaping the event you are enjoying."

On that note, most people in the room bowed their heads. Armed with the knowledge that Zhāng's death was definitely a murder, Keoni and I glanced at each other and then scanned the room to see if anyone was behaving in a less than respectful manner. As a semi-retired journalist, I wondered how the city's reporters would react when they learned belatedly of the death.

Jason then cleared his throat and continued. "As each of you checked in today, you received your envelope with this morning's clue. I want to assure you that the professor's passing has not altered the nature or sequencing of the hunt's clues. Let me remind you that today's cocktail hour will begin at five-thirty. After that, you're free to enjoy the evening as you wish. This might be a good opportunity to use some of the coupons for restaurants and entertainment you received in your packet of fliers and brochures.

"I think that's all for this morning's announcements. As usual, please speak with me or another board member if you have any questions. And now, you may open the clue you have been given."

As everyone rushed to open their envelopes and depart, Keoni put up his hand to keep Dan, Margie and me in our seats.

"Let them all dash out while we take a moment to analyze this challenge. I've already moved the car to the street, so we can quickly go around the block to maneuver through town, or shoot onto Nimitz Highway, if we need to get out of the downtown area."

"Like yesterday, I think we should look at the map of the island and consider the radius of the stated mileage. Then we can analyze the individual elements of the clue," said Dan.

First Annual Aloha Scavenger Hunt
Day 2, Clue 4
Shortest distance to your destination: 16.5 miles
In a neighborhood of homestead homes, this theatrical sanctuary for largely pacific creatures of sea and land faces a shore once invaded by an Asian singularity before the median of the prior century.

"Given the distance, we can ignore anything *makai*—oceanside—of this hotel. That leaves going West, or across the Ko`olau Mountains to the windward side of the island," said Keoni.

"What about going through Waikīkī and around Diamond Head?" I asked.

Abruptly, Keoni announced. "Hmm. You're right about our direction. This is another easy one. Our destination is Sea Life Park."

"How can you be so sure?" I asked.

"It's the use of the word *homestead* followed by the phrase *theatrical sanctuary*. There are other places on O`ahu with homestead housing, but I just read a description of Sea Life Park in one of the brochures we picked up at the opening party, and that phrase was used."

"What do you think the reference to an *Asian invasion* is about?" asked Dan.

"I'm not sure," replied Keoni. "But saying that the incident occurred prior to 1950 makes me think it may refer to the capture of a Japanese naval officer who ran his midget submarine onto a beach the night of December 7, 1941, after the attack on Pearl Harbor."

Having determined our probable destination, we gathered our belongings and headed for the car. Since Keoni was experienced in navigating between downtown and Waimānalo, I insisted he drive. We were soon headed southwest on King Street. After a few turns, we were on the H1 Freeway traveling east.

When H1 ended, we were dumped onto Kalaniana`ole Highway, which took us directly to Sea Life Park.

We appeared to be the first of the Hunt's contestants to reach the Park. We were facing a large outdoor entertainment venue. Seeing a small sign for participants of the scavenger hunt, Margie identified our team and was given four passes for the day.

She smiled up at the large Hawaiian man and asked coyly, "I don't suppose you have any tips you can share with me about where I'll find the pot of gold at the end of today's rainbow?"

"Now you wouldn't want me to spoil the day for any of your other friends, would you?" he said with equal warmth. "I can say that the sparkling blue of the sea will match the eyes, if not the shirt, of your greeter."

"Well, that didn't help much," moaned Margie as she turned back to us.

"So how do you think we should approach this task?" questioned Dan.

"Well, it's too bad we're not supposed to split up," commented Keoni. "It's like a house-to-house search, and that's something I've had plenty of experience with."

After looking over the map of the Park, we began making a loop to check out the grounds in general. Given the name of the Park, we zeroed in on exhibits focusing on dolphins, sharks, turtles, sea lions, and penguins. After an hour of wandering from one to another, we decided we would have to attend the special shows. We knew we had to remain in formation as a four-person team to win the task's prize. Therefore, we opted to watch the signature act, the Dolphin Cove Show.

Sitting in the open-air theater, I tried to keep my mind on the scavenger hunt, instead of the body in the hallway of our hotel—or the one in my vision of a similar crime that seemed to occur decades ago in an old Honolulu hotel. This was not too difficult, since the synchronized swimming and aerobatics of the dolphins were dynamic, and we were surrounded by *keikis* of several ages who shouted their glee with each spectacular move. As we were departing from the show, my cell phone rang. Caller

ID indicated that the caller was my neighbor Joanne. I knew she would not be ringing me unless something important had occurred at home.

"I'm sorry to interrupt your vacation, but I thought you'd want to know that someone has broken into your home...but nothing major's been damaged."

She was speaking rapidly and her tone was brusquer than usual. "There's no sign of their entry or exit, but they were in the kitchen long enough to disturb items on the counter and break the soap dispenser. Also, Miss Una's food dishes are empty and her water bowl's been overturned.

"We've looked everywhere and can't find her anywhere. The pet door in the garden window above the sink is opened wider than usual and the pot of flowers you keep on the *lānai* table below the window's been smashed. I'm wondering if some animal other than Miss Una got into the cottage through the garden window."

After assuring Joanne I would be home fairly quickly, I moved to catch up with the others in my party. Just then, a fellow contestant squealed her delight in winning the challenge by finding the Elvis impersonator who was our official greeter. We joined the crowd that had gathered to watch her having her picture taken with the good-looking man wearing a bright blue aloha shirt. Although she received a white and yellow plumeria *lei*, the winner was informed that she would be awarded her prize certificate at cocktails that evening.

As we signed in to register for having solved the morning's clue, we were told there were no further challenges for the day and we could enjoy Sea Life Park throughout the afternoon. By that point, we had toured most of the Park's exhibits. With my needing to dash home, Keoni and our friends decided to play at Kaupō Beach Park across the road. I was glad we had thought to place our swimwear and beach toys in the trunk of my car.

Leaving my crew behind for sun and surf, I pulled out onto Kalaniana`ole Highway and headed home to resolve the crisis at hand. Once I was in Lanikai, there were a couple of cars in front of me. Just after I turned onto my street, the car in front of me suddenly braked and then sped away from me. As there was no one behind me, I slowed and looked in both directions before proceeding. On the right side of the road I saw what had caused the driver's erratic behavior. Unfortunately, I realized there was nothing I could do for the cat that had been tossed without care to the edge of the road. After parking in my driveway, I called Joanne and told her about what had just occurred.

"I'm going to check, but I'm pretty sure the cat is dead. At least I know Miss Una is all right since she's sitting in front of Ming Ho's house staring at me. I'll call you as soon as I've been able to grab her."

I quickly confirmed that the kitty on the roadside was dead. Sadly, it looked like she had recently given birth. Turning away, I advanced on my own little darling. "I'm sorry about your friend," I said kneeling. Then I extended my hands. "Let's go home now, baby, okay?"

After staring at my hands for a moment, Miss Una turned and ran behind a shrub. Not knowing my fleet-footed companion's intentions, I followed slowly. Since I knew the Ho family was on an extended vacation to visit family in Taiwan, I was not concerned about their questioning my presence. All I had to worry about was setting off their alarm system.

As I pulled a bush away from the latticework running along the base of their porch, I heard a chorus of meows. I looked closely and saw that there was a small doorway standing slightly ajar. Bending down, I pulled it toward me and found Miss Una surrounded by five small furry shapes. Backing away, I pulled out my cell phone. "Joanne, I think I've just solved a couple of our neighborhood mysteries. If you'll put some toweling in that garden basket of yours and come across the street, I'll show you my discovery."

Soon, Joanne joined me, and we carefully picked up the wee kittens. Prancing ahead of us, it was clear that Miss Una did not require any encouragement to return home. When we arrived at my kitchen, we found that Izzy and Samantha had tidied the room and re-freshened Miss Una's food and water. Knowing our human scent would no longer be a problem with the kittens' mother, we crowded around the basket and gently lifted out the quivering balls of orange-striped fluff. At their incessant crying, we placed them gently in front of bowls of warm milk Samantha was setting out.

"They're so cute," said Izzy enthusiastically. "I'm glad they're old enough to drink from a bowl instead of needing to be bottle fed. I was thinking of getting a pet or two for my niece Malia's children—now that they're old enough to understand the responsibility. These little kitties are the perfect answer to that need."

"Well honey, it's going to be a couple of weeks before they can be adopted out," said Joanne pragmatically.

"I'll check with Anna Wilcox, the manager of my condo, and see if any of the owners or renters are in the market for a pet," I said.

"Isn't her cat Miss Una's mother?" asked Samantha.

"Yes, she is," I replied.

As though on cue, Miss Una jumped up to the counter in front the open pane of the garden window above the sink. Sitting tall and silent, she watched the proceedings below her. She then nudged Joanne who was standing with her back to the counter. "And what do you desire, sweet little girl?"

For a few moments, the two carried on an unspoken dialogue. "Oh, you think our home needs a little mascot of its own, do you?"

Miss Una meowed once and pressed her head into the hand extended to her. "Well, I guess that settles this litter's future," laughed Joanne.

I nodded. "Unfortunately, their mother hasn't survived to be offered a home. If you ladies will watch over our guests, I need to call Animal Control."

After arranging for removal of the kittens' mother, I called Keoni to update him on the felonious feline break-in at our home. He told me our scavenging crew had enjoyed as much sun as they could tolerate. I verified that The Ladies could handle the increased burden of five kittens and hit the road.

Moving against rush hour traffic, our party made it back to

the hotel in time for leisurely self-renewal prior to the cocktail party. At precisely five-thirty, we walked into the crowded ballroom. I thought of three reasons why so many attendees had arrived early. First, we've completed two days of hunt events, with several prizes having been awarded. Second, to build suspense for the overall scavenger hunt, the prize for today's single challenge had been kept a secret. And third, well, there was the issue of Professor Zhāng's death. For all of these reasons, the room was buzzing with intense conversation.

As Jason Chin began addressing the crowd, he gained the immediate attention of everyone. "I hope we didn't disappoint you too badly by keeping today's prize a secret, but we wanted to make sure you'd all be here tonight. I won't delay the suspense any further so if Linda Tan will come forward, I will present her certificate for wining today's single challenge." Since she was seated close to the podium, she quickly reached Jason's side.

"I'm pleased to announce that nearly every one of our hunters solved the clue and made it to Sea Life Park. However, with such a large venue, there were many potential check-in points and you were the first contestant to determine that the Elvis look-alike was our greeter. In keeping with the nautical theme of the day, I am pleased to announce that you have won a day of deep-sea fishing for a party of six."

I heard a slight groan beside me. "Now that's the one prize I would have enjoyed winning," declared Keoni with a shake of his head.

After giving Linda her certificate and escorting her off the platform, Jason completed his spiel for the night. "Before I send you off for another evening of entertainment on your own, please remember that tomorrow night is our beachfront *lū'au* at beautiful Paradise Cove. Unless you insist on driving, transportation is provided by the Hunt. We don't want to be late for the sunset procession of the Royal Court, so please meet me in the hotel lobby at four-thirty to board our buses. As to the menu and content of the evening's entertainment, I urge you to read the venue's brochure."

When Jason dismissed us, everyone returned to their conversations and sampling of the extensive *hors d'oeuvres*. We had been a foursome for most of the last few days, so our group decided to break up and mingle with as many people as we could. While Dan and Margie concentrated on getting to know our competition, Keoni and I turned to foraging for information that might be useful to John Dias.

Having spotted a couple of off-duty police officers, Keoni drifted off toward the back of the room. I decided to find the UH professor of linguistics who had been chummy with the murder victim. Since I did not remember the man's name, I asked Nathan to check the records of prize winners. By the time I managed to track David Fox down, the number of people in the room had thinned considerably. I introduced myself and mentioned that Keoni and I were customers of Pinky's Pupu Bar and Grill and said we would look forward to meeting him and his wife at a future dinner.

After that, I could not think of what else to say, aside from expressing my sorrow for the loss of his colleague. The man's reply was short and did not lead to further conversation. I excused myself and departed before I could say something I might regret later. Now that we were acquainted, I could always refresh our contact and pursue a specific line of inquiry, when and if I had one.

Although there had only been one clue to solve on the hunt's second day, I was far more exhausted than on the first. Everyone else on my team may have been refreshed after their afternoon at the beach, but I was grateful when they agreed to have dinner in the hotel's restaurant. Beyond sharing an appetizer of grilled shrimp and Caesar salad with Keoni, I did not notice much of the meal. Anticipating another day on the hunt and the evening *lū`au*, we all decided to go to bed early.

Despite my good intentions, the call of the oversized whirlpool bath was too much to resist. I was certain that the luxury of a long soak in passion fruit infused Epsom salts would ensure a peaceful night. Later, held in the loving arms of Keoni, I did slip into a deep sleep for an unknown period of time. But whether I was affected by recounting my vision to JD early that morning, or by looking at photos of the victim *in situ*, something had stimulated a revisit of my vision, and I experienced little rest that night.

*   *   *   *   *

I again feel myself ascending in the elevator of the old hotel. This time the scene is in vivid color, but with a tinge of brown at the edges. There is a crisp clarity that allows me to appreciate the intricate design and patinaed bronze finish of the wrought iron cage of the elevator. For a while, I study the hexagonal black and white tiles on the floor framing the medallion of the Chinese logogram. I glance up to a scroll domed ceiling and down again.

The elevator stops. The door slides open and I step out. I look back and realize that a smaller metallic version of the floor medallion is embedded in a rosette at the back of the elevator. I again face the triad of windows covered with delicately patterned ivory sheer curtains. Framing them are floor–sweeping deep green velvet drapes held with tiebacks. Below, worn dark wood floor boards are covered by a burgundy wool runner with a herringbone pattern I recognize from childhood.

My first vision of the vintage hotel had been experienced with minimal detail and in total silence. This time I hear a conversation between two men from outside the windows. As a pulse of air moves the curtains, I see the sash of the center window is raised. The language spoken is clearly Chinese. The tones remind me of the Yue dialect spoken in Shànghǎi, the birth city of the Wong sisters who own the Makiki Sunset Apartments where my grandniece Ariel died.

I pause, flashing to the memory of Pearl Wong's revelations of her early childhood during my clandestine investigation of her apartment complex. The scene now surrounding me freezes. I again recall Pearl's description of the Shànghǎi meeting of her Chinese mother and Hawaiian-Chinese father after the First World War. Again, I sense her sorrow at describing the impact of the Great Depression on China...and the tragic death of her mother during the birth of a son who also died. I picture the cloud-filled night in which Pearl and her older sister Jade escape the 1932 Japanese at-

tack on their city. A mixture of sadness and expectation fills Pearl's description of the parting from their father and oceanic voyage with their amah Chu-Hua Lee from Hong Kong to Honolulu. Again, I hear Pearl clarify that one's surname is put before given names.

Abruptly, the curtains before me are moved by a gust of wind. I am stunned to hear "Lee Chu-Hua" mentioned twice in soft words that reach up to my ears. Inexplicably, I often understand foreign words spoken in my visions. But that is not the case in this scene. I understand only those three words. Lee Chu-Hua. I know this is the Chinese sequencing of the name of the Wong Sisters' amah.

The conversation I am overhearing from outside the building continues for only a short while. I count several seconds of silence. When one of the curtains moves again, I peer out. I see only an empty street below. It is the somewhat seedy Honolulu Chinatown of my youth.

I turn back to the hotel corridor and walk, as before to the right. When I arrive at the "T" in the corridor, I turn to the left. Ahead lays the body I expect to find. The dark carpet provides a suitable backdrop for the man in the wrinkled vanilla-ice-cream-colored suit. I see no socks in the brown and white spectator wingtip shoes sticking out from the cuffs of his tapered pant legs. Above the jacket is the narrow collar of a vintage Alfred Shaheen aloha shirt featuring a brown kapa print with hibiscus flowers. Against a wide baseboard of dark wood, leans a straw fedora with a feather in its brown band.

I look to the left and see that the door to number 312 is narrowly ajar. The opening yawns wider and I look within. Again, I watch the elegant woman conduct her meticulous search. Viewed in color, I realize her suit is a deep red crêpe de Chine. With her back to me, she inspects the space below the single unmade bed. She then rises and looks at the rest of the room's furniture. She opens the drawers of the single nightstand, small dresser, and secretary's desk of mahogany wood. As in my first vision, she next opens the door to what I know is a dimly-lit closet with dressing room.

I find myself immediately behind her, as she examines the pockets of the garments hanging on the left. When she has com-

pleted this search, she turns and peers into a large oval Cheval mirror resting against the back wall. It is so discolored by age that I cannot see her features clearly. She then turns her attention to the strapped leather suitcase laying open on a luggage rack to her right.

With practiced movements, she explores each compartment, her hands seeking anything that may be hidden from view. She stands back for a moment, then reaches forward and pulls out a straight-edged razor from an open leather shaving kit. She flips it open and begins slashing at the lining of the suitcase, to no avail. Nothing has been revealed...Except, that I see a gold ring on one of her fingers.

It almost seems like the object of my attention knows I am present, for she has kept her back or side to me the entire time. Having ended the task at hand, she stares again at the mottled mirror. She then walks forward and pulls it toward her to examine its backside. Angry at the lack of results, she shoves the mirror against the wall and sighs deeply. After repositioning a strand of hair loosened from her French twist, she brushes her skirt and, like a sophisticated character in an old movie, she shoots the sleeves of her jacket and adjusts a handkerchief in her breast pocket. For a moment, I smell the fragrance of roses.

Abruptly, the elegant woman brushes past me through the bedroom. I move behind her to the doorway of the room, again struck by how tall she is. I watch as she stoops to pick up something from the floor of the hallway. She then steps across the corpse she seems to regard as being of no consequence. With purpose, she turns toward the hallway intersection. I stare at the man on the floor. Despite the blood that has dripped down his face, I realize his eyes are almond shaped and that there is a slight yellow tinge to his suntanned skin. The door to the vintage elevator cage clangs open and shut.

*   *   *   *   *

"Natalie, Natalie. Come out of it. You're okay. You're with me...at the hotel," said Keoni soothingly.

He cradled my back and slowly rubbed my arm. "Where are

you, Natalie?"

"I'm at the hotel...the other hotel. He's still dead, but this time I saw his face. I think he's Chinese. But he's not old like Professor Zhāng. Not old at all."

I shuddered and turned to face Keoni. "We've got to call John."

"It's only two-thirty. It's not like we can send John back in time to save a man who's already dead. JD usually goes for a workout at six. We'll call him then. Okay?"

"Mmhm. You're right, that man isn't about to rise up any time soon."

CHAPTER 6

I will now put forth a riddle unto you...
**The Book of Judges, The Bible, King James Version
[circa 6ᵗʰ Century BCE]**

Although I was unable to return to sleep, I tried to remain still and quiet to let Keoni get some rest. Finally, at five thirty, I got up and took a shower. Reversing our usual roles, I approached our bed with a morning eye opener of spiced chai tea.

"Good morning, honey," said Keoni opening his eyes. "Did you get any sleep?"

"Not really, but I feel quite good after snuggling with you for a while," I responded.

Sitting up in bed, he took the cup I offered and looked at the clock on the night stand. After a couple of sips of tea, he said, "I think it's time to see what JD's up to."

Within moments, Keoni had confirmed an early meet with his old partner and disappeared into the bathroom. John arrived an hour later. He was pleased that we had readied a carafe of coffee and a few items from the basket of fruit, breads, candy and nuts that was delivered to our room each day.

"Glad you caught me when you did, Keoni," said John. "I skipped the club and just went for a quick run."

"That's more than I'm up to these days," replied Keoni, glancing at the ankle he had injured in helping to solve Ariel's murder.

While we ate, I caught John up on the few new details from my expanded vision of the mid-twentieth century murder in

Chinatown. After glancing through his notes, John offered a summation.

"The bottom line is that this time you saw everything in color and you've determined that the murdered man was young and Chinese. The vic was in a vanilla-colored suit and brown and white spectator shoes. His shirt looked like a vintage Alfred Shaheen, featuring a brown *kapa* print with hibiscus flowers. Leaning against the wall above his head was a man's straw fedora with a feather. The woman who was searching room 312 wore a dark red suit, white blouse, and black high heels. In this second vision, you saw a gold ring on one of her fingers. That means that she might have been married—or she had money herself, or someone give her an expensive gift. Does that cover everything?"

"I think so. Except for the conversation I overheard. I don't know very much about Chinese names, so maybe the sounds I heard have multiple meanings and occur often in common speech. But it seems odd that all three parts of the name, *Lee Chu-Hua*, were said twice, in the traditional sequence of last name followed by given name."

"Didn't you tell me that although the Wong Sisters' *amah* brought them to Honolulu before World War II, she returned to China after the girls were grown?" asked John.

"Yes. Sometime between 1950 and 1953."

"Well, that fits with the rest of your descriptions being mid-twentieth century," said Keoni.

"True. But that raises the question of whether Pearl's *amah* was somehow involved in the murder I saw in the old hotel," I said, contemplating the ramifications of such a scenario.

The Lieutenant nodded. "Well, if that's it for your news, I have a little of my own. Since our first conversation about *my* case, the CSI team has gone through the professor's suite. So far, there's only one item of interest. I'd like to see what you both think. But before I go into that, I can tell you we found no suspicious fingerprints, sign of a struggle, or other evidence of foul play. There's no wallet on him, which made us think it was a simple theft."

"His suite was not on this floor, so why was he here?" Keoni asked.

"That's a great question. Except for you two—and that woman who just departed to change rooms, there was no one booked in the suites surrounding the location of his body," added John.

"That's a departure from my vision. I felt like 312 *was* my victim's room," I noted. "But I could be wrong; I didn't see a key by his body or any ID in the hotel room."

John nodded. "Well, what I want to show you is a Scavenger Hunt clue that looks intended for tomorrow's event. It was in the inbox of the vic's email account on his laptop."

Keoni looked at me. "I'm happy to help, JD. But I hate to see Natalie, Dan and Margie disqualified from participating in the hunt."

"That's not a problem. There's no conflict with the hunt. You see, the clue I'm going to show you is a fake. I've already checked with Jason Chin and what I've got is *not* a legitimate clue. The real clues are in the hands of just three people, *not* including the professor. He never received one until all of the contestants did. And *no* one has received any clues via email, not even members of the Hunt's board of directors. In fact, no information about any clue has been released prior to the day and time of the challenge."

Although printed on plain paper, the clue looked like the others we had received so far.

First Annual Aloha Scavenger Hunt
Day 4, Clue 6
Shortest distance to your destination: .9 miles

The ancient masters were subtle. In the new town of our forebears lies a building with a triad of windows topped by church-like arches. Traversing all floors is a hidden door that needs no lock. In the hub of the wheel, resides the revered Song Lady of the White River who hears the cries of the world. Like the Sage, be guided by what you feel...magnify the small...so that without substance can enter.

"Hmm. The font and layout look the same as the official clues we've seen," commented Keoni.

"The text is rather long and vague, but the poetic rhythm is similar," I added. "It mentions the Song dynasty, which fits with tomorrow's theme of Chinese New Year. Overall, it reads like a Chinese proverb."

With a furrowed brow, Keoni sipped his coffee. "My first question is *why* did the professor receive the fake clue? The second is *who* sent it to him? And then we might ask, why was it sent to the Professor two days prior to the contestants being handed the real clue? What was in the subject line of the email?"

"It just read, *Chinese New Year*," stated John.

"Was there a message?" I asked.

"No, the clue *was* the message. It wasn't an attachment," John explained.

"Has Jason—or anyone else on the board— indicated whether anything in the fake clue parallels any part of the actual clue scheduled for distribution tomorrow morning," queried Keoni.

"Nope. There's not a single element in common with tomorrow's real clue number six. Of course, I've got a couple of CSIs analyzing it. But with you two in the midst of this event, there's always a chance you might run across something of interest. If you can think of some way to solve the riddle, it's fine with me for you to pursue it—as long as you don't reveal that this text is a fake clue in the scavenger hunt."

Our conversation halted for a moment. Sipping my coffee, I wondered how the clue fit the current murder, or the one in my vision. I also thought of the ramifications of what I had overheard in the corridor of the old hotel. "One thing I'll do is call Pearl Wong. I've been meaning to check on how her sister Jade is doing. It shouldn't be too difficult to dream up a reason for asking her advice on what I'll call a *riddle*. If I see her in person, I can slip in some question about her *amah* Chu-Hua Lee. It'll simply be another round of storytelling for her—but this time I'll keep the conversation short and to the point."

"Sounds good to me. Just keep the source of the clue under

wraps," said John, putting his cup down. "How you handle the vision is up to you, provided there's no linkage to my case. You know there's no way *I* could go to Pearl and ask about *your* hearing a name from *her* youth during one of your visions. Does she even know about your visions?"

"No. There are very few people who know about my dreams and visions. Not even Margie has any inkling of them and I've known *her* for decades."

"Hmm," was John's meaningful response.

"I guess we'd better get started with the hunt. But I'll call Pearl sometime this afternoon," I said.

"Before Natalie sees her, we'll make a copy of the *riddle*, stripped of any reference to the hunt," declared Keoni.

I knew we were running late, but I was surprised when I heard a knock at the door. As Keoni went to see who our company was, John put his notebook in his jacket pocket and I folded the copy of the fake clue.

"Oh. I didn't mean to interrupt anything," said Margie entering the living room.

"Hello, Margie," said John.

"Hi, John," she replied. "Terrible about the death of the old professor. With him being a foreigner, there must be a nightmare of extra paperwork for you...having to deal with the Chinese Consulate and all."

"Well, it's not something I would have asked for," said John. As he rose, he gave me a steady look. "Thanks again for the coffee. I'll see you two later."

Keoni walked him to the door and I heard a couple of muffled sentences. When Keoni returned to the room, Margie was seated in a chair with her back to him. Keeping a straight face, I glanced up to see if he needed to pass me a subtle message from officialdom. He merely shrugged and opened his hands outward. I took that to mean that I was on my own about whether or not to reveal my visions to Margie.

Through the years, I have told her nearly everything about my life. But I have always had mixed feelings about disclosing my little secret to anyone, including her. Being uncertain of where the day, let alone the rest of our week in Honolulu might lead, I decided to maintain the *status quo* and save a revelation of my visions for another time.

Glancing around at Keoni, Margie asked, "Are you helping the good Lieutenant with his latest case?"

"I'm just going to keep my eyes open for anything unusual that comes up," Keoni answered smoothly.

"Well, you two have certainly experienced enough death recently. But I guess it's like any other life's work, at least for you Keoni—once a cop, always a cop. I just came to let you know that Dan has moved our rental car out of the parking structure, in case we want to take two cars today. Natalie, I thought maybe you and I might want to scoot back ahead of the guys to get dressed up for the *lū`au* tonight."

I nodded and dashed off to brush my teeth, grab a bottle of sun block, and drop the fake clue into my suitcase. When the three of us arrived in the ballroom, Dan had already secured seating for us. I could not tell if the tables at the front of the room were filled, but it looked like there were clear sight lines from Dan's vantage point.

The room was crowded and full of chatter, but I heard nothing of particular note. The next half hour passed quickly. Full of breakfast and Jason Chin's humor, everyone seemed anxious to launch the morning's hunt.

First Annual Aloha Scavenger Hunt
Day 3, Clue 5
Shortest distance to your destination: 22.9 miles

Are you aboard to pay homage to one of our island's two pastoral treasures of the Industrial Age? At the center of the world's largest verdant puzzle is a golden icon that has grown in popularity with tourists and locals alike since shortly before the millennium.

Looking down at a fistful of brochures for Island entertainment venues, Margie quipped, "How about you two provide us with another chorus of the solution to the clue."

"Mm," responded Keoni. "It's too great a distance to be toward the ocean. And we've already been northeast on the windward side of the island. I'd guess we're going north or northwest today."

"The two *pastoral treasures* are sugar and pineapple. Even though they no longer impact the economy as they once did, there are pockets of both crops growing across the state," I added.

"With a distance of nearly twenty-five miles, we're clearly heading out of town," said Keoni resolutely.

The men had parked our vehicles near each other, so we decided to take whichever car was closer. As we were walking from the hotel, Margie sorted through several brochures we had added to our collection that morning. "There are a couple of places that look like they're quite a ways out of town. First there's the Sugar Plantation Village. It's in Waipahu," she said looking at a map with driving directions.

"How far is it?" asked Keoni, unlocking my car.

"Well, there are two ways for getting to Waipahu, and both are less than fifteen miles...a bit short of the goal for today," she answered. "That leaves the Dole Plantation. It's, uh, right on target. About twenty-three miles for both ways to get there—from here to Wahiawa, that is."

"That fits. They've got the world's largest maze, with a planting of a giant pineapple right in the middle," I said in summation. "And that's *green, verdant, with a golden center.*"

"Sounds good. Let's take H1, followed by H2," declared Keoni, plotting our course.

Considering how far we were traveling, we decided to take both cars. Margie teamed up with me in my car, and Keoni joined Dan in the rental. With open cell phone connections, we moved out of town. Knowing Dan's continual desire for sustenance, I was glad that the Dole Plantation has a restaurant. Although we were again driving against rush hour traffic, it took nearly an hour to arrive at our goal.

Since the Dole Pineapple Plantation is large, we knew we needed to hurry to the center of the Maze. Nearing our goal, we saw a Hilo Hattie look-alike making a *lei*. She had a very efficient system of production. A galvanized tub of loose plumeria blossoms sprinkled with water sat half way under the card table on which she was working. Another tub on her right was covered by an umbrella to keep the sun off the *leis* she had completed. In front of her table, a third tub offered bottles of water in ice for anyone arriving thirsty.

Just as we were approaching her table from the front, Evelyn Souza, followed by her husband, came dashing in from the rear. Out of breath, but victorious, they claimed their position as the first contestants to solve Clue Five of the scavenger hunt.

"Yahoo," she shrieked. "I did it, didn't I? Are we the first to arrive?"

"Yes, you are. Please sign in and I will present you with your certificate," replied the *tūtū*. "Also, there will be no other challenges for today. Your next scheduled event is the *lū'au* tonight."

Quickly signing the ledger, Evelyn accepted the envelope holding the description of her prize. "Am I glad to win this," gloated Evelyn. Turning to us, she nearly shouted, "It's a gold bracelet with charms representing life in the Hawaiian Islands!"

After such a disappointing turn of events, Margie, Dan, Keoni and I went to lunch at the on-site restaurant before considering our next activity. Dan and Margie had not been to the plantation before and they decided to stay and take the scenic train ride and walk through the entire maze. Keoni and I decided to return to town and catch up on emails and phone calls.

On the way back to the hotel, I listened to messages on my home phone line and found a few that needed immediate attention. Surprisingly, there was one from Pearl. Listening to her restrained voice, I was saddened to learn that her sister Jade had died. I had spoken to Pearl a couple of times during the last year and had had a feeling that despite Jade's apparent renewed health, the woman would not live much longer.

Considering Pearl's devastating news, I decided to call her from the quiet of our hotel suite.

"Hi Pearl, this is Natalie Seachrist. You've been on my mind. I'm very sorry to have been out of touch."

"It is good of you to return my call so quickly. A couple of months after Jade and I saw you at Ala Moana Shopping Center, she had a setback in her health and died. I did not call you, or many other people in our lives. This was because I wanted to honor her desire to gift her body to the Medical School of the University of Hawai`i. Until the students completed their studies of her, I could not plan a celebration of her life."

"I understand. She seemed to be doing so well when we met," I said, avoiding my inner voice that had told me that was not the case.

"Although she saw you only that one time, Jade mentioned you occasionally, wondering how *you* and your brother were doing without your grandniece in your lives."

"Nathan and I are doing as well as may be expected. I'm so glad I had the opportunity to meet Jade. I could tell that she was a gracious woman and that she genuinely regretted how Ariel died at your apartments."

"That is true. But do not feel bad about Jade's passing, Natalie. She had a good life and through the scholarships she funded, she enhanced the lives of many young men and women and their families. Even in death she has continued to help others. She was an organ donor and through the months since she died, she has helped restore health to several people. Even medical students at the University of Hawai`i have benefitted from the gift of her body."

There were tears in my eyes and I swallowed before responding. "I'm so sorry for your loss Pearl, but you must feel pride in this final gift she gave."

"Oh, yes, very much. It may not be the customary way for Chinese, but then little in our lives has been traditional. Nor will the celebration I am planning for this Saturday. It is only a day after Lunar New Year, and there will be only one aspect of our gathering that reflects our mother's culture. We will be releasing Chinese wish lanterns at sunset after a picnic."

Pearl explained that she had just received Jade's ashes from the University Medical School and wanted to celebrate her sister's life without further delay. She was inviting the residents of the apartments, as well as the students and medical personnel who had been involved in Jade's final illness, or the gift of her organs and body. We continued to speak for a few minutes and I told her that barring any scheduling conflicts on Keoni's part, we would both be at Saturday's memorial celebration.

When she politely inquired about our recent activities, I had an opening for mentioning our participation in the scavenger hunt—and the poetic message I had found.

"We were in Chinatown for some Chinese New Year activities and ran across an interesting riddle that reads like a Chinese proverb adapted to Honolulu. It made me think of you and Jade and I was wondering if you could help me figure out what it means."

I then read her the false clue and asked what she thought of it.

"I see why you believe it refers to Chinese culture. Mention of the Song Lady speaks of the Song Dynasty, which was from the tenth to the thirteenth centuries. And I would say that the phrase *hearing the cries of the world*, refers to the Buddhist *bodhisattva* of compassion, *Kuan Yin*—or as it is written in modern Hanyu Pinyin Chinese transliteration, *Guānyīn*. I would be delighted to help you examine it further if you could bring me a copy of your message on Saturday. In the meantime, I will be thinking of its potential meaning."

I thanked her for her offer and promised to call her back soon. Within a couple of hours, Keoni and I looked like we had stepped out of a *Honolulu Magazine* advertisement in the mid-1970s. We each wore classic Tori Richard's aloha wear and the plumeria *lei* we had been given at the Dole Plantation. On top of my long black and gold *muʻumuʻu*, I wore a seed pearl choker, with matching earrings and bracelet. Knowing there would be a lot of sand beneath our feet that evening, I wore a new pair of gold-toned gel sandals for practicality.

As we listened to a prolonged commentary on Hawaiian culture and history during the bus ride to Paradise Cove, I wondered if the facts contained in our tour guide's script might prove useful in solving clues during the next two days. Although I knew most of the material, I found the trip out to the leeward coast as entertaining as a tourist. By the time we arrived, we were ready for some liquid refreshment. True to their advertising, we were greeted with *kuku`i* nut *leis* and Mai Tais. I was delighted with the balance between the Curacao and lime juice.

After our day on the hunt, my foursome was more interested in watching the fun than participating in Hawaiian sports, games of chance, or the *huki lau* (a communal pulling in of fishnets). Drinks in hand, we strolled the grounds as attendants in traditional Hawaiian dress enhanced our experience of old Hawai`i. As a mature woman of some life experience, I enjoyed watching the young Hawaiian men who were accomplished at *o`oihe*, spear throwing, and `*ulu maika*, the rolling of stone disks. The tourists who attempted to copy their movements were thoroughly entertaining as their alcohol-enhanced improvisation provided unexpected thrills and spills. Hopefully, those who had been imbibing were taking the bus back to Honolulu, rather than driving themselves.

Even by torch light, our front row seats offered a clear view of everything. Except for the lack of a single *lau lau*, the food was excellent. A salad bar was offered for those who disliked Hawaiian food, but I couldn't imagine anyone except a vegan or vegetarian foregoing the succulent underground roasted pig. And while pork was the centerpiece of the menu, local fish with a macadamia nut crème sauce was a close second in popularity. I was especially pleased that sweet *kalo* rolls were available.

Following the feast, there was a review that included a beautiful presentation of Hawaiian culture through music and dance, and even a Samoan fire knife dance. Although the MC for Paradise Cove conducted most of the show, Jason Chin managed to get in a couple of jokes about *poi* as he presented the Souzas with the exquisite gold bracelet they had won that day. Evelyn got a little too excited about her good fortune. As she preened and shook the jewelry gracing her wrist, she stumbled and had to be helped back to her seat by Jim.

The evening was long, and I was very glad we had not driven ourselves. On the bus ride back from the *lū`au*, I fell into a troubled sleep. Urged by the beating of Hawaiian war drums, a Chinese dragon chased Hawaiian warriors up into the hillsides of Nu`uanu. Then I watched as the warriors of O`ahu were picked off by what looked like World War II howitzers, rather than the late eighteenth-century cannon I would have expected to see. As the bus jolted to a stop, the scene of hillside warfare faded and a life-sized statue of *Kuan Yin* standing at the Pali Lookout morphed into a cloud that floated into the stratosphere. Since these scenes had unfolded in living color, rather than the faded sepia tones of my visions, I doubted that I needed to consult with John Dias about what I had just seen.

Shaking off the remnants of my dream, I stretched and reached for my bag.

"Back in the land of the living?" asked Keoni.

"I guess so."

"Is it safe to ask what you were dreaming about?"

"What's up, Natalie" Margie inquired. "Having a nightmare?

"No," I laughed. "Just a follow up on the *hula* show—except that my dancers were Hawaiian warriors."

CHAPTER 7

The real voyage of discovery is not in seeking new landscapes but in having new eyes.
Marcel Proust [1871 - 1922]

When our party of revelers entered the hotel, the lobby was empty, aside from a trio of men with regimental haircuts exiting the sports bar. After bidding everyone goodnight, Keoni and I went up to our second suite of the week. This time, we were being treated to VIP quarters that were vast and luxurious. Huge tropical floral arrangements stood on elegant *koa* furniture in every room. The master suite included a bathroom with a whirlpool tub large enough for group R & R and a bed that enveloped one in silken sheets. And in case anyone got bored, there was a sophisticated television and sound system.

Despite the amenities of our beautiful suite, the week was wearing on me and I could not wait to fall back asleep—even if I had to watch dragons, warriors and a giant Kuan Yin. For most of the night, I experienced peaceful rest. Shortly after four in the morning, I awoke refreshed but thirsty. I poured a glass of water and sat in the living room to avoid waking Keoni. Leaning back in the ergonomic white leather recliner, I soon fell into that state I often experience between consciousness and sleep.

* * * * *

I hover in the midst of clouds, looking down on a classic waterfront scene in Shànghăi. I realize that little changed between the pre-World War II time of the Wong Sisters and when I first visited in 1980.

In an instant, I stand at the front of a walled residential compound. I hear the laughter of children. The gate swings open and I see two little Chinese girls at play, dashing around a traditional bride's wedding sedan chair resting on its bamboo poles at the back of a small outbuilding. The scene is familiar because Pearl Wong once described it to me. It took place shortly before she and her sister Jade escaped from Shànghǎi with their father and amah *during the Japanese attack on Shànghǎi in 1932. I next picture the girls parting from their father and their ocean voyage aboard the RMS Empress of Britain from Hong Kong to Honolulu.*

I cringe as I feel the deck rolling beneath my feet. I close my eyes for a moment and try to separate myself from the ship's movement. When I open my eyes, I am staring at the pier alongside Honolulu's Aloha Tower. No cityscape of high-rises stands beyond the water's edge. The hillsides above are not crowded with roads and homes reaching nearly to the top. In front of me, I see the girls and their amah *being greeted by their father's family and friends. The Wong sisters are clearly overwhelmed by the numbers of smiling Chinese and Hawaiian people of all ages, who press* lei *upon* lei *around their necks.*

I stare as Chu-Hua Lee separates herself and walks toward the tower. I hear no dialogue. Two middle-aged haole *men in pinstripe suits and felt fedoras await her. They behave deferentially toward the diminutive woman approaching them. Judged to be of humble stature and little importance in her homeland, here she walks with the sure steps and perfect posture of a well-respected person. She nods slightly upon reaching them, extending her hand to accept their handshakes. She then holds out a small box tied in string and one large envelope. The trio shares a few words before Miss Lee turns and retraces her steps with equal decorum.*

The scene shifts. I am standing in the hallway of the Honolulu hotel in which Keoni and I are staying. An elevator door opens. Professor Fù Hán Zhāng exits. He is dressed in the white suit in which he will die. A small straw hat compliments his brown and white spectator shoes. Again I recognize that the suit, shoes, and hat are similar to what I saw in my vision of the mid-twentieth century murder.

Oblivious of my presence, the Professor turns without hesitation to the right. He pauses briefly at the hallway's T-junction. He looks down at a sheet of paper in his hand and then up at the room numbers on the wall. He then turns left and walks forward with a look of expectation on his face. From the top of the corridor, I watch him knock on the door at the end of the hall. The door opens, and he enters a suite that will be luxurious like the one I am staying in.

I begin to walk down the hall, but as in the Chinatown hotel of my initial vision, I am stopped as though by a glass wall. There is no sound and no variance to the full color in which I watch this scenario. Within a short span of time, the door to the suite reopens and Professor Zhāng exits. Projecting confusion, he walks toward me unsteadily, rubbing his lips.

The door to the suite swings open again. A tall willowy female in a flowing silk dress, long evening gloves, and high heels emerges. Everything she wears, as well as her clutch purse and large tote bag, is in blood red. Large round sunglasses and a broad-brimmed straw hat prevent me from seeing her features. Quickly closing the door, the woman hangs a do-not-disturb-sign on the outside of the doorknob. She turns back toward me and silently strides on shapely legs toward the man who has stopped abruptly. She reaches into her purse and pulls out a small pistol with a squarish pearl grip. Stepping behind her prey, she squeezes the trigger. Once.

There is no sound. The man falls diagonally across the floor. The woman stares at the paper that has fluttered to the floor. She snatches it up and glances around before moving away from the man for whom she has no further need. With no awareness of my presence, she breezes past me with a scent of roses and walks down the hall. There she turns, presumably to continue her purposeful stride to the elevators.

I stand alone for a few moments, staring at the dapper little man who had loved Hawai`i since watching Charlie Chan movies in his youth in Shànghǎi. For a moment I contemplate what he had experienced in his life: the multiple attacks on and occupation of the city once called the Paris of the East; the dissolution of the

Republic of China; the ascendance of Mao Zedong; and, the rise of the People's Republic of China. How did this impact his childhood, his years as a student and then as a professor of numerous languages? Knowing his interest in the world beyond the Central Kingdom, I suspect this scholar fulfilled the promise of his given name, broadminded. For such freedom of thought, he probably spent time in house arrest or even prison. Finally, after surviving everything else, he dies by violence in the island paradise he had admired from the silver screen.

*   *   *   *   *

Thursday morning Keoni and I arrived for breakfast a bit later than usual, since I had to call John Dias and report the vision I had just experienced. Except for the piece of paper that had been in the Professor's hand, there was little for John to add to his case notes. When we entered the room, the only seats available in the ballroom were at a table in the rear. I wondered if news of Professor Zhāng's death had attracted greater participation in the hunt.

"Welcome to day four of the Aloha Scavenger Hunt," announced Jason Chin. "I have only one announcement for you before we open the morning's clue. This is the start of Chinese New Year and I don't think I'm giving away any secrets by telling you that that is the theme of our activities today. Before you head out, we want to remind you of the many special events taking place just a few blocks from here, including a noontime lion dance for kids at the Chinese Cultural Plaza.

"And tonight, we will be participating in a traditional Chinese New Year dinner at Legend Seafood Restaurant, beginning at six o`clock. Let me add a final hint for assuring you survive, if not thrive, in what we've planned for you. I suggest you put on your walking shoes, because while today's adventures may be short in mileage, there may be many turns you will need to make in order to complete your several assignments. Now let the day begin. Same game. Same rules. You may now open your first clue of the day."

First Annual Aloha Scavenger Hunt
Day 4, Clue 6
Shortest distance to your destination: .8 miles
From showcased bounty of sea and land, an image of strands of shimmering seeds awaits you in a bed of yawning mouths.

"Well, it's nearby," declared Margie.

"That's true. Let's dump most of our things in the trunk of the car," suggested Keoni. "Less to carry, but nearby if needed."

"Good idea," said Dan. "With the Chinese New Year dinner tonight, I'll bet that all of today's challenges will be centered on Chinatown." Glancing at my gel sandals, he asked, "What about your shoes, ladies? Are you up to a day of pounding the downtown pavement?"

"No. I'd better switch shoes," I said, giving in reluctantly.

When the elevator reached the lobby, I waved everyone ahead and sat on a sofa to put on my walking shoes. A short while later, my daily bag of healthy snacks and gel sandals were stashed in my car. With large bottles of water, we headed west on South King Street.

"You didn't even pause to consider another direction, Keoni," Margie observed as we moved toward Chinatown.

"With clients in the core of the city—and having put in a few years as a beat cop—I'm pretty familiar with storefronts in every direction. We're talking about less than a mile. The waterside shops at Aloha Tower would be too far. And there's nothing in the middle of the financial institutions, office supply stores, and urban colleges that cries *bounty of sea and land*. That leaves Chinatown, which we've agreed fits the theme of the day."

"True. And I'm sure it's a retail store," I added.

"I know we're supposed to stay together, but we aren't tied with a leash," commented Dan. "Why don't we spread out a bit?"

"I think that's splitting hairs, but I guess it's not really breaking the rules. Why don't we work as couples, going in and out of every other doorway? That keeps us only a few feet from one another," suggested Keoni.

Soon we were prowling the many shops on the roadways that run perpendicular to King Street. It seemed like we ran into a hunt contestant or two every few feet. Our strategy seemed to be a template for several other teams. I spotted the Souzas following our zigzag pattern, as well as the college kids who had captured the first prize at the Pali Lookout. A couple of times I saw the father-daughter combo that had solved the second clue. From her lingering at windows, I got the impression the girl was more interested in shopping than solving clues.

"The phrase *shimmering seeds* does not have to mean food," observed Dan, as we paused for a water break.

"It could be something decorative," suggested Margie.

At that point, I noticed a crowd gathering at the front of one of the semi-open markets. Gesturing, I checked for traffic and dashed across the street.

"It's a good thing there's a cross-walk in this block," chided Keoni when he caught up with me.

We crowded in among the mixture of scavenger hunters, tourists, and local shoppers in time to see big Jim Souza shake his head.

"What's up, Jim," I asked, sliding in next to him and Evelyn.

"We almost did it," he harrumphed. "A minute earlier and Evelyn would have had some more jewelry."

He pointed to a large poster above a fishmonger's counter. There in shimmering glory were images of pearls lying in open oyster shells.

"What was the prize?" I asked.

"Beautiful cultured pearls, in a necklace, earrings and cuff links," responded Margie.

Dan signed in with our greeter, a Chinese man appearing as an affluent merchant might have before World War I. His ensemble included a black silk *tángzhuāng* coat with Mandarin collar, gold silk vest with a dragon pattern, a tasseled black skull cap, and black cotton shoes.

Dan returned to us with the next challenge in hand. We moved out of the market to analyze our assignment.

First Annual Aloha Scavenger Hunt
Day 4, Clue 7
Shortest distance to your destination: .4 miles
Sacred words from the Sage reach out to those who
can see within the brushed wash of sapphire blue.

"I'm getting tired of losing by only a couple of minutes. This destination may be close, but there are a lot of stores in this small area," I complained.

It was noon and we were not bound by the team-in-tandem rule. So even though we might lose another challenge, we decided to take a food break. While the men opted for *teriyaki* beef sticks and `*ahí sushi*, I decided to introduce Margie to one of my favorite local ices, *liliko`i*.

Our tightly-knit group unwound as we slowed to enjoy our in-transit mid-day repast. When Dan stopped in at a shop featuring fishing paraphernalia, Keoni paused to call a couple of clients. Margie and I played hop-scotch through the doorways of storefronts that beckoned us with varied soft and hard goods. Motivated by her upcoming redecorating project, she decided to spend time looking at Asian ceramics.

Meanwhile, I continued on with my own window shopping, admiring the many attractive displays for Chinese New Year. In a theme dominated by miniature orange trees and scattered cherry blossoms were verses of Chinese New Year poetry that had been penned on red paper by talented modern calligraphers.

Across the street, I saw a door painted in bright red enamel. Beside it was a window with another elegant exhibit. At the back of the waist-high display was a Chinese screen. Within rosewood and brass framing, its three panels of painted silk showed classic vignettes of Chinese culture. Included were the Great Wall and the Forbidden City of Beijing. Laborers toiled in rice paddies, panda bears climbed eucalyptus trees, and beautiful women in colorful silk *cheongsams* danced with fans.

In front of this background were numerous antique books, calligraphy brushes and ink sticks. Surrounding these literary materials were the twelve animals of the Chinese Zodiac in carved rosewood. The scene was enchanting. I leaned in to examine it more closely.

As my eyes panned across the visual fairytale, I realized that the center of the display was an illustrated copy of the *Tao Te Ching*. Having written an essay on Chinese philosophy in college, I knew about the debate regarding the date of the book's composition and its authorship. Usually it is credited to Lao-Tzu, a sixth-century BCE philosopher and Zhou Dynasty official.

This antique edition featured beautiful illustrations and translation by the noted Scottish sinologist James Legge. Immersed in the beauty of the overall display, I glanced up at the screen. Faintly imprinted on clouds floating across a blue sky, were the same words as the passage in the open book below. And that was the solution to the current clue—a message from the Sage in a sapphire sky.

Choking back my desire to shout out my discovery, I looked at my watch. It was twelve fifty-five. At one o'clock the men rejoined us and we went into the shop in tandem. Directly ahead was a long counter with a cash register. Displayed prominently behind it was a poster with the symbol for "luck" printed upside-down to invite good fortune to enter.

An elderly gentleman attired as a Chinese scholar greeted us in character and delivered a short philosophical monologue. Dressed in the traditional black-trimmed white silk *panling lanshan* robe and black cap, he added a sense of history to the occasion. As he bowed, I felt honored to have solved one of the hunt's vaguest challenges.

There was only one thing disappointing in my having solved this clue. I would have to wait until this evening's Chinese feast to receive my prize—the beautiful book in the window.

Since we were the only people in the store, we decided to take a quick peek at the third clue of the day. The proprietor, Bertram Fong was very pleased to let us see the book in which he had inserted another clue centered in Asia.

First Annual Aloha Scavenger Hunt
Day 4, Clue 8
Shortest distance to your destination: .3 miles

*Both East and West of the Nipponese Sea, smiling fe-
lines beckon hungry guests and the prosperity they
ensure. Awaiting you today is one whose Bengalese
eyes look out on the promenade of the Dragon.*

"Again, it's in the neighborhood," said Dan. "I get the reference to the Sea of Japan, but I'm not sure of its significance."

"I think it refers to both sides of the sea—China and Japan,"
I suggested.

"That sounds appropriate, but don't forget Russia and Ko-
rea," added Keoni.

"Well, *feline* is a no brainer. And the reference to something
from Bengal sounds like a tiger," said Margie.

"Okay. So far that gives us, *in China or Japan, there are smiling cats who call out to people who are hungry*," ventured Keoni.

"Now it's *my* turn to say, *no brainer*," I said gleefully. "It's a
maneki neko or beckoning cat. At least that's what it's called in
Japanese. I don't know the Chinese phrase, but they're the por-
celain cats with the waving paw you see in Asian restaurants.
They're believed to attract good fortune and customers."

"How many Asian restaurants are there in Chinatown?"
mused Dan.

"A few too many for my taste. It could take the rest of the
afternoon to find the right one," Margie moaned.

"Oh, I think we can narrow it a bit further," said Keoni with
a smile. "The *promenade of the Dragon* sounds like the Chinese
Cultural Plaza. There can't be more than a half-dozen restaurants over there."

"Isn't that where there's going to be a lion or dragon dance
to open our New Year's dinner?" I asked.

"Yes," nodded Margie. "I was reading about it in a brochure.
The Queen of the Narcissus Festival is going to greet us for this
evening's *Lóng wǔ*, the Dragon Dance."

As Keoni circled the Cultural Plaza on a map, I took another look at the clue. "I don't understand the Bengalese tiger part," I said.

Margie looked over my shoulder for a moment. "It's really talking about the eyes of the cat being Bengalese...like a tiger."

Without further delay, we moved onto the plaza to make the most of our lead. Once we were there, we zigged and zagged through restaurants facing onto the plaza. By this time, we frequently saw other scavenger hunters looking around.

"I remember Jason Chin remarking that the destinations would be visible from the street," said Keoni. "The only beckoning cats we've seen so far have been inside near cashiers. Why don't we do what we did earlier—work as couples approaching every other storefront, until we find a cat that's visible from the sidewalk?"

While his idea was sound, it did not bring us success. Cruising a second quadrant of storefronts on the plaza, we heard a whoop of success from a rival. Ahead we saw a crowd gathering as one of the young policemen John Dias had mentioned waved his award certificate in the air. When we were able to work our way to the front of the crowd, I found the solution to the mystery of Bengalese eyes ...this *maneki neko* had eyes that had been shaped from polished tiger eye stones.

Ever the glutton for punishment, Margie wanted to know what prize she had missed by a hair's breadth.

"My girlfriend is going to be thrilled. I've won a necklace, bracelet and earring set made from tiger's eye and sterling silver!" declared the young policeman who looked like he had been pulling double shifts the entire week.

We knew there was still the chance of winning a daily challenge or the grand prize the next day. Accordingly, we dutifully checked in with our greeter, a young Chinese girl dressed completely in red. She was the quintessential bride of southern China. She wore a traditional two-piece silk wedding dress, which included a tunic with golden dragon and phoenix to represent the joining of male and female. Her outfit was completed with embroidered soft-soled shoes and a tasseled bridal crown with pearls. Proudly pinned to her tunic was a picture of her great-grandparents on their wedding day.

Once our foursome had returned to the hotel, we took a while to clean off the grit from our day's adventures in Chinatown. As cocktails would begin at six, we had ample time to outfit ourselves elegantly...except for our footwear. Margie and I had chosen to wear flat sandals to let our tired feet breathe through the cooling hours of the evening. Not knowing how late we would be partying, I brought a light shawl for each of us.

We had spent the entire day in Chinatown, but were so involved with the hunt that we had little opportunity to appreciate the ambience of the community. That evening, we departed from the hotel feeling like tourists who had never been to Chinatown. No matter how many times you have participated in Chinese New Year celebrations, it is always a new experience.

As we neared the Cultural Plaza, celebrants dressed in traditional red for the New Year increased in numbers and bombastic behavior. With people jammed in around us, Keoni and I had fallen behind Dan and Margie. The scents and sounds of the holiday atmosphere were almost intoxicating. We enjoyed our leisurely pace holding hands like a young couple in love for the first time.

While waiting for a pedestrian light to turn green, I glanced around at the century-old structures. "Look up there. That building across the street to the left. The windows look just like the ones in my dream," I said excitedly.

"You're right, it does resemble what you've described" said Keoni, squeezing my shoulder. "It's too bad it looks like it's in the middle of renovation. I think we're going to need some backup to pursue this possibility." He pulled out his phone and dialed quickly. "Hi, JD. Keoni here. Sorry I'm missing you. Natalie and I are walking through Chinatown. She's found a building with windows like the ones she described to you from her, ah, dream. In case you don't get this message soon, I'll text you the building's address and the name of the contractor whose sign is on display—and a picture, while I'm at it."

We crossed the street so Keoni could snap a photo and take

down the sign's contact information for John. We admired the four-storey stone fronted building for a few minutes, and then I texted Margie to apologize for wandering off. The closer we got to the plaza, the numbers of people in the street ballooned to the point that we could barely move forward. Regardless of whether you believe in the philosophy behind all the hoopla, it is fun to join in the communal spirit of the annual festivity.

For me, the only negative aspect was the overuse of fireworks. Every once in a while, we heard a large explosion of firecrackers and could smell their remains building in the air. In several cultures, especially Asian, the fire and noise are intended to drive away ghosts, evil spirits, and bad luck. While those may have been major concerns in another age, I was more concerned personally about the issue of public safety if anything went wrong with any of the fireworks, no matter their size. With ordinances regarding the legality of consumer fireworks changing periodically, there is a parallel rise or fall in injury and even death on holidays in the Islands. Thank goodness we now live in Windward O`ahu, where the fallout of fireworks is minimal in comparison to downtown.

On the positive side of the day's celebrations, there had been numerous performances of music and dance, as well as civic groups parading through the Plaza in exuberant recognition of the Year of the Wood Sheep or Goat. Knowing a *wŭ lóng* dragon dance, was scheduled to begin at the time of our dinner, I was hoping to arrive at the restaurant before it began. Luckily, we were able to slide into the space the O'Haras were holding for us beside the doorway. As we eased in between them, Margie passed each of us a brochure explaining this aspect of traditional Chinese New Year.

CHAPTER 8

Every year have bounty in excess.
Chinese Proverb

I have watched many dragon dance parades before, but never understood their historical and cultural significance. According to the brochure I was reading, the dance of the mythical dragon originated about two thousand years ago during the Han Dynasty. The dance welcomes good fortune and wellness at the beginning of the New Year and scares off lingering evil spirits. Associated with Chinese agricultural cycles, the dragon is viewed as a river spirit, whose breath creates the clouds that bring life-giving rains and fertility to the land and its people.

Representing the *yang* force of the *yin-yang* element, the good-natured creature is believed to be the custodian of life's seasons, attracting health, long life, prosperity, and even heavenly affirmation of imperial authority. Viewing themselves as directly connected to their mythology, the Chinese people often refer to themselves as *lóng de chuán rén*, Descendants of the Dragon.

Most of the troupe performing this dragon dance were dressed in gold *cheongsam* costumes with red embroidery. They were practitioners of *kung fu*, with a strength, agility, and musical prowess that imbued the performance with the dignity and strength associated with the mythical creature they had constructed for the event. To allow repeated use, the dragon was made of durable fabric, rather than *papier mâché*.

The dancers' movements simulated swimming or flying, as

they manipulated the poles up and down within the head and body of the 100-foot dragon. The undulating pattern was reinforced by improvisational music with a strong back beat provided by drums, flutes, cymbals and gongs. Since the dragon dance was being performed at sunset, a torch bearer led the parade and battery-powered lights highlighted the colors of the scales and the horn on the head of the dragon.

Excited by the shimmering magical quality of the show, I entered Legend Seafood Restaurant as hungry for cultural tidbits, as I was for the superb feast we were about to enjoy. The restaurant is noted for exquisite *dim sum* during the day and sophisticated seafood in the evening. Within the streamlined modern décor, I was again taken with the stunning chandelier that lights much of the main dining room. Despite the numbers in our party, I was hoping they would be serving some of my favorite dishes that night. After verifying our reservation, we entered the banquet room.

At each guest's place was a red packet of *lucky money*, such as Chinese children traditionally receive during New Year's celebrations. Looking at the menu in front of my napkin, I knew I would not be disappointed in the evening's fare. My eyes skipped through the delicacies being offered, including: my favorite appetizer, deep fried taro puffs; Lunar New Year soup with tofu and pork balls; crispy Peking duck with sweet steamed buns; whole steamed *onaga* (a red-skinned snapper); and eight-treasure rice pudding with red bean paste, sugared dried fruit and lotus seeds. No wonder the fees for the week's events had been so high!

As dish after dish arrived, we visited with fellow contestants and board members from the scavenger hunt, and the non-profits benefiting from the event. With toasts from our table, as well as the podium, I was pleased to remember that none of us would be driving that night.

Throughout the meal, Keoni maintained a polite demeanor, while monitoring his smart phone. I knew he was checking to see if John Dias had gotten our message about the building in Chinatown.

"How's it going these days, Keoni, as a peeping eye?" quipped Dan about the third time Keoni glanced downward.

"I'm on vacation this week, remember?" Keoni replied quietly.

"You said you were keeping your eyes open for the Lieutenant," said Margie.

"So far, Natalie and I have been spending our time with you two, and I think you'll agree there hasn't been much to pass on to JD," said Keoni smoothly.

Dan gave Keoni and me a searching look, but taking the hint from our reticence, said nothing further. Nevertheless, I was nervous about whether we would be trapped into revealing what we had been doing with and for John—and worse than that, that our sleuthing was based on my visions. I was glad that my concerns were short-lived. Both of our companions were tired, and Margie had broken the strap on her sandal. Therefore, she and Dan slipped out of the room during a long round of applause to catch a cab back to the hotel before the presentation of prizes.

I was also tired, but Jason Chin provided an entertaining program with frequent references to Chinese New Year customs. It seemed appropriate that a Chinese woman from Maui had won the pearls in one of today's challenges. When I was awarded my copy of the *Tao Te Ching*, I thanked my teammates, who were generously allowing me the privilege of adding the volume to my library. The young policeman who won the tiger's eye jewelry set an excellent tone for the closing of the evening. After insisting that his girlfriend join him at the podium, he dropped to one knee and proposed to her. Fortunately, she quickly accepted, and the applause was deafening.

As a crowd of well-wishers pressed forward to congratulate the couple, Keoni and I said a few farewells at our table and scooted out the door. Part way to the hotel, we got a call back from John. After receiving Keoni's message, he had called the contractor listed on the sign in the building's window. With a team of subcontractors pulling an all-night shift, he had been able to schedule an immediate tour of the property.

* * * * *

As we approached the Chinatown building I believed to be the site of my vision, John stepped out of his new Ford Fusion Hybrid. "Hi, guys. Thanks for the heads up. At least I had a chance to grab some *sushi* before our moonlight rendezvous with the past."

"Not to brag, but we just enjoyed a full-on Chinese New Year feast," gloated Keoni.

"That's it. Rub it in. The last time I had that luxury was five years ago. I usually end up pulling late shifts or all-nighters during Chinese New Year. Before we go in, you should know I told the owner I'm checking out several buildings in the area about an old case—and that as my former partner, Keoni, you're consulting with me."

"That explains our presence very well. You won't believe what happened today, John," I said. "I found the answer to the second clue of the day and won a copy of the *Tao Te Ching*."

"Good for you," he replied. "I know you're supporting the cause of helping women and kids at risk in Hawai`i, but it's nice you've gotten a little something in return."

"It really *is* good for *our* purposes," I said. "Keoni and I talked about it, and I'm going to put a copy of the fake scavenger hunt clue inside the book and tell Pearl Wong I found it there. That will fit in nicely with what I've already told her."

"Sounds good. Run with it," John said encouragingly.

He then punched in a few numbers on his cell phone and spoke briefly. The door to the mysterious building opened almost immediately. We were greeted by a young man in a white T-shirt with a kaleidoscope of paint splatters.

"Hi. I'm José. I'm the architect's assistant. I got a call saying you'd be dropping in."

"Sorry to interrupt you, but I need to go through the property," said John, flashing his badge. "You don't have to stop your work, but we need to look over the place—from top to bottom."

"Sure. The boss said to do whatever you asked. Everything is pretty much open. You can go through it all. If you don't need me, I'll go back upstairs. A painter and I are working on the penthouse on the top floor, if you want anything."

As I stood at the probable site of my first vision in this round of murders, a mixture of feelings washed over me. The scarred outside walls of brick and plaster betrayed little of what I had seen in my vision. Stepping within, we entered a land of chaotic reconstruction.

"Tell you what," began John. "Why don't you take the lead, Natalie? Keoni and I will follow behind. Tell me immediately if you see something from one of your visions. Anything, even if it's not exactly the same—just give me a running commentary, like you did when you looked through the crime scene photos of Miriam's murder."

"All right, John," I replied, moving ahead of him. The barren rooms of scraped walls and woodwork did not resemble what I had seen in my vision. Swipes of paint and swatches of fabric in the first room gave a hint of the designer's sense of the building's future, but no indication of its past. When I first saw the windows from outside, I was sure I had found the building I envisioned. But after going through the ground floor, I doubted myself. As we prepared to move upstairs, we found the elevator had been blocked off. John called José and learned that the elevator was filled with the last of the former owner's furnishings, so we would have to take the stairs.

We located the narrow staircase in the back corner of the building and began climbing. We paused at the second and third floors, but I felt no sense of *déjà vu*. Everything was dirty and cluttered, but I could tell there had been numerous small rooms laid out along a narrow hallway.

On the top floor, I found several rooms that remained intact. None of them seemed related to the murder I saw in my vision. But then we caught up with José and his companion in an open space running across the front of the building. There, I faced the windows that had caught my attention from the street. And at the end, I saw an old-fashioned cage elevator car—in decorative wrought iron.

"Look John," I said excitedly. "The windows, just like I saw them. And the elevator. Well, it's black, but everything else about it is exactly what I saw."

For a moment, the three of us stood looking up at the two workers who were poised on ladders, sanding crown molding below the cove ceilings. Drawn by something intangible, I approached a worn luncheon table full of paperwork. As I tried to politely peek at the assortment, John and Keoni walked toward José.

Calling up, John asked, "Can you tell us anything about this building and the way it might have looked originally?"

"Or, maybe fifty or sixty years ago?" added Keoni.

Climbing down from his ladder, José said, "Sure. I've been through a lot of historical information on this project." He gestured toward the table. "There are some enlargements of old photographs you can look at."

At his invitation, I began actively sorting through the photos he had indicated. Luckily, the man did not ask what my official role was.

"This building has been through several incarnations. Originally there was a shop on the ground floor, offices on the second floor, and the owner's family lived on the top two floors.

"Through the decades, there were decreasing numbers in each generation of the Shēn family that owns the building. With their changing needs, the configuration of the building was altered. Eventually, they consolidated their living quarters onto this floor. After that, they remodeled floors two and three to accommodate a small hotel for travelling Chinese businessmen. I guess it was what we'd call a boutique hotel today."

"This top floor has always been a family space?" I inquired.

"Yes. Evidently there's something funny about the family trust. The person inheriting the building has to live here to claim his inheritance. But when Bō Shēn inherited the building after his uncle died a year ago, he refused to live in the mess the place has become. That's why we were brought in."

Seeking a connection to my vision, I asked, "You say the hotel rooms were on the second and third floors?"

"Yes. Emphasis on *were*. When my boss was called in on this project, he was given the keys, some old photo albums and two weeks to formulate a design for the remodel.

"Since Bō hasn't been sure about some of the design details, we've been concentrating on removing many of the interior walls and generally prepping the shell of the building. Right now, Bō's conferring with his fiancée about configuring their personal living space. Once we have their input, we'll know which parts of the building to devote to commercial purposes."

"I know you said the elevator is full of furniture. But could you turn on some lights inside, so I can see how the interior is finished?" I asked. "Also, do you know if it's always been black? The cage, itself, I mean?"

"Yes, and no. If you can wait a minute, I'll move one of our work lights, so you can take a look. As to your second question, except for a few brass pieces, the metalwork used to be a bronze tone, which we're hoping to restore."

I looked over at John and Keoni. "If you'd two don't mind spending a little extra time, I'd like to check out the elevator."

The Lieutenant shrugged and nodded.

I glanced at Keoni and thought about the romantic week we were supposed to be enjoying. He returned my look without expression. The call was mine.

"Okay, José. Let's go for it," I said.

The man pulled over a ladder with a large halogen light dangling from it.

Speaking softly, John said, "With a corpse in the morgue and no physical evidence, I'm yours for the entire night if it'll yield anything useful."

Within a few minutes, I had the confirmation I sought. Although the outside of the elevator's cage was now black, what I could see of the interior displayed the brass and bronze finishes I recalled from my vision.

And although there were several pieces of furniture stacked along the sides, I could see a scuffed hexagon of black-and-white tiles on the floor, featuring a Chinese character set in a black frame. At the back of the cage, the same design appeared on a metal medallion.

I stood back from my investigation and found that John was ready for my response. He may have been waiting for a detailed report, but I simply gave him a thumbs-up sign. At that moment, John called me back to the table.

"Take one last look at the building's past life, Natalie. Tell us what you see."

A single long shot of one of the old hotel's hallways confirmed that this was the setting of my vision. "Even though the photo is in black and white, I'm sure that's the carpet runner I saw—it has the same herringbone pattern. And the floor? The boards look the same, a bit wider than what we use today. The molding looks right too. And even though I wasn't paying attention to the walls, I think I remember that flowered wallpaper."

"Are there any pictures in color? Going back in time?" John asked José.

"Yes, Lieutenant. But after looking at them for any architectural significance, my boss returned them to the owner."

"Do you know what kind of drapes were on these windows?" I asked

"Yeah. Across the glass were sheer floor-length curtains with a tiny floral pattern. And I know there were deep green velvet drapes at the sides of the windows. We even have an old tieback."

With that revelation, our Chinatown investigation ended for the night. John thanked José and told him he would call Mr. Shēn if he needed anything further. As we exited the building, he said he would see if there was any record of a murder occurring on the premises. Declining his offer of a ride back to our hotel, we resumed our night-time saunter. When we arrived in our suite, we decided it was too late for a soak in the whirlpool and settled for a brief dalliance in the shower.

* * * * *

Having decided to skip a shower, we slept as late as we could before joining Margie and Dan for breakfast. The room was buzzing with recognition of this being the last day of the hunt. Jason Chin kept his commentary to a minimum, probably saving his final jokes for the banquet that would cap our week-long adventure.

After our late-night exploration of the Shēn Building I was hungry. Fortunately, I had the opportunity to choose a variety of options from the extensive breakfast bar. We then opened the morning's clue and quickly saw the distance we would be traveling across the island. Thank goodness I had stoked my inner fires.

> ### First Annual Aloha Scavenger Hunt
> ### Day 5, Clue 9
> ### Shortest distance to your destination: 14.3 miles
> *For more than a century, the sharing of bento boxes and lunch pails, saints' days and Lunar New Years, encouraged the merging of the myriad cultures of Hawai`i. On this, the final day of the First Annual Aloha Scavenger Hunt, we invite you to the park that celebrates the peoples of Europe and Asia whose labor crowned the Islands' first agricultural industry "king".*

This time, Dan took the lead in solving the challenge. "Well, this looks fairly simple, even for a mainlander. Tuesday, the challenge was Sea Life Park. Wednesday, it was the Dole Plantation. The giveaway to today's clue is that last phrase about the *agricultural king*. With pineapple already having been featured, the answer to this challenge has to be the Sugar Plantation Village inside the Waipahu Cultural Garden Park."

Keoni looked up from the brochure he was reading. "You've got that right. The mileage is on target. The only thing I'm debating is our route...should we take H1 or H2? How desperate are you all to try and win this challenge?"

I looked at Margie who was smiling in anticipation. "I hate to put a damper on the morning, but I don't think there'll be many people who'll miss this clue. Those kids on motorcycles should be able to scoop this one up without much competition from the rest of us."

Margie accepted the inevitable and said, "It sounds like an interesting place and it'll be fun to get out of town for a while."

"Okay then. We'll take the slightly more scenic route along H2," decided Keoni.

Our guess was correct. We arrived at the outdoor museum to find many of our fellow contestants ahead of us. The property includes a couple dozen old plantation homes and other structures dating back nearly a hundred years. With so many sites to explore, there was no telling who might be the first to find the scavenger hunt greeter.

I found it fascinating to view the artifacts of the people who had made Hawai`i an agricultural success. Listening to the melodious voices of tourists, I thought about the mix of peoples, food, and music that had merged through the years. As the guides reminded us, people from many parts of the world had contributed to the life we enjoy in the Islands today: Polynesia, Europe, the Americas, China, Portugal, Japan, Korea, the Philippines, Puerto Rico, and Okinawa.

Even though there was no restaurant, we were treated to samples of sugar cane and delicious fruits which the immigrants had brought as seeds from their homelands. We were standing near restrooms, sucking on sugarcane, when we heard someone's victory yell. Turning toward a building that displayed vintage tools, we spotted a growing circle of our fellow scavengers.

"Okay, who won this challenge?" asked Margie.

Being taller than his wife and me, Dan called out the answer. "Your prediction was on the mark, Natalie. It's the guys on bikes, again."

"What's their prize?" I asked.

"A train set surrounded by a miniature sugar plantation that one of the park docents created," Keoni responded.

Knowing we were still eligible for the grand prize, we signed in and picked up an event survey. Our greeter was a young Portuguese man dressed as a nineteenth-century water boy. Seated on an old dented bucket, he serenaded a growing audience with classic `ukulele pieces on an instrument he informed us he had inherited from his great-grandfather.

After learning this was the final challenge of the scavenger hunt, we spent a short while admiring the workmanship on the tiny elements of the scene surrounding the vintage Lionel steam train. The miniature plantation surrounding the train track featured tiny people in ethnic garb engaged in the various processes of growing sugar.

Although we were going to a final banquet for the hunt that evening, we needed a bit of sustenance to make it through the day. Meeting another of Dan's culinary goals, we decided to have plate lunches at a classic diner in Waipahu. Between the four of us, we had the most popular items on the menu. We began by sharing some `ahi sashimi and octopus poke. With sides of two scoops of rice and macaroni salad, our entrées ranged from beef teriyaki, to chicken adobo, Korean kalbi ribs with kimchee, and grilled shrimp. All of it flavorful, but not too spicy.

Despite the late night, Keoni and I agreed to Margie's suggestion of a round of cocktails after we arrived at the hotel. As we enjoyed the view from the top floor lounge, we conducted a personal summation of the week we had just experienced. Keoni and I managed to steer around the topic of Professor Fù Hán Zhāng's murder. This was easy to do so since our most noteworthy sleuthing had been the night before, after Margie and Dan returned to the hotel. Our cocktail hour conversation centered on planning further adventures, on the mainland or perhaps in Asia.

After a brief rest, Keoni and I donned our best attire for the final event of the hunt. Although the men wore aloha shirts with dress slacks rather than tuxedos, most of the women arrived in elegant long dresses and exquisite jewelry. As it was the last opportunity we would have to do a bit of detecting for our friends at HPD, Keoni and I separated to work the room. Even so, we arrived at our assigned seating ahead of the O`Haras. We quietly compared notes on potential clues to solving Professor Zhāng's murder. But aside from a consensus that the killing of the professor was the low point of the hunt, no one had volunteered any information that would help solve the mystery of why the man was killed—let alone who might have committed the crime.

Gradually, our table filled with contestants who shared interesting stories of their struggles to solve the challenges of the hunt. Everyone agreed that although it had been an expensive event, it was a unique and fun way to raise money for several non-profit organizations. By the time Jason Chin took the microphone, I was anticipating another great dinner and a quick trip to dreamland.

"ALOHA!"

This time the room gave him the resounding response he desired.

"We haven't had a chance to go through your survey comments, but I'm pleased to announce we'll be inviting all of you back for the Second Annual Aloha Scavenger Hunt next year!"

Tired as I was, I managed to contribute to the enthusiastic applause that followed. While the audience enjoyed a first course of kale and bacon salad, Jason introduced a few noteworthy people and regaled us with his favorite anecdotes of the week. Conversation subsided as we finished our entrées of baked `ōpakapaka, with a complex stir-fried rice.

Jason seemed to realize that many people were exhausted from the week's events and picked up his pace. While we enjoyed coffee or tea and tiramisu made with Kona coffee, he quickly awarded the grand prize of the hunt. The room grew quiet as Miss Hawai`i pulled a name from a large basket woven of *lau hala* leaves.

"Drawn from a pool of all contestants who completed each of the hunt's nine challenges, the winner of the twelve animals of the Chinese Zodiac in carved jade is Mary Stover from Pawtucket, Rhode Island."

How lovely that the winner of the grand prize was someone who came from a distant point! She would remember her Hawaiian adventure with pleasure and become the best word-of-mouth advertising the event would have on the East Coast. After a few final jokes and a heartfelt entreaty to come to the next hunt, Jason left us to make our final farewells to one another. Margie and Dan expressed pleasure in participating in the event, but I could tell they were disappointed they had not won any of the prizes, so I resolved to send them a set of the Chinese zodiac animals.

As we rode up in the elevator, I appreciated the fact that we had paid for an eighth night and were not departing until the next morning. Although it would have been wonderful to enjoy the hotel's amenities, Keoni and I were both so tired that we wasted no time in falling into bed.

Knowing Dan and Margie were going to a timeshare on Maui, we slept late on Saturday morning. When we awoke, we enjoyed a romantic soak in the whirlpool tub full of bubbles scented with orange blossom oil and savored a leisurely room service breakfast.

"This has been a wonderful first vacation together, honey," declared Keoni.

"It has, hasn't it? We've had nearly free room and board—if you don't count our hefty donation to a worthy cause. And we have a beautiful antique book to add to our growing library. Who could ask for more?" I replied.

"Well, one or two less murders."

"Mm, that's true. But at least none of that is connected to us personally."

"Point taken, Natalie. Now, why don't I call for a final accounting for our bill and a bell hop to help with the luggage, if you think you can manage to cram everything back into our bags."

"No problem, my dear. I got a couple of large shopping bags from one of the stores downstairs to contain the overflow."

CHAPTER 9

*Very often it happens that a discovery is made whilst
working upon quite another problem.*
Thomas Alva Edison [1847 - 1931]

We were soon in the car and headed back home. Suspecting we might be too tired to handle a round of grocery shopping, I had frozen some dairy products before leaving for the scavenger hunt. And since we would be attending the memorial barbecue for Jade Bishop, I felt we could squeak by in the food department for another day. Unfortunately, that did not release me from doing laundry. Luckily, with a wardrobe containing more than one *mu`u`mu`u*, it would not be difficult to come up with something to wear that afternoon.

"While you ferry us home, I'll catch up on some communications for Hewitt Investigations," said Keoni, opening his tablet.

By the time we pulled into the driveway, I was ready for a stroll on the beach. Keoni had received a client's SOS text, so Miss Una and I would be enjoying that walk alone. After depositing our luggage in our bedroom, he departed for a day of unscheduled client appeasement. That meant I would be on my own for Jade's life celebration as well. After a week of constant togetherness, I could not complain.

I popped a load of delicates in the washer and set the rest of the laundry aside for attention that evening. Next, I put away our toiletries, accessories and jewelry. Soon the suitcases were cleaned and airing out in the guest room. I then declared the house ready for normal operation. Having eaten a large breakfast, I decided to skip lunch. While Miss Una's food and water bowls were full, I found no trace of her in the house. With our week-long disappearance, she might have given up on us. I sloshed on some sun block, pulled my hair back with a scrunchie and put on a swimsuit faded by several seasons of sun. Grabbing my old straw hat, I shoved my feet into my worn rubber sandals and went out the back door.

As I suspected, I spotted Miss Una in The Ladies' garden. Beneath a plumeria tree, I spied her playing with Izzy and the five kittens we had rescued.

"Hi, Natalie," called out Joanne from her weeding of a row of strawberries. "Did you have a good time on your in-town holiday?"

"It was wonderful," I said, leaning over the back gate. "Except for the minor issue of a man found shot to death in the hotel hallway, almost in front of our suite."

"Oh, dear. I hope it's not anyone you knew," she said.

"I did actually. He was a very nice man. In fact, you've all met him. He was one of the Chinese professors on our infamous cultural outing last summer in Kawai Nui Marsh."

"Oh, my goodness! Has his death been resolved?"

"No. So, don't be surprised if you spot John Dias visiting," I replied. Steering the conversation to a more pleasant topic, I observed that Miss Una seemed to be having a good time with the kittens.

"Oh, she's quite the little auntie. They're already plumping up from the diet we're giving them. Looking ahead to adopting them out, I've been watching to see if she has a favorite."

"I'm sure she'll love whichever one you choose as her playmate," I affirmed. "I have to go to a memorial this afternoon and Keoni is working with a client, so I don't want to suggest a potluck supper we might have to cancel. What about tomorrow? Do any of you have anything scheduled?" I asked.

"Nothing we can't rearrange. We've all been looking forward to hearing about your scavenger hunt adventures."

"Great. Let's say a sundown rendezvous at the hot tub," I said. I then waved at Izzy and returned to the house for Miss

Una's lead. When I entered The Ladies' yard a few minutes later, Miss Una came trotting over to me. I slipped on her lead and she pulled me toward her play group.

"My, she sure seems ready for an adventure," observed Izzy. "You know, she's had a great time supervising all of us."

I chuckled at the image of Miss Una standing with a pointer at a chalk board. On this walk, my favorite feline agreed to go all the way to the beach. However, she kept to her established rules: I was allowed to take her onto the sand, but after a few yards, she sat down on a large rock. Not knowing how long I would be standing at Pearl's barbecue, I did not mind a short walk. It felt good to sit alone with her at our neighborhood seashore and observe the birds calling to one another as they flew over distant boats.

Aside from showering and dressing, there was little I had to do before my engagement. Except for the riddle I wanted her to examine, Pearl had not asked me to bring anything to Jade's memorial. When I was ready to leave, I went into the office to slip the note with the puzzling message into the *Tao Te Ching*. Keoni had re-written the fake clue so the penmanship would not resemble mine. I looked at my desk and found Miss Una sitting on the book. She was clearly reluctant to relinquish custody of it.

$$* \quad * \quad * \quad * \quad *$$

I walked toward the back of the courtyard at the Makiki Sunset Apartments feeling sorrow on several levels. Just as I was reflecting on the death of Ariel that had introduced me to Pearl Wong, the diminutive woman materialized and came toward me with a welcoming smile. When I expressed sorrow for Jade's passing and apologized for Keoni's absence, she surprised me with a hug.

Stepping back, I said, "This is the book I won as a prize in the Aloha Scavenger Hunt, and here is a card with the riddle that sounds like a Chinese proverb."

"I look forward to examining them both. This should be an interesting project. I have glanced through my Chinese copy of the *Tao Te Ching*, but to be honest, I will be better off reading the

English text first. What a shame that Jade is not here to assist, as she was fully literate in several Chinese dialects."

"I can only imagine the many ways you must miss her. I truly appreciate your helping with my little mystery, Pearl."

"It will be my pleasure. As I get older, I find there are not enough mysteries in life. I always enjoy learning something new, and this will be a stimulating exercise for my mind."

I nodded, and she asked me to join the other guests while she took the book to her apartment for safekeeping. I was greeted like a returning friend by handyman Al Cooper and Maria Espinoza, a long-term resident. Other residents, like Cory Lowell were equally glad to see me. Excitedly, he asked his mother for permission to come over to me.

After giving me an enthusiastic hug, he asked, "How's Miss Una? She must be very big now, like me."

I laughed and held him out for a quick appraisal. "Yes, she's a big cat now. And I can see that you're going to be as tall as your mother before long."

"Maybe as tall as my dad," he said with a smile. "He's had to go away again, but we're going to take a trip to the mainland to see my Grandma."

"That sounds like fun. I hope you'll have a wonderful time," I said smiling as he ran back to his mother.

At that moment, Pearl returned carrying a shopping bag and a box of assembled Chinese wish lanterns. Everyone came forward to collect paper and pen to write a message for one of the biodegradable lanterns that would soon float into the sky. The activity gave us all the opportunity to feel involved in celebrating Jade's life—and it was certainly better for the environment than balloons in the air, or paper boats with candles clogging waterways.

"While you write your thoughts for the wish lanterns, I will share passages from some of Jade's favorite authors," announced Pearl.

After we sat down at one of the picnic tables surrounding the two barbecues, Pearl cleared her throat and began speaking in the loudest voice I had ever heard her use. Without any reference materials, she recited moving passages from the works of Walt Whitman and Ralph Waldo Emerson, as well as Lao-Tzu and the Dalai Lama. Listening to her gentle, almost lilting voice, I realized that she was closer to her Chinese culture than she sometimes indicated. After pausing for a moment of silence, Pearl urged us to follow her to the dragon fountain. There we released our wish lanterns into the shimmering heat of the late afternoon. As they floated upward, I thought of the lifelong love and support the Wong Sisters had shared.

By the time we returned to our seats, Al Cooper and Mrs. Espinoza had laid out dishes, utensils and all the food people had brought. Being a typical Island potluck, the buffet offered food for every taste, with a variety of salads, breads, meat, and seafood that smelled amazing. While we ate, I enjoyed stories of Jade's generosity told by some older residents and a few young people I had never seen before.

While Pearl visited with each guest, I carried a glass of champagne back to the black dragon fountain. It is amazing how time and occasion can alter one's feelings about a place. While this had been the scene for solving the mystery of Ariel's death, today I felt all right with even the painful cycles of life. I looked over at the celebratory gathering and thought of the people I knew who had died in the last year and a half. They would all be missed sorely, but I was pleased that the joyful lives of Ariel, my Auntie Carrie and Jade would be appreciated for many years.

Suddenly Pearl was standing beside me. "I am sorry that Keoni was unable to be with us today, however I would like to invite you to join me in something, Natalie."

"I'm pleased to do anything you wish, Pearl."

"If you can spare an hour or so, we will take a short trip in the neighborhood. All right?"

"That's fine. There's no way of knowing how late Keoni may be, so I consider myself free for the evening. But before we leave, can I help tidy up after the barbecue?"

"No need for that, my dear. Al will take care of everything. If you will wait here for a moment, I will get my handbag."

Walking across to the parking lot, I wondered which vehicle Pearl would be driving—her old Chevy Silverado, or Jade's classic Mercedes. Momentarily, we were seated in Jade's black beauty and driving downhill to Wilder Avenue.

"You've mentioned that you and your twin Nathan enjoyed playing in Makiki as children," Pearl commented.

"Yes. Every day after returning from school, I played hopscotch while he rode his bicycle with training wheels."

"That was the year Jade was your teacher at Punahou?"

"Why, yes it was."

"We may not be next to the school where she worked, but it seemed ideal when we had the opportunity to buy the apartments. You may have wondered why we have remained here in the humblest of our properties. But you see, some of our tenants have been recipients of the scholarships Jade funded. By our being on the premises, we have been able to watch them grow in knowledge and life experience. And, except for the horror of your grandniece Ariel's death, we could watch over them and try to keep them safe."

I did not know how to respond. I merely nodded and continued to look out the window.

"With Jade's passing, I have decided that it is time for me to leave the care of the apartments to someone younger. I think that with his awakened sense of humanity in the aftermath of Ariel's death, Al Cooper will make an ideal manager."

"Where will you go?" I asked.

"Jade's assisted living condo is paid for and while I may not require all the services available, it offers a lot of amenities I can use—and it has a lovely view. Of course, I have no intention of stagnating. While I still have my health, I am thinking of doing some traveling—beginning with the land of my mother's ancestors. I need to learn what kept our papa there. I learned that after we left, our papa remarried and had three more daughters. Before I too pass on, I have thought they might like to meet someone from their father's earlier life and learn about his family in Hawai`i."

Maneuvering expertly, Pearl parked the large car. As we got out, she moved to the trunk. "Can you help me hold up the lid?

There is something I need to get, but it takes more than one person to open it. We kept this car so long because it is so comfortable to ride in, but now that even the trunk lid is unreliable, it really is time to get a new vehicle."

With my help, Pearl pulled out two large carryalls that smelled of incense and candles.

Stepping onto the sidewalk, I looked around and realized we were standing beside a segment of the fence of the Makiki Cemetery. "Did I tell you that Nathan and I used to play in the cemetery? We were quite proficient at getting in, even when the gate was locked."

Pearl laughed. "It is funny you should mention that, Natalie. Jade and I used to sit on the balcony of her condo for hours," she said, gesturing to a high rise above us. "We enjoyed watching people of all ages and backgrounds coming and going on holidays and during funerals—including children playing on the hillside around the headstones."

Pearl reached into her pocket and pulled out a key. It looked worn but well-polished. By her familiarity, I knew she had used it for many years.

"This isn't the main entrance," I said, looking at a non-descript gate to our right.

"That is so. You might call it a back door for a few of us who have very long-term relationships with the cemetery."

There were a couple of hours before darkness would fall and Pearl had no difficulty in leading the way through the headstones. Part way up the hill, she paused to look down toward the center of the city. We were standing near the point of my vision on that first day of summer when my grandniece Ariel had died. I realized that, in a way, this was where my relationship with Pearl had begun.

After glancing at me, she turned and continued uphill. Within a couple of minutes, we had reached her goal. In front of us was a crypt built of local stone and mortar, accented with black wrought iron fencing. A plaque on the gate announced that this was the resting place of Hiram Wong. This seemed at odds with what Pearl had originally told me. Should I remain silent, or ask what I was thinking?

"What a beautiful burial site for...for your father. But I thought you said that neither you nor Jade ever saw your father after you left China."

"That is true. We had thought that with the escalation of war in China, he would soon follow us. But after December 7, 1941, we knew we would not see him before the hostilities ended."

"Yet here is a crypt with his name on it," I said in a neutral voice, looking around.

"Yes. Our *amah* always spoke of Papa joining us eventually."

"So, is this crypt, mm, your father's? Did he indeed rejoin your family, if only in death?"

"No. Although we planned for him, he never came. As I told you, we never again heard *from* him—or *of* him—after our departure from Hong Kong. Periodically Lee Chu-Hua—or Chu-Hua Lee, as her name is said in English—received mailings from Hong Kong. But she never told us what they contained, or from whom they had come."

"I'm a little confused, Pearl. The crypt is your father's, but neither your father nor his body ever returned to Hawai`i."

"That is correct, Natalie. What I have not told you, or anyone, is that through the years this crypt has served as a private vault for a few of our keepsakes from our home in Shànghǎi."

"I don't mean to be too personal but let me see if I understand all this. You and Jade never saw or heard from your father after you left China?"

"That is so."

"And you and Jade brought things from your Shànghǎi home that have been stored here since 1932?"

"Well, actually it was Chu-Hua who brought our family's keepsakes aboard the ship in 1932. I don't know where she stored them initially. I may have told you that she returned to China in the early 1950s, leaving only a letter and a key to this crypt for Jade. By the time I knew anything about these matters, the crypt had been in use for many years. When my sister first brought me here, the plaque with our father's name was already showing wear. Of course, there are many families that buy such above-ground burial vaults in advance of anyone's passing."

"Well, all of this must have been quite a surprise for you," I observed.

She nodded and glanced around the cemetery before withdrawing what looked like the ornate key to a castle from her pocket. Reaching forward, she opened the gate that was topped by two cherubs holding a heart between them. Stepping through, she turned to beckon me into the small plot of perfectly trimmed grass. Once I was beside her, she turned to lock the gate. Together we approached ornate double bronze doors. Pearl then inserted the same key in the lock set in the right-hand door.

"As you can see, the size of the crypt is considerable," Pearl said.

"Yes. It is," I answered, trying to look politely at the expanse of the Wong Sisters' miniature home.

"Please wait for a moment while I light our way," Pearl instructed.

She then picked up one of the carryalls and walked forward. Soon I saw light coming from long slits of windows at the top of the structure.

"All right," she called out to me. "You can come in now."

I entered the single room. Even with several wall sconces lit, the corners of the interior walls were barely visible. I was amazed by the number of Chinese antiquities that greeted me on every side. The perimeter was filled with narrow cabinets and tables of rosewood in various shapes. Some of the tables were covered with silk cloths. Peeking out at the bottom of some were shipping crates and a couple of old wooden fruit crates. Facing a family altar were two chairs of carved mahogany set with mother of pearl. Their backs featured dragons whose talons reached down onto the chair's arms. The seats were covered with white silk pillows stamped in gold with what I recognized as the Chinese symbol for longevity. They looked like the ones I had seen in a photograph in Pearl's dining room featuring Pearl, Jade, and their mother Yüying.

On every flat surface in the room were beautiful vases, carvings and statues of cinnabar, *cloisonné* and jade. "There seem to be more keepsakes here than in your home."

Pearl laughed demurely. "Many items have come and gone during the years. If I were to take inventory, I would have to decide whether to count some things singly, or as part of a set."

She turned to me and took the bag I had carried in. She pulled out an orchid plant made of several shades of jade and placed to the side of the altar. "Many years ago, our *amah* began investing our seed money in properties. The first was our downtown bungalow. As I believe I told you earlier, after that she made a variety of investments for us in both residential and commercial properties. At some point, she decided that we should have a family crypt."

As Pearl focused her attention on the altar, I felt honored by her obvious desire to have me share in this time of reflection on the life and death of her sister. I watched quietly as she drew out a beautiful urn of white jade with red veining from her bag. She placed it reverently on the altar and then lit the surrounding candles and sticks of incense. Finally, Pearl moved a Buddhist rosary to rest in front of the urn. She beckoned me forward and I saw that one of the sacred statues was a seated Kuan Yin holding a small incense burner in her lap.

The elegant figure perched upright on an open lotus flower in a garden of miniature flowers of rubies and sapphires, set among supporting leaves of emeralds held up by thin gold stems. From an article I had researched years earlier, I recognized the value of the artifact. It was fashioned from pure white jade with yellow-brown *sucrosic* crystalline accents on the edges. The sugar crusts made this a very rare piece of jade. The piece also featured layers of hollowed out images called *Lou* carving which became popular during the Song Dynasty.

Gesturing for us to sit, she said, "As you may have surmised, I am not a religious person, Natalie. However, I honor the beliefs of our Mother and Lee Chu-Hua by performing certain ceremonies, at what they would term *auspicious times*. Kuan Yin, known as the Goddess of Mercy, is worshipped by the women of South China more than those in the North. Like the Christian Santa Maria, she is believed to help women in times of trouble, especially those seeking to become mothers. She also watches over unfortunates who may be ill, lost, or senile. While this depiction of her is rather colorful for this somber purpose, I feel she will be a good companion for my dear sister.

"With Jade's passing, I wanted you to share in my visit here today. Through the years, we allowed the plaque on this crypt to be viewed as announcing a truth. But as you now know, our father never returned to the land of his birth. I feel I owe it to the memory of your grandniece Ariel to acknowledge that this has been the repository of the wealth that Ariel's killer sought in his sick quest for treasure."

The shock I felt must have registered on my face.

"The pressure of his search for our family's treasure aggravated the mental condition that was already impacted by the drugs he took. This is what brought him to the action resulting in Ariel's death. My dear, I am so sorry for the role our family's deceit played in that sweet girl's death."

"Oh, Pearl," I said, hastening to put my arms around her fragile shoulders. "What a burden you have carried. I thank you for revealing this secret of your lives. But Nathan and I know there was nothing you, or your sister, could have done to prevent her death."

"Jade and I debated telling you the full truth. I made the decision to wait until her passing, since, as you have said, there was nothing any of us could do to change what had happened."

"Thank you for sharing all of this with me."

"Shall we rest for a moment?"

"Yes, of course."

We sat back in our chairs, and for a few moments, Pearl held the prayer beads in her hand and intoned some Chinese words softly. I remained still but watched her from the side. After a few moments, she looked over at me, smiled faintly and sighed.

"Thank you, Natalie. You are the only person with whom I could share this moment."

Pearl then brought out two silver goblets and a small split of Champagne. We sat for a short while, sipping our effervescent wine and inhaling the heady fragrance of incense while looking through the flickering candlelight at the statues on the altar.

*   *   *   *   *

After Pearl dropped me off at my car, I thanked her again for including me in the celebration of Jade's life—and for her personal revelations. As I headed home, I thought about what I had learned. At one level of consciousness, I felt a profound sense of closure regarding Ariel. Prior to Pearl's disclosures, it had seemed that my grandniece's death was without reason. Although I had never blamed Pearl or her sister for what happened, I had felt confused as much as angry about her demise. At least now I could understand the depth of the killer's obsession with rumors of hidden treasure.

My time in the Wong family tomb had also allowed me to feel I had shared in the sisters' lives on a deep level. While they may have benefited from the wealth of their parents' success in business, their lives in a new country paralleled the experiences of most immigrants. Unlike many other immigrant children, in addition to learning a new language and living in a society with unfamiliar customs, they grew up without the love and guidance of their parents. After completing their education, the one person who had been there throughout their youth was suddenly removed, and like their father, never heard from again.

At least they had received legal and financial direction from their family lawyer. And although Jade's eventual marriage to the man who had protected the sisters' nest egg may not have overflowed with love, they seemed to have enjoyed a comfortable companionship. While I might never know the full extent of what Jade's husband, Richard Bishop Senior had done for them, obviously the women had not just survived. They had thrived.

CHAPTER 10

It is a capital mistake to theorize before one has data.
Sir Arthur Conan Doyle [1859 - 1930]

Once behind the wheel, I phoned Keoni and told him I had accomplished my mission and had some new information on Pearl and her family. After learning he was just beginning his trip home from the North Shore, I realized he would require a substantial dinner. And although I had enjoyed the barbecue, I would not last through the night without another caloric influx. After stopping in Kailua for *Niçoise* salad and pasta primavera, I considered the challenge met.

At home, I checked my messages and I called John Dias to inform him Pearl had received the copy of the *Tao Te Ching* I had won in the scavenger hunt and the text of false clue number six. I speculated she would have a solution to the clue's riddle within a couple of days. John responded positively and announced he had just received the initial autopsy report on Professor Zhāng and was hoping we could get together the next day.

"Sorry that I'll be breaking in on your Sunday. But I'll be in Lanikai for a round of golf at Mid-Pac Country Club and would like to have both of you look at the report."

"No problem John. Keoni is handling a round of emergencies with clients today. I'm free until next week, when I'm scheduled to interview the chef of a culinary school."

"Great. My tee time is at eight, and with three of us in the party, I should be through by eleven."

"That sounds good. *We* might even get in some exercise before you arrive. There'll be leftovers from tonight's dinner, so let's make it a working lunch," I offered in closing.

After Keoni arrived home, we spent a while looking over the notes each of us had been compiling. Keoni's, of course, were focused on the technical details of John Dias's case. My notes centered on my visions of the mid-twentieth century demise of the man in the vanilla suit in the hallway of the Chinatown hotel—as well as that of the similarly clad man in the corridor of our hotel in Honolulu.

By that evening, life was settling down. Everything from our week's holiday had been cleaned and put away. Miss Una was delighted to play with the scraps of paper we generated in the office. Later, she nestled down with us during a couple of classic British comedies on PBS television. Of course, I am sure her favorite part of having us home was being able to eat fresh food on demand.

The next morning, we decided a swim at the beach was more important than tidying the yard or restocking the kitchen. Because we would be gone for a prolonged period of time, I was glad to find Miss Una playing with the kittens in The Ladies' backyard. After gracing us with a nonchalant glance, she returned to licking the face of the smallest female kitten. Izzy had named her `Ilima, since she is orange and white and our family of felines was usually found at play near the large flowering shrub of the same name.

By the time John arrived, Keoni and I were showered, dressed, and sitting on the front porch looking at the fountain's new pattern of synchronized color changes ranging from pink to purple. The light show had been one of Keoni's latest DIY projects. Joanne told me that Keoni had seen me watching a display at Costco and bought the LED light kit as a surprise.

John must have showered before coming over; despite his girth, he looked as sleek as if he were courting a new girlfriend. I was tempted to ask what he had planned after leaving us but decided that might be asking for too much personal information. For privacy, as much as convenience, we again gathered at the kitchen table. Within minutes, the three of us were sharing our individual perspectives on John's case as we munched on cold cuts, leftover salad and hand-pressed apple cider.

"In addition to the autopsy, I have a little news that should interest you, Natalie," announced John. "As promised, we've begun researching the source of your original vision. So far, we've been able to confirm some of what the three of us were told during our tour of the Chinatown building. There's always been at least one shop on the ground floor. After World War I, the Shēn family *did* convert the two middle floors into what we'd call a boutique hotel today.

"Now that we have a Chinatown address, we're looking into mid-twentieth century murders," said John. "Of course, a case that old means paper—a lot of paper—because HPD hasn't had the resources to digitalize everything going back that far. Nothing has shown up on our radar yet, but we're cross-checking with cases of missing persons. Your description of the perp in your vision sounds like a pretty savvy woman. If she had the skills to go through a room the way you described, there's no telling how she might have disposed of an inconvenient body.

"It's too bad we don't have four seasons in the Islands. If we did, you might have been able to pin down a time of the year by the temperature, or the wearing of overcoats, or—what did my Mother call those things she put over her heels in the winter?"

"Galoshes?" I asked.

"Yeah, galoshes," John replied.

"You're right about my inability to pinpoint the time of year," I said. "The only thing I can say about time is that I think my vision took place in mid-day, with full sun. And since most days are sunny in Honolulu, that doesn't get us very far in determining the month."

"Another unknown has to do with the dead man's ethnicity. You've ID'd him as looking Chinese. I'm willing to accept your identification ethnically—with one big proviso. There's no way of knowing what his *nationality* was. He could have been a resident of Hawai`i, a tourist from the mainland, or a foreign national from Taiwan or Hong Kong.

"And there's the possibility he was from the People's Republic of China. Mao Zedong and his buddies may have locked down that country for the most part, but there were still people who managed to escape from his workers' paradise. In addition, there's also Singapore, Malaysia and the Philippines, which all have Chinese populations."

"It sounds like my suggestion that the murdered man I envisioned was Chinese has opened up more questions than it solved," I said with disappointment.

"Don't worry about what you can't answer now. Most everything you've shared with me from your visions has eventually been proven true. Think of me as the case stenographer. I'll just keep notes as we go along. We'll see what it adds up to later. All right, Natalie?"

"Sure, John. One thing at a time," I responded.

"To get back to what we know so far. I can tell you that Hotel Shēn catered to Chinese businessmen traveling to Hawai`i and beyond. In the run-up to World War II, there may even have been some hanky-panky going on with call girls working out of the place. As you probably know, Hotel Street has been a red-light district for a long time. What few people are aware of, is that in that period before World War II, the industry was actually government supervised—to minimize the chances of both crime and disease. With the thousands of single men working on the plantations and a growing number of military personnel, there was an obvious need to be filled.

"Martial Law was declared on December 7, 1941, following the Japanese attack on Pearl Harbor and other parts of the island of O`ahu. Every aspect of life in the Islands became subject to official scrutiny. As I said, *women of the evening* were already being supervised by officialdom. With the growing need for female companionship for the military, they were brought in from the mainland. To maintain control, the women were given short-term contracts and assigned to specific houses in the red-light district where they lived as well as worked. Except for a few supervised outings to Kailua Beach park, they were not allowed out of their restricted neighborhood. Amazingly, with condoms being issued to the men using their services, there were few case of sexually transmitted diseases."

"I knew part of the story, but your research has really added to my understanding of the era...and that aspect of life in historic downtown Honolulu," said Keoni grinning.

For a moment, I looked at my companions with barely concealed anger. "Well, you two can act like this is a joke. But I've always had a certain respect for women who, for one reason or another, have had to make their living horizontally. It isn't called the oldest profession without reason. After all, it caters to men. And it is men who have continued to control a world in which for many women, and children for that matter, there is no other means of earning a living."

The smiles slipped off their faces. John Dias said nothing. He looked down at his shoes. Keoni knew he was in trouble. "I'm sorry, Natalie. I didn't mean to be so flip. Pardon the expression, but JD and I have both worked the streets for a lot of years. I also respect many of those women. In fact, there were quite a number of crimes on my watch that would have gone unsolved without their tips and active help."

"All right. I'm sorry I got so upset. But if you had read some of what was in Miriam's journals, you'd understand why I responded as I did. As to the business at hand, I don't have your resources, John. I've been thinking about how I could obtain some information that wouldn't normally come out in a police interview. I think that if I can talk to the owner of the Shēn building in a relaxed atmosphere, I may learn something that could help your inquiries," I suggested.

"And how do you plan to schedule a meeting with Bō Shēn?" asked John.

"Well, I am a journalist. I'll tell him I'm writing an article on Chinatown...That participating in the scavenger hunt gave me a chance to appreciate the rich culture of the area. I can say that I accompanied Keoni on his tour of the building with you and was so impressed with his remodeling project that I'd like to write a story about the reconstruction process—and how dedication to honoring one's family's wishes is reflective of the Aloha Spirit.

"I think that'll get me an interview with him. And when he's giving me the grand tour, I'll ask some questions about the generations of his family living together."

"Well, I guess you couldn't get into too much trouble doing an interview. But don't tell Bō Shēn very much about the scavenger hunt, or the details of Professor Zhāng's death."

"That's a given. I'm excited to track down the identity of the dead man in my first vision. When we were in the building the other night, I recognized the elevator and the green drapery tie back. If I'm with Bō Shēn, I might be able to get him to specify the remodeling that's been done through the years."

"Yeah. But remember that this man wasn't alive during the time frame of your first vision. He's two generations later. Who knows how much redecorating the family did in that time?"

"Well, there were those photo albums on display. I'll bet that as a little boy, members of his family told him all about living in the old building. If I can compare the images from the albums against what he tells me, maybe we can piece the story together like a quilt. My only concern is getting him to agree to my recording the interview, which will lessen note taking, as well as make review easier."

"Okay then. Go for it," said John in conclusion of that issue. Moving on to the primary topic of the day, he began pulling files from his briefcase. "This is starting to become a habit. Per regulations, I'm keeping the report under my supervision. But I'd like your responses to what is said, and unsaid," John declared with a tight smile.

He then shuffled through the files and began distributing them. "Here you go. By now you should know what to expect. Natalie, you're going to focus on the Summary Autopsy Report. I'm only going to show you a few pictures. You've already seen the victim in a vision. I don't think there'll be anything gruesome or surprising—just a distance shot of the hallway before the vic was moved and some shots of the suite at the end of the hall. Like you said, the Professor and his killer could not have been in the hotel room very long, because the place was pristine—not even a tissue in the trash."

Turning to his former partner, he said, "As for you Keoni, I want you to look everything over. Once Natalie starts giving me her feedback, we may get an idea for putting aspects of the case in focus. Your input may not be part of the official investigation, but I'm open to inspiration from every direction."

Opening a file he had retained, John pulled out several 8 x 10 photos. He spread them out for both of us to examine. While there was nothing that surprised me in the pictures, I found the pooled blood around the professor's head a bit depressing. I sighed and tried to put myself in the right frame of mind to be of assistance in the investigation.

"I'd like to ask you to do something a little differently today, Natalie," requested John, pulling out a pad of yellow lined paper. "I'd like you to put the report on your left, and this pad to your right. Here's a sharp pencil to write your immediate responses to what you see as you work your way through the report. As usual, I don't care what they are. Just note anything that strikes you as particularly on-target, slightly off-target, or missing—or maybe something that isn't even relevant to the report itself. Maybe you'll think of a new topic for me to research, or something the CSI team might not have considered looking for. Anything and everything is welcome. Okay?"

I nodded and proceeded to align the pencil and notepad per instruction. Then I opened the folder. On the left, I saw a picture of the crime scene with an outline of the victim's body. On the right was a single page summary of the ME's initial findings. The form had not changed since I saw Miriam's last summer. It opened with a fill-in-the-blank section requesting information: name of the decedent; case number; and dates of death and autopsy. Again, Dr. Marty Soli was the examining physician who performed the autopsy. The findings, of course, were wholly different.

The body is that of an adult Asian male measuring 67.4 inches and weighing 169 pounds. The body is normally developed, of unremarkable health, and appears consistent with the given age of seventy-two years. The victim was received wearing an off-white leisure suit with a tan and off-white bamboo print aloha shirt from the Hilo Hattie collection and brown and white wing-tip brogues without socks....undergarments, include a white cot-

ton singlet T-shirt and boxer undershorts...vintage silver Mickey Mouse watch with curved rectangular face and three-quarter-inch wide black leather band on left wrist. All items of clothing, except the undershorts and socks, were bloodstained. The shirts and suit jacket have brain matter splatter consistent with a gunshot wound to the head.

I have only seen Mickey presented in round watches, so the mention of a rectangular face caught my attention. The next information was less entertaining.

...the scalp hair is black and silver, straight, and short...Fingernails, short, even, no signs of struggle...The patient has no surgical scars, but numerous ones on the abdomen, back and extremities, possibly indicative of repeated beatings during several periods of his youth and mid-life years...avulsion fractures of the volar plate of the left middle and ring fingers is also consistent with possible torture...

Considering the decades of multi-phased revolution in the People's Republic of China, I was not surprised to learn that Professor Zhāng might have been tortured. Regarding the single gunshot that ended his life, the description was to the point.

...a 3/16 inch close-range penetrating gunshot wound on the left temple, at 3 inches below the top of the head and 4 inches left of the anterior midline...A hemorrhagic wound track passes rightward, backward, and downward causing patchy subscapular hemorrhage...extensive damage to the bases of the left frontal and left temporal lobe...a distorted .25 caliber unjacketed lead ball was lodged and has been recovered from inside the right ear canal.

At least the man's death would have been nearly instantaneous. The preliminary toxicology screen indicated no presence of prescription or illicit drugs and only a small amount of alcohol. As to his final meal, he had consumed rice crackers with a curried tofu spread and a tropical rum punch. Neither the food nor the beverage seemed to account for the vertigo he had displayed in my vision.

"There's nothing surprising in the autopsy, JD," observed Keoni. "GSW to the head. Single round .25 caliber. Obviously, a small weapon, John. What do you think it was?"

"Given the caliber (and what Natalie envisioned), the weapon's probably something like a Baby Browning, which has been manufactured since at least the 1920s. No one reported hearing anything, so some kind of silencer was used. Old weapon or new, the silencer was probably a custom job. That'll be another avenue to explore. Since the MO and the victims' attire is the same for the murders of both Professor Zhāng and the vic in Natalie's visions, the perp may very well be the same. If that's so, she probably used the same vintage weapon."

"What about the shot itself? Does it look like a pro killed the professor?" Keoni asked.

"Nah. More like a lucky shot. No pro would plan a crime with a weapon like that. In keeping with Natalie's vision, I think the perp was a woman who was just carrying her weapon of choice."

"But what about blatantly committing a murder in the hallway of a Honolulu hotel? Who'd be dumb enough to do that?" I asked.

They both looked at me.

"From what you told me, Natalie, the victim didn't get very far into the hallway before being shot. My first guess is that it was a spur of the moment crime. Or, maybe I should say it was a crime of convenience. If *you* knew that guests at that end of the hall had checked out earlier in the day, the perp may have as well. So far, there's no indication of a connection to the hotel. But if she has some kind of position in the hotel, or maybe one of the businesses on-site, she could easily have known about the arrivals and departures of groups of travelers like a sports team. Of course, that doesn't explain what she was doing in that suite. There were no guests registered in it at the time."

"Mm. I see what you're saying. I guess the same questions can be asked about the murderer in my initial vision. What was the connection between the woman I saw and the Shēn Hotel? Why would she think she was safe to commit a murder in a public building in the middle of a day?"

"Maybe it wasn't a business day? Maybe it was a Sunday, when no one would have been in the downstairs shop? Or maybe there was an event like a parade or something? But then, the only noise I heard was that conversation between those men outside the building," I said in summary.

Reaching over to squeeze my shoulder, Keoni said, "Those are good questions, Natalie. But don't go crazy trying to keep track of every possible lead. That's JD's job. We don't even know if the murder you envisioned is related to the murder that happened in front of our hotel suite."

"Keoni's right. Don't drive yourself nuts over your vision OR my case. I'm grateful for every idea and theory you come up with, but I've got to follow protocol in my investigation. Like I said, I'm keeping track of the details and we'll just have to wait to see how the pieces come together."

*　*　*　*　*

When Miriam's Ladies came trooping through the back gate late that afternoon, Keoni and I were ready for some neighborly conviviality in the hot tub. It had been some time since we had all been together, and Keoni and I were not the only ones with news. While we had been gone at the scavenger hunt, The Ladies had been endeavoring to find homes for the kittens.

Although they were still too small to be adopted, it looked as if they would all have homes when the time was right. Earlier that afternoon, Anna had called Joanne to say she had two potential adoptive families at my Waikīkī condo complex. Izzy was taking a male and female to her niece's children down the street. Best of all, our neighbors were going to keep `Ilima, who has been the object of Miss Una's frequent grooming. If any of these plans failed, Nathan had promised to take a kitten as a mascot for the women at Hale Malolo.

"That's wonderful," I said. "You know, some people can be so ignorant that they don't neuter their pets. And if they decide they can no longer care for a cat or dog, they just release them at the beach. I guess they think the animal can survive on their own until someone else materializes to offer them a new home."

"That's been true for as long as I've lived here," said Joanne. "Occasionally, Miriam and I would care for a litter of kittens we found in the neighborhood. But it was a struggle and so disheartening if we had to let them go to a shelter. In the early days, both Miriam and I were traveling, and we couldn't offer a permanent home to even a single cat. Thank God for Izzy's large family."

"I think it was a win-win for a lot of the kids. My family never had to make an effort to find a pet. We gave away any cats we found in a basket, with a collar, and food, and toys," said Izzy with a laugh. "It was a great learning experience in sharing."

"And they were all neutered," added Joanne.

"You two must have had quite a week. We heard the newscasts about the man who was killed at your hotel. But we never connected him with the Chinese doctors we met on our tour of Kawai Nui Marsh last summer," said Samantha.

"Once you explained the incident, Natalie, I took a look at the newspaper article that had announced his death. Even with the suit and tie he was wearing in that formal picture, I recognized him right away," added Joanne.

"He must have really enjoyed his visit to the Islands last year. After learning about the scavenger hunt, he offered to help plan the event," I explained.

With a flick of his eyes in my direction, Keoni added, "He might not have known our local community, but his familiarity with Chinese New Year was a definite asset."

"What a shame. The tour was such a great experience for him and then when he came back, he died so horribly," remarked Izzy.

"At least it was quick," said Keoni, almost under his breath.

For the rest of our play time, we regaled our guests with stories of our week in Honolulu. Once we moved the conversation to the specific challenges of the hunt, we were able to avoid revealing the details of our involvement in the investigation of the professor's murder. Joanne was very keen on hearing each of the hunt clues. She and Izzy did very well at guessing their solutions. Samantha enjoyed learning about the artistic prizes that had been awarded. As expected, Izzy's favorite topic was the daily menu we enjoyed.

CHAPTER 11

Study the past if you would define the future.
Confucius [551 BCE - 479 BCE]

I went into overdrive on Monday morning. First, I followed through on my conversation with John Dias and called Bō Shēn to set up a meeting on Wednesday. I then conducted a telephone interview of Chef Akira Duncan in preparation for my tour of his culinary school. I had enjoyed my conversations with him immensely and planned to take classes with him after completing my forthcoming article on Pacific Rim specialties.

Next, I caught up on snail mail, email, and phone calls. Most of these items were mundane matters. However, after the delightful week Keoni and I had enjoyed with the O`Haras, I wanted to plan another adventure with them as soon as possible. I knew that Margie's focus would soon be on remodeling her home. Perhaps a getaway to Las Vegas would make a great mid-project break. She had other ideas.

"Let's do something more exciting. How about a trip to Japan?"

"That's already on the horizon. One of Keoni's old buddies has a long-distance relationship with a girlfriend in Sapporo. We've been thinking of visiting Japan before she retires. I have a feeling she'll be calling Honolulu home sooner than later, if Stan Carrington has his way."

"If you don't mind widening your party to include us, what about taking in the Sapporo Snow Festival? The ice sculptures are supposed to be phenomenal!"

"That's exactly what we had in mind. Stan recently told Keoni he's going over for this year's festival. That's where he met Tamiko. He told us she loves to coordinate vacations for the families of the U.S. Navy personnel in her department. I'm sure she'll be glad to help with our itinerary."

"We should be able to have the perfect holiday with an entire year to plan," said Margie. "Speaking of ideal outcomes, how's your investigation going?"

"My investigation of what?" I asked, hoping her inquiry was not what it seemed.

"Come on, Natalie. You and Keoni are far more involved in Lieutenant Dias's murder investigation than you let on."

"Well...you know Keoni was his partner. It's natural that John would ask his opinion occasionally."

"That's not all. I've seen how John looks at you, and I don't mean to say he's leering at you."

"With budgets what they are, I'll admit he sometimes asks me to draw on my research skills for him."

"Mmhm. Maybe someday you'll trust me enough to tell me what you're *really* doing."

"I don't know what you're talking about. As to our trip, why don't we also go to the ancient capital of Kyoto? I've always wanted to see the temples, castles, and art in that city. My father spoke of it often after returning from deployment to Asia. Once he brought me an exquisite *geisha* doll. You may have seen it in the bedroom. It's in a beautiful glass display box."

I was relieved that she let go of the topic of murder. We signed off in anticipation of a delightful holiday. I then I turned to bill paying and writing out a list for the grocery shopping. These activities did not require much concentration and I ran lines of potential dialogue with Bō Shēn through my mind simultaneously.

I had researched the man on the Internet and learned he was quite wealthy. There was no way of confirming his net worth, but I knew he owned several properties in downtown Honolulu and a couple of commercial buildings on Maui. Although he sounded young on the telephone, he looked about thirty-five in his Chamber of Commerce photo. If so, he had had about ten years to grow whatever assets he inherited from his family.

In preparation for meeting with Bō on Wednesday, I presented my outline of questions to John Dias. I breathed a sigh of relief when he gave his approval to the direction of my planned inquiries. He suggested I focus on stories of people who seemed to have dropped off the edge of the world—the world of the Shēn Hotel, that is. His only caution was for me to guard my safety.

I had never conducted an interview that I knew could lead to criminal proceedings. Therefore, I did a run through of the interview with Keoni playing the role of Bō. In spite of knowing the man could not have been involved in the 1950s murder, Keoni insisted on driving with me into town on Wednesday morning. He also instructed me to have my cell phone set for instant re-dial to him in case I felt threatened in any way. I did not object to the force of his words because I knew he was trying to ensure my security without interfering with my work.

We parked the car and my vigilant knight settled into the sports bar of the hotel where we had just spent a week. As I approached Chinatown, the rich scents of food and flowers were tantalizing. I walked anxiously toward the building that might hold the keys to two murders. The exterior of the Shēn building had been pressure-washed since we last visited. Its sparkling stone cornices and pediments reminded me of a woman who has had her hair restyled and is feeling elegant. Looking upward, I admired the arched clerestory windows. They were what had first caught my attention when I was looking for the building in my visions.

I could delay no longer. I wiped my shoes on the new welcome mat, inhaled deeply and entered. I was surprised to hear the tinkle of bells as I pushed the door inward. I looked behind me and saw three bells attached to the back of the door. They seemed like an homage to the past. A man I had not met before stepped forward to greet me. He was wearing faded blue jeans, a speckled painter's cap and a less-than pristine University of Hawai`i tee-shirt. Despite his appearance, he carried himself with the demeanor of an executive.

"Hi. You must be Ms. Seachrist," the lanky Chinese-Hawaiian said. He extended his hand. "I'm Bō Shēn. Welcome to my personal urban renewal project."

We shook hands and he beckoned me into an area that looked prepped to become a retail store. "You'll see we've made some progress," he declared with pleasure.

"You certainly have. You've finished the drywall, and everything looks painted down here. I like the dove gray you chose for the walls," I replied. "How're the upper floors coming along?"

"Eh, we're getting there," replied Bō, less enthusiastically.

We took the elevator up to the fourth floor and I again admired the metal work of its vintage cage. It would be beautiful after being restored to its original burnished bronze finish. Stepping out onto the building's top floor, I noted few improvements since my last visit. Bō tossed his hat on the foldable luncheon table and ran his hand through his rumpled black hair.

We sat on opposite sides of the table. I saw that several new folders and photo albums had been added to the previous collection. I suggested we go over a few basics before we toured the premises and I was glad Bō agreed to let me record our conversation.

On the first page of a large notebook, I entered his full name and those of several members of his family. On subsequent pages, I had written down the questions I planned to ask him. We worked our way through them and his photos, achieving a relaxed pace that resembled two friends catching up after being apart for years.

Bō then handed me a tanned brown leather album highlighting major dates in the life of the building. In a voice filled with pride, he talked me through images of the building's life: its groundbreaking, construction, and dedication; the opening of the original store and offices on the second floor; and, his family's initial move into floors three and four. I closed the album and steered the conversation as John Dias had suggested.

"Thank you so much for the wonderful tour through the decades! I think I have the timeline for the businesses, but can you tell me more about your family?"

He laughed, opened a folder and pulled out a couple of heavy linen sheets of paper. He passed me one and said, "This has got to be the first-time grandma Alana Huang's efforts in genealogy have been useful. How about I go through the family tree with you? It's my dad's side of the family, since it's the men who have inherited the property."

I nodded. Thanks to the beautiful family tree his maternal grandmother had created, I would not have to keep notes on marriages, births and deaths.

"First there was *the greatly truthful one*, Jūnlì Shēn. He emigrated from China's Guǎngdōng Province in the late nineteenth century."

Bō paused. "Do you want the whole story of the family? I don't know what you need to know and I don't mean to get carried away. My Tūtū Alana died when I was twelve. Going over the old pictures and family tree was our way of connecting, especially after she got sick."

"I've got all afternoon, Bō. I still don't know what direction I'm going in for my article, so go ahead and tell me anything that comes to mind. I'll sort it all out later."

"Okay. Here goes the story of the Shēns in Chinatown, Honolulu. When Jūnlì arrived in the Islands, the sugar industry was going strong. After his initial contract as a laborer expired, he kept his job, because he had a real skill with languages and the bosses used him to keep harmony between the different ethnic groups. Also, he was a member of a *hui*, or *huay* as we say in Chinese. You know what that is?"

"Sure. I've written about how those ethnic support groups helped members get ahead in the countries where they emigrated."

Bō nodded. "Jūnlì made some good investments through those men and then went to work for one of them. As for the family, he had planned to send for the wife and daughter he'd left in China. But his prospects for doing so evaporated after the Chinese Exclusion Act was passed by the United States Congress in 1882. For although the Hawaiian Kingdom was not directly affected by that law, it needed to support of the vital sugar industry that relied on exports to the U.S. Accordingly the Hawaiian government also restricted immigration from China. This meant that Jūnlì was unable to bring his wife and daughter to the Islands as laborers and he couldn't afford the exorbitant expense of paying for their travel himself. Soon after, he married Lehua Yi, a local Hawaiian-Chinese woman and they had six kids.

"You've probably heard of the epidemic of measles that killed a quarter of the Hawaiian population in the eighteenth century?"

I nodded but did not interrupt the flow of his story.

"Well, in the nineteenth and early twentieth centuries, epidemics of leprosy, influenza, cholera, whooping cough, and even bubonic plague, hit Honolulu. Between illness and the great Chinatown fire in 1900, Jūnlì lost his wife and all of his kids except his second son, Xiǎochén."

"What a way to begin life in a new country," I commented.

"It was that way for a lot of families back then, even if they weren't immigrants. That's why a baby's first birthday *luau* is so important in the Islands."

With the mention of a baby *luau*, I thought of my parents dying in a car crash while on their way home from one. It had been hard to cope with at the time. But in retrospect, it seemed appropriate that they had died together, after enjoying a celebration of family.

Bō didn't seem to notice my momentary loss of attention. "It seems fitting that his surviving son, Xiǎochén, was named for a new morning. When his son was grown, Jūnlì had quite a nest egg. That's where this building enters the picture."

He then picked up two of the larger albums and we paged through them for a few minutes. Whoever assembled the red velvet volumes had obviously enjoyed the project. The tabs framing each picture were ornate and pasted in perfect alignment with the edges of the pages. One photo that caught my attention was of the family in formal dress. The male members wore suits of the era; the females, long *cheongsams*. They were arranged on and around a Victorian settee that appeared to have been upholstered in velvet. I wondered if it matched the green drapery tie I had seen in my first visit to the site.

By the time we set off on our exploration of the building's physical history, I was processing so much information that I was second-guessing the questions I had outlined. I did not really know what I was looking for and needed to remain open to whatever direction the interview might take me. Bō was in no rush. I used the adjusting of my mobile recording set-up as an excuse for walking slowly, which allowed me to pull my thoughts together.

On the first floor, Bō explained that the space had sometimes held two shops at a time. I learned that all of the tenants had had either familial or *hui* connections. Vegetables, dry goods, fabrics imported from China and cigars from San Francisco, had all passed through the retail stores of the Shēn building. Interesting, but I was much more intrigued by the post-World War I family hotel on floors two and three.

When we stepped out of the elevator on floor two, I could see a few more changes had occurred since my initial tour. A couple of supporting posts had been exposed and there was one inner wall standing with two rectangular gaps. I might have seen them before, but their possible importance had not registered with me.

"It looks like you've nearly completed the demo here. I imagine a project like this turns up some surprising things. Has there been anything that caught you or the contractor's team by surprise—like old newspapers, or maybe hidden treasure left behind by a guest?"

"It's funny you ask that, Natalie. You see those rectangular recesses? José has found several of them. Maybe they date back to some redecorating. It's like someone was playing hopscotch up and down a couple of the walls. With patches on the old lath and plaster and dry wall of the inner walls, it seems like someone was either hiding something or searching for something. But we've taken everything down to the studs and haven't found the crown jewels."

We laughed, and I jotted down this unusual detail of the current remodel. "So, what do you think the niches were used for?"

He shrugged his shoulders. "We haven't figured that out. By the time the hotel went in, the family wasn't that large, so the third floor living quarters had been sacrificed for the hotel. At first, I thought the recesses might have been for the family altar. But there wouldn't have been any reason to move the altar more than once or twice, and they aren't really large enough for an altar."

This was another element that tallied with my vision. Clearly someone had been searching the premises for something of value. But how did the search of the dead man's suitcase fit into a longer scheme of cutting into walls throughout the building? If the woman I saw in my vision was responsible for all of this, she had to be connected to the family in some way that spanned the decades from the middle of the last century until today.

I glanced around and hunted for something to say. "I can see where the old inner walls were located. The rooms look small and the hallway narrow. Aside from size, how would you compare your family's hotel with the boutique hotels of today?" I asked, wanting to see how his description would compare with my vision.

"The main difference is the bathrooms: The Shēn Hotel had only a single bath on each floor that all of the guests shared."

"How were the rooms laid out?"

"Like you said, they were small. Each one had a closet with a rack for suitcases and bars to hang clothing. At the back there were small dressing rooms with *Cheval* mirrors leaning against the back wall. Furniture wise, every room had a single narrow bed, night stand, small desk, and a dresser."

"What was the lighting like?" I asked, reaching for more details.

"Except for some lamps, the main lighting was provided by wall sconces—one inside the door of each bedroom and one inside the closet."

"Were there any other furnishings? Artwork? Mirrors?" I asked.

"There were water color and pastel art pieces painted by the women in my family. They weren't very good, but I've kept a couple for sentimental reasons. Mirrors? In addition to the ones in the dressing rooms, some of the rooms had mirrors over the dresser or desk. The beds, night stands and dressers were all from the same furniture line, but the desks and lamps were mismatched, as if someone bought them at different times and places."

As he listed several features that I recalled from my vision, I had to fight to keep from revealing the excitement I felt. So far, everything fit my recollections of the drab hotel room I had seen.

"What did you do with the furniture and other things?"

"I sold what I could. Most of it was pretty worn. A few of the older pieces had some value, but a lot of them had been replaced through the years with low-quality junk. This hasn't been a hotel for decades. By the time I came along, these areas were just a lot of unused space that was ideal for playing hide and seek with my friends."

As we took the elevator to the third floor, I wondered how to pursue this line of inquiry smoothly. Looking at the small space, I pictured it full of the furniture I had seen on the night Keoni and I took the tour with John Dias. What excuse could I dream up for expressing interest in the building's old dressers and desks?

"I've been doing some remodeling myself lately. I inherited my aunt's cottage in Lanikai. It's a vintage Hawaiian bungalow."

"That's great. Does it have a Dickey roof, with extended eaves that make it look Asian?"

"Yes. Most everything else is typical American craftsman, but the roof is strictly Island style," I said with a laugh.

"You know, my grandaunt Toitoi had dreams of my becoming an architect. I remember studying Charles Dickey's work. He was a great architect, but that roof line is what he's remembered for," Bō added. "What have you been doing with *your* architectural treasure?"

"Well, between the termites and dry rot, there's been a lot of reconstruction. But we've tried to honor the home's original features. Of course, the kitchen and bathrooms needed to be modernized and there's been some expansion.

"My boyfriend and I are through with the structural work.

We're now into decorating. I'm looking for a few unique furnishings. It sounds like some of the desks from the old hotel may be from the right period for my project. Where did you sell them?"

By the time we arrived back on the fourth floor, I had the name of the store that had taken the vintage furniture I hoped would match my vision. As we settled back at the table, I thought about moving our conversation to another topic of concern. I really wanted to explore the possibility of a link between the Shēn family and the Wong sisters, or more particularly, the sisters' *amah*.

What were those men discussing outside the hotel in my second vision? I had a feeling the incident occurred around the same time Miss Lee returned to China. I wondered if she had delivered some object to the Shēn family's scion before she left—as she had to the two men at Honolulu Harbor in 1932.

Bō was clearly up to date on his family history. But how could I introduce a person outside of the family? Someone he may never have heard of? At a time before he was born? Even if I found a way to ask Bō about Chu-Hua Lee, how would I explain *my* knowledge of her, or my true concern about her possible connection to his family? I would have to put that topic on hold until an opportunity allowed me to pursue it.

"So, what have you decided to do with the building?" I asked.

"According to the family trust, I don't have much choice. If I want to retain ownership of this building. I have to officially *live* here. Fortunately, the hotel conversion was done on a shoe string, so aside from the inner walls and doors, there hasn't been a lot to take apart. I'm going to put a penthouse on this floor and move my real estate offices into floors two and three. As to the first floor, I'm sure someone will be interested in such a premier retail space. My biggest concern is keeping my fiancée happy about living downtown, while staying with the rules that apply to modifying an historical building."

"Just make sure you include your sweetheart in designing the bathrooms, kitchen, and closets."

He grinned broadly, "Oh, she doesn't let me do anything without her input."

I smiled and steered him back to his family.

He paused for a moment and then picked up the thread of his story. "By the time Jūnlì's son Xiǎochén inherited the building, he and his wife Lìlíng had had five kids. She was a mail-order bride—kind of in reverse. Lìlíng Yang didn't come from China, but San Francisco. You see, her father visited Honolulu, and being related to someone in Jūnlì's *hui*, he was wined and dined by the old men. When he heard that the name of the man's daughter meant *plum-tinkling of jade pendants*, Jūnlì declared it was an auspicious sign and arranged for her to marry his son.

"The family prospered in the 1920s, but like the first generation, they lost a couple of kids. When Xiǎochén's eldest son Xing wanted to go to college on the U.S. mainland, his father sent him to San Francisco to live with Lìlíng's family. Let me think. What's next? Well, eventually Xing was joined by his sister. Xiǎochén wasn't too upset when she married a California merchant, but he was disappointed that his eldest son joined that man's business and remained on the mainland. That left the younger son to inherit this building.

"Named for the wind, my Great Grandfather Fēng was a whirlwind in commerce, especially real estate. It was his idea to convert the second and third floors into a small hotel. You could say that's how *I* ended up in real estate—despite my degree in art."

"I'm amazed at how you've memorized your family history. You even know what everyone's name means."

"That's because of Tūtū Alana. She really lived up to the meaning of her name—*awakening*. She thought it was important to know your roots. Of course, being a little kid, I was more interested in fire engines and ships."

"Well, I'm certainly grateful for the beautiful family tree she created." I replied. "Did your family enjoy the hospitality business? Did you have regular guests who returned often?"

"I guess so. At first, most of our guests were business men coming and going from China. With the global prosperity of the 1920s, a lot of people were investing in international enterprises."

I had my opening. "That's true. I know a family from Shàng-hǎi that exported furnishings and antiques. They have relatives here in Hawai`i as well as China. Maybe your family knows them. Hiram Wong was the father."

"Gee, that's a long time ago. Tūtū Alana recorded special friends and frequent guests, but I don't remember that name being in her diaries."

"How wonderful that you have her diaries," I said, recording that little gem of information in my notes.

He nodded. "Yes, it is. She died when I was a kid and it's one way to feel close to her. Now, where was I? Great grandfather Fēng. He married Lani Wilcox, a Maui girl and they had two sons and a daughter. By the late 1930s, everyone knew war was coming. I've even heard a story of people playing bridge the night of December sixth and speculating that a Japanese attack could come by the next day. And as we know, it did.

"My Grandpa Chāng was named for *prosperity* and his elder brother Bàozhǐ for *wisdom*. They were less than a year apart and were nearly inseparable. After Pearl Harbor, they both joined the Army. But they weren't in the same units. My grandpa was a regular soldier, but his brother was a whiz at languages like his grandfather. He served as a translator of both Japanese and Chinese. If it hadn't been for the war, he'd probably have become a scholar.

"Say, I don't know if you can use it for your article, but my Granduncle Bàozhǐ had a real gift for calligraphy. I've got some of his beautiful scrolls."

"I planned on including pictures of the building and family in my article. Maybe we can squeeze in a picture of your Grand-mother's family tree, along with a piece of Bàozhǐ's calligraphy."

"Gee, that would be great." He paused again. "I guess I'm losing steam. Where was I?"

"World War II," I replied.

"Oh, yeah. At the time, there was a single store on the first floor. It was restricted by wartime rationing, but the hotel remained a good source of income. The guests were primarily military and government personnel, and there were a lot of them.

Unfortunately, when the tourist industry took off after the war, there were too many new hotels for us to compete effectively."

"What was life like for your family following the war?"

"For most people it was like you'd expect. The soldiers were coming home, and life was getting back to normal. But things were a little different for our family. My great-grandmother Lani had died during the war. Great-grandfather Fēng was getting tired of trying to manage the hotel, and the growing number of properties the family owned.

"Both my grandpa and his brother served in the Allied Occupation of Japan. Grandpa Chāng returned first, in 1948. He married his high school sweetheart Zhīlán Ing and in a few years my father was born. He was named Kāng, for *wellbeing*. I guess that was to celebrate how lucky they felt to have survived the war.

"When my granduncle came home in 1951, he wasn't alone. We never learned the exact story of how they met, but Bàozhī arrived home with a war bride. Being an *Ainu* woman from the Japanese island of Hokkaido, Toitoi Naiporo originally spoke barely any English and only a little Chinese. But somehow, she already knew her name had the homonym of *toy-toy* in English. According to family stories, she never failed to make the most of that little joke. Maybe her coming from Japan just after the war made her feel insecure and possessive of my granduncle's attention.

"My Auntie Toitoi was hardly the wife my great-grandfather Fēng would have picked for his son. Nevertheless, the family welcomed her. She's a real sharp woman. She worked very hard to learn English and everything she could about Hawai`i and our family. From the beginning, the two brothers and their wives were very tight.

"It's just too bad the fun didn't last for long. With ancestors from southern China, the Shēns have traditionally enjoyed fishing and boating. One Sunday when the young foursome was out on the water, there was an accident. My grandma Zhīlán fell in and drowned. It was very strange, for both of the women had gone into the water, but only Toitoi came out.

"Grandpa Chāng never got over Zhīlán's death. Not long after that tragedy, his brother, Bàozhī, took a trip to Hong Kong and was never heard from again. My grandpa was pretty lonely the rest of his life, but he never remarried or even dated. I think Auntie Toitoi always hoped the two of them would end up together. But no matter how she tried to catch his eye, he only saw her as a sister."

CHAPTER 12

...let there be search made.
Ezra 5:17, *The Bible KJV* **[circa 440 BCE]**

I was dying to tell John and Keoni that I had verified a member of the Shēn family *had* gone missing during the mid-twentieth century. And with all the details that matched my vision to the old Shēn Hotel, I had proven I had not experienced a mere dream. Aside from the need to identify a murderer or two, my primary question was: What happened to the body I saw in my vision?

Unfortunately, I could not go running out the door. What would I say? "Sorry. I got what I was after and now I have to report my findings to HPD." Somehow, I doubted that comment would be well received. Besides, who could say what the future held? Aside from the possibility of solving a couple of murders, there might be a magazine article in the story of the Shēn family. To move toward either goal, I needed to complete my interview.

"My goodness. What happened to your granduncle Bàozhǐ?"

"We're not sure. A couple of weeks before Christmas in 1953, he was packing for a trip to China and then he was gone—never to be heard from again. I've been told he was doing an errand for the family, traveling by sea on the luxury liner the SS President Cleveland. After a stop in Manila, the ship pulled into Hong Kong, where Bàozhǐ was booked at the exotic Repulse Bay Hotel. Even though he was traveling economy class, the trip wasn't cheap. Whatever he was supposed to do must have been important for his father to spend so much money.

"The ship he was travelling on originated on the West Coast.

When it arrived here, everyone in the family went to the Aloha Tower for Boat Day. Music, *leis*, streamers flying, it was a festive time for the local community, as well as the tourists. We think Bàozhǐ must have visited with someone debarking, because years later we found a dinner menu from December the sixth, during the San Francisco-Honolulu leg of the cruise. It was in the desk drawer of the hotel room he used as an office."

This was another item to put in my mental file drawer. It confirmed that Bàozhǐ, heir apparent to the family business, frequented a wing of the old hotel on a regular basis.

"I remember looking at the menu as a teenager and wondering how much food a person could eat at one meal. Some of the dishes sounded great—especially to a Chinese-Hawaiian kid used to stir fry and hamburgers. There was roast saddle of spring lamb, risotto Milanese, and mocha éclairs. There was also some strange stuff. I never have learned what *long branch potatoes* are, or *coco honey*."

"So, your granduncle just disappeared?" I asked, hoping there might be some clue as to what had happened to the man.

"Yeah. No one in the family could go to the harbor for his departure because the family store was holding a holiday sale of crafts created by local artists. They weren't surprised when they didn't hear from him for a couple of weeks. But after that, Tūtū Alana said they had expected at least a post card. On the day the ship was due back from the cruise, my great-grandfather insisted on going to the wharf alone. He didn't come home for a long time. I was told that when he finally returned, he took my Grandpa Chāng into Bàozhǐ's office. They stayed there for a couple of hours. After that, my granduncle's name was never mentioned. I only learned about him from my Tūtū Alana."

"Wow. That's quite a mystery! And it's never been solved in all this time?"

"No. In fact, both my great-grandfather and my grandpa died without ever talking to me about Bàozhǐ's errand for the family, or his disappearance."

I shook my head in honest amazement. "Your family and this building certainly have a fascinating history. But I don't mean to interrupt your story. I think you were getting close to your own chapter, Bō."

"That's true. But I'm afraid there's not much left to tell."

"What about your parents? We left the story with your father as a toddler. You said he was raised by your Grandpa Chāng and your Grandaunt, Toitoi."

"That's right. Except for losing his mother, Kāng, my dad, had a normal childhood. He grew up in this building, went to Chaminade University and married the girl next door. And then I came along. My mother, Amber Huang, was hoping to return to school, once my father's career was established. But she never realized that dream.

"You see my parents had taken a trip to Japan because my father was attending a conference on international finance. He had gotten a job right out of college as an assistant to an investment banker. The guy was nice enough to include my mom on the trip. I was just a baby and my mom had debated whether she should go at all. But Grandpa Chāng and Auntie Toitoi assured her I'd be fine. I guess they had a great trip until it all ended on August 11, 1982."

That date rang several bells in my memory. What I was thinking was not good.

"They were returning on Pan Am Flight 830 from the Narita Airport near Tokyo. A bomb had been placed aboard by a Palestinian terrorist. When it detonated about a half hour out of Honolulu, a Japanese teenager died in the explosion. Sixteen other people were injured, including the kid's parents and mine. Mine survived long enough to be taken to the hospital, where they died from complications from their injuries within a week of each other. If it hadn't been for Captain O`Halloran, everyone aboard might have died. But he managed to get the plane to Honolulu and made an emergency landing.

"I was a teenager in 1996. That was when the restored 747 was used as a prop in the film *Executive Decision*. It was really strange, sitting there with my Grandpa and Auntie. I was looking at the plane where the trajectory of my parents' lives ended before I even got to know them. The bomber was eventually caught and put away for what our family had been told would be forever. But he's free now, due to some plea deal with the Feds. He was released in 2013 and deported to an unknown country. And the man who instigated that terrorist act (and others) is still being hunted—with a $5 million reward on his head."

What could I say? All I could think about was that except for accumulating wealth, each generation of the Shēn family had been unlucky in their travels. If I were Bō, I doubted that I would be very interested in travel of any kind.

"I remember the case. It was linked to the 15 May Organization. I'm sure Abu Ibrahim was hoping to make his mark by taking down everyone on the flight."

"You have quite a memory, Natalie."

"Just part of being a journalist. Even if you're not reporting on a big story, the details of anything so horrific stay with you." I did not mention that the same terrorist organization was responsible for the death of a colleague of mine.

"So that's why my family is so small. But I'm not complaining. I was raised by my Grandpa Chāng and Auntie Toitoi...and my great-grandfather until his passing. My Grandpa was easy going, but my Auntie had firm expectations. She wanted me to live up to the family's heritage. I've failed to meet both of her expectations: I'm not a Chinese linguist and I'm not an architect."

"But you've done well with real estate."

"Now that I'm good at. Of course, I was given a great starting point. And my Auntie's been a lot of help. I take care of the properties on O`ahu. But since my Grandpa died, she's taken over everything on Maui."

"I guess she must miss him quite a bit."

"Yes. I think with raising both my dad and me, she kind of hoped they might end up together. But he never got over my Grandma Zhīlán."

I nodded my understanding. "Well, Bō, you have quite a family story."

"I hope you got enough for your article."

"Oh, yes. You've given me a lot to think about."

*　*　*　*　*

I left the Shēn Building and made a bee line to Keoni. On the way, I called John Dias.

"You were right, John. A member of the Shēn family went missing. His name was Bàozhǐ Shēn. He was Bō's granduncle, the older brother of his grandfather Chāng. Supposedly he went on a cruise to Hong Kong in 1953 and was never seen again."

"Whoa, Natalie. You're off and running and I'm playing catch up. Let me grab the right notebook. Better yet, where are you?"

"I've just left the Shēn Building. I'm meeting Keoni at the lounge of the hotel where *your* murder took place."

"Great. I'm in the neighborhood. I'll meet you in a few minutes."

While hurrying to our rendezvous, I called Keoni to catch him up on our change in plans. John arrived at the bar shortly after I did, so I did not need to tell the story of Bō's missing relative twice.

"Okay, Natalie. Tell me all about your meeting with Bō," requested John.

"The interview went well. He thinks I'm writing an article about his family's hotel. It really could be a great piece. I've also confirmed several aspects of my vision. There *is* a Shēn family member who disappeared in the mid-twentieth century. Bō's granduncle, Bàozhǐ Shēn. He supposedly went to Hong Kong in 1953 and never returned."

"Let me get this straight. The man who owns the Shēn Building now is Bō Shēn. The guy you think was the vic in your vision from the 1950s was a man named Bao?"

"That's half right. His full name was Bàozhǐ Shēn. He was the older brother of Bō's grandfather Chāng. This is the family tree Bō gave me during my interview. I'd like to keep it, but Keoni can make you a copy in the hotel's business office while you and I finish talking," I suggested.

"Fine."

I studied the document before handing it to Keoni. He left some cash on the table for our tab and departed.

"I didn't get many details about his granduncle's disappearance. And, I'm not sure how much you could learn from my interviewee, since the story pre-dates Bō's birth by about three decades."

"Well, give me what you can."

"Okay. Although departures are almost as important as arrivals in Hawai`i, the family had to work the day the SS President Cleveland was departing for Hong Kong. Nobody went to the harbor to see Bàozhǐ off. It takes about two weeks to get to China, so the family wasn't surprised when they didn't hear from him for a while. But they never even received a postcard. The man simply left one day and never came back. End of story."

"You say the guy disappeared during a trip to Hong Kong—but are you sure he ever made it off O`ahu?"

"If he did, he's not the star of my vision. But how does a man making major preparations for a trip abroad get killed in the family hotel a floor or two below their living quarters without anyone noticing? How and when was the body moved? By whom? And, where did it end up?"

"Those are the questions of the day. At least I've got his name and the approximate date he disappeared. Good starting points. I just hope somebody filed a missing person report. That'll be my ticket for meeting Bō. I'll say I'm investigating old cold cases. Of course, that's no guarantee I'll find a link to *my* current case, or enough info to officially open a file on Bàozhǐ."

"I'm sorry I couldn't get anything else during my interview," I remarked, looking up as Keoni slid into the booth.

"Thanks, partner," said John, as Keoni passed him a copy of the Shēn family tree. "I'm grateful for everything you two give me. But this time your vision is a real shot from the unknown, Natalie. You've seen a murder from the past, which may or may not be tied to another in the here and now. Both victims are Chinese. Both wore white suits with aloha shirts and two-toned brogues. Straw hats that we assume belonged to the vics were seen just beyond the bodies that were stretched diagonally across hotel corridors. The crimes are separated by less than a mile—and, more than sixty years. That's curious, don't you think?"

"I guess so."

"Well, before we part, I should mention that no new leads

have emerged in Professor Zhāng's case. He came here alone. It doesn't look like he flashed money, jewelry or other signs of wealth. There were no public displays of drunkenness, drug use, or womanizing. And no intrigues have been uncovered within the scavenger hunt organization. So, I might as well follow up on the Shēn family's missing uncle. Now that I have a specific name and nearly exact date, it's going to make our search for a mid-century missing person report a lot easier. Is there anything else you can think of to narrow the search for Bàozhǐ?"

"I don't think so, John. I'll go through my notes and let you know if I've overlooked anything. Also, I'm still waiting for Pearl's evaluation of the hunt's false clue number six."

"Great. What about you, Keoni? Any hot topics you can think of for me to pursue in checking out Natalie's vision or the Shēn family gossip?"

Keoni played with the swizzle stick in his bourbon and ginger ale for a moment. "Just one thing. Did the family have the man officially declared dead—maybe for insurance claims?"

*   *   *   *   *

I easily get motion sickness and so refrained from looking at my notes on our trip home. We chatted about some of the small details in my interview and the colorful tourists Keoni had visited with in the lounge.

"Some of these people travel all of the time. I met one couple who does nothing but take cruises," said Keoni eagerly.

I looked at him in astonishment. "You sound like that's something you'd like to do. Are you planning to make it a boys-take-to-the-sea kind of adventure? You know it's nothing *I* would ever want to do."

"Ah, the sea sickness thing. A lot of new treatments have emerged since you last traveled by sea."

"That may be true, but even the thought of being out of sight of land makes me woozy," I said to rebuff his unspoken image of standing on the promenade deck of an ocean liner.

"Just a thought, honey. We had such a great time with Dan and Margie and I thought you might be up to another vacation."

"Now *that* I'm open to planning," I declared. "In fact, Margie mentioned wanting to go to the Sapporo Snow Festival and I told her about Stan and Tamiko. How do you feel about pursuing that trip to Japan? Maybe next winter?"

"Sounds good to me. By that time, I hope to have a full-time assistant for my business, so I shouldn't have any problem taking off for a couple of weeks."

Keoni went directly to the shop he had built at the back of the garage when we got home. Knowing Keoni would be busy for a while, I turned to reviewing my interview of Bō. I listened to the recording as I went through my notes. Aside from explanations of people in his family tree, Bō had provided several points for future consideration. Foremost, the probability that his granduncle was the man I saw murdered in the Shēn Hotel.

Next, he had mentioned finding a menu from the ship's sailing from California to Hawai`i. This may indicate that Bàozhǐ had met with someone disembarking from the ocean liner on which he was about to depart. In addition, there was Tūtū Alana's diary. I remembered the journals that Miriam Didión had kept. Perhaps the diary had entries that would explain incidents in the Shēn family history—or better yet, reveal a person of interest in the case of the missing or murdered granduncle. Finally, I now knew where Bō had sold the furnishings from the Shēn Hotel.

At sunset, I shut down my computer and tried to clear my mind of murderous thoughts. Keoni and I closed the day by enjoying margaritas in the hot tub. Next, we had a light supper on the *lanai* with grilled *teriyaki* chicken sticks, the rest of our luncheon salad, and fresh rolls Izzy had made with chives from Joanne's garden.

"So what's up with Miss Una's new buddy?" asked Keoni.

"In about two weeks, `Ilima's siblings will go to their new homes. Then there will be just our little darling and The Ladies' kitten romping through the garden."

"The reason I ask is that our smallest neighbor came scratching at the garage door, all on her own. I'm wondering how long it's going to be before she's going to be able to go in and out of Miss Una's garden window?"

"Not for several months, dear. She'll have to grow quite a bit before that'll be an issue."

"Well, if she's going to be part of our extended family, do you think I should put in a doggy door at ground level?"

"I fear that would be overkill. You know that Miss Una's window access is how `Ilima's mother gained entry to the kitchen. If we do what you're suggesting, we'll be inviting in all small creatures at ground level."

Who says retired cops are hard hearted? Leave it to my sweetheart to think of something so accommodating for the kitten from next door.

*   *   *   *   *

On Thursday, I uploaded the recording of my interview of Bō with my new voice recognition program. It took a while to train it for my voice, but once I saw how quickly the material could be edited, I was sold on the technology. Next, I finalized preparation for my interview of Akira Duncan. The chef had been born in Japan. His father was an attaché with the U.S. State Department and his mother a secretary at the Embassy in Tokyo. Akira had grown up sampling many of the cuisines of the world as he traveled with his parents.

When his father retired and accepted a local position with an international company, the young chef entered Kapi`olani Community College's culinary arts program. After stints in the kitchens of Island resorts, he went to Europe for advanced training. By the time he married into a family of French restaurateurs, Akira had been awarded a silver medal in the Bocuse d'Or Concours Mondial de la Cuisine. After his father-in-law died, the couple pocketed their inheritance and moved to O`ahu. With a successful restaurant in Honolulu, he opened his culinary school a few miles from his home in Kāne`ohe.

That's where I met with him on Friday morning. Professionally, I was meeting with Akira Duncan to learn about the nuances of the Pacific Rim cuisine he served in his restaurant and taught in his school. Personally, I was there to decide if I was ready to enroll as a student. Given my limited kitchen experience, I needed to begin with a class in kitchen basics. If I managed to conquer that, I could move on to something delectable…like appetizers or desserts. Well, maybe not desserts. I cannot even produce a decent cake from a box mix.

Akira was a personable man. No wonder he was capturing the interest of foodies and the media. Keoni and I have dined at his Honolulu eatery—a fusion of Pacific Rim and classic Japanese specialties. I am not fond of *sushi*, or fish with scales, but Akira's seafood dishes are receiving acclaim from even the most jaded reviewers. As we looked over his evolving menus, I realized the man had often met or exceeded culinary trends by as much as a year.

As we began our tour of the school, I confessed that I was interested in culinary courses personally. He smiled and asserted that even a challenged cook could improve their skills while enjoying the process. By the time we viewed a class in session, I was determined to complete my article and sign up for the class in basic knife techniques. We ended our meeting by scheduling appointments for a photographer to shoot both the school and the restaurant.

That afternoon I took some mail to The Ladies that had been delivered to our home by mistake. Izzy insisted I join Joanne and her for afternoon tea. I told them about the article I was planning and announced my decision to take a cooking class. They wholeheartedly encouraged me. Izzy offered to help me with my homework assignments and Joanne promised to keep me supplied with produce for practicing my knife wielding skills. Before leaving, I elicited promises to keep my culinary studies a secret until I had completed my first course.

The next morning, I got the call I had been anticipating from Pearl Wong.

"As you asked, I have looked over the *Tao Te Ching* you won during your scavenger hunt. I must say this book is one of the most beautiful editions I have seen. You know I am not fully literate in Chinese, and therefore cannot comment on the translation, but the illustrations are certainly exquisite."

"I'm quite delighted with my prize. It's one of the finest volumes in my library."

"The riddle you discovered in the book of the *Tao* is most interesting. To help you understand it, I have examined both the English version you gave me, Natalie, as well as Jade's Chinese copy. Again, you must remember my limits in translation. It seems to me that the writer of your riddle wove portions of chapters together with his or her own words. Do you have a copy of the riddle with you?"

"Yes. It's in the office. I really appreciate your helping me with this little mystery, Pearl. Ah, here it is. I am now looking at the riddle."

The ancient masters were subtle. In the new town of our forebears lies a building with a triad of windows topped by church-like arches. Traversing all floors is a hidden door that needs no lock. In the hub of the wheel, resides the revered Song Lady of the White River who hears the cries of the world. Like the Sage, be guided by what you feel....magnify the small...so that without substance can enter.

"Although it would be better if we were meeting in person, I do not wish to delay in giving you some feedback. I have written down my findings, but you might want to take some notes while I explain the phrases from the *Tao* I have found within your riddle."

"That's an excellent idea. I'm at my desk and if I put you on speaker phone, I can input my notes into a computer file while we speak."

"Very good. I must say this little project has been a welcome break from the paperwork I have been doing regarding Jade's passing. I do not mean to sound like my sister the school teacher, but I did some research to put the words of the riddle in perspective."

Putting my legs up on the desk and the keyboard on my lap, I geared up for what I knew would be a precise, if complex, report. "All right Pearl, I'm ready to record what you've learned."

"As you may know, the *Tao Te Ching* is comprised of two parts. The first consists of chapters one to thirty-seven and the second, chapters thirty-eight to eighty-one. The author of your passage has drawn on both parts of the book. I have been able to pin down the chapters that were sources of much of the riddle.

"*The ancient masters were subtle*' is the first line of Chapter 15. The words, '*In the new town of our forebears lies a building with a triad of windows topped by church-like arches. Traversing all floors is a hidden*' must be the words of the riddle's author, since they are not found in the *Tao*.

"*Door needs no lock*' concludes the fourth line of Chapter 27. '*In the hub of the wheel*' is a reworking of the end of Chapter 11. '*Resides the revered Song Lady of the White River*' are also the words of the author of your riddle.

"*Who hears the cries of the world*' are your author's words, but they are a traditional description of the Bodhisattva Kuan Yin who watches over those who suffer.

"*Like the sage, be guided by what you feel*' is a rephrasing of text from Chapter 12. '*Magnify the small*' is the opening of the fourth line of Chapter 63.

"*So*' has been inserted before '*that without substance can enter where there is no room*' which is the final sentence of Chapter 43."

"That's amazing work, Pearl! So, the majority of the riddle is from the *Tao Te Ching*?"

"Yes. That is true."

"Does the riddle itself make sense to you?"

"It seems to suggest where the reader can find Kuan Yin— that is, a tangible representation of the demi-god—like a statue or figurine. When I recognized the reference to the *bodhisattva*, I did some additional research. Kuan Yin was originally a male demi-god in Indian Buddhism, named Guān shì yīn. By the time of the Song Dynasty in the mid-tenth century, he was being integrated into Chinese culture as Kuan Shih Yin, a female, revered by both Buddhists and Taoists. Although there is a vague reference to the statue's hidden location, I do not understand linking her to the White River."

Well, I had an idea of where the goddess might be: somewhere in the Shēn Building.

CHAPTER 13

Everything must have its roots, and the tendrils
work quietly underground.
The Tao Te Ching [circa 600 - 400 BCE]

I began the new week by writing the first draft of my article on Akira Duncan. I knew it would go through at least one major change after the photo shoots of his restaurant and school. Looking at the menus from the former, and the course descriptions of the latter, I knew what images I wanted to accompany my text. Obviously, I couldn't include quotes from Keoni or me, but with Evelyn and Jim Souza being retired restaurateurs, their observations would be ideal.

While sipping cinnamon sun tea at lunch, Keoni glanced through the three pages of the first draft of my article. "Looks good, honey. You even mentioned my favorite appetizer—crab cakes with green onion on a bed of locally grown watercress. I sure wish Akira would open a restaurant on this side of the island."

"I agree. I'm glad you like the piece," I responded, wondering if Akira's recipe for the crab cakes was included in the appetizer course at his school.

"I know you've been working with your stash of *alaheʻe* wood while waiting for the appointment with your new clients on the North Shore. If you aren't meeting with them for a few days, I wondered if you'd like to help me check out the furniture Bō said he sold to an antique shop. I'm hoping to find a piece or two that matches what I saw in my vision."

"No problem, Natalie. I've got about a week until my next

appointment. Once I evaluate their needs, I may be locked in for a few days. Until that time, my schedule is clear."

In the morning, we set off in Keoni's truck, in case I found something that would be a great addition to the cottage. *Memories Antiques* was a delightful place and I enjoyed every moment we spent there. While Keoni strolled through the store's stock of antique koa furnishings, I approached the owner. She told me that she had not yet prepped the furniture from the old Shēn Hotel, but if I wanted to see it, I could check out the warehouse across the back parking lot. I waived at my partner and exited through the back door.

I have never minded a bit of dust when I am on the hunt for a bargain...or a key to an incomplete article. At the moment, I did not know if I was more interested in an acquisition for the cottage, or a clue that would solve the mystery of the man who had died in that narrow hotel hallway so many years ago. Wandering through the cluttered space, I found a number of furnishings that would complement the style of my Auntie Carries' home.

Eventually, I spotted a corner stacked with odds and ends that looked like what I had seen in the hotel's elevator. I located the mahogany drop-leaf desk I had seen in my vision of Room 312 covered with shabby silk lampshades and stained lace doilies. Since I had been invited to look through the warehouse, I felt I could not get in much trouble for making the most of this opportunity to do a little sleuthing with my shopping.

I found a folding card table and quickly erected it beside the desk. I pulled a pair of nitrile gloves and a package of tissues from my purse. With my hands covered, I cleared the top of the desk and began opening its sizeable drawers. I had no idea what I might find, but if there were anything that qualified as *evidence*, I wanted to protect it. I drew the desk toward me, one corner at a time. I walked around the lovely old piece. Aside from a few scratches that I knew could be buffed out, it was in great condition.

I then pulled a chair on wheels over and sat down. I opened the drop leaf and found numerous mini-drawers and cubicles, some of which had inner, almost hidden compartments. I examined everything carefully but found nothing but a lot of dust. I had the same result when I pulled out the side drawers as far as I could. I was disappointed but refused to give up. At that moment Keoni appeared.

"I see you've found something, dear. For the house or the case?"

"I'm not sure. With respect to the first option, it's beautiful and would go nicely with what we've already got. Regarding the second, well I haven't found anything yet."

Keoni walked around the desk as I had. Like me, he did not find anything noteworthy. Removing the center and side drawers, he stacked them carefully out of the way. He pulled the small flashlight he carries from his pocket and started to kneel down. Just then his phone rang out a few notes of a Scott Joplin ragtime piano classic. Straightening up, he glanced at the caller's name and then gestured that he needed to take the call.

He stepped out the open back door and I contemplated my options. Bō and I had discussed the rectangular niches his construction crew had uncovered in the walls of the Shēn Building. They must have been used for something valuable. Maybe even the family's antiquated furniture had concealed some treasure they needed to keep secret.

I may not be able to do any heavy lifting, but there was no reason I could not take a peek at the inner structure of the desk. I dropped a cushion from a nearby chair onto the floor, picked up Keoni's flashlight and knelt down. Glancing from the stacked drawers to the space within the desk, I noticed something strange. It was obvious that all of the drawers had been shortened. I crawled under the desk and felt the sides and back.

"If Miss Una were here, I'd suspect you found a new cubby with her hiding in it," exclaimed Keoni.

I pushed back and looked up. "I've found something. I'm positive there's a hidden space behind these drawers, which have been shortened by about four inches."

After conducting his own investigation, he gave me his appraisal. "I think you're right, Natalie. This desk has definitely been modified. If you want it for the house, we should buy it and continue our little investigation at home."

We were home in less than an hour. After Keoni removed its drawers, we carried the desk into the workroom at the back of the garage. Within a minute, we were joined by Miss Una who seems to know when something exciting is unfolding. Despite the strong smells of wood shavings and paste wax, she jumped onto the workbench for a good view. Keoni picked up a LED lantern and began a careful examination of every surface of the desk.

"There's got to be a mechanism that releases a door. But the back is completely smooth. I don't see anything that's been added; all of the wood pieces match in color and grain."

"Maybe the trigger for the door to the compartment is on the outside. Or maybe there's a sequence of actions you have to complete before it'll open. Like a Chinese puzzle box. I'll get on the Internet and look for descriptions of hidden compartment latches," I suggested.

"That's possible. If the alteration of the drawers was a custom job, the same may be true for the mechanism that opens the hidden compartment. I'll get started on cleaning the wood below the desktop."

As I was reading through a second website on furniture construction, Keoni yelped and called out my name.

He greeted me with a hug as I entered the workshop. "I looked everything over again. Even the decorative brads, in case they were drawer pulls. I'd given up and was giving the drawer rails a last rub. As I was reaching forward, my hand slipped and bounced against the back. And, *voilà*, the mystery of the hidden door is solved. It's opened by a Quaker lock; you just push against the panel to open it."

I moved closer. "What's a Quaker lock?"

"A spring lock."

"So, what did you find?"

"Do you think I'd spoil the unveiling of your find? I just popped it closed. You can do the honors.

Grinning, I said, "Then give me your flashlight and gloves."

I pulled on the Nitrile gloves, bent down and pushed against the panel as directed. It made a small popping sound and opened. I pulled the top of the door toward me and a couple of objects fell into my open hand. I rocked back and got up.

"There really was hidden treasure in the Shēn building. All these years and nobody found it, or should I say them? There may not be a jade statue but look at what I did find." I opened my hand slowly, revealing two small scrolls and an onion skin letter envelope.

"Let's go inside the house to examine everything. I think happy hour has arrived early," said Keoni, wiping his hands on a rag.

Soon we had thoroughly cleaned our hands and were seated on the sofa in the living room. Keoni was sipping a glass of his latest batch of sun tea with passion fruit juice, while I enjoyed a glass of Sterling Pinot Grigio. On the coffee table were the scrolls, the letter envelope, a box of gloves and a roll of soft paper towels. With gloved hands, Keoni carefully wiped a few of Auntie Carrie's crystal paper weights. Then he unrolled each of the scrolls and set the weights on the edges to keep them open.

"The calligraphy is beautiful. The slightly larger scroll looks older and rather formal," I declared. "Maybe it's some kind of family or legal record. I'm pretty sure that this letter envelope is similar to others I've seen dating from around the Second World War."

After Keoni carefully unfolded the letter envelope with the blade of a slim letter opener, I examined its content. Written by Bàozhǐ, it was dated December 10, 1953.

> *Honorable Father—*
>
> *As I prepare to embark on the task you have asked me to undertake on behalf of our family, I wish to thank you for the trust you have placed in me.*
>
> *While I feel positive about my ability, I recognize that I will be relying on unknown people in an unfamiliar land. If anything occurs that prevents my success, I want you to know I will have done my utmost to accomplish our goal.*
>
> *If you have found this letter, these may be my last words*

to you. And while this may not be the path we have envisioned our lives taking, my only regret is in having failed you. If indeed I have been unable to return, please comfort my wife Toitoi and ask my brother Chāng to care for her. For the sake of our family's future, I pray his son will grow up to fulfill the dreams of our esteemed Jūnlì. If people could follow the ancient way, then they would be masters of the moment.

Below the English text was a Chinese character that I assumed was the man's personal seal, followed by the Shēn family symbol. Beneath that was a vertical line of Chinese characters.

* * * * *

When I called John Dias, he told me he had caught a new case involving multiple murders and couldn't view our latest finds until Tuesday. We made it a lunch date to compensate for his taking time to come to Lanikai. It seemed like only a day when John arrived at our door. After we finished our meal of left-over stir-fried chicken and vegetables, John methodically refolded his napkin and launched into an update.

"At the moment, I'm trying to figure out a way to balance my schedule. My new case, involving two cousins by the name of Comacho, could impact drug use across the Islands, so the hours I can devote to the case we're dating to 1953 are few. Being at a dead-end with Professor Zhāng's murder, I'm in a catch 22. And if I can't find a link to the Professor's case, I've got no excuse for rooting around in one from sixty years ago. But if I can pull some of the threads together, it'll be different. Then I can have Detective Ken`ichi Nakamura take on more details of the new case while I slip in some cruising through the last century."

Keoni and I nodded and remained silent.

"Speaking of which, I've managed to do a little walking and knocking in the area surrounding the Shēn Building. There's one thing I can tell you about ethnic neighborhoods—the members of the community hang together through time. In my brief tour, I found several families who've worked within a half-mile radius of the Shēn Building for decades. There's also one couple who, like the Shēns, have lived in their building since before World War II. Everywhere I went, people of every age wanted to show me photos of how the Chinatown neighborhood has changed. One thing I've seen plenty of is herringbone-patterned carpet. And I've looked at more than one image of men dressed in white leisure suits.

"I've also learned that, while the Shēns aren't leaders of their neighborhood, they're solid supporters of the Chinese community. I get the feeling that if the Shēns hadn't suffered so many deaths in each generation, they would've played a larger role in local Chinese society. Looks like every member of the family has been well-known and liked—except Bō's Auntie Toitoi, who's considered very controlling."

"Have you found people who knew Bàozhǐ?" I asked.

"Anyone who's old enough remembers both of the Shēn brothers. I guess they were similar in their trim builds, good hair and popularity with the ladies. Looks like there were a few broken hearts when the one married a girl from the 'hood and the other brought home a war bride from the land of the enemy. The local women were really let down after Chāng's wife died. Some of them had thought they might get another chance at him. But no way. Not with Bàozhǐ's quasi widow in the picture. I guess she made it clear that no woman needed to apply for the apparent opening in the family. But Chāng wasn't in the market for a new wife. Ever.

"As to Bàozhǐ himself, he was declared dead seven years after he went missing. With Toitoi, officially a widow, she collected a nice little packet of insurance money from two policies. Not enough to live in grand style, but it gave her a start in real estate. And now she's a full partner in Shēn Commercial Properties."

"What about Bō's parents?" questioned Keoni.

"They don't get much mention, but I guess that makes sense. It looks like the threesome of Kāng, his father, and Auntie never hit the Honolulu limelight. Bō told you most all there was to know about his father Kāng. His folks met in college, married, had him, and then were gone. They didn't live long enough to make their mark. International terrorism was a relatively new thing for this country. Their deaths were horrible and changed the entire Shēn family dynamic. I think that's when Toitoi took the reins in most every aspect of their daily lives."

"So, where *is* the infamous wife—well, his widow?" I asked.

"On Maui. I guess she doesn't make it over here very often," John replied. "She's been hard to run down, especially since we can't pull her in for anything officially. She seems to spend a lot of time island-hopping on her boyfriend's yacht.

"She's getting up in years, but she's pretty spry for an old broad. And good looking. I'll bet some of her wealth gets spent on plastic surgery."

"What about Bàozhǐ? Have you found any trace of him?" I asked.

"Or his body?" added Keoni.

"We're talking pre-computerization. You know how time-consuming it is to go through old files. Most cases before the eighties have yet to be digitalized. As to the hardcopy files, there's mold and water damage, not to mention the misfiling of records. Besides all that, I can't exactly announce why *I'm* going through a case that old, let alone put a CSI team on it. Like I've said before, once I can uncover some kind of link to the current case, it'll be a different story.

"Even if I had a body, there are few finger print data bases going back to the 1950s. At the time there was no real cooperation between state and regional law enforcement agencies, let alone the Feds. It was a decade after Bàozhǐ's disappearance before the states even got around to using fingerprinting for drivers' licenses. If a perp wasn't in the military or working for a government agency, his or her prints weren't available to public safety officers. And if they never made it into the record back then, they're certainly not available to me now.

"In short, I have found no evidence of Bàozhǐ as a missing person or any unidentified John Doe in 1953. What I've got is a case from the past that I can't prove is related to the current one on my plate. So, although I've barely scratched the surface of this old case, I'm skidding to a stop."

On that depressing note, we moved into the living room and settled around the coffee table.

Looking at the scrolls and letter envelope Keoni had placed in clear plastic archival bags, John asked, "So what have you got here?"

I described our adventure at *Memories Antiques* and finding the secret cubicle at the back of the desk. It was doubtful that Bàozhǐ's letter to his uncle was related to the current murder, so our opening it would not compromise the chain of evidence. None of us speak or read Chinese, so there was little to say about the scrolls. The age of the larger one seemed to preclude its having anything to do with whatever happened to Bàozhǐ.

John put his notebook away. "Well, thanks again for everything you've been doing. Unfortunately, if I can't find any trace of Bàozhǐ's body, your efforts may be leading nowhere. The similarity to my current case is too uncanny to ignore, so I'll continue exploring every hint of a clue to it. But like I've said, without direct links, I can't call in the CSI team. Therefore, I'm tempted to have you return to Pearl Wong for a little more help."

"I'm happy to do that, John. What shall I tell her this time? I've already shared the *Tao Te Ching* with her, including the note with the unexplained "riddle" in it. We know she's capable of keeping secrets, but I should be able to avoid discussing Fù Hán Zhāng's murder. I'll tell her these things may relate to a crime dating back several decades."

"I think she's right, JD," said Keoni. "As you've said, currently there's no link to Professor Zhāng's death. As long as we don't say anything about *that* case, we're just doing a little digging into the past. We could even say it may relate to one of *my* old cases, but we need to maintain silence until we're sure."

"You've always known how to present your case to a jury. My hands *are* tied until I come up with some definitive evidence." He paused to think. "Okay, this is how we'll do it. Give copies of everything to Pearl. Tell her about the article you're writing and explain you found these items in a desk from the old Shēn Hotel. This is all true and this approach will give you a chance to see how she responds to the Shēn name."

"All right, John. I know she'll enjoy having another assignment," I responded.

"Also, I'm going to ask you to do a little knocking and talking. As far as Bō and his team of remodelers know, I'm not in the picture at this time. I told him I'd get back to him if I needed anything further, but I'm not going to call him again until I've got something tangible to move on.

"But *you've* established your credentials as a journalist, and he's probably mentioned your project to a few people. So, I want you to go back into Chinatown and interview people who work or live in the area. Tell them you're looking for more stories on Chinatown's buildings and families. Don't forget to put your safety first. Why don't you think up some pretext to go with her, Keoni—as her photographer, intern, or whatever."

"Sure. And what do you want us to do with this evidence?" asked Keoni pointing to our latest finds.

"For now, put it in that fancy safe you had installed. We'll see what happens. If we get something I can run with officially, the lost can be found—and acted upon."

*   *   *   *   *

The photos of Akira Duncan's school and restaurant had not yet been taken, so I had some lead time to complete my article. And since Keoni had taken measurements of a client's offices after our meeting with John on Tuesday, we were both free to play detecting journalists on Thursday. Before driving into Chinatown, we dropped off the materials for Pearl to translate. She was delighted to have something new to occupy her mind. Following John's guidelines, we described the project as a continuing personal mystery I hoped would aid me in writing a feature article. After another disclaimer that she was an amateur linguist, we parted from her with clasped hands and warm smiles.

"I would say that was an auspicious beginning to our new phase of discovery, darling," I remarked as we got back in my car.

"Revving up for Chinatown, are we, dear?" asked Keoni. "Auspicious indeed! The next thing you'll be doing is a re-interpretation of Charlie Chan."

"Now don't laugh about that classic—if politically improper—series of movies. They may have mocked Chinese culture on the one hand, but they introduced the American public to an intelligent leading man who was supposed to be Chinese. That's a great advance from the days of the Chinese Exclusion Act. And some Chinese, like Professor Zhāng, actually liked the funny character and his derring-do."

As we crept into downtown Honolulu, Keoni asked, "Where do you want to begin this morning's adventure? JD's already visited with Bō's immediate neighbors. Maybe we should widen our investigation."

Glancing at a map of downtown Honolulu, I considered all the blocks we had walked during the scavenger hunt. "How about we begin at the store where I won the book? If the owners have been there very long, there's no telling how many stories they could have collected about the neighborhood."

When we entered the bright red door of the bookstore, I was pleased to see the elderly gentleman we had met before. With a duster in hand, Mr. Fong was standing on a stepstool in front of a glass-fronted bookcase. He looked down and smiled.

"Ah, the lady who won the *Tao Te Ching*. I hope you are enjoying the book's art as well as its text," he said with genuine interest as he came down to greet us.

"Oh, yes. It's become one of the most treasured books in my library."

Showing his age as well as his politeness, he waited for me to offer my hand and shook it gently. Turning to Keoni, he provided an obviously firmer handshake.

"And how are your friends? I believe they said they were visiting from the mainland."

"They're fine. In fact, she's beginning some remodeling for which she is delighted to include some of her Chinatown purchases."

"Excellent. It is gratifying that our culture continues to spread across the world! And what may I do for you today?"

CHAPTER 14

I know enough of the world now to have almost lost the
capacity of being much surprised by anything.
Charles Dickens [1812 - 1870]

I reintroduced myself as a journalist and explained my
desire to gather stories of the local architecture and
families. When I mentioned the Shēn Building, he volunteered that he had spoken with one of Bō's neighbors who had
said the building was being included in a forthcoming magazine
article. Mr. Fong then graciously offered us tea, and we sat at a
small table near the front window for over an hour. He told us
his family had lived over the shop in past years, although his son
now has a tailor shop upstairs and his daughter-in-law works as
a Vietnamese translator.

As we talked about the evolution of the neighborhood, I
noticed that a few events had triggered the greatest changes:
plagues; two major fires; two world wars; statehood; hurri-
canes; and tidal waves. While that last category usually affects
Chinatown in indirect ways, sometimes the impact is surprisingly direct.

"When Hurricane Iwa struck the Islands in November of
1982, residents of Chinatown, like many of those across O`ahu
and Kauai, experienced power outages. Thanksgiving celebrations that year often relied on menus of food barbecued to prevent spoilage. In the following weeks, many surprising things
emerged, including the discovery of a body in a warehouse where
a blown compressor resulted in an old freezer's meltdown."

Suddenly I realized what he was saying. If I had not had Keoni beside me, I do not think I could have constrained my over-whelming desire to leap up and shout, "Are you kidding me?"

Fortunately, with just a slight movement of Keoni's knee, I remembered to keep my emotions reeled in. That did not, how-ever, help me gulp down the mouthful of tea I had nearly splut-tered across my companions. But since I was the journalist pur-suing an unknown story, I knew I had to step fully into my role.

"That must have been quite a shock. I was in the Caribbean on assignment and missed the storm by a couple of weeks. When I returned home from such missions, I always tried to catch up on local news by reading old issues of the *Honolulu Star-Bulletin* and the *Advertiser*. I don't remember anything about that event. Of course, there were so many things that happened during Hur-ricane Iwa, I guess it must have slid past me."

Mr. Fong grimaced slightly. "So many people were affected by that storm. I don't think there was much news coverage of the discovery of the body. It was not like today, with instant re-ports—even from kids with their smartphones. Of course, the neighborhood knew about the body. It was found in the ware-house owned by the Ching family. At that time, they owned a few markets and three restaurants. They used to joke that every time one of their kids married, they had to start a new business."

"I know who you're talking about. Wasn't Richard Ching the head of the family? My auntie used to buy fresh produce from their Kaimukī market," commented Keoni.

"Yes. The original market and restaurant were founded by his father, but Richard was the real businessman in the family. By the time he had been in charge for a few years, the family owned half a dozen markets and a couple of restaurants. Offer-ing free delivery to homes and businesses all over this side of the island, allowed the Chings to develop a loyal customer base. I think that if the stores had spread to Windward Oʻahu—or even the North Shore—they would have been able to compete with the larger chain stores."

"So what happened? Why didn't they stay in the retail food business?" I wondered aloud.

"Well, just before Iwa, Richard had a stroke. And then, with the problems at the Sand Island warehouse, the grocery side of the business just wound down. One of the kids wanted to move off-island. One of the markets lost their lease. Once your luck turns, well, it turns."

"You're right, Mr. Fong. A lot of things in life depend on unforeseen events. So who did they find in the warehouse?"

"That we never learned. After everything calmed down, no one was reported missing, and no one came forward to claim the body. It was really strange. You see, the body had been in that freezer for many years."

"The police never discovered the deceased's identity?" questioned Keoni.

"I don't know what the police found out. All we learned was that it was a man, fairly young, Asian. We never heard anything else," concluded Mr. Fong with a shake of his head.

"What an amazing story," I said honestly. "I don't know how it might fit into my article, but who could I talk to if I want to learn more?"

"Well, the Chings aren't in the grocery business any longer, but they still have several restaurants in Honolulu, and one on Kauai. The closest one is over at the Cultural Plaza. It's owned by Richard's granddaughter. I forget her name, but I think her mother still helps out when things get busy. It's a creative take on Asian fusion.

"It's kind of Chinese *dim sum* meets Korean barbecue. You sit wherever you want. They bring around the *dim sum* carts, but you can also have the stir fry chef cook your favorite mix of meat, vegetables and sauces. Of course, by the time they return with your order, you've usually had another round of the appetizers. It's a successful enterprise even though they're only open for lunch and don't have a liquor license."

"What's the name of the restaurant?" I queried, hungry for both lunch and the story of the unknown man found in the Ching family warehouse.

Keoni and I were soon on our way to a new culinary experience.

"Do you think the popsicle from thirty years ago is your

missing Bàozhĭ?"

"Do you have to be so gruesome," I asked, nearly giggling at the image, despite the respect I felt for Bō Shēn and his family.

"Sorry. Morgue humor is what got me through a lot of sad cases," said Keoni.

"I doubt the sincerity of your apology, but I get the need for emotional release."

By the time we arrived at Lily's Dim Sum and Stir Fry, I was ready to eat anything they brought out from the fragrant kitchen. When the *dim sum* cart arrived at our table, I had already looked over our neighbors' choices. The problem was that everything looked so good: pot stickers; grilled shrimp; *mu shu* chicken and pork with pancakes; skewered meats; even some kind of *tempura* style vegetables. It was an eclectic menu and exactly what I desired. Keoni however, had designs on a stir-fried medley of meats and vegetables topped off with a Korean garlic sauce.

As we munched our first round of appetizers and drank a delightful house blend of oolong tea, we looked over the history of the Ching Company printed on the clean paper placemat I had grabbed from another table.

"Mr. Fong was right. The Ching family used to have several markets in Honolulu," I confirmed.

"Like I told you, my auntie used to shop at the Kaimukī store. I think they delivered to my grandma's home a couple of times when I was visiting during school breaks," added Keoni.

"So how are things going with the family abode? Did your folks decide to keep it or sell it?"

"Well, after all the research you did at the time of Ariel's death—and the possible link to a visit by Queen Lili`uokalani, I've convinced them to keep it in the family. One of my cousin's sons is living in it with a couple of his buddies from the University. It may not be a permanent solution, but it sure beats the wrecking ball."

On that happy note, we finished our meal. With the lunch crowd diminishing, I took a chance and I asked to speak to the owner. Lily was on a run to the bank, but her mother was available. For my purposes, that was probably better. After introducing myself as a freelance journalist and Keoni as my friend, I said I was writing an article on historic Chinatown. I then referenced my interviews of Bō Shēn and Mr. Fong. After Mrs. Ching confirmed that she had heard of my project, I expressed interest in learning more about the story of the body that materialized after Hurricane Iwa.

"In the aftermath of the storm, it was a question of doing what was most important. If something wasn't at the top of the list, it didn't get done. In a couple of weeks, life started to settle down. But for some people, life was changed permanently.

"My grandfather had died the year before, and my dad had a stroke a month before the storm. He was our family's rudder. But after the stroke, he couldn't communicate fully, and his memories were vague and muddled. Our family had several markets and a couple of restaurants at the time. We were finally figuring out how to handle things without his daily input when Iwa struck. Soon after, one of my brothers (who'd been running two of the markets) needed to move to Kauai. His wife's family had lost most of the cottages at their small resort and they needed help to rebuild.

"In those days, few people worked with a business plan. With each generation, our family just kept opening businesses to provide everyone with a job. By the 1980s, there were less kids coming along, and fewer of them wanted to go into food service. The very thought of maintaining the varied stock of a market frightened me. Besides, I was too young to step into the management of one, let alone two markets."

She paused and motioned for one of the servers to bring us a fresh pot of tea. After we all had a cup in our hands, she took a sip and continued.

"We were luckier than a lot of people. Not a lot of damage to our buildings. Only one market was totaled. We were in the middle of cleaning up and preparing to do a full inventory, when we got a call about our Sand Island warehouse. Warehouses in that area have served the needs of restaurateurs and grocers for a long time. Like others, we used the place for storage of many things: produce, meats, and dry goods, plus old equipment, furniture—even decorations for Chinese New Year.

"Also, we provided space to friends and neighbors who couldn't afford warehouses of their own. For a small business, it was the most cost-effective way to store products and supplies. Sharing space is nothing new in our culture, or any immigrant society. But as things piled up over the years, the warehouse became cluttered. By the 1980s, we couldn't identify items that had been stored during the time of our father, let alone our grandfather.

"With everything else that had happened, we weren't surprised when the manager of several area warehouses called to say the storm had caused a prolonged blackout. The worst news was that the compressors of one of our refrigeration units and two freezers had broken down. But with the meltdown of the freezers, some horrible smells emerged after a few days. And as the cleanup crew worked their way through the building, they found a locked freezer in a back corner that had the worst odor.

"Imagine the shock of breaking the old padlock and finding a man dressed in just his underwear. He'd been shot in the head and stashed there, rolled up in a tarp. The cops came immediately. They were followed by the coroner. The body had been there for a long time and it didn't hold up too well in the defrosting process. With our grandfather dead and our inability to communicate with Dad, we couldn't determine who owned that freezer. It wasn't even on our inventory sheets.

"I was pretty young when it happened. It made a lasting impression—on everyone in the family. In fact, it was the last straw for our grocery business. We quickly sold the buildings where our markets were located and the warehouse. Within a few months, we were completely focused on the restaurants.

"Time moves on, but you never forget something like that. We never did learn who the man was...or how he ended up in the freezer in our warehouse."

*　*　*　*　*

After Keoni and I left Mrs. Ching, we debated whether to continue canvassing businesses in the plaza. It seemed more logical to check in with John. Even if we had no forensic evidence, I felt confident that the mystery of Bàozhǐ's disappearance had been solved. With the details we had gleaned, there might be enough data for the good Lieutenant to track down the case of the 1982 unidentified corpse in storage.

When Keoni could not reach John by phone, he left a message and we headed to Lanikai. I was still keyed up from the success of our adventure when we arrived home, but too drained physically for a walk to the beach. With the end of the day approaching, we put on our swim suits, grabbed some large beach towels and glasses of orange mango juice, and eased ourselves into the hot tub.

"I think I've figured out why you've enjoyed being a detective."

"Mmhm," mumbled Keoni, focusing on rubbing my feet.

"It's the adrenaline, right?"

"Partly. But I don't see how that fits into today," he replied.

"For you, it might be the result of the rush from physical confrontation that drives your adrenaline. But except for a couple of my scary visions, it's the thrill of confirming a truth I've only suspected that's a rush for me—even if it emerges in a dusty archive or an interview."

"And what about your nightmare experiences as a journalist? Are you going to deny the physical rush of a bomb going off in your vicinity?"

I pulled my feet off Keoni's lap and moved to sit opposite him. "I'll agree with that. But it's only happened a few times. It's not like I was a front-line war correspondent."

For a few minutes we sat there steeping in warm water and old memories. Just as my eyes closed, I heard a faint "meow" in my ear. Looking behind me, I found Miss Una's new playmate seated on the towels I had piled on the table behind the spa.

"Hello, `Ilima. Aren't you the brave one. I guess you missed your mentor's message about the unknown dangers of bubbling water. Speaking of Miss Una, where is she?"

Like most felines, her only reply was a vague flick of an ear in the direction of the master bedroom. When we emerged from our shower a half-hour later, we found both kitties playing tag on the *lanai*. I checked our voicemail and saw that John had left a message. After touching base with Keoni, I returned the call and suggested he join us for cocktails and maybe a late dinner at Buzz's restaurant. I wasn't sure how hungry I would be, but the salad bar was great, and I have never known Keoni to turn down a good steak grilled over *kiawe* wood.

Given our vague dining plans for the evening, I was uncertain about what I should offer in the way of *hors d`oeuvres*. Keeping it simple, I set out small dishes of macadamia nuts, chunks of dried pineapple, sourdough pretzels and a wonderful goat cheese from the Big Island. Light, but enough to fortify the men until we wandered down to Kailua Beach for that late supper I had suggested.

Again, John looked rather dapper despite the long hours he had been working. I decided it was time to learn the source of this upswing in his appearance. What emerged from our usual banter was surprising. Evidently Medical Examiner Martin Soli had a new assistant who was young, charming, and already smitten with our good friend.

"So, all those trips you've been taking to the Coroner's Office lately have offered fringe benefits," said Keoni, opening a couple of bottles of Weasel Boy Ale.

John grinned and turned his hands outward. "I will admit that some of the more gruesome aspects of the job are improving. The only problem is that Lori Mitchum and I can't go out for a quick lunch or drinks immediately after work."

"Why not?" I asked. "Has Marty turned into an ogre? Or is he feeling threatened by the competition?"

John laughed. "The answer to your second question is simple; Lori is Marty's cousin. And besides, he's married. Lori's doing an internship with him. Once she's through with that, she's got one more semester of a master's program at UCLA. As to your first question, we don't go out as soon as she's off duty because after a day in the morgue, she's dying for a shower."

"Here's a third question. Aren't you robbing the cradle?" I teased.

"Hey, she's not that young. Just switching careers," he countered, defensively.

"Oh, another long-distance relationship," said Keoni. "That's been one of your best excuses for avoiding commitment, my friend."

"It's *early days*, as the Brits say. We'll see where it goes. I'm about at the point where I'm considering retiring. If things work out with Lori, I might just speed up that timeline."

Keoni offered a shake of his head in response and we moved out to the covered portion of the *lanai*.

"When do we get to meet Lori?" I asked.

"How about after we've found Bàozhǐ? He hasn't been seen for nearly three decades, but I think it's a safe bet he'll show up in her lab as soon as anywhere else...So, how did today go? You sounded excited on the phone, Natalie."

"Well, we may have pinpointed his current location," offered Keoni.

"Wow. What did you two learn?" questioned my second favorite cop as he pulled out his notebook.

Within a few minutes Keoni and I had caught John up on the discoveries we made during our saunter through Chinatown.

Keoni turned to his old partner seriously. "What's the game plan from here?"

John snapped his notebook closed. He then set it on the glass topped coffee table and laid his pen beside it. Leaning back, he sighed.

"Well, let's begin by summarizing what we know so far— thanks to your excellent research. I don't know how you do it. Not only is *what* you've found amazing, but the way you've managed to stitch it all together blows my mind.

"First, you had a vision of a murder in the middle of the last century. Almost immediately thereafter, I landed a case with a similar setting at the Honolulu hotel where you just happened to be participating in a scavenger hunt. I found a fake hunt clue, which you took to Pearl Wong for a little off-the-books explanation. The text may have looked like the other clues, but it was really some kind of riddle for finding something of value that was concealed. That something of value might be a statue of Kuan Yin.

"Then you located a building in Chinatown that is remarkably similar to the site of the murder in your vision. When we toured the building, you found architectural features, décor, and photos that jibed perfectly with your vision. You subsequently interviewed Bō Shēn, the owner of the building. In that interview, you learned that his granduncle Bàozhǐ Shēn had disappeared in 1953—at the time the man was believed to have departed for Hong Kong aboard the luxury liner the S.S. President Cleveland."

Keoni and I nodded in agreement with his review.

"Based on Bō's revelation that he had sold the old hotel's furnishings, you tracked down a desk you saw in your vision. You bought it and located a hidden compartment with a letter envelope written by Bàozhǐ and two scrolls. You took copies of those things to Pearl Wong for her analysis. And you've interviewed a woman whose family's Sand Island warehouse suffered a power outage during Hurricane Iwa in October 1982. After the compressor on a freezer blew, a putrid smell triggered discovery of a body that had probably been frozen three decades earlier. How am I doing so far?"

"Great. And if you didn't look so elegant, I'd ask if you want to put your feet in the spa," I teased. "Of course, you could borrow a pair of Keoni's trunks."

"I think I'll pass. Otherwise, I'd have to go through the hassle of dressing again," he responded, taking a long sip of ale.

"So where were *you* during the 1982 hurricane?" I asked.

"I was right here. In fact, I was on duty for nearly a week. Hurricane Iwa arrived when I was on my first round as a cadet."

"What do you mean, *first round*," I responded.

"JD is a member of an elite squad of HPD officers who have gone through the academy twice," said Keoni.

"Well, it's not like I washed out. I just came down with a case of mono and had to take a little break."

"Mono? The kissing disease? I hope she was really hot," joked Keoni.

"Hold that thought. Several members of my family had it. You *can* get it from more than kissing, you know."

"So, if you hadn't graduated from the academy, what were you doing officially?" I asked, picturing him in a cadet's uniform.

"Anything I was told to do. At first it was sandbagging. Then taping and boarding windows and glass doors. Once the storm hit, and the power went down, I was running errands, directing traffic, and rescuing stranded animals. It was quite an intro to the back alleys of our fair city. In fact, it was a confusing time for even the most seasoned men. I don't mean to sound gender prejudiced, Natalie, but there were few women on the force back then.

"I remember one who had made sergeant. She'd been an educator and was a sharp cookie—and I don't just mean with the tests and paperwork. She was good on the street, too. But some of the old timers grumbled whenever she left a room. She wasn't in my chain of command, so it didn't affect me one way or the other. But I do remember one time when I almost took on a sergeant who was about to retire. He made some crude remark, and I recall thinking that if it had been my sister he was talking about, I really would have taken him outside for a little one-on-one."

I was proud that John had stood up, at least mentally, for the rights of women so long ago. "What's next?"

"Well, I think I've got enough evidence to warrant an official look see: I have the name of a man who disappeared in mid-December 1953. And, in 1982 a body fitting his description was found defrosted after twenty-nine years in a freezer. This should be enough evidence to authorize me to go through the records to track the body that was found. If I'm lucky, I'll be able to have the John Doe body exhumed for DNA testing."

"How do you plan to present this to your captain?" queried Keoni.

"I'll tell the truth—a truncated truth, that is. Admittedly, I haven't gotten very far with the case that started all this—Professor Fù Hán Zhāng's murder. However, I *can* say that learning he was seen talking to members of the Chinese community gave me cause to do some walking and talking in Chinatown. And while listening to the stories of old timers in the area, and looking at their photos, I saw one of the missing hotelier Bàozhǐ dressed much as the Professor was in the downtown Honolulu hotel.

"Then I can say that tonight, when we met for cocktails, you told me about a mysterious body that had been in a freezer for about three decades. This made me curious about the possible link to the story of the Chinese man who went missing in the 1950s. And that brings us to my decision to look into both of those cases for a potential link to Professor Zhāng's murder. Do you think that'll fly with the captain, Keoni?"

"I think you've got enough pieces of the puzzle to justify cruising through a few old files."

By the time we finished our drinks, nibbles and storytelling, we all decided to pass on dinner. After John left, Keoni and I zapped some popcorn, sliced a couple of apples and put on an old Masterpiece Mystery. After a little connubial bliss, I fell into a deep sleep. At least for a while.

CHAPTER 15

Patience and tenacity are worth more than twice
their weight of cleverness.
Thomas Huxley [1825 - 1895]

A s sometimes happens, instead of a night of peaceful rest, I slipped into one of my visions. It began in the sepia tones I've experienced since my first vision as a young child.

*   *   *   *   *

This night, I am lying on a misty hillside in the Koʻolau Mountains, watching rain-filled clouds drift above me. My eyes slowly close.

When I reopen them, I am sitting on a cloud that floats toward Honolulu on a sun-drenched day. For a moment I hover on the town-side of the hills, wondering if I have moved back to the mid-twentieth century. Viewing the tall buildings of my current life, I know that I am in the present.

I hear a man's voice call out in Chinese. I do not know the meaning of his words, but I know that I must go to him.

Within a second, I stand just inside the door of a room in the hotel that hosted the Aloha Scavenger Hunt. A man is seated at a desk with his back to me. I am able to see that he's looking at a flier that appears to be an advertisement for a condominium development. He then closes the folder containing the flier and looks up at the screen of a laptop computer. Before him is the image in silhouette of a woman dressed in a long silk cheongsam, *sunhat, and very high heels. From the top of her head to her ankles, she is a picture in red, except for a thick carved bracelet in creamy white jade that looks like it belongs in a museum or the finest of jewelry emporiums. I cannot see her face, but assume she is Asian because of her delicate proportions, sleek black hair, and attire.*

A chiming bell announces the arrival of an email. After opening and reading the short message, the man punches a couple of keys and the printer to the left of the computer spits out a sheet of paper. His gray head turns toward the lower right of the screen, where I know there is a clock. He pauses for a moment. Then, with a few keystrokes, he replies to the sender. He rises and pulls a jacket away from the back of his chair. With a smooth motion, the man puts on the ivory colored linen suit jacket. He steps to a dresser to the left of the desk and pulls a red rosebud from a vase. He snaps the stem and places the shortened flower in his lapel. He looks up into the mirror and I realize I am staring at Professor Zhāng.

He turns back to the desk and picks up the printout. He folds it twice and slips it into his breast pocket. Smoothing his lapels, the professor smiles broadly and exits the room. I walk beside him down the hallway. We ride an elevator up several floors. I wish I could warn him about what is going to happen. The door opens. We step out. He pulls the paper from his pocket, glances at it, and then up at the sign in front of us. As in my other visions, we turn to the right and move toward a T-junction.

The professor looks at another sign and turns left. I walk slowly behind him to the suite at the end of the corridor. I stop a few paces from the double doors. My companion inhales deeply, pulls his shoulders up and back, and straightens his tie. He raps on the door to the right. Barely a moment passes before the doors open inward. The bright light of the hallway contrasts with flickering candlelight in the suite's foyer. Standing before him is a tall woman dressed in a crimson dress of hand-painted silk. Below a broad brimmed felt hat, her long black hair is swept to the right and wrapped with gleaming gold wire. She beckons the professor with the fingers of both hands. I see a vintage Elgin gold watch on her wrist and smell the scent of roses.

With a feeling of dread, I watched the rest of the scene unfold as before. I only wished I did not know what was going to happen.

*   *   *   *   *

On Friday morning, I placed a quick call to John to give him the new details that were revealed in my latest vision. He quickly confirmed one of my new pieces of information. Yes, the professor *had* been wearing a rose in his lapel.

It seemed we all had homework to do. Keoni was beginning analysis of a new client's McMansion on the North Shore. I had the article on Chef Duncan to complete and the potential one on Chinatown architecture and families to contemplate seriously. As for John Dias, his schedule was filled with investigating the deaths of a couple of druggy cousins, as well as the case of Professor Zhāng.

Now there was a chance of proving a link to the murder I had seen in my initial vision. At least with that case, Keoni and I had made some progress. We had the name of Bàozhǐ Shēn, the approximate date of his death, and the location of his icy interment for twenty-nine years. If he had ended up in a John Doe grave in the early 1980s, it should not be that difficult for our clever lieutenant to have the body exhumed. That is, if his captain agreed to the plan.

It took me most of the day to polish my article on the culinary school, which I immediately emailed to my publisher. The following morning, I enjoyed a swim before turning to outlining key points from my interview of Bō Shēn. Mid-day I got a call from Pearl Wong. She had completed her analysis of the riddle. Although I was prepared to go into town and take her to lunch on Monday, Pearl offered to come to me.

When I asked whether she was up to the drive, she said that Al Cooper would chauffeur her since she had a few silver pieces she wanted Heritage Antiques to have restored. While I was delighted to have her come for lunch, I was not sure what to do with Al, for whom I still had mixed emotions. I was glad to learn that since he had not been to Kailua for many years, he would be enjoying a stroll at the beach park while Pearl and I visited.

I was very pleased that Pearl was coming to White Sands Cottage. I knew that she and my Auntie Carrie would have liked each other. I doubt that Keoni understood why I was so concerned that the house look perfect, but I felt as though my auntie or parents were coming. It was rather like a final stamp of approval that would announce my home had passed the white glove inspection I had heard so many friends in the military speak of while vacating base housing.

Accordingly, Sunday became a whirlwind of activity after an early walk at the beach with both Keoni and, for a rare occasion, our feline companion. Even Miss Una knew there was something special about the day. She, like most cats, dislikes the vacuum cleaner. But having to endure both the vacuum and the floor steamer was more than she could stand. When I arrived in the kitchen with the steamer, she jumped onto the counter and exited through her garden window. And when I went out to sweep the back *lanai,* I saw her through the back gate playing with `Ilima in Joanne's garden.

With Keoni gone, it would be a quiet girls' luncheon. There was no way I could compete with the feast of Asian specialties Pearl had previously shared with me, so I decided to offer simple American picnic fare. Not of my doing, of course. Looking in the refrigerator, I saw that there was grilled chicken Keoni had cooked the night before. To that I would add Izzy's signature potato salad, fragrant fresh bread from Agnes's Portuguese Bakery, and sliced tomatoes from Joanne's garden, drizzled with balsamic vinegar. To cap it all, I would serve peach-infused sun tea. I might not be much of a cook, but I could certainly arrange a nice buffet.

Al and Pearl arrived promptly at noon on Monday. His bright smile and warm handshake confirmed he had never learned of my suspicions of him at the time Ariel died. I was glad, since he had proven to be a good friend to the Wong sisters and residents of the Makiki Sunset Apartments. As he departed for his time in sun and sand, I was glad to note that while Pearl and I enjoyed our visit in the privacy of my home, he would be only a phone call away if Pearl grew tired.

After accepting a glass of tea, Pearl expressed interest in seeing Auntie Carrie's cottage. We began the two-dollar-tour in the living room, where we found Miss Una lounging on top of the mahogany desk that had been Bàozhǐ's hiding place.

"Why hello, Miss Una," said Pearl, reaching over to stroke the cat's soft fur.

As she bent over, Pearl's beautiful *Taijitu* necklace swung forward. As the late morning sun struck the gold edge of the Yang half of the symbol, Miss Una's paw came upward to swing it to the side. We laughed and moved on with our explorations. In each room, Pearl commented on the tasteful remodeling Keoni and I had done and found something of particular note.

In the dining room, Pearl spoke of having met artist Delores Kirby, whose serene painting of Kāne'ohe Bay hung above the drinks cart. The *geisha* doll my father had brought from Japan caught her eye in my bedroom. Moving up to the case, she asked if she might examine the doll more closely. With my immediate permission, she lifted the glass and carefully hoisted the doll from its stand. After a couple of moments, she turned to me with a wide smile.

"Oh, Natalie. This is a superb piece. She is a *maikoiko* doll, an apprentice *geisha*, created by the master artisan Hirata Gōyō. She dates from the late nineteenth century. Look at the detail of the carved head and body, the exquisitely applied oyster shell lacquer, and the red silk brocade decorated with fine gold thread."

My father always told me to take great care of the doll. Now I understood why. With everything Pearl had said, by the time I needed it, that thoughtful gift might help pay for a couple of months of care in a nursing home.

Eventually, we arrived in the kitchen where Pearl recognized Auntie Carrie's prized Spode teapot in the Indian Tree pattern. As we moved into the dining room, we chatted about memorable meals we had enjoyed. Ever the perfect guest, she protested that I had worked too hard as we filled our plates from the food I had laid out on the built-in buffet. During lunch, I told stories of the cottage and my Auntie Carrie, while Pearl looked out the French doors at the lush backyard.

"No wonder you do not miss life in town, Natalie. You and Keoni have created a wonderful home for yourselves. Whenever we visit on the telephone, I shall picture you in your lovely sea-

Burrows-Johnson

side cottage."

"Of course, I trust we will be seeing one another in person as often as we visit by phone," I replied.

We smiled and quietly finished the fresh strawberries I had dipped in a shell of chocolate for dessert. After refilling our glasses, we went into the office. I was glad the room was large enough to accommodate a loveseat for occasions like this. I gestured for Pearl to sit while I opened a drawer and pulled out some exam gloves. From another drawer, I retrieved the evidence bags containing the scrolls and letter envelope.

I was lucky to have possession of them, since John Dias did not yet have a green light to officially pursue the case of Bàozhǐ. He had given me permission to tell Pearl that I might have stumbled across an old murder case, so I offered an edited version of the story of the Chinese man who had disappeared long ago. I sat down beside Pearl and handed her a sheet of paper.

"Here is a copy of the scroll I'm about to show you." I then pulled on the gloves and unrolled the small scroll I removed from one of the bags. I held it up so that she could easily compare it to the copy in her hands.

"Mmm," she said, nodding. She glanced at the scroll briefly and indicated that I could return it to the bag.

"This is remarkable. It is the Chinese version of the riddle you found in the book you won," she said, handing me several sheets of paper with her analysis.

Pointing to the top one, she continued. "You know there are varying translations for Chinese characters, and certainly for each Chapter of the *Tao Te Ching*. I have rechecked the citations I gave you originally and I think they are fairly accurate."

"Thank you Pearl, for all you've done. And please don't worry about the details. It's not like I'm trying to publish a paper on Chinese linguistics. An expert can always be brought in later if needed."

I then pulled out the second scroll and carefully unrolled it.

She smiled slightly and nodded periodically as she read through it. "As to this scroll, you are right that it is a formal document. It is the will of a man named Shēn Fēng, or as we say in

English, Fēng Shēn. This will is unusual in a couple of aspects. Surprisingly, the liquid assets of his estate are divided equally among the living members of his family. But disposition of the family home follows the ancient rules of primogeniture—the property conveys to the eldest son, as long as he agrees to reside on the premises. In fact, there is a clause that specifies that each generation of the family must live in the property in order to inherit it.

"It is lovely to see a family using this traditional means of communication. Some of the scrolls I have seen previously are true pieces of art. In this case, although the calligraphy is nice, I do not think the author would have had the skills with which to embellish his words with art."

After replacing the scroll in the plastic bag, I brought out Bàozhǐ's letter so that Pearl could look at the Chinese characters at the bottom.

"Ah," Pearl said. "Now this is the hand of a man who was master of his brush. There is such energy in his work...a superb sense of rhythm in the flow of the finely spaced elements."

"His family has told me he was a fine painter. I'm looking forward to seeing some examples of his work. In fact, I may put one in an article I'm writing," I revealed, replacing the letter in its protective cover.

"How wonderful," Pearl responded. "I anticipate you will be impressed with his work." She paused momentarily. "Is this an artist whose work I would know?"

"No, Pearl. In fact, I am sad to say he died as a young man, leaving only a few pieces of his art. In fact, it is his death that is now being investigated."

"What a shame," she declared with honest sorrow. "In addition to his calligraphic skill, he had a deep appreciation of the highest principles of our culture. The passage he chose for concluding this letter to his father is from the *Tao Te Ching*. The words are simple, but the thought behind them is complex. *If people could follow the ancient way, then they would be masters of the moment.*

"I have tried to think of anything else I can tell you about the riddle. The only thing that occurred to me is that the beginning is an attempt to describe a building I would say is here in Honolulu. Given the age of the scroll I have just seen, I would say it is in Chinatown, since it was then the center of the Chinese community."

"I agree with you, Pearl. In fact, I believe I've located it."

"How exciting!" she exclaimed. "You are closing in on the solution to the riddle."

"Yes, it's a giant step. But I've been inside and there is no sign of a statue of Kuan Yin of any kind or size."

"Ah. Well, there is another aspect of the riddle I have considered."

"Oh?"

"It is the reference to the White River. You see, the White River is the source of something rather special. White Jade.

"Do you recall the seated Kuan Yin on my family altar? The one with the incense burner held in her lap?"

"Of course. It's one of the most exquisite pieces of jade art I've ever seen."

"The jade from which my Kuan Yin was carved came from the White River region of China. It is unique for the sugar-like crystals on its ridges. If the stone from which it was carved had stayed in the river very long, those crystals would have been eroded. With or without such crystals, or gems like those embedded in my piece, the Kuan Yin referenced in your riddle also appears to come from the White River and the Song Dynasty. And, like my piece, it may actually come from the Southern Song Dynasty, dating it to the twelfth to thirteenth centuries C.E."

"That's amazing! It seems like you've accounted for everything described in the riddle."

"If this is all true, Natalie, you may be looking for a very valuable piece. I only wish I could tell you the meaning of the latter part of the riddle, alluding to where the Kuan Yin *resides*."

"Hmm. Well, that's been the major question since the beginning."

"You said you found both of the scrolls and the letter in an antique desk?"

"Yes. I interviewed the young man who is the current owner of the building I believe the riddle speaks of. He told me he had sold most of the old furnishings. Out of curiosity, Keoni and I went to the store he mentioned. As soon as I saw the desk that is now against that wall, we both agreed it would harmonize with several pieces of Auntie Carrie's furniture, so I bought it. While cleaning it, we found a hidden compartment behind the center drawer and that is where we found he scrolls and letter.

"When I mentioned the details of my recent adventures to Lieutenant John Dias, he suggested this may all relate to that unsolved case he's been looking into. Unfortunately, he can't do anything about it until he verifics a few legal issues."

"Oh, my. Well, as you asked, I have not mentioned this project to anyone. And I will not. Ever. But I am honored that you sought my assistance, minor though it may have been."

"There's nothing minor about the help you've provided. I'm now hopeful that the answers to my questions will come to light, eventually. And I look forward to sharing the facts with you after everything is resolved."

"I shall look forward to that day, Natalie."

*   *   *   *   *

After Al picked up Pearl, I tried calling John. He did not answer, so I left a simple "no real news" message that seemed sufficient for the time being. When we finally spoke that night, I told him Pearl had declared that the first scroll in Bàozhǐ's desk was a Chinese version of the fake riddle in our scavenger hunt. This meant that the riddle pre-dated the hunt by several decades. While the quote from the *Tao Te Ching* at the end of Bàozhǐ's letter to his father would have meaning to Bao and his family, I could not see any relevance to either his death or that of Professor Zhāng. As to the second scroll, the will of Fēng Shēn confirmed that the men who had inherited the Shēn Building were required to live in the property. *Why* was the question? I was pretty sure the answer to it brought us back to the riddle's hinting at the location of a hidden statue of Kuan Yin, and any other family treasures.

On Tuesday, my article on Chef Duncan appeared in *Windward Oʻahu Journeys*, the new magazine that had hired me. It was their second issue, and the reason I had accepted the assignment was the beautiful photography they featured. From early morning to evening, I received calls of interest and congratulation. There were two I especially cared about: Akira Duncan and my publisher Harry Longhorn.

I was pleased and touched that Chef Duncan called to thank me for featuring the key elements of his interpretation of Pacific Rim cuisine. I was also happy that Harry proclaimed my work a success. After words of congratulation, he amazed me with a long-term proposal.

"I know you refer to yourself as *semi-retired*, Natalie, but would you consider a regular gig?" Harry inquired.

I was surprised. "What do you have in mind?"

"Let's call it a column to follow-up on your current article. Would you like to be our wandering food and drink writer? Not the usual food column that simply reviews local restaurants and bars. It'd be more of a *following Natalie Seachrist around our island* series."

"Mm, you've caught my interest. I'm not a real foodie. I don't have the professional vocabulary to qualify me to write a traditional food and wine column. But what you're describing could be really fun...if you think I'm qualified and like my style."

"With all the years you spent traveling the world, I think this is a no brainer. But I don't want to overwhelm you. Why don't we say an initial run of six articles?"

"That means six months?"

"Yes."

"Do you pick the topics...locales? Or do I?"

"Hmm. Well, I have two destinations I'd like to see the magazine feature—just because they're so popular with tourists, as well as our local community. But that doesn't mean you can't add additional elements along your way. As to the rest of the series, tell me what you think would be of interest to our readers. Although we're focusing on the windward side of Oʻahu, I think we should take in the entire island. Okay?"

I laughed. "All right, I'm in. What's my next assignment?"

"How do you feel about beginning with Haleiwa Joe's at Ha`ikū Gardens in Kāne`ohe?"

"I love it. It's one of our favorite places."

"And whom do you mean when you say *our*? If I'm not being too personal..."

"My life partner is Keoni Hewitt, of Hewitt Investigations. He's a former HPD detective. I've known him for several years and we became personally connected last year—during an unfortunate death in my family."

"I'm sorry about the death of your loved one, but I'm glad you'll have someone to enjoy your culinary adventures with," concluded Harry.

"So it's all right if I take him along with me?"

"Absolutely! And why don't you include his responses to your adventures. Remember what certain political stars have said, *two for the price of one.*"

"I love the idea. And I'm sure Keoni will as well."

"You've got nearly a month to put the next piece together. Why don't you outline what you'd like the article to encompass, and the type of images you want to include? It seems like you and Andy Berger have already established a good relationship. I really liked the photos you had him take of Chef Duncan's school and restaurant. The only change I'd like to suggest is that in the future, I'd like at least one of the shots to include you or Keoni. Is that all right with you?"

"Sure. At least it's okay with me. I'll have to get Keoni's stamp of approval, but he's a pretty easy-going guy. All I have to say is *good food* and he happily joins in the fun."

When I hung up the phone, I felt delighted with the new direction my life was taking, professionally. In addition to earning a little extra money, I would be sampling good food and drink while enjoying the company of the love of my life. Who could ask for more? Well, maybe the knowledge that a foodie would bring to the assignment. But at least I was planning to do something about that.

Inspired by my new column, I called Chef Duncan's school.

With all Keoni does to enhance our living in Auntie Carrie's cottage, I have been inspired to elevate my ability as a cook. While sitting on hold, I looked at the brochure Akira Duncan had given me. The couples' classes looked tempting, but I knew I needed to start at the beginning. When a perky sounding young man came on the line, I signed up for a three-session course on basic knife skills. The first thing I would learn was the choosing, sharpening and storing of cutlery. I inquired about supplies I might need for the first class and was told the school would provide an eight-inch knife from a custom line Chef Duncan had designed. However, I was welcome to bring my own knives. Looking at a knife sitting on my kitchen counter, I wondered how the decades-old cutlery I had received as a wedding gift might compare with knives forged more recently.

CHAPTER 16

Friends are as companions on a journey, who ought
to aid each other to persevere...
Pythagoras [circa 570 BCE - circa 495 BCE]

After registering for the cutlery course, I dashed next door to let The Ladies share in my delight at embarking on a new program of self-improvement. As always, their generosity extended to ensuring I had the ingredients to make a salad. Beyond that, I had to decline any obvious increase in the flow of food from Joanne's garden to my kitchen. If I allowed them to provide too much produce for practicing my knife skills, Keoni might learn of my delving into continuing education of the culinary variety.

By the time I returned home, the afternoon was nearly over. Either Keoni or Miss Una could arrive at any moment. After a day on the road, I was sure Keoni would enjoy a bottle of beer. For dinner, I made a quick salad from the latest gift basket of Joanne's produce and thawed out a piece of *mahimahi* from the freezer sufficient to feed all of us. With initial food preparations complete, I looked at the clock. At that moment Miss Una popped into the kitchen through her garden window. She seems to have her own sixth sense that alerts her when a treat is being prepared for her.

While the cat shows affection for the people in her life, it was good she would continue to enjoy the company of little `Ilima as a playmate, when the rest of the kittens went to their adoptive homes. I was also glad I no longer had to worry about Miss Una spending every night peering into The Ladies' backyard. After making sure that Keoni and I have retired for the night, she now takes up her guard stance on top of Bàozhǐ's desk. The few times I have left it open, I find her lounging on the blotter, poking at the drawers and cubby holes. If we had not already found the scrolls and letter envelope, I would be tempted to think she was trying to hint at something hidden within.

That night, Keoni did not arrive home until nearly sunset. By the time he had showered, there was barely any twilight left to appreciate in the dining room. Happily, the crystals of Auntie Carrie's chandelier sparkle in any level of light, guaranteeing our supper was consumed in the romantic atmosphere I had envisioned.

"How was today? You were gone so long I thought that your client might have had a break-in."

Keoni laughed. "Nothing that dramatic. But the place is huge. Do you remember the booming Hawai`i real estate market from about the 1970s to the early 1990s? When the old Kahala properties were being gobbled up by foreign investors? A lot of high-end buyers would remodel or replace an old house, sometimes building right up to the property lines and put in multiple air conditioners that drove their neighbors crazy."

"Yeah. That happened in a lot of the old neighborhoods, especially since some lease-hold property owners were raising leases rates so high that the average family couldn't afford the payments. Worse yet were the conversions from lease-hold to fee simple. The cost of the land was so prohibitive that some people abandoned the houses they'd been paying mortgages on for a long time, or even owned outright."

"Well, looking at that house today reminded me of those years. It's an overbuilt property, owned by a corporate entity that's providing a holiday haven for their well-paid executives. But I can't change things. They're paying my fees, which allows me to help with our little conversions here in Lanikai."

"I take it you aren't impressed with the North Shore Mc-Mansion?"

"In one word, *no*. All that money and none of the taste you would expect from people in such high tax brackets. At least most of the big players in this neighborhood have a sense of place, if not time. You'll have to admit that most of the McMansions surrounding *us* look appropriate to a beach setting."

"That's why I wanted us to redo this cottage ourselves. I didn't want Carrie's home to turn into something she would never have recognized. I knew we could make the improvements essential to our enjoyment without destroying its character. Of course, it wouldn't have happened without your technical oversight. Here's to you, my love, for everything you've done to bring the old girl back to life," I said, raising my glass of tea.

"And I thank you my dear, for the trust you placed in me. I've enjoyed just about every part of our work. Speaking of which, if you'll wait a moment, I have a little something I've been saving for a special occasion."

With that, Keoni got up and went out the back door. A couple of minutes later he returned with a cardboard shipping box. Through the flapping ends, I could see newspaper covered objects.

"Sorry for the lack of gift wrapping, but I've been stockpiling items as I've finished them."

"What have you been up to?" I asked, bending over the box he set beside my chair.

"You know it's been some time since we began working on the cottage. And I thought it would be good to commemorate how far we've come. But with your visions and Professor Zhāng's murder...Well, time just got away from me."

After removing its wrappings, I stared at the first item. I was overcome with joy and sadness. It was a large salad fork and spoon set I knew he had fashioned from some of the *alahe'e* wood from Kawai Nui Marsh.

"Oh, how beautiful. They're perfect. You remembered my story about burning Auntie Carrie's salad set at a barbecue when I was a kid," I said with tears in my eyes.

"Well, I don't know what the original set looked like, but I saw the condiment utensils of monkey pod wood in the buffet, so I copied their style. Makoa helped a lot. Of course, being a master woodworker; he has all the tools for shaping and finishing. Speaking of finishing, everything's been rubbed with several coats of beeswax."

"Perfect. We could have used them earlier tonight, dear."

I continued opening the packages of Keoni's woodworking projects with growing excitement. There was a set of cutting boards that would be lovely when we entertained. Next were carved corbels for the front porch and rosettes to use as accents in several places. And, at the bottom of the box? Three custom ceiling medallions. Every piece a unique creation that Keoni had fashioned to elevate the craftsman style of White Sands Cottage. Auntie Carrie would be proud to see her home shining so beautifully in the twenty-first century!

The next day, we both stayed home. After a morning swim, we wandered from room to room, deciding where to install Keoni's wonderful creations. I paired his fork and spoon with my grandmother's cut glass salad bowl on the bottom shelf of the Italian inlaid tea cart in the dining room. Then I set the cutting boards on the side of the buffet. Best of all, the concealed hinges Keoni had placed on the back of each medallion allowed us to install them around ceiling light fixtures.

While we were enjoying glasses of sparkling wine in the hot tub that night, we got a call from John Dias. When John suggested we meet in town between his visits to yacht clubs and marine supply stores, I quickly suggested a club where my auntie had enjoyed reciprocal benefits because of a membership she had maintained in Massachusetts. That membership encompassed her entire family. As long as I paid the minimal dues, I could enjoy the amenities and activities wherever such memberships are honored.

"I forgot you enjoyed this little perk," commented Keoni as we approached a table overlooking the ocean.

"When I lived in town it was easy to hop on the bus and drop in at one of the Waikīkī yacht clubs. But once we took on remodeling the Lanikai cottage, I never gave yacht clubs another thought. But then as I was paying the annual dues, I realized how much I had enjoyed the drinks, brunches and especially the view."

I then opened my purse and pulled out a card the size of my driver's license. "This is for you, Keoni. On a whim, I called the Massachusetts club to see how they define *family*. And guess what? With all of today's blended families and life partnerships, they leave it up to their members to define *family*. With our being partnered and sharing the same address, I got you an associate membership allowing you to enjoy reciprocal privileges wherever it's honored."

"How thoughtful of you, honey! These reciprocal memberships will be ideal for my meeting with clients, and they'll come in handy when we start traveling."

Knowing I needed to check in at the desk, we had timed our journey to arrive ahead of John. By meeting after the lunch hour, we were able to get a table at the rail overlooking the water. Watching the boats bob in their slips made me think of my father's naval career. Although he had loved my mother and me very much, he never tired of the ocean. If he had not been forced to retire with thirty years of service, he would have died in uniform. But he enjoyed a wonderful retirement with my mother. Even when he had been on duty overseas, he had managed to fit in romantic holidays with Mom. I was often amazed at how they scooted in and out of exotic places.

"Hey, guys. Front row seats?" asked John as he came up beside me. "Hello, sweetheart. How's my favorite psychic?"

He leaned over to give me a peck on the cheek. Then he sat down between Keoni and me.

"I wish you wouldn't call me that. You know that isn't true," I said with a shake of my head.

"Yeah, yeah. I know. Just an occasional dream. Right?"

"Yes, John. And lately they haven't been all that useful," I said wistfully.

"I wouldn't say that. We just haven't pulled the pieces together yet. After all, this time we're dealing with cases from both yesterday and today."

For once we all ordered the same menu item: Hawaiian style shrimp po'boys. We then prepped our personal variations of iced coffee and settled down to listen to John summarize his rounds of detection. He began by reaching into his breast pocket and pulling out a small folded piece of paper. He opened it and smoothed out the creases. After laying it on the table so we could both read it, he cleared his throat.

"Here's a copy of the two characters found on the back of the photo of a beautiful young Japanese woman. They mean *snow woman*, which can be a description of a woman. Or, combined, they form the Japanese name *Yuki-onna*."

We nodded and waited for him to continue.

"We found the picture inside the dive suit from one of the two vics we found in the dinghy off Fort Kamehameha Beach. Neither guy had any ID or other personal items on him, so the pic's the closest we came to personal evidence. The characters were printed by hand with a bit of a flourish, so the techies are leaning toward them representing the woman's name.

"There's nothing distinctive about the girl. Except for that potential name, the only thing we've got to go on is that sleek one-piece black swimsuit she's wearing. I've got a member of the forensic team looking into a possible designer or manufacturer. Of course, the clothing industry is now a huge international market, so I don't know how much that avenue of investigation will yield. But even if the suit came from Japan, the girl could be from here or even the mainland.

"As to the nondescript stretch of beach she's standing on, there are no trees, rocks, or buildings; nothing to distinguish the location. I've got a couple of people analyzing the photo itself and the elements of the image: angle of the sun; time of day; time of year; type, size and topography of sand. Of course, the goal is to determine the geographic location of the beach, and so far, all I can tell you is that it's not here in Hawai`i."

"Aside from being a double homicide, what's this new case about?" Keoni asked.

"The usual. Drugs. It doesn't take much to progress from doing drugs to selling drugs to murder. Once we had the victims' fingerprints, we knew who they were—a couple of low-level scumbags from Maui. Given that they were found near the air base and the airport, the Feds were on top of it from the beginning. Fort Kamehameha was absorbed into Hickam Air Force Base a long time ago. It's not really open to civilians, although a service member or their family can bring guests. Of course, it doesn't look like those two were part of a family outing. Anyway, once the Feds declared the case had nothing to do with the military—let alone a terrorist attack—the ball was volleyed back into our court.

"Probably just your average hit in a drug deal gone bad. Maybe professional. Maybe not. The bodies were almost on top of one another. The one on the bottom, the younger, took a clean GSW to the forehead. The other one caught a double tap. Probably the first was to his shoulder as he was trying to get away. Then a shot to his back. When Marty Soli got the bodies, the initial fingerprinting was confirmed by DNA. The older guy, Jesse Comacho, was in the State database as well as CODIS. This brings us to the link between the two vics—and to drugs.

"As I mentioned before, we're looking at two cousins in this case. Jesse Comacho was thirty-three; his younger cousin, Jimmy, was twenty-eight. The initial tox screens show Maui Wowie for both, with exposure to more than a little heroin in the younger one. I don't know if it's a question of *Chasing the Dragon* or from an *a-bomb*. Beyond that, there was a hint of China White heroin ingrained in some of the creases of their hands. Seems like whatever they were involved in proved fatal without an overdose.

John glanced at me. I am sure my face telegraphed the reality that I had no idea what he was talking about. John's eyes moved from me to Keoni, who was nodding.

"*Chasing the Dragon* is when the user inhales heroin from the smoke and vapors produced after heating heroin. An a-bomb is a cigarette with a mixture of marijuana and heroin," explained Keoni, who had obviously kept up on street drug slang since his official retirement from HPD.

I couldn't add anything to the conversation, so I just nodded.

"These two idiots are twigs on the branch of a fine local family tree. At least until this generation. Their dads and granddad had tough but well-paying union jobs on the docks. The Comacho family has a small parcel of land in `Ulupalakua—upcountry

Maui. Somehow, they got their relatives to give them control of the property. That's the source of the cousins' personal stash. But it isn't enough to bring in the kind of lifestyle these two jokers seem to have been seeking. No education. No jobs. Losers from day one. Easy pickin's for any crime boss seeking brawn and no brains."

Keoni sat passively through John's summation. I wrinkled my nose at the thought of another family tree with a declining number of branches.

"If they were really as dumb as they seem, they were tiny cogs in a larger wheel. What did they do to invite murder? Why were they in those waters between the airport and Hickam? And why didn't the perp or perps just sink the boat at sea, with the bodies and any forensic evidence? I haven't a clue today, but the CSIs are on it, and who knows what they'll find.

"Speaking of clues, I thought we might get somewhere looking into the IP address of the sender of that fake clue in Professor Zhāng's case. But that went nowhere. It ended up that the sender used one of the computers in the hotel's business center. There are so many people going in and out of that place, there's no way of knowing *who* might have sent it. There are only two things we have figured out about that email. One, it was sent about forty-five minutes before the vic died. Two, whoever sent it didn't want us getting too close, because the keyboard was sparkling clean, no fingerprint in sight."

"Even if there had been prints, a keyboard in an office open to all the hotel guests might have had a lot of smudges," I observed.

We paused for a moment, as the waiter brought refills of rich iced coffee.

"To get back to the case of the cousins united in death, unlike the Professor's case, I've got plenty of leads. In fact, I've found so many links to unsavory people, places, and activities on Maui—and every lock-up in the state—I might just as well open our files of mug shots for the last fifteen years and throw a dart. The only way to narrow the connections to these players is looking into that teak dinghy. Rather high end for those two boys to be playing in."

"Is that what you're doing today? Checking out the greater world of yachting?" asked Keoni.

"That's right. The techs are looking into the scuba suits the guys had on, and a few odds and ends that were in the dinghy. But I said I'd hit the pavement and get educated on old teak boats. So, what's up with you two?"

"Well, it looks like I might be using yacht clubs as my shoreline offices," said Keoni.

I explained our reciprocal status with local yacht clubs, courtesy of Auntie Carrie's East Coast membership.

"Gee, after today's little luncheon, I may need to visit your mobile offices from time to time for a consultation," said John.

"That works for me. Do you need a consult today?" asked Keoni jokingly.

"I don't know. How much do you know about old style dinghies?"

"Not much. But I've been thinking of looking into a little vessel that could slide down the boat ramp at Kailua Beach," answered Keoni.

"Really, dear?" I asked.

"Yes. Something small enough for me to handle alone, but large enough for a little deep- sea fishing."

I shuddered at the thought. "Obviously something for one of your outings with the boys."

"Where's your sense of adventure, Natalie?" queried John.

"Don't ask," cautioned Keoni. Turning to me reassuringly, he said "You won't even need to clean or cook the catch, honey."

"If you're serious about a little maritime sightseeing, you can join me in researching the dinghy," said John. "Looks like it might be a vintage Cheoy Lee boat. Probably built in Hong Kong somewhere in the `50s or `60s. The bigger issue is determining what boat it was connected to."

Keoni looked across at me. I nodded immediately.

Just then my cell phone rang. Looking down, I saw that the incoming call was from Shēn Properties. Leaving the men to settle the bill, I walked a few feet away. Bō said he had found some of his granduncle's art and suggested our getting together. Since it looked like Keoni would be joining John for the afternoon, I agreed to drop in at the Shēn Building shortly. I then returned to the table and set up a cocktail hour rendezvous back at the yacht club with John and Keoni.

When I arrived for my meeting with Bō, I was pleased to see that a lot of progress had been made on the remodeling. Except for a couple of open walls showing those mysterious niches, the first floor appeared nearly ready for occupants. Bō said that once the walls were fixed and some crown molding and baseboards had been installed, he could move his offices onto floors two and three. As to the top floor, he couldn't wait to show me the layout for the new living quarters.

When the gate to the elevator opened, I had a clear view of its interior. The inset black and white medallion of hexagonal tiles on the floor had been refurbished and shone like the day it was installed originally. Looking up, I was amazed at the workmanship of the logogram repeated on the back wall. Although it was set in a bronze-like metal frame, the center was comprised of glistening small tiles that again announced the Shēn family name. I guess repetition is a constant feature with some designers.

We exited the elevator and I was amazed at the openness of the layout. There was a lot of finish work to complete, but the samples of flooring, cabinetry, and fixtures for the kitchen and baths were streamlined but elegant.

"Oh, Bō. This is going to be a wonderful home for you and your honey. She has to be very happy with the decisions you've made."

"Thank you for your positive comments, but to be honest, the decisions have been almost entirely hers."

After we had completed a brief walk through of the top floor, we sat down at the luncheon table that remained by the clerestory windows. In front of me were several unframed paintings, most of classic Chinese landscapes.

"I was lucky to find these. They'd been shoved on top of some furniture my Auntie Toitoi was planning to get rid of. She's never liked anything that isn't the best in design and material. I once heard she'd insisted on re-structuring the configuration of some of the rooms in this building."

As we looked through the pieces, I encouraged Bō to tell me more about himself.

"I think I've told you that my Auntie Toitoi has always been here to encourage me. As a kid, she insisted I go to Chinese language school. But unlike my great-great-grandfather and Bàozhǐ, I've got no gift for languages. When I entered UH, she wanted me to become an architect and said I should begin my practice by gutting this building. But with my dyslexia, I couldn't handle the math and science. That's why I ended up studying art on the mainland—all of the beauty of architecture, without so many technical challenges. While I was at the San Francisco Art Institute, my Auntie fantasized about my becoming a classic Chinese painter. She even made me continue studying calligraphy with an old scholar long after it was clear that I had no talent with a Chinese brush.

"Once I'd graduated, I took off for Europe in hopes of finding my own path in the art world. But I never found a niche for my scattered interests and talents. I ended up bumming around for a couple of years, sketching portraits for tourists and occasionally getting an assignment to help friends in art restoration. Then my grandpa took ill. It was clear that my art career wasn't going anywhere, so I came home and took over the family's commercial real estate business. That way Grandpa could relax a bit and concentrate on his health, with Auntie Toitoi looking after him and this building.

"Last year it looked like his cancer had gone into remission. He said it felt like he had a new chance at life. We took a phenomenal world cruise together—after putting the business on autopilot with my Auntie overseeing the day-to-day details, here and on Maui. You see, a few years earlier, our business really took off. Initially, one of my distant cousins ran things in Lahaina, but by the time my grandpa died, that man was ready to retire. So, when my grandpa died, and I took on this building's redesign, my Auntie moved to Maui and took up the reins there. Since then, she's built that office into one of the top commercial property companies on the island. She actually makes more money than I do and has a home only a few can dream of.

"I get over occasionally. It's a great place for boating and her boyfriend has a really amazing older Chinese yacht with all kinds of classic features carved into the teak. It's where I go when I need a break. In Europe, I fell in love with the gondolas of Venice and the houseboats of Amsterdam. I've always loved boats, despite my grandmother dying in a boating accident. I guess boating is in the genes. My mother's family once lived on junks in the harbors of southern China."

CHAPTER 17

But the father answered never a word.
A frozen corpse was he.
Henry Wadsworth Longfellow [1807 - 1882]

I walked out of the Shēn Building into a late afternoon rain shower. With all the concrete in downtown Honolulu, wind patterns through the city corridors have changed over time. Today, I was shielded from breezes that might be brushing the sand on the open beaches and enjoyed the soft patter of drops on my shoulders and cheeks. By the time I got to my car, I was a bit damp, but still in good spirits.

I may not have learned anything pertinent to either of the murders on my visionary screen, but the joy of seeing Bàozhǐ's art had lifted me to a level of elation similar to the day Keoni and I moved into White Sands Cottage. I sensed new horizons, while immersed in the beauty of a past I may not have lived, but whose images touched me as though drawn from my personal memories.

Most of Bàozhǐ's work was on sheets of paper and rolls of silk. Unlike western art, traditional Chinese paintings are created with the same inks as calligraphy, rather than oils. The use of these fragile materials makes such works all the more precious—when executed by a master. I was no art critic of Occidental, let alone Asian art. But I could tell that if this man had lived a long life, he would have continued to grow as an artist. Executed with Chinese brushes, many of his pieces featured misty mountains, juniper trees, waterfalls, and Buddhist temples drawn from the ancient dynasties of the Central Kingdom.

Yet, even these classic studies presented a crispness that fore-shadowed contemporary Chinese artists like David Lee who is now associated with Hawai`i. For a moment my mind drifted, as I realized that this artist has the same surname as the Wong sisters' *amah*. Since the name is as common as Smith, I doubted if there was any relationship her.

I was glad I was not far from the yacht club where I was meeting Keoni and John. Within a few minutes I had left the car with the valet service and was seated at the same table where we had enjoyed lunch. Not knowing what my companions might want to do that evening, I declined a complementary appetizer and ordered a glass of the white wine featured for Happy Hour. Sipping the cool Castle Rock Riesling, I recognized this was the first time I had been out for a drink by myself in more than a year. In my life as a journalist, I found that enjoying my own company was a good thing. And although I have experienced turbulence and tragedy in both my personal and professional living, I remain a happy person in most circumstances.

Watching the movement of people and boats in Waikīkī Bay, I thought about the subjects of Bàozhǐ's art. With the tradition-al inks, silks and ancient brushes of his culture, he had painted meaningful glimpses of Island life. Beyond the expected scenes of flowers, land, and sea, he had captured: a women's work gang harvesting sugar cane; children of several ethnicities racing through the surf; and an elderly Japanese man repotting an or-chid.

The way his artistry enveloped me reminded me of the environment Pearl Wong maintained within her family crypt. Beyond a shared Asian aesthetic, the artifacts within the crypt reflected a similar richness of material, design and execution. This was especially true of the seated Kuan Yin in white jade with sugar crystals on the ridges of her crown and the fall of her gown. If someone in the Shēn family possessed such a statue, they must have experienced similar feelings when looking on her countenance.

But where might that object of incarnate beauty and spir-itual ecstasy now reside? The Shēn Building had been stripped to the studs. Its mediocre furnishings were not included in the restrictive terms of the family trust and had been sold. I was pleased to have found and bought a desk I recognized from my vision. I was even happier to have found scrolls with the original Shēn family will and the letter from Bàozhǐ to his father.

I wondered if I should return to the antique store for another look at the furniture that came from the Shēn Building. But surely a hiding place large enough to accommodate the bulkiness of even a small statue would have been obvious in the simple furniture I had seen in the warehouse.

When Keoni and John returned from their sojourn through all things marine, they each ordered an Australian beer on tap. I had not been to leeward O`ahu for a while and suggested we stay at the club for a casual supper of appetizers. But when our waiter told us there was a seafood buffet on offer, we quickly changed course. The abundance of fresh fish with fins appealed to the men; that with shells seemed the ideal conclusion to a wonderful day for me!

Once we had filled our plates, we settled down to a serious discussion of the several murders we were examining. Since we had arrived early, there was no one sitting close enough to overhear our conversation. That was good, because the details of my afternoon's immersion in art appreciation were few compared to those that were revealed from the men's walkabout.

"After looking at the pictures I had, the guy at the marine shop said the dinghy was a real beauty. He confirmed that the boat was built by the Cheoy Lee Shipyard," said John. "And being constructed of teak, he thought it must have been built mid-twentieth century, at their Ngau Chi Wan Yard in Hong Kong. The company actually began in Shànghǎi, but after Mao Zedong conquered mainland China, the company relocated to Hong Kong."

"That shipyard is highly respected for its quality of naval architecture and construction," added Keoni. "Even a dinghy receives as much attention as the yachts and commercial vessels they build. The story of the company is pretty interesting. When constructing the large old teak yachts, a family of carpenters often lived on board, until completion of the structure. And while they were working, they added their own unique carvings of dragons to distinguish their work from their colleagues."

John rejoined the story. "That's how the guy ID'd the manufacturer so quickly. With the trashing the dinghy took, one of the seats had come loose and I had a photo of some carvings on the underneath side."

"So where does this lead?" I asked.

"Well, it confirms that this little boat would have been built for a yacht," he said, tapping a photo. "If we can find a yacht that looks similar in age, design, and finish, it could be our ticket to finding the murderer of the dynamic duo from Maui. And the clincher to proving that connection may just be those carvings," John finished with a look of expectation. "If the yacht this dinghy belongs to is really valuable, you've got to wonder why the killer let it go if he's the owner. Of course, the yacht, and/or the dinghy, could have been stolen. Regardless of those questions, I come back to wondering why the perp didn't just sink the boat at sea and avoid the chance of getting caught."

"Perhaps the cousins had escaped from the yacht before they were killed," I speculated.

"She's got a point, JD. It sounds crazy for a little boat to escape from a larger one, but something could have happened to interrupt the hit," Keoni suggested.

"Anything's possible. Maybe another boat approached, or the young men looked dead, and the perp took off—on the yacht, or another vessel," John said with a nod. "And once the yacht departed, the cousin who was alive managed to get the outboard motor working before he croaked. Even if the killer had returned to finish the job, the dinghy was gone."

"Sounds like all you need is the Mother Ship to put it all together," Keoni said with a laugh.

"Easy for you to joke. Every case I've got on my desk right now presents more questions than answers."

"That's not entirely true. Tell Natalie about the call you took," urged Keoni.

"Okay. A glimmer of light at the end of one hallway. Looks

like we're making headway in the mystery of the missing Bàozhǐ. You know, when I initially checked on him, I set the contents of your vision to the side. I tried to look at his disappearance as a simple missing person case, dating to December 1953. Of course, I was concerned about the lack of digital records. But there's one nice thing about really cold cases—the population you're looking at is small compared to today. And therefore, the number of John Does is even slimmer. Despite that, the hardcopy files I was searching were pretty deteriorated and I wasn't getting very far.

"Then I caught the Fort Kamehameha case and had to shift gears. That's when I asked Ellie, a CSI tech, to look into the John Doe case from 1982. When I checked with her this morning, she said she'd found the case number for the unidentified man in the freezer. She called later to report on the case notes. Too bad they didn't yield anything new on that John Doe. She did say that when Hurricane Iwa hit; there was a power outage and, a week after the power went back on, it was discovered that the compressor on a freezer was blown and everyone got a mega surprise—a defrosted, youngish Chinese man."

At that point, we got up to revisit the buffet. While John and Keoni piled their plates with *ahi* in several preparations, I opted for *Kūohonu* crab cakes. In silence we focused on our entrées. After cleaning his palate with a sourdough roll, John resumed his report on the discovery and minimal investigation of the 1982 corpse.

"I found one thing interesting. The victim was only wearing a sleeveless singlet-style undershirt and boxer shorts. There was no sign of the snazzy suit, shirt, shoes, or hat you saw in your vision. And not much forensic evidence to pursue—just a .25 caliber GSW to the head. There was no tracking of DNA in those days, but there wasn't complete disintegration of the finger tips, so they got a few prints. Unfortunately, there wasn't a data base of fingerprints for holders of drivers' licenses in most states or territories...and certainly no national system for reference.

"HPD left the case open, but since no one ever came forward to claim the corpse, there wasn't anyone around to make a fuss. He was eventually planted in a grave for the unknown. At least I have the grave marker number."

"He served in World War II. What about tracking the finger-prints through his Army records?" I asked.

"That should be pretty easy, now. And today we have DNA tests, which should prove decisive, since we've got Bō Shēn and some other family members on Maui for comparison.

"Of course, the freezer is a secondary or even tertiary crime scene. We're assuming the man was murdered in the old Shēn Hotel. Soon after, he was transported to the freezer, where he was deposited with a hope he would be forgotten. And who knows how long he might have lain there without being discovered. You know how those old commercial freezers were—real workhorses, twenty to thirty, or even forty years of life.

"With all the time that's passed, even if we find the murderer, I doubt that the vehicle used for moving the body could ever be found. I already know that the freezer's been disposed of. So, where does this lead? To the John Doe grave, that's where. Since there's no evidence field, the main thing we've got to examine is whatever's left of the body. I'm getting an exhumation order, in hopes of performing a little DNA analysis with the latest tests available."

"The beauty of the here and now," I commented. "And what comes after proving your John Doe *is* Bàozhǐ Shēn? How do you plan to connect his case to that of Professor Zhāng?"

"Hey. One mystery at a time. I've still got zip on the Professor's case. But hope springs eternal. I'll just keep moving, one step at a time and hope it all comes together."

*   *   *   *   *

Our trip home that night seemed short. Looking out at a mist-filled night sky and listening to Mozart on our local NPR station, I was almost as relaxed as I had been that afternoon. But by the time Keoni and I arrived home, I felt restless again. Although John might be able to get an order for exhumation of the body he thought was Bàozhǐ's, there were so many questions that did not have easy answers jamming my brain.

Keoni asked whether I would enjoy soaking in the hot tub.

I declined, with regret. But after looking deeply into my eyes, he could tell I needed to wrestle with my intruding demons by myself. With the promise of a morning swim, he kissed me good-night and went to bed. I put on a cotton shift and went to the kitchen. After verifying that Miss Una was well supplied with food and water, I poured myself a glass of sherry.

I then moved into the living room, so I would not interrupt what I hoped would be a peaceful night for Keoni. I took a long sip of the fortified wine and stretched out in the wingback re-cliner. Within a few minutes, Miss Una came in to check on me. At first, she jumped up behind my head, mewed, and played with my hair. Then, satisfied that I was in place for a while, she moved to the top of Bàozhǐ's desk, which I had left closed.

When she rubbed the brass lamp on top to the point of near-ly dropping it to the floor, I got up to open the drop-down door to reveal the writing area. As expected, she jumped down and made a couple of circles on the ink blotter before lying down. I stood there for a moment stroking her fur. Somehow it did not bring me the peace it usually did. I returned to my chair and drink. Even without the benefit of actual music playing, strains of Mozart wafted through my mind and my eyes closed for a short period.

Somewhat later, I heard a persistent scratching noise. I opened my eyes and looked for the source of the sound. Need I have wondered? Miss Una. But what was she doing? She was lying on her side on the desk, idly playing with the corner of a cubby hole. I couldn't stand the continuing sound of her claws against the wood. Perhaps I was getting a migraine, because the sound seemed amplified beyond a normal range.

"What are you doing, my little darling? Can't bear to see me sleeping more deeply than you?"

Ignoring me completely, she concentrated on dislodg-ing something I could not see from my chair. I approached the desk with curiosity, as well as dread that she could have adopt-ed a new and destructive behavior. Standing over her, I quickly caught sight of her objective—the corner of a piece of white on-ion skin paper. Nudging her away, I picked up a pencil and used the nub of its eraser to free the paper from the crevice in which it was lodged. With only the bottom left corner of a single sheet, there was no way to tell what the dimension of the original had been. The message was obviously incomplete, but the thought behind it was not.

so I wonder... how she could repay with infamy
with all our family had done.
I must be wrong

The handwriting looked like that of Bàozhǐ. The paper and ink appeared to be the same as that on the letter we had discovered with the scrolls. But without a date, there was no way to know if this document, like the letter we had found earlier, had been written at the time of his scheduled departure for Hong Kong. Also, the penmanship looked as though the writer had been rushed, as though anxious that he would be discovered.

Leaving the fragment of paper in the desk, I picked up the cat, closed the desk lid, and returned to my chair. Having accomplished her goal, Miss Una promptly settled down on my lap and fell asleep. How nice for her. I was now wide awake. Even after a couple of sips of sherry I remained so. Myriad questions filled my mind. Who was the *she* to whom Bàozhǐ referred? What was her act of infamy? Why did he think he must be wrong in his assessment? What could be so terrible that he preferred to be wrong than right? Better yet, who could be so important that he wanted to be wrong?

I mused briefly. Then I decided to go to work. When in doubt, I return to the simple list-making process my mother had taught me so long ago. With a little effort, I encouraged Miss Una to hop up on the back of the chair. I got a pen and steno pad from the desk and settled down again. I headed the first sheet of paper, "Questions regarding Bàozhǐ Shēn."

Concerning the latest find in the desk, the essential question was *who*? Who was the woman he could not trust? Was she the one who killed him? If the scrap of paper I had just found was written at the time he returned from war, it could refer to the wife of his brother Chāng. But Zhīlán Shēn had not lived very long, and I had not heard anything negative about her in my conversations with Bō. Who else could it be? John Dias had not mentioned any female neighbors or girlfriends in the short period between Chāng becoming a widower and Bàozhǐ's disappearance.

The only woman Bō had discussed at length was Bàozhǐ's wife Toitoi. Bō had not said much about the years following World War II and most his references to her had been positive. If she were the murderer, what could have motivated this war bride to kill her husband of only a few years? As to the decades after Bàozhǐ's disappearance, she had played the role of surrogate mother for Kāng and later Bō.

Despite these positive aspects to her role within the Shēn family, there was one issue that reflected negatively on her. More than one person mentioned her keeping women away from her brother-in-law Chāng. Had she been so jealous of him that she had actually done something against the family?

The woman I saw in my vision had coldly executed Bàozhǐ and methodically searched the furniture in the room he used as an office. She had thoroughly examined the few clothes hanging in the closet and suitcase—and savagely slashed the lining of the open suitcase. Altogether, it demonstrated that the woman was fully capable of making the holes in the walls of the Shēn Building.

Of course, to do that, she would have needed a substantial excuse. And she would have needed to restore the walls to a normal state when she was through with each of her searches. That would indicate she had a close relationship with the family. Of the few women mentioned in the Shēn family story, Toitoi was the only one with continuing access to the Shēn men and the building in which they resided throughout the latter twentieth century. And Bō told me the woman had "restructured" some of the rooms. That could account for the niches and holes in the walls of the Shēn Building.

By the time Bō arrived as a cogent youngster, Toitoi would have had plenty of opportunities to complete her investigations of the property. If she had found what I was assuming to be the Kuan Yin mentioned in the fake scavenger hunt riddle, she would have escaped with it at the time. Unfortunately, Bō's grandfather Chāng was not alive to answer the questions that were streaming down the pages of my notes.

Working backwards through the few clues I had, I contemplated the riddle's hint at the location of the statue of Kuan Yin. How had the artifact gone missing? Who had hidden it? Did they move it periodically? Did anyone in the family know where it was? Surely Fēng, the father of Bàozhǐ and Chāng had known. Bàozhǐ was Fēng's eldest son. According to tradition, he would have been the next in line to learn any family secrets. But then the older son disappeared. Did Fēng share the secret with the younger brother Chāng? Or had he gone to his grave without revealing where the Kuan Yin was hidden?

Next, why was the scroll containing the riddle hidden in Bàozhǐ's desk? Did he know its meaning? Was it a document that would have been passed by hand, from generation to generation, accompanied by an oral presentation of its meaning? And if the location of the Kuan Yin was not an issue, why was the man sent to Hong Kong? Judging from both the contents and the tone of the letter Keoni and I had found, he did not take his responsibility lightly.

So why did he anticipate the possibility of failure—a failure that could result in his death? Was Hong Kong his true destination? Or was it merely a starting point in his journey? At the time, the government of the People's Republic of China was not friendly to people who breached its borders. Where else might he have been going?"

Like Pearl Wong's family, the Shēns came from Shànghǎi. Pursuing that line of inquiry brought me back to Chu-Hua Lee. I was sure I had overheard her name in the conversation between the two men outside the Shēn Building in my expanded vision of Bàozhǐ's murder. But when I had mentioned the Wong family name to Bō, he denied knowledge of any connection to his family. As to the Wong family, Jade was dead, and Pearl had seemed forthcoming with the scanty information she possessed regarding the departure of Miss Lee. Aside from hearing the woman's name, the only link I had was one of time: Miss Lee had departed for China at about the same time the elder Shēn brother disappeared.

My thinking was becoming jumbled. I took a final sip of sherry and leafed through my evening's work. There were no answers to the questions that filled the pages of my notebook. Knowing there could be no immediate resolution to the issues I had raised, I set the book aside and reclined fully in my chair. I then pulled at the velour throw I keep over the back of the chair for such occasions. Wrapping it about me, I sent a loving thought to my sleeping sweetheart and envisioned joining him for a bit of sleuthing through a film *noire*.

When Keoni gently woke me in the morning. I was still in a bit of a daze and gratefully accepted the cup of tea he had brought me. Then I explained my late-night discovery and the questions I had listed. While trotting to the beach for our swim, we continued our discussion of Bàozhǐ's doubts about some woman and my suspicion that his elusive wife Toitoi was the sole murderer in my visions.

After some frolicking in the gentle surf, we dropped down onto our towels for some rare time in the sun. Fortunately, we had planned ahead and lathered each other with fifty-plus sun screen before leaving home.

CHAPTER 18

Sit down before fact as a little child, be prepared to give up every conceived notion, follow humbly wherever and whatever abysses nature leads, or you will learn nothing.
Thomas Huxley [1825 - 1895]

L et's look at the case—or should I say cases—from the beginning," Keoni proposed. "You had a vision of Bàozhǐ Shēn's murder a couple of nights before we went into town for the scavenger hunt. A day after the hunt began, Professor Fù Hán Zhāng was found murdered in our hotel corridor. We don't know of any connection between the two deaths. From the visuals you've described, we've got two men dressed in similar attire, who were killed in Honolulu hotels—sixty years apart. The other strong visual is the woman, or women—tall, slim and dressed in red. Except for the color palette, the specifics of their wardrobes are not identical—but how could they be after all those years. Also, they both had long, black, or brownish-black hair. And they both wore high heels. Did I get everything?"

"Just about, Keoni. There are only two points you missed—a rose in the lapel of professor Zhāng and a gold ring on the hand of the first woman. I don't know which hand it was on, so I don't know if it was a wedding ring. I do know that I didn't see one on the hand of Professor Zhāng's killer, undoubtedly because of her gloves. I must say I would never be able to identify either of them: The first woman never turned around; the second one wore a broad-brimmed hat and sunglasses. They both had long hair that was about the same in color. But the first wore hers up in a classic French twist, while the second had pulled hers to the side with a gold ornament. Of course, when I think of the number of times I've changed my hair in just three decades, the matter of style is insignificant."

"Furthermore, with a good hairdresser, her hair color could easily have been kept dark. I don't really know the height of the murderous women I saw—just that they were both taller than I am—and since I've known some women who manage to wear heels until they die, the women's height and their shoes are not an issue. Bàozhǐ's killer wore a suit. As I said before, the killer of Fù Hán Zhāng wore a long-sleeved dress, gloves, hat and sunglasses. Frankly, the Professor's killer could have been wrinkled and covered with age spots, but I wouldn't have noticed," I added.

"Aside from needing to determine a link between the victims, the key question is, could the same woman have murdered both men? We have to remember that she would have aged sixty years between her crimes," summarized Keoni.

"That, my dear girl, brings us back to Bō's auntie. From what you've just said, the same woman could have committed both murders. Nearly all of the actors in Case One, Bàozhǐ, are dead. Without a confession, we can't substantiate a firm motive, or even establish Toitoi's movements at the time of her husband's disappearance. Fortunately, soon JD should have confirmation that the John Doe he's located *is* Bàozhǐ.

"As to Case Two, the murder of the Professor, you've just had a vision of him before and during his murder. Is there anything about that vision that bears further consideration? Some detail you haven't mentioned. Some aspect that JD should be looking into?"

"Uh, I don't think so. In fact, it's all starting to blur. Maybe I'm coming down with a migraine. And if that's the case, I shouldn't stay in the sun any longer."

We then picked up our towels and headed home. Once we got into the air conditioning and I drank a tall glass of water, I felt much better. By the time we got out of the shower, I was delighted to have Keoni lightly massage my neck and back. That's as far as our play time went, since I soon slid into a somnolent state. An hour later I awoke feeling clear headed. After wandering through the house in search of Keoni or Miss Una, I found myself alone.

Checking our message chalk board in the kitchen, I learned my sweetheart had gone to the hardware store. For once I was able to reach John Dias on the first try. Briefly, I filled him in on the scrap of paper I had found in the desk and our deliberation on Bō's Auntie Toitoi being the perpetrator in both cases. He responded by saying that the John Doe corpse was being exhumed momentarily and that the autopsy would follow—if no other case took precedence.

Since he said there was no reason for him to take immediate custody of the torn note I had found, I added the baggie containing it to the other evidence in Keoni's safe. After that, I returned to bed with an ice pack to ward off a return of the pre-migraine state I had experienced earlier. It was noon by the time I finally got up. I found Keoni in his workshop happily finishing a couple of cornices in *alahe`e* wood to embellish the entry into the dining room. When I asked about the status of the client on the North Shore, he said he had completed preparations for installing custom security screens. Until they arrived, his calendar remained clear.

Keoni was not ready to break for lunch, so I fixed myself a smoothie with some of the sweet strawberries Joanne grew in hanging baskets. Next, I re-checked my voicemail. There were only two calls, and both were invitations. Nathan called wondering whether Keoni and I would like to attend a neighborhood barbecue on Sunday. I called to confirm our availability and asked what we could bring to the festivities. Ever the skeptic, Nathan declined my culinary offerings and suggested we contribute a jar of Keoni's latest sun tea and a couple of bottles of wine. It had been some time since I had attended a block party at Nathan's home. I looked forward to seeing the Souzas, as well as the newcomers being welcomed.

The next call was from The Ladies at Mokulua Hale. They wanted to know if I would like to join them that afternoon to introduce the kittens to the joys of walking on leads. Since I was feeling better after my morning of rest, I decided that wrap-around sunglasses and a large sunhat would enable me to join in the fun. When I walked through the back gate into their garden, I found the adventure had already begun.

Being unaware of Miss Una's whereabouts, I had taken her lead so that she could maintain her preeminence as `Ilima's mentor. As suspected, she was watching the proceedings from a perch on a low branch of the plumeria tree closest to the covered *lanai*.

"My, don't you all look busy," I said in greeting.

All three of The Ladies held leads that ended in bundles of diminutive catly perfection. Each kitten was a variation of a Creamcicle color palette, but that was where the similarities ended. The perennial mischief maker was trying to nibble through her lead. The one who slept most of the time, simply sat down and refused to participate in the event. The two noted for their mewing choruses seemed to be competing for the honor of hitting the highest note.

As Miss Una was removed from the equation, I snapped my lead on one of the two kittens remaining without connection to a human. `Ilima. She was the only one who had been named, as she would be remaining at Mokulua Hale. Her noteworthy behavior was her constant attachment to one sentient being or another. During daylight hours, it was Miss Una to whom she clung. In the evenings, when she was restricted to the house, it was Samantha with whom she kept company. I wondered if her behavior stemmed from being the smallest of the litter.

"Obviously, there's no way to employ the commands one would use with a dog," said Joanne, shaking her short afro curls. "At least we can get them accustomed to being on leads."

Izzy piped up. "That'll be good when they have to go to the vet."

"Or for any ride in the car...or a walk on the beach," added Samantha.

"Don't get your hopes up about combining a cat and a car. Miss Una has never adjusted to that experience. As to the beach, she doesn't like the sand, let alone the sight of dogs," I said.

"I have a plan regarding that last problem," said Joanne. "I think the grand finale of their course will be in having Nathan's dog Kūlia join in our animal behavioral training."

"You should be forewarned that while he's a friendly dog, he thinks cats were created for the pleasure of romping. The only reason he doesn't take after Miss Una is that she's whacked him severely on the nose several times," I explained.

"Then we'll have to make sure she's in attendance on the big day," affirmed Izzy.

After we completed our cat obedience session, we released the kittens to play with Miss Una. Settling around the white wrought iron patio table Miriam and her husband Henri had brought from France, The Ladies and I enjoyed a peaceful tea time. While sipping tall glasses of Keoni's latest concoction of sun tea and mango juice, I filled everyone in on my new column and assignment to review Hale'iwa Joe's at Ha'ikū Gardens. They were happy for me and gladly accepted my invitation to be my guests the night I re-sampled the restaurant's menu.

When I returned home, I called Harry Longhorn, at *Windward O'ahu Journeys*. I explained my desire to make my first article a celebratory piece. He immediately agreed with the theme. I offered to pay for my guests, but he said that the magazine would be pleased to underwrite a small kick-off party for the column. After that, he mentioned he was setting up a webpage so that readers could interact with me. He also announced that he wanted me to write a blog to further the magazine's visibility in social media.

"I really want to be a team player, Harry, but all of a sudden my role has grown beyond what we discussed initially. You know Keoni and I are planning to take an occasional holiday—beyond O'ahu."

"That won't be a problem, Natalie. In fact, it's perfect for us. If you're on the road, you can take some pictures and keep a diary for any special column you want to write later. As to handling our readers' emails, we may begin by just posting their comments and you won't have to respond to them personally.

"For the launch of your own blog, why don't you come up with some teasers for your first columns. Maybe you could look back over articles you've written in the past and come up with a few commentaries about your previous professional life. I promise we'll compensate you appropriately for the effort. We'll even provide you with a good camera for those times when Andy isn't available."

Harry was very persuasive. He seemed to have an answer for everything. By the end of our conversation, I had decided to go with the flow. If the column became too much, I would renegotiate our agreement. For the time being, it would be a great way for Keoni and me to enjoy some of O`ahu's more interesting food, beverage and entertainment offerings.

As I disconnected, I glanced at the clock on my laptop. It was too late to make any other business calls. I did not feel motivated to begin an outline of potential columns—let alone cruise through my old files for items that could be reworked for blogs. With professional topics off the day's to-do list, I opened the freezer. Although there was plenty of food, I could not muster the energy to plan or execute a full dinner. At that moment, I heard the garage door opening.

It is truly wonderful that Keoni is relaxed about domestic issues. Sometimes I think he is grateful simply to have someone with whom to share laundry day and take-out pizza. Sensing our schedules were about to become congested, I suggested we settle in for a night of bread, cheese, fruit and, since I had had a migraine, spiced tea instead of wine. He immediately accepted my idea and suggested another round of old movies. I agreed, as long as they were not murder mysteries or dramas. Soon we were ensconced on our bed, surrounded by good food and lots of pillows for a wonderfully relaxing evening. Somewhere in the middle of a romantic comedy with Debbie Reynolds and Cary Grant, I fell asleep in Keoni's arms.

All it takes for me to feel truly energized is a good night's rest. In the morning, Keoni and I enjoyed a walk to the beach, accompanied on the first leg by Miss Una. We had brought our towels to have a swim. Luckily my joints did not scream in protest at the cool temperature of the early morning tide.

"So, what's on your agenda?" I asked.

Keoni smiled. "I got a text and it looks like the screens for the North Shore McMansion are on the island and scheduled for delivery in a few hours. I'm thinking I should be there to make sure there's no problem with the dimensions or finish work. If everything's in order, I can begin installing them tomorrow. What about you?"

"I've got a date with the past. Harry has asked me to produce a few blogs in advance of launching the column. He suggested I go back through my files for any items that might fit in with my initial articles. With Ha`ikū Gardens being the locale of my first column, I thought I would look up a few pieces on gardens that have impressed me over the years."

"That sounds great. You might want to reference the Dole Plantation Maze. Even if they don't have a fancy restaurant, it might be a good site for one of your columns."

"I've already got that on my list. I thought maybe I'd ask the Souzas to join us for another adventure there. If I hold off on that piece for a few months, I can reference the Aloha Scavenger Hunt to provide some advance publicity."

"Sounds good, Honey."

After a meal of tea, toast, and yogurt, plus fresh papaya from our own tree, we separated to follow our individual schedules. By noon I had found several pieces I had written on gardens around the world. Just looking through the pictures that accompanied my articles reminded me of the joy of strolling through their varied offerings.

Some of the most luscious foliage I have ever seen is in Buchart Gardens in Victoria, British Columbia. Walking beneath the rose arbors of the century-old plantings was delightful. I could almost hear the laughter of young women in full-length gowns strolling on the arms of their beaus. Other images came from a tour I took through England. There, the charming gardens of small quaint cottages matched the grace of far larger and more elegant gardens on both sides of the Atlantic Ocean.

Perhaps my favorite memory occurred while exploring the

parts of Denmark from which my mother's family had emigrated. While there, I visited Copenhagen's Tivoli Gardens on a summer's evening. Beyond taking pleasure in the expected aroma of flowers and the sights of the amusement park, I had enjoyed the strains of *Carnival Joys* played by the Gardens' orchestra. The piece was composed by Hans Christian Lumbye, *the Strauss of the North*, who had served as Tivoli's music director in the nineteenth century.

After my morning saunter through floral memories, I enjoyed a smoothie of strawberries and coconut milk and a soak in the whirlpool tub. Later that afternoon, I received a call from Lieutenant Dias. The verdict was in. The body found after Hurricane Iwa had been identified as Bàozhǐ Shēn. Following protocol, John had called on the man's next of kin as soon as he received the ME's report. By the time he arrived at the Shēn building, Bō had prepared himself to receive unpleasant news.

"Of course, the guy was shocked. Who wouldn't be? I began by telling him that while I was looking into some old cases, I'd heard a couple of anecdotes about families in Chinatown—including the story of his granduncle's disappearance in the early fifties. Then, I told him about the John Doe who was found in the freezer meltdown after Hurricane Iwa. After that, there was no way to gloss over the fact that Bàozhǐ Shēn had finally been found.

"I was glad that once the initial impact had passed, he expressed curiosity about how the identification had been made. He'd never met his granduncle, so his ability to absorb the details objectively is not surprising. There was no way I was going to have him looking at the original pics of the corpse that had defrosted after thirty years in a freezer, let alone what it looked like after another three decades in the ground. I told him that we'd been able to run the two fingerprints the techs got in 1982 against old Army records from the Second World War. This confirmed the man's identity. With the two cases linked, and the John Doe declared to be his granduncle, I gave Bō a general overview of the autopsy performed in 1982."

"I don't know how you can handle this part of your work,

John. It's bad enough that you have to deal with crime and unrepentant perpetrators. But I can't imagine having to tell someone that their loved one is dead. When Ariel died, Nathan told me how impressed he was with your kindness, sincerity, and steadiness. But how you can do it, over and over again—not knowing how the families and loved ones will respond to whatever you tell them—is totally amazing."

John paused for a moment. When he spoke, I could tell that my words had affected him. Perhaps he was reliving a moment when speech had failed him. After clearing his throat, he continued.

"You're right, Natalie. It isn't easy to tell a woman that the man she sent off to work in the morning has been found dead in a seedy hotel room with a hooker. I guess the worst scenario is telling a couple of kids that their Mom won't be coming to pick them up after school—ever again. But somehow you get through it, as best you can.

"That's why having a partner is so important. If you're lucky, you each bring something different to the game. You know what I mean? One of you is good at the physical take-downs; the other's good with the interviews. And if neither of you can handle interaction with vics or their loved ones, hopefully there's someone on tap who can address that."

"So, what's next John?" I asked. "Has your team found any connection to Professor Zhāng's case?"

"You're getting ahead of things, again. I just identified a man who's been missing since the middle of the last century. That's a major accomplishment. But I can't jump from Bàozhǐ Shēn to Fù Hán Zhāng without something tangible to show the powers that be. Up to yesterday, the only link I had was your visions. Today I've got two glimmers of light to guide me. The first is a fistful of photos. The second item I'm leaving as a surprise for you.

"You see, when I met with Bō, I got some pictures of his granduncle. Many were taken at what we'd call a block party, just days before his scheduled departure for China. There he was, all decked out in the suit, shirt, hat, and shoes you've described. That allows me to say, *Isn't it interesting that the attire of the vics in two cases separated by sixty years is pretty much identical.*

"Of course, a lot of men have worn white leisure suits. Unfortunately, I can't point to crime scene images that are also parallel. And, unlike Zhāng, there's no shot of Bàozhĭ lying on the floor. Could be I'll end up solving one case but not the other, if I can't find a way to join them officially. You know?"

"Yes, John. I understand that's a possibility. But you've got me intrigued about the surprise you have for me."

"You'll learn about that soon enough. Let me have the pleasure of surprising *you* occasionally. And I want you to know how much I value your help. No matter how things play out, I don't want you to feel like you've failed in some way. If you hadn't come forward and revealed your first vision of a man in a white suit, we wouldn't be returning the man's remains to his family. Of course, I'll be thrilled if we can solve the mystery of his murder. As to the Prof's case, we're moving forward inch by inch. If we're able to cross the finish line in that race, it could be your input that will have led to a successful resolution."

"If my visions help you or anyone else, John, I'm happy to share them. And I certainly understand that you can't use them as a basis for prosecution—even if I could identify a murderer."

"So, we're good to move forward then?"

"Definitely! Like I said, the ID is definite. Bō let me take a swab of his mouth and those results are in. Again we have confirmation that the man who was buried as a John Doe, after being frozen for nearly three decades, *is* Bàozhĭ Shēn. The original autopsy on the John Doe remains found in 1982, as well as the preliminary findings on the exhumed remains prove it. Since *both* of the autopsies refer to him, I'd like you and Keoni to look them over. And, I promise there's a little something you'll find interesting."

Because John did not want to share Bàozhĭ's two autopsies with the public—and could not yet justify our involvement in his investigation—I suggested we have another meeting around the kitchen table at White Sands Cottage. The only time John could come was before he played a round of golf in Ewa Beach. That meant getting up rather early, but at least the issue of food and drink was simple: Kona Coffee and bagels with fruit.

When John walked in the door, he was dressed for the golf course, but carrying a garment bag, which he asked to hang in the front hall closet. Somehow, I had the feeling that he had an engagement with a certain person from the morgue on his schedule for later in the day. I could not wait to meet the alluring Lori Mitchum, who was clearly making an impression on his daily life, but I limited my conversation to the purpose at hand.

Despite the early hour, he managed to insert a bit of humor as he strolled into the kitchen.

"Ah, the fragrance of finely blended Kona coffee! Got a shot of bourbon? We can enjoy an early morning of mixology with our toxicology."

Keoni and I groaned, as expected.

"These days I like to separate mealtime from murder," said my personal detective.

"Well, I do feel bad about starting your day with another glimpse at the seamier side of my work."

"At this point, I'm getting used to our little conferences on autopsies—as long as you minimize the photos and restrict the technical verbiage to summary reports," I responded.

CHAPTER 19

Nothing clears up a case so much as
stating it to another person.
Sir Arthur Conan Doyle [1859 - 1930]

S oon we were settled around Mom's old Formica table. As I put together our light breakfast, Keoni showed John the scrap of paper Miss Una had found in Bàozhǐ's desk.

"You're right," agreed John. "This implies there was a woman in the guy's life who was up to some kind of mischief. As you said, the list of possibilities is rather short, and unless the date of this note goes back a while, it points in the direction of Bō's Auntie Toitoi. Of course, the majority of the text is missing, along with a date, so there could be someone else in the picture. But I've never heard of any other woman on Oʻahu at the time, except Chāng's wife, who was already dead by the time Bàozhǐ wrote the letter to his father before his trip."

I brought over the coffee pot and sat down. The room was quiet for a few minutes, as we focused on our mugs of coffee and plates of fruit, bagels and cream cheese. After wiping his mouth politely with the edge of his napkin, John reached down for his briefcase.

"Let me begin by showing you a couple of pictures Bō Shēn gave me yesterday. I'm probably going to have to get back with him to identify individuals in the group shots, but at least I can show you Bàozhǐ in his prime."

We looked down at several photos of varying sizes. It seemed like the majority were taken by an old Kodak box camera. John must have been reading my mind.

"These are pretty good for the time. I asked the techs about the camera, and they guessed it was a Brownie 127, which was the hottest thing back then."

"It looks like many were shot at the old hotel," observed Keoni.

"That's what Bō said—although there were a couple taken by neighbors, when his granduncle was out parading around in his new traveling suit. But because the family was having a holiday sale in the store and couldn't go down to the harbor, they threw Bàozhǐ a party ahead of his ship's departure and that's where most of the pics were taken.

"Before I go any further, here's a pad of paper for you, Natalie. I'd like you to take notes the way you did with the Professor's autopsy. Don't take time to formalize your thoughts, or censor how you write them down. Just record anything that comes to mind, no matter how trivial or unconnected it seems."

"Sure."

At that point, Keoni was recording his responses to the pictures in his electronic notebook. I was pleased there were no unsettling images—if you could ignore the depressing thought that within a couple of days, this handsome young man would be dead.

"When you're through with these, you can look at the Summary Autopsy on the exhumed remains, Keoni. The report I'm going to show you, Natalie, is from 1982, when the John Doe was discovered in the freezer meltdown. Everything has been recorded by typewriter and handwritten note. There's a case number, but obviously no name for the deceased. There were no belongings with him, other than the T-shirt and underwear he wore. Not much of a forensics report. The freezer was a secondary crime scene, but if we were investigating today, there'd be a lot a CSI team could do."

While the names, case numbers and dates of autopsy might be different—and the forms themselves—this summary report paralleled that of Professor Zhāng's in more than one aspect.

The deceased is an adult Asian male measuring 68.9 inch-

es in length. The weight of the deceased at the time of his death was guessed to be approximately 165 pounds. He was between twenty-five and thirty years of age. Despite the degree of decomposition, it appears that he was in good health at the time of his demise. The body arrived at the morgue wearing only a white cotton singlet undershirt and brown and white striped cotton boxer undershorts...The undershirt is stained with blood and brain matter...hair on the scalp is black, straight and short...fingernails are clean and even...Analysis of the remaining skin indicates no surgical scars and no signs of bruises ante mortem or postmortem...Time of death is impossible to pinpoint, but occurred approximately thirty years prior to discovery of the corpse in the Sand Island Warehouse...Cause of death is a gunshot wound on the left temple, 2.6 inches below the top of the head and 3.7 inches left of the anterior midline...A hemorrhagic wound track passing rightward, backward, and downward was caused by the bullet ricocheting in the interior of the skull...extensive damage to the bases of the left frontal and left temporal lobes...although the bullet was not recovered, a .25 caliber lead bullet is suspected to have produced the gunshot wound...

As might be expected, there was no modern toxicology screening. I was glad that, like the Professor's demise, death had been immediate. I passed the report to Keoni and looked at John, who sat expectantly.

"Well, it reads about the same as Fù Hán Zhāng's autopsy, John."

"Yep. As Keoni has seen in the autopsy of the exhumed skeletal remains, the COD is confirmed to have been a single round .25 caliber bullet. And here's the kicker...your surprise for the day...the entry wound on Bàozhǐ is nearly identical to the one found in the Professor's cranium. There's a slight but distinctive indentation on the left side of the wound from the bullet. If that doesn't show the two cases are linked, I don't know what would! And as soon as Dr. Soli realized that fact, he was on the phone to me."

I froze for a moment, trying to absorb what I had heard. "So, the same person *did* kill them both?" I asked, incredulous that my visions had been proven to link to a real case in the here and now, as well as to one dating from my youth.

"Again, you are proven to have the *gift*, my dear," confirmed John.

I caught my breath and looked over at the file in front of Keoni. "Do I have to read that report too?"

"There's no need at this point. We're talking a skeleton. COD is a no-brainer. A single gunshot wound to the head. But beyond the distinctive bullet, the only thing I learned from that report is that the cheek bones of Asians are angled forward more than in Caucasians. As to anything else, I'm waiting for the toxicology reports. With nothing but bones to work on, it'll be a while before they come in, unless there's something that pops up in the cursory tests. But did you see anything unusual in the report, Keoni?"

"Just that it parallels what we already know about the Professor's death. As you've said, the big news is that the two cases are linked by the distinctive GSWs in both victims' skulls. Too bad you only have the bullet from the Professor. It would be great if you had shell casings from both murders. They would strengthen the finding that the same gun was used in both cases. Since the ejector would have made the same indentations each time the gun was fired, each bullet fired from it would have been impacted similarly, thereby producing nearly identical wounds."

"True. That's what we have. Hey, it doesn't look like you've written anything down, Natalie."

"I think we've already discussed everything in my visions. I don't see anything startling here—except for the staggering announcement you've made about the wounds."

As if on cue, John's phone rang.

"Dias here. Yes...Uh-huh...Yeah, that's pretty important. Have you touched anything? I'd appreciate it if you'd all back off and wait until I get there. Mmhm. About forty-five minutes, depending on the parking. Thanks. I'll see you then."

Keoni and I had remained quiet during John's call, but we were anticipating good news since he had a goofy grin on his face.

"Wow. You won't believe what Bō Shēn just told me. His team was gearing up to refinish floors, and they found a bullet."

"Where? Was it on the second or the third floor?" I asked.

"On the third. With a silencer, the Shēn family being on the fourth floor wouldn't have heard gun fire. And if the crime occurred prior to business hours, there wouldn't have been anyone on ground level to hear a scuffle upstairs."

"Okay. But how did the murderer, especially a woman, get the body out of the building without anyone noticing?" I asked.

"Another item for the list of *What ifs* and *How comes*," John replied, putting the reports and photos back in his briefcase.

"As you just heard, I've got to get back into town. Depending on what I find, I'll be pulling in the CSIs for a stroll through the decades. Too bad about all the work Bō's been doing. I have a feeling there's going to be a hold on his remodeling. Oh, please hang on to those little evidence bags you've been saving for me.

"Thanks again. It's beginning to look like we're going to be able to prove the two cases of the men in white suits are related. That's a huge step forward, even if there's no conclusion in sight."

I walked John to the front door, pulled his garment bag from the closet and wished him continued luck with his investigations. Next, I filled a travel mug with coffee for Keoni's trek across the island. He had no idea how long his visit to the North Shore would be, so I decided to dedicate myself to outlining my initial magazine column and blogs. Within a couple of hours, I had completed my homework and felt prepared to move forward with my renewed life as a journalist. All that was left to be done was to book the column's launch party at Hale`iwa Joe's at Ha`ikū Gardens.

With thoughts of the forthcoming festivities, I picked up Miss Una from Keoni's desk and walked into the living room. After dropping her on the back of my favorite chair, I turned on a selection of Mozart concertos. With both of us set for a short nap, I leaned back in the recliner and closed my eyes. After the excitement of my early morning meeting with John, I should not have been surprised to experience another time away from concrete reality.

*　*　*　*　*

I open my eyes to a blurred and fading view of my living room. I look around and focus on Bàozhǐ's desk. Suddenly, I see myself seated there, with an old-fashioned fountain pen in hand, I look down at a blank sheet of white paper positioned in the center of an old-style brown leather blotter. I glance up and see Miss Una on the top of the desk. Everything then turns to the sepia tones of most of my visions.

I now stand outside of Room 312 at the Shēn Hotel. Miss Una is perched on my shoulder. Why is she here? She has never been in any of my visions before. The door to the room that Bàozhǐ uses as an office is open. He is seated at his desk. I notice the side of his bare leg. He wears brown shorts, sandals and a tan aloha shirt with palm trees. He is bent over, writing something on a sheet of white onion skin paper. A beautiful, tall, and willowy woman passes me and enters the room with a feline expression on her face.

"There you are. I wondered where you were," she says in a purring voice. She is not a native English speaker, but she is easily understood. In more than one way. This stunning woman could attract any man she chose.

"Hello, Toitoi," he replies almost curtly, smoothly folding the paper on which he had been writing. "I'm getting organized for my trip."

"How can you possibly leave your toy-toy? I will be so lonely without you," she says in a cloying voice as she approaches his side.

The man does not respond to the joke about her nickname. "As I have told you before, my father has asked me to do something for the family."

"Why can Chāng not do it for him, this errand that is so important?" she asks pouting.

"I'm the eldest son, Toitoi. There are some things only the eldest son can do. You should understand that."

"I know only that you brought me here promising to be with me always. Why cannot I go with you, on this errand?"

"You'd be bored. I couldn't be with you all the time."

"Why not?"

"Because there are some things I must do alone."

Pressing against him, she rubs his neck and shoulders. With almost a whine, she asks, "What do you and your father discuss when you are locked away in this room? Is there something you are not telling your wife? Am I not truly your toy-toy?"

Looking up at her steadily, he says, "We discuss nothing that concerns you. There are some matters that pertain only to the family."

"But I am now your family. Surely as your wife I should know about everything that pertains to you and our family."

The man sighs. "I've explained this to you before. Since we won't be having any children, there are some things that will involve Cháng and his son Kāng in the future, not me. Not us."

In an instant, the woman's behavior changes. Practically hissing, she asks, "How can you mention this? At a time when you are preparing to be gone. This unfortunate...circumstance...is not of my doing. We discussed this before we were married. You said nothing would ever come between us. You promised to always take care of me."

"I have honored my word. You've been cared for very well since coming to Hawai`i. And you will always be cared for. Even if I do not return from China, you'll continue to be taken care of, Toitoi. I'm sure your friends have mentioned the insurance that some of the war widows receive each month. I've made similar arrangements for you."

A sly smile softens the woman's face. "Oh, Bàozhǐ. How thoughtful of you."

"Now if you don't mind, I need to get back to my work," he says turning away.

"Very well, my husband. I will prepare a special dinner for you and your family tonight."

"Thank you. I always enjoy your cooking."

The woman turns abruptly on her heel, her face now a mask frozen in displeasure. She brushes past me and exits the room rapidly. Over her black sheath dress, she wears a red silk scarf that flows across her shoulders and long black hair. Her black patent leather heels leave deep depressions on the carpeting. Beyond the cool elegance of her clothing, hair and makeup, it is the piercing blackness of her eyes and icy facial expression that chill me.

*   *   *   *   *

When Keoni checked in with me later that afternoon, I told him about envisioning the legendary Toitoi in her youth.

"That insurance might not have been much, but you should have seen the smile that appeared on her face when he told her about it. The way she looked around that room and spoke of Bàozhǐ's private conferences with his father, it's clear she was watching everything that took place in the hotel. And those eyes. She's definitely not someone you'd want to cross in broad daylight, let alone a dark alley. I have no trouble picturing her with a saw carving up the walls of the Shēn Building—or with a gun in her hand. In fact, I'll bet you it was her husband who gave her the gun for protection. Little did he know he'd end up on the receiving end of its barrel."

The next day, I got a call from John. He wanted to fill us in on his latest meeting with Bō Shēn. Thanks to Keoni's collection of fine electronics, I was able to put our favorite lieutenant on a good quality speaker phone. Again seated in the kitchen, my honey and I pushed our chairs together to minimize extraneous noise.

John immediately shared his findings. "Bō greeted me at the door. We went right up to the third floor. His team has finished putting in insulation and drywall on the perimeter of the building. But they haven't rebuilt the inner walls, because it's easier to refinish the old wood flooring without them in place. I can see why no one noticed the bullet before. For one thing, no one knew a murder had been committed there."

"And the place sat unused for decades. When I interviewed him, Bō said little about the old hotel, except for playing in the rooms as a kid," I added.

"From what I could tell," John continued, "the bullet is lodged in an old screw hole at the edge of a hallway floor. It wasn't protruding very much, so I can see how the casing was picked up without the perpetrator noticing the bullet. The perp would have thought the bullet was lodged in the vic's skull. The way the bullet was positioned in the floor, I didn't want to touch anything. So, I shot a couple of pictures with my cell phone and put in a call to the CSIs, informing them that the case of Mr. Shēn had just heated up.

"We had a while to wait, so Bō took me up to the fourth floor. As we passed through the front hallway, I saw the art you mentioned, Natalie. That Bàozhǐ really was a great artist. Bō then gave me a tour of everything he's done in the penthouse and showed me the plans for what's he's going to do everywhere else. At the moment, the building is at that in-between point— some rooms look ready for an ad in a magazine, and others are still bare to the studs.

"To keep Bō happy, I avoided mentioning that depending on the lead CSI's investigation, he might have to delay implementing his plans—at least on the third floor."

"I'll bet that would really thrill his fiancée," I said with a laugh.

"I'm sure you're right about that. Fortunately, the crime scene is one floor below the penthouse, so the love birds should get to move into their new home on time. I was blown away when Bō took me into the refurbished living room. What a pad. Not exactly what I'd expect a bachelor with means to have, but I guess that fiancée of his has been involved with the remodeling. There's already a huge rug and some leather furniture still wrapped in plastic. But what really caught my eye was a fireplace across from the entry."

"What kind did he choose, JD?" asked Keoni.

"It's one of those electric wall mount jobs. Sleek, long and narrow; brushed metal finish. And even though the flames look real, they're coming up from a bed of glass pebbles. Really cool."

"Your age is showing again, JD," observed Keoni. "The word 'cool' is no longer cool."

"What should I say?"

"Well, if you want to sound a lot younger, you could say, *sick*" I suggested.

After harrumphing, John continued. "Whatever. So, where was I? Oh, yeah. On the mantel was a row of pics, and right in the middle was one with Bō, his Auntie Toitoi and her boyfriend, Brian Yamaguchi. They're on an old teak yacht, standing along a rail on the bow. And guess what's below, riding the water just below the name of the boat?"

"No way," exclaimed Keoni.

"Yep. The dinghy that's been haunting my dreams. No Comacho cousins, but you can't get everything you wish for."

"That's amazing, John," I exclaimed. "So, what's the name of the craft?"

"It's *Moku laki milimili*. The literal translation is *yacht lucky toy*. Not exactly a traditional use of the Hawaiian language. But the boat's a vintage model and it was probably rechristened by Toitoi's sugar daddy. He must love that woman a lot to name his luxury plaything what amounts to, *Toitoi's lucky yacht*."

"How exciting. It looks like a lot of the puzzle pieces are materializing," I said grinning.

"Mmhm. I've just got to draw them together. Since Bō invited me into his living quarters and the photo was in plain sight, I should be able to go back to it any time I need. So, four murders in three cases, spanning two islands. And the linchpin to it all appears to be one woman—although the Comachos were not taken out with a .25 caliber Baby Browning."

"So how did you control your enthusiasm after your photographic discovery?" I asked.

"Well, that was the hard part. I had to smile and make nice while we finished the tour. If I didn't have several cases to solve, it would have been fun. That kitchen he's putting in is enough to make anyone a chef. Satin finished *koa* wood cabinets. Anti-bacterial quartz counter top; fancy glass backsplash. Center island on huge casters that lock in place. A lot of stainless steel and hand-blown light fixtures. My favorite part was a faucet right over the stove for filling big pots with water. Man, you could sure boil a lot of pasta or lobsters with that.

"And then there was the master suite. King-sized bed on a raised platform. Sun screens, drapes, sound system, huge drop-down TV screen, all controlled by a single remote. And the bathroom? More *koa* cabinets. Italian glass sinks. A whirlpool bath with a miniature waterfall for the faucet. And a shower you could hold a party in."

"Where was your excitement about architecture and design when we were renovating Auntie Carrie's cottage?" I asked.

"It was actually your projects that got me started on appreciating home design. Now whenever I'm on a case that's rough on my heart and gut, I take a little time out to see if there's anything interesting in the crime scene that I can utilize when I can finally afford to redo my condo."

"Now there's a memorable image of our tax dollars at work," Keoni said with a snort.

"So, what's next, JD?"

"Right now, most everything is in the hands of the techs—except for the research on Toitoi and her boyfriend and their connection to the cousins from Maui. So far, I can tell you that Mr. Yamaguchi is a slippery character. His name shows up in a lot of nasty cases, but you wouldn't know it from his jacket. There's nothing in that file except a couple of misdemeanors as a young man. He must have been taken under some sharp criminal's wing at an early age.

"Quite the respectable man in his community. Owns a couple of restaurants and a club in Lahaina. Major donor to a lot of popular causes—kids, the food bank, the environment. But underneath all that? The whispers are loud and lethal. Women employees who just disappear. But every time he's pulled in for a little sit-down with the authorities of several agencies, nothing actionable comes to light.

"And surprise of surprises, there are some upcountry properties he owns with Toitoi—suspiciously not far from the charming Comachos' land. The unofficial suspicion is that the land is yielding some botanical recreation for wealthy visitors staying in a resort he's part owner of. Yep, a real gent."

"Now that you've got the name of the boat, you should tap your buddies at the Coast Guard for anything they might have on the guy," suggested Keoni.

"Already on the agenda. In fact, I've got a meeting with them tomorrow to look into any open or closed cases on the high seas that involve the lovebirds, the Comachos, and/or any of their known associates. I've already got Ken'ichi Nakamura looking into the history of Yamaguchi's yacht."

"Sounds like you've got everything in hand," I said.

"Close enough that my palms are itching. I should have some new info by early next week. How about we rendezvous at that yacht club again—I could sure go for another one of those shrimp sandwiches."

"They *were* pretty good. I also liked the sweet potato fries—the waffle cut adds a little something special," I observed, wondering if I would learn to use a mandolin in my culinary classes on prepping fruits and vegetables.

Looking up at the calendar on the refrigerator, I realized my first class was coming up next Thursday. I would then have to offer an excuse for my absences from the house. Thankfully, I had chosen a daytime course, so I can simply add the time to a shopping trip. Maybe in the future, I could talk Samantha, or even Izzy, into taking a course with me. That would give me company, as well as a reason for my prolonged absences. Not that Keoni has ever questioned my schedule, but I still want to keep my adventures in the culinary arts to myself until I have something to brag about.

CHAPTER 20

One may smile, and smile, and be a villain.
William Shakespeare [1564 – 1616]

T he rest of the day passed with only a little excitement. The block party at Nathan's was particularly enjoyable. Most guests brought their favorite dishes, and like Ariel's life celebration the year before, the cooks were encouraged to share their recipes. Even though Nathan had told me to bring only wine and tea, I cheated and took some of The Ladies' potato salad that had evolved to include elements of both Izzy's and Joanne's recipes, with potatoes, macaroni, and mayonnaise, plus green onions, and dashes of Dijon mustard and Louisiana hot sauce.

Half way through the evening, Nathan presented Dr. Adriana Gonzalez as his new girlfriend. I had watched a few sparks flying between the two during the scavenger hunt, and now their relationship was official. With his granddaughter Brianna still at college on the mainland, I was glad Nathan had someone with whom to share the highlights of his life. And although they had only known each other a short time, they seemed quite cozy. Their relationship certainly proved that a beautiful woman can bring a spring to the cadence of a man, regardless of his stage of life.

Early Monday afternoon, I got a call from John announcing that the ME's office was releasing Bàozhĭ's body. Perhaps that was a misnomer, since there was only a skeleton remaining after three decades of interment of an already decomposed body. By this time, bone samples for toxicology reports and evidentiary purposes had been taken. Beyond those issues, there was almost no evidence to analyze. The deceased's underwear, as well as the freezer in which he was stored for decades, had been disposed of long ago. Since revelations of my visions would not be admissible in court, it was good that John now had the evidence of a bullet in the floor of the Shēn Hotel to establish the probability of the crime scene at which the man had died.

With the release of the body, Bō Shēn was able to schedule re-interment of his granduncle's remains for Wednesday afternoon. After the many years that had passed, it seemed like a rush, but there was no reason to delay the event. With just a couple of days to plan, I think that only Bō's neighbors were given classic handwritten invitations. The rest of us received phone calls. It was not surprising that like the *amah* of Pearl Wong, the Shēn family had arranged for burial plots at the old Makiki Cemetery.

There would be no traditional funeral procession. For despite the number of Chinese who were expected to attend, there were too few Shēn family members to warrant it. Also, the residents and business people of Chinatown who would attend were elderly and incapable of walking for any prolonged time or distance. Therefore, the coffin would arrive unceremoniously at the cemetery in the funeral home's hearse.

I am certainly no expert on burial customs—Occidental let alone Asian—but I doubted there would be many traditional elements in the reburial service. Although the man who had died had been the elder son, he had predeceased his father and left no sons. Above all, he had been murdered. These were all issues that overturned the expected order of life. And within traditional Chinese culture, such irregularities were feared to attract bad luck, including accidents or even death.

A high percentage of religious Chinese people practice Mahayana Buddhism, which is concerned with the balancing of positive and negative energies. Bō did not seem especially religious to me. Even if he were, I wondered what kind of rituals could address all of these unfortunate circumstances. In the minds and hearts of some people, I doubted that the use of harmonizing crystals, burning incense, or offering prayers to the family's ancestors would mitigate the possible impact of Bàozhǐ's unfortunate demise.

I was right in my speculations. Bō might respect Chinese traditions that were intended to prevent bad luck, but his arrangements were clearly tempered by the realities of the twenty-first century. The first deviation from Chinese cultural norms was the lack of multiple days of prayer for the soul of the deceased. The next was the absence of a wake. Given the incomplete state of the Shēn Building, even if such an event was desired, there were no statues of deities to cover in red paper. Nor were there any mirrors needing removal to prevent the coffin's reflection, which is believed to invite additional death. And, it was unlikely there would be an altar table with candles, incense, or food for the spirit of the departed. I did wonder if according to tradition a gong had been placed to the left of the entrance to the Shēn Building to announce that a male family member had died.

On the day of the graveside service, the weather was cool and clear. Out of respect for Bō, Keoni and I wore light colored aloha wear. Unfortunately, although I knew I was not supposed to wear open toed shoes, my white gel sandals were the only footwear that would allow me to walk through the hilly cemetery. When we arrived, we found the gate open and manned by one of Bō's oldest neighbors. With so many men in Hawai`i possessing white slacks and shirts, it was not surprising that the attire of the day was in harmony with both aloha wear and Chinese funeral customs. Aside from the black band on his left arm, you would not have thought the man directing us was dressed for a funeral in the United States.

I was grateful for Keoni's support as we climbed up to the gravesite. As we joined the sizable gathering, I was surprised to recognize many people I had passed on the streets of Chinatown recently—as well as individuals frequently mentioned in the media for their success in finance and real estate. In addition, there were people like Keoni, John Dias, and I, who had been involved in the investigation of Bàozhǐ's disappearance.

One person was noticeably missing. But while Pearl Wong had played a large role in helping me understand my visions and the objects I had found in the dead man's desk, no one in the Shēn family knew of her participation. As I glanced toward downtown Honolulu, I realized how near we were to the Wong family's crypt.

Bō Shēn stood at the head of a mahogany coffin with a semi-circle of mourners surrounding it. He was dressed in white shoes and pants, but since he was a couple of generations removed from the deceased, he wore a pale blue shirt rather than white. Tied to his left sleeve was a black ribbon. On one side of him stood a young woman of mixed heritage in a soft white cotton shift. She kept her eyes down and maintained a demure demeanor. I suspected she was Bō's fiancée.

On the other side of Bō stood a tall slim woman I recognized as his aunt Toitoi. Although she wore the expected color of black for the widow of a Chinese man, there was nothing reflecting the traditional symbols of sorrow or poverty in her attire. The mid-calf dress she wore was made of shimmering silk, like the scarf that adorned her sunhat. At least the hat was black, instead of her signature red. And, although she wore large dark sunglasses, it was clear that she had not foresworn applying makeup to her smooth skin. The most obvious concession she had made for the solemnity of the occasion was wearing black leather flats.

Toitoi was clinging to the arm of a distinguished Japanese man. Although he was clearly eligible for membership in AARP, I was certain he was at least ten years younger than she. Unlike her, he had made no attempt to keep the white from his hair. Since he was wearing sunglasses, I could not tell his expression. But knowing Yamaguchi's history, I suspected that behind the innocuous exterior was the head of a major crime group in Hawai`i. Of course, there is nothing like aloha wear to make even a master criminal look like a harmless tourist.

By that point, my emotions were in turmoil. Somehow Keoni knew that I was on the verge of a headache, or a vision, and he cradled my waist to afford me the greatest degree of support. I tried to remain calm, but in front of me was a woman I suspected to be the cold-hearted killer of at least two men. Even without the benefit of my visions, she should be viewed as a person of interest in the disappearance of her husband. Of the three elements the police consider in any murder, she had possessed both the time and opportunity to commit the crime.

But what was her motive in either case? I could see none for the murder of her husband. The Shēn family had received her with open arms. As John had already discovered, she had even received payout from two minor life insurance policies. Beyond that, she had continued to receive the support of the family in the intervening years. And now she was Bō's full partner in a major real estate operation on two islands. As to the Professor, I could not imagine how she had met him, let alone conjure up a motive for her killing him.

As Keoni rubbed my back, I refocused my thoughts on the occasion at hand. Beside Bō was a picture of the deceased on an easel. At the foot of the coffin was a small table holding a beautiful white orchid plant, lit white candles and burning fragrant joss sticks. Beneath a nearby tree, a young man played mournful melodies on a traditional Chinese flute. Perhaps because of fire regulations, there were no firecrackers or the burning of paper representations of items from daily life or faux money to bring happiness to the departed. The single ceremonial component I recognized was the chanting of ancient prayers by a Buddhist priest standing near Bō.

Once it was clear that all of the expected attendees had arrived, Bō glanced subtly at the priest, who brought his incantations to an end. The young man then addressed the gathering. First, on behalf of himself and his aunt, he thanked everyone for their attendance. After that, he described Bàozhǐ and his artistry—and noted his having been a pious son who died at a time when he was to make a significant journey on behalf of his family. I might have been disappointed by the lack of details regarding the journey that was never undertaken, but the sincerity of his words reminded me of how much a family can demand of its members.

There was not much to the service beyond Bō's comments. As his voice stilled, the flautist resumed performing classical Chinese melodies. As the music ended, Toitoi and Yamaguchi both removed their sunglasses. I was struck by the frozen look on Toitoi's face. After a couple of moments, Bō and his party bowed three times to the coffin. Bō and Toitoi then turned to greet those who had come to pay their respects to the deceased and his family. The first to approach them were a group of seniors from the family's neighborhood. I watched with interest as Bō's presumed fiancée handed each person a couple of envelopes. I knew the white one would contain some kind of candy and the red one a coin to ensure the recipient got home safely. I noticed that a few people received a third envelope that I thought might be an invitation to a dinner celebrating Bàozhǐ's life.

Calmly and with theatrical solemnity, Toitoi played her role as the widow well, nodding with a sad smile to each person who offered sympathetic words of condolence. The only give-away to me as someone who knew her actual role in her husband's death was that fixed expression that remained in place the whole time. Was she a superb actress? Or, was she more than a bit insane, after the many decades of the charade?

When Keoni escorted me over to express our condolences to Bō, several of my assumptions were proven correct. After shaking hands with the current scion of the Shēn family, we were introduced to Toitoi and then her companion. As I approached her, I saw no indication that she knew who we were—or that we had been involved in the investigation of her husband's murder. She did not even acknowledge Keoni and stared intently at my shoulder. It was all I could do to refrain from calling out, "Your day will come, in the not too distant future."

Brian Yamaguchi smiled politely and shook our hands. When Toitoi remained fixated on me for an inordinate amount of time, he nudged her. His smile did not slip, but his eyes narrowed cruelly. I could tell he was indeed the man John Dias had pegged as having a curriculum vitae of activities spanning a full range of criminal pursuits. Fortunately, Keoni continued to keep me calm. Just the touch of his hand on my back eased my tension and reminded me that we were there to observe the dynamics of the group, as well as to provide support for Bō. The next person we met was the young woman of Asian and Caucasian heritage who continued to stand with Bō. When he confirmed that it was his fiancée, Leah Coombs, I was tempted to compliment her design work in the Shēn Building. At Bō's prompting, she pressed three envelopes into my hand with an amiable smile. Although I was anxious to read everything, I merely slipped them into my pocket.

In the midst of greetings and farewells, we lost track of John. We had seen him when we arrived, but he was probably watching the proceedings from a distance that allowed him to see almost all of the people in attendance. As Keoni and I turned to join the crowd drifting downhill, I felt a shiver of cold energy pass through me. Glancing back casually, I saw Toitoi looking vacantly toward the city with that same frozen smile on her face. But her paramour was staring angrily toward a figure poised beside an old headstone with Bertram Fong. Although the man stood in profile, there was no mistaking the posture and stocky build of Lieutenant John Dias.

In the moments it took for us to reach the headstone, Mr. Fong had departed. John wasted no time in expressing his view of the evil duo he was now investigating intensely. "What did you think of our persons of interest, Keoni? The man's idea of dress up is downright pretty—almost the same quality of threads as the old Frenchman during the Didión case last summer. But from what I can tell from his file, the stuff this joker's been into shows he doesn't begin to have the class that Frenchman displayed in even the little pinky ring he wore. By the way, what did you make of those tats peekin' out from below his shirt cuff?"

"Not much, JD. I could tell they weren't from a homegrown prison job. But there wasn't enough showing to tell if he's connected to the Yakuza, or just a rich bad guy with an artistic flair."

"I can't argue with any of that, guys," I said. "But did you catch that plastic look on Toitoi's face? It seemed like she wasn't really present. Maybe all the years of intrigue are getting to her."

Once we were out of sight of the day's star players, I opened the third envelope Leah had given me. It was an invitation to join the Shēn family for a Consolation Feast at Legend Seafood Restaurant, where we had enjoyed a sumptuous Chinese New

Year celebration. When we arrived at my car, I passed the keys to Keoni. "I'm too drained to drive, dear," I explained.

Taking the key fob from me, he opened my door and checked the car's well-polished exterior for any tampering, as he had always done as a police detective. After adjusting the driver's seat and mirrors, he said, "We've got a couple of hours until the dinner. What would you like to do?"

"Why don't we park at the Chinese Cultural Plaza and check out the shops. We might find something that would complement our blend of Auntie Carrie's furnishings and ours."

"What are you looking for?"

"I don't really know. Let's just wander around until we see something interesting in a window.

With that agreement, we zigzagged along the streets, doing more window-gazing than actual shopping. The only thing that really impressed me was a poster in our favorite bookstore announcing an upcoming auction of antiques from Asia and the Pacific Rim. Taking a quick perusal at the display of discounted hardcover books, I was delighted to find one on the life of Lao-Tzu that would make a perfect companion to the copy of the *Tao Te Ching* I had won.

While paying for the book, we identified ourselves to the young salesman and inquired about the owner's wellbeing. We were told that he was not ill but had taken the day off to attend a neighbor's funeral. We then explained that we had just come from the service ourselves.

"My grandfather was pretty sad when he learned what had happened to his friend Bàozhǐ. He used to say he had always hoped the guy was out there somewhere, wandering around with amnesia or something. But when Bō Shēn called to say his granduncle's body had been found, there was no more daydreaming."

"I take it he knew Bàozhǐ Shēn pretty well," Keoni stated.

"Oh, yes. They went to high school together and served in the same Army unit in World War II. My grandpa came home first, but the two of them reconnected after Bàozhǐ got back. Of course, my grandpa hadn't married yet, and as he said, with his friend bringing home a clinging war bride, they didn't get together very often. And then Bàozhǐ was suddenly gone. While on an errand for his family. It was an issue of shame for the Shēns, who never mentioned him after his disappearance.

"And now after all those years, Bàozhǐ is identified as the man who was found in that warehouse after Hurricane Iwa. That really hit my grandpa. He couldn't grasp how no one had put the pieces of the two mysteries together. But I guess everyone thought the guy was overseas when he went missing. And, no one considered the possibility that the body they found in the freezer might have been their neighbor."

I nodded my head in concurrence with the sorrow he expressed. At that point Keoni informed me that we had only a half hour until the dinner. I completed my transaction and confirmed that we would be seeing Bertram Fong at the memorial feast.

When we arrived at Legends, we were immediately directed to a private dining room. I looked around and saw that John Dias and Mr. Fong were conversing again. After we were seated, tea and a sweet white wine were offered by the servers. As always, the food was delicious. But the atmosphere was far different than that of the Chinese New Year dinner we had attended.

Careless chatter was wholly absent. The conversation we did hear was subdued, perhaps by the knowledge that the man we were honoring had been murdered. One thing we learned from our companions was that in keeping with the rest of Bàozhǐ's Life Celebration, the evening's menu reflected his personal preferences, as well as Chinese tradition.

When I glanced at the head table, Toitoi's face bore another smile that did not reach her eyes. The most significant point in the evening was Bō's evident grief when he raised his glass of wine in a salute to his granduncle's service to his family and country. No one else may have noticed that at that moment, Toitoi was looking down at her plate and muttering softly to herself. I could have been mistaken, but the shape of her lips indicated she may have been speaking in her native language.

I knew it was going to be a long evening and decided to go to the Ladies room before the meal was served. I was not the only one with that idea. There was a rather long line in wait for use of the well-appointed facilities, but it moved fairly quickly. As I was washing my hands, I looked up into the mirror over the sink. What a shock to see Toitoi staring at me. Or should I say my shoulder.

"The lady with the cat," she whispered hauntingly.

Before I could think of a response, she was gone. The room was still crowded, and I could not tell if she had gone into a cubicle or returned to the dining room. A few minutes later, I was back in my seat contemplating how I could tell Keoni about what had just happened. Before I could strategize a way to slip it into the hushed table talk, a waiter arrived with the first course.

The sweet lychees in an almond gelatin (with a hint of champagne), was intended to ease our sorrow. There was also roast pork, whose rosy hue signifies good fortune. Representing the Eighteen Buddhas was a vegetarian dish of eighteen ingredients known as Buddha's Delight. Like most Chinese dinners I had attended, there was chicken cooked with lots of garlic and vegetables, as well as steamed rice. My favorite dish was the Peking duck, believed to help the spirit of the dead safely cross three rivers to heaven.

On the way home, Keoni and I both expressed surprise that no one had hazarded a guess about who could have killed Bàozhǐ—or what the motive for his murder might have been. But the presence of HPD Lieutenant John Dias may have put a damper on any audible speculation. Knowing John would be in touch with us as soon as he had some news, we refrained from calling him, but that did not mean that my emotions had stopped simmering. Between anticipation of a resolution to the murders I had seen in my vision and taking my first cooking class, I lay awake for much of the night.

* * * * *

I looked at the time again. Three o`clock. Ante meridian. Thursday. My date with my culinary destiny had arrived. I was so excited that it was difficult to stay in bed. At dawn, I opened my eyes and found a tail hanging in my face. I slipped out of bed and went to the kitchen. I sprinkled some feline dental goodies on top of the dry cat food and then began boiling water to make a carafe of French press coffee. To avoid waking Keoni, I went into the guest bedroom *en suite* bathroom for a quick shower.

As the warm water relieved my morning stiffness, my mind drifted away from my entry into adult continuing education. With the approaching alignment of several murders, I could not wait to discover what the overall picture would be. Four men were dead: two near clones of one another in appearance yet separated by decades; and two who were biologically related and found in an old teak dinghy. How do the four fit together? And what or who was at the center of this multi-dimensional puzzle? It appeared there were two people: Toitoi *and* her lover Brian.

How long had the pair been together? I doubted that their relationship dated to the mid-twentieth century. Brian Yamaguchi was probably not involved in Bàozhǐ's death, since he would have been a teenager in the early 1950s. No, for that first murder, the investigative team is left with the not-so-poor, not so little Toitoi—the war bride who thanked the man who brought her to a new life by killing him. I wondered what John was learning about her background. If Yamaguchi was part of the Yakuza, I wondered if Toitoi herself was somehow connected to that elite criminal organization.

At that point, Keoni entered the shower and I shut down further contemplation of things criminal. In a short while, I was dressed and moving back to the kitchen. I pulled two pieces of Izzy's apple and oat dump cake from the freezer. After plating them, I zapped them in the microwave for a moment and then sliced tree-fresh papaya, apple, bananas and a few of Joanne's strawberries over the top. Finally, I blended a little vanilla extract and agave syrup into some fresh cream cheese as a topping. After placing food, coffee, dishes and silverware on a tray, I proudly went outside to set a romantic table for a breakfast healthy as well as flavorful. What an accomplishment!

I was feeling very domestic at the moment. I might not be a true *gourmand*, let alone a *gourmet* chef, but at least I was moving beyond a lifetime of adolescent encounters with food selection and preparation. If nothing else, I would soon be able to work efficiently with the set of cutlery I received as a wedding gift decades earlier. And, I hoped I would be learning about the succulent foods I could prepare with those knives.

Of course, Keoni knew nothing about my agenda. He had told me he was having a final session with the owner of the North Shore McMansion on maximizing the features of his new computerized security system. That was great for me because it meant I did not have to be concerned about the dear man until the end of my own event-filled day.

CHAPTER 21

The murdered do haunt their murderers, I believe.
Emily Bronte [1818 - 1848]

Once he was gone, I took the time to tidy the kitchen and plan dinner. How wonderful to discover a package of lasagna from Kalapawai Market in the freezer. With the mealtime dilemma solved, I wrapped my knives in some tea towels and placed them in a beach bag I had bought during our week in town. Next, I had to think about preparing myself.

I could not do much about my nervousness, so I contemplated my wardrobe options. Not knowing what I might be expected to do, I decided to wear a blouse with a pattern to mask potential food accidents and a skort for ease in movement—not to mention avoiding any embarrassing revelations about my preference in undergarments. As to footwear, I did not have much choice. I had been directed to wear close-toed shoes. The most comfortable ones I had were therapeutic walking shoes that felt great on my arches and provided a bit of strength training for my calves.

After all my anxiety, the day unfolded easily. Knowing that it was imperative to establish good relations in the community, Chef Duncan was in the kitchen to greet us, even though someone else would be conducting our rudimentary class. Generous in spirit, as well as time, he took a moment to introduce me as the journalist who was helping to put his school and restaurant on the map of world gastronomy. The afternoon session passed without any culinary disasters or injuries on my part. And I left with a new-found appreciation for the blades with which I could shape gourmet delights!

During the relatively short trip from the culinary school to my cottage, I relived my day with a call to The Ladies. I was delighted that their speaker phone allowed me to talk with both Izzy and Joanne. As I shared the high points of my exploration of the world of proper cutlery usage, I contemplated how I might augment the menu I had planned for dinner that night. When Joanne offered me another basket of salad ingredients, I jumped at the chance to practice my new skills with French and paring knives. And, although I had not received instruction on it, I was tempted to apply my crinkle cut knife to the edges of cucumber rounds and carrot sticks.

As I was putting the lasagna in the oven, John Dias called to announce he had new information that warranted a mid-day rendezvous at the yacht club. After confirming Keoni's availability, I called John back to set up a meeting, and to pry some answers from him.

"Too bad, so sad. I'm not giving you anything until I see the whites of your eyes," he said, almost gleefully. "But I think you'll agree the wait was worth it. And by tomorrow, I may be able to up our prospects for solving the trinity of cases we've been looking at."

Well, that was all he was going to divulge at moment. He left me wanting a lot more, but there was no point in pouting about what I could not change. On to the next subject of the day—dinner. Although I was serving a trustworthy entrée, I wished my class had included some exciting dressings for the vegetables I was about to prepare. Ah, well, another day, another chance for discovery on many levels.

The evening proved to be all I had anticipated. For me, the highlight of the dinner was the salad. Despite my initial desire to apply what I had learned in class, I kept it simple. I tossed fresh spinach, tomatoes, and sweet Maui onion with a macerated strawberry vinaigrette recipe I found online. Keoni is so used to my augmenting prepared foods, that he did not suspect I had ventured into actual creation of any of the elements of our meal, certainly not the dressing.

We followed dinner with a long soak in the hot tub beneath a starry sky. There we finished a bottle of Mount Horrocks Riesling from the Clare Valley in South Australia. I was pleased to support a vineyard that had earned its designation as an organic enterprise.

The next morning, I slept in until roused by the aroma of fresh coffee. After serving me a cup with the perfect amount of French vanilla coconut milk and agave syrup, Keoni sat down on the edge of the bed. He set his cup on the nightstand and reached over to gently rub my legs.

"You know there's going to be a fair amount of walking in our day, Natalie. Why don't we substitute a swim for our usual walk on the beach?"

I looked up and smiled at his thoughtfulness. Even when I do not complain, Keoni is very sensitive to my movement challenges. As I got up, I realized I was a bit stiff and that my aching joints may have disturbed his sleep the night before. After putting on an old swimsuit I use for non-social events in the surf or spa, I grabbed my old sun hat of braided banana leaves. As I locked the back door, I called out to Miss Una who was seated on the *lanai* table. Per her established routine, she escorted us through The Ladies yard to the edge of the path leading to the beach. Then, with a flick of her tail, she turned around for some playtime with the kittens.

By the time we were prepared for our trip into town, the winter sun was warm but not too hot. The drive up the Pali Highway was especially nice since there had been some rain and a couple of the upward-flowing waterfalls were visible. When we entered the metropolitan area, there was little wind and the temperature was warm enough that I was glad I had dressed as I had. I was also grateful that I had remembered to bring a fine-mist sunblock to re-apply if our day lengthened unexpectedly.

We were lucky to park near the yacht club, but my hip was already announcing it would have been happy to keep the day's exercise to our swim. Once we were seated at the edge of the *lanai*, I eagerly drank from a tall glass of iced tea with a stalk of pineapple core as a flavorful stir stick. John arrived within a few minutes and we all ordered shrimp po' boys with sweet potato waffle fries. When I commented on the benefits of the cut on the fries, John said, "Gee, aren't you little Miss Chef."

I laughed off his words but realized that if I continued to demonstrate my developing kitchen skills and analysis of food preparation, Keoni would soon figure out what I had been doing with my increasing hours away from home. Fortunately, we were all so hungry that there was little conversation for several minutes. As the food on John's plate diminished, I itched to launch my quest for a concise update on the three cases.

Beating me to the punch, Keoni inquired, "So what's up, JD? How are things going?"

"Well, I guess I've kept you waiting long enough. It looks like a lot of the puzzle pieces are falling into place. The biggest forensic news is that the CSIs have again confirmed the ID of Bàozhǐ. This time through his bone marrow. And, they've found a few specks of his blood near the bullet that was discovered on the third floor of the Shēn building."

Keoni and I nodded awareness that this clearly pinpointed the locale of the man's death.

"As to the grieving widow, Toitoi has a very interesting background. Also, her boyfriend is *not* connected to any great crime family, Yakuza or otherwise. Finally, the Maui Wowie Comacho cousins are strictly small-time hoods."

"Okay. That was the overview. How about those little details I love so much?" I asked.

"Where shall I begin?"

"Why don't you start by telling us about Toitoi's arrival on our shores?" I suggested.

"I can do better than that. To begin with we've confirmed that she's Ainu…they're a minority people from northern Japan. Bàozhǐ was translating testimony from former prison guards at the time Toitoi met him. She had some kind of menial job around the Allied Occupation troops stationed on Hokkaido—that's where most of the *Ainu* live today.

"During the war, she worked in an armaments factory. Since

it was virtually forced labor, there was no question of her being a war criminal. Once the couple decided to get married, there was nothing standing in their way except a lot of red tape. By the way, if it hadn't been for the war, her life would have been quite different. It looks like the Imperial Japanese Army did more than force her to help their war effort; they wrecked her plans to become a *geisha*.

"Evidently, she was an apprentice *geisha*, when the war on the Asian mainland was heating up. She was lucky she wasn't forced to become what they called a *comfort girl*, to keep the troops happy, if you know what I mean."

Keoni and I nodded our knowledge of the women forced into roles of indentured servitude as mistresses to members of the Japanese military, and even prostitution. Sometimes poor Japanese families sold their daughters into such lives. But beyond whatever money they received, or patriotic duty they thought they were performing, their families assumed the girls would be better off.

There were also Korean and Chinese women who were pressed into such service. Regardless of their origins, for many of these *comfort women*, shame, as well as financial considerations, prevented them from returning to their families after the war.

I grimaced. "I know that's all true, but it's hard to hear spoken aloud."

"The bottom line is that as the bride of an American serviceman, Toitoi's prospects improved greatly. And she was lucky that the Shēns, unlike many American families, greeted their war bride with hospitality. That's the backstory of Yamaguchi's dearly beloved.

"I have no idea of how or when those two met. His dad was a club owner and drug runner for a long time before Brian arrived on the scene. We're guessing Toitoi might have known his father first. With *that* man's connections for moving people and products between the islands, *he* might have been involved in moving Bàozhǐ's body to that wharf-side freezer. But unless our widow comes clean about everything, I don't think we'll ever know the finer details of her husband's murder."

"I wouldn't hold my breath on that happening, JD," responded Keoni, shaking his head.

"So, what's the professional profile of Brian Yamaguchi?" I asked.

"As I told you, he's into the entertainment scene in Lahaina. Nothing funny about his restaurants—although they can be a means for laundering a bit of cash or hiding a person. But the big question is that club he owns. More than a couple of women have disappeared from there. We also think he's a silent partner in some strip joints. Speaking of which, that's where the Camacho cousins come in. The older one has worked as assistant manager at Yamaguchi's restaurant, his nightclub, and a couple of those strip joints."

"To sum up Yamaguchi, he's a small fish when it comes to high crimes. His nefarious activities seem to be limited to pimping, minor drugs, and moving people—not necessarily to their liking. We looked into other members of his family since his old man was dirty. But there wasn't anything worth pursuing. Like many of Hawai`i's early Japanese immigrants, most of those with the surname Yamaguchi were plantation workers who came from the southern island of Kyushu. That doesn't mean they're all clean, but today's crime families aren't bound by ethnicity or locale of origins."

"What do you think would have provoked Yamaguchi to kill the cousins?" I wondered.

"I haven't a clue. All around, they're pretty far down the food chain. Their backyard Maui Wowie crop is too small to attract much attention. Maybe they were trying to move up to the next level. All we've found so far is that they're a couple of minions who didn't have the smarts to stay out of waters infested by sharks.

"Yamaguchi's yacht provides him with both means and opportunity—for moving bodies, as well as questionable products. And while I doubt that he would have planned to lose the dinghy that matches his yacht, it may have simply gotten away from him."

"Where's the boat now?" asked Keoni.

"She's down that pier on the right," replied John, gesturing ahead.

"Can we look at it?" I asked.

"Look all you want. In fact, there are a couple of good-looking boats you might want to check out, Keoni."

"Great. We're about through with lunch and it's fairly early. We might as well take a tour while we're here," Keoni happily replied.

"Maybe I'll join you," John responded. "Nothing like letting the bad guy watch the lasso tightening on him. Yes, Yamaguchi knows he's under a microscope, around the clock. Before coming to lunch, I checked in with my eyes on the yacht, and unless they've gone over the side, both Brian and Toitoi are on board. They saw all of us at the funeral; maybe our visible presence will prompt some unexpected action."

"You've got watchers on the pier, but have you had an opportunity to check things on the yacht?" asked Keoni.

"No probable cause to justify getting a warrant. As to going aboard without one—well, chain of evidence is always my biggest concern. I'm grateful for what I learned from those items you found in Bàozhǐ's desk. But, I doubt that we'll be able to use them in court. We're pretty sure Toitoi's the source of the fake clue—at least the one in English. But even if we can prove Toitoi can read Chinese, there's no way to prove if, or how she directly utilized those scrolls. As to anything that might materialize *now*, it's all got to be properly discovered, bagged, and tagged. Know what I mean?"

"So, you haven't been able to prove a connection between the dinghy and the yacht," I commented with disappointment.

"Not yet. But the CSI unit isn't through with it. So far, we've established that detail of unique dragon carvings indicate both crafts were manufactured by the Cheong Company. If they come up with anything, we should be able to get a search warrant. With that, I'm pretty sure we'll find something like a few fingerprints to link the cousins to Yamaguchi's boat as well as the dinghy. And that should lead to solving the Comacho case. But if

I can't tie Toitoi to anything, she could walk on the murders of the men in white."

"I can't bear the idea of her getting off without any consequence for what she's done. Even if she didn't pull the trigger on the guys in the dinghy, I know what I saw in my visions. Maybe the murder of her husband was triggered by passion. But the murder of Professor Zhāng was clearly premeditated."

"I'm sure you're right about that. From your vision, it's clear she lured him to an assignation. Whatever the bait, it ended up as an assassination."

"That's pretty poetic, for a non-writer," quipped Keoni.

We finished our meal and I dashed off to the ladies' room. Then, we began our stroll down the pier. Keoni had been talking about getting a small boat for recreation and fishing since before we moved into Auntie Carrie's cottage. As we made our way down the rows of varied crafts, John and he sounded like salesmen at a boatyard.

"So, what are you looking for, Keoni?" inquired John.

"I started thinking about boats seriously when you and I were working that diamond heist with the Coast Guard years ago. Just looking at their vessels reminded me of some fishing trips I took to Maui. When Natalie and I were prepping the cottage, I got a chance to study some of the boats around the neighborhood and at the Kailua Beach boat landing."

"Well, you've got a lot to sample in the slips in this yacht club. In addition to your million-dollar yachts, you've got day cruisers, boats built on a modified fishing trawler design—even the occasional outrigger canoe."

"What about a gently-used teak boat?" I asked, thinking of their classic beauty, as well as Yamaguchi's toy. "You know I'm always worried about safety. I wouldn't feel comfortable with you being out at sea on something relying on oars or wind alone."

"There's too much maintenance in the wooden boats, honey. That's why there aren't many being built today. As to your concern for my safety, I can assure you that's high on my list of priorities in everything. I wouldn't consider any vessel that doesn't have an engine."

"Does that mean you're considering a motorsailer?" queried John.

"Sails are a lot of work, but a motorsailer might be ideal," responded Keoni.

We walked a little farther. When John and Keoni spotted a man sitting on the deck of a sleek sail boat, we stopped. Within a few short minutes, I had learned more than I ever wanted to know about anything putting to sea. The worst part for me was looking toward the cabin. I could just imagine being seasick and locked into that small space for entirely too long. I stood on the pier patiently while Keoni and John enjoyed a full tour. When they rejoined me, I learned the boat was available for purchase—a bargain at just under one hundred thousand dollars.

We then passed larger boats with and without sails. I guessed the price tags of many were in excess of a million dollars. Next up for consideration of things nautical was a catamaran with a helicopter landing pad. Now that was something a retired cop really needed. Well, if his business grew into an international security conglomerate, it could prove useful. After a couple of jokes, we moved on to a smaller catamaran.

At that moment, John received a call and turned away. After a couple of grunted responses, he clicked off and turned to face us with a serious look. "You won't believe it. Toitoi and Yamaguchi are on the move. Our way. The big question is, do you two want to stay here, or move out of their way. As I've already said, I'm game to take them on. I'll leave it to you, since they already know me and are aware that they're under surveillance."

"Let's go for it. Whether we talk to them or not doesn't matter. We can play that by ear," I said with a rush of adrenalin spreading through my body...like Keoni must have felt every day he was a detective.

John, Keoni, and I stayed where we were, slightly to the right of the walkway. Within a few minutes, I spotted the couple heading toward us. Brian Yamaguchi looked like any Island man on a bright Hawaiian day at a yacht club: shorts, aloha shirt and deckers. Toitoi was wearing her signature red, displayed in a mid-calf length *pareau*, a straw sunhat, dark glasses, and spiked heels.

But while he carried himself with the same decorum he had at Bàozhǐ's funeral, she seemed to be unsteady. As they neared us, Yamaguchi paused and looked from me to Keoni, to John. Toitoi, who had been moving more slowly, suddenly caught the heel of her shoe and staggered into her boyfriend. As though they were merely companions for a day, he steadied her but then pivoted to move back toward his yacht.

Then the woman who had caused heartache for the people closest to her, came to a standstill. Her body trembled noticeably. With a shaking hand, she removed her sunglasses and stared toward us. She opened her mouth, but no sound was uttered. With all I had observed in these few moments, I wondered if she was drunk, on drugs, or had gone completely bonkers.

With a moan, she pointed and said, "You can't be here. Neither of you can be here."

As she continued to stare, John calmly asked, "Who can't be here, Toitoi?"

"Bàozhǐ. He stood at the foot of my bed with his suitcase. He whispered, *You want to find the treasure? You will soon see the man who can give you the secret to the treasure of Kuan Yin.* He was right. I did see him."

She swallowed deeply. "I knew who he was right away. He, he looked like Bàozhǐ, only shorter and older. He was right there in the Chinatown book shop where I had gone to learn what the riddle meant."

Her voice softened. "But he would not tell me. No one has been able to tell me the secret of the riddle. I have searched everywhere. I asked him why he was here. He told me about the scavenger hunt and when I offered to give him a tour of the island, he invited me to have a drink. I showed him the riddle and asked him to help me find her—Kuan Yin—he smiled at me like I was a child, and said she was not real. He said there was no treasure...just the faith you blow into the wind with the prayers you waste on her. "Such a foolish old man. Worse than my husband. I told him I would bring him proof that the statue of the goddess did exist. When I went to his hotel and showed him a letter from Bàozhǐ's father, he laughed again. But I showed him. I showed him that I was someone he could not laugh at. I showed him, just as I showed Bàozhǐ."

Suddenly, Toitoi opened the small red clutch bag in her hand and drew out the baby Browning that John suspected was the weapon used in both of the killings I had seen in my visions. We all froze. I watched John slowly look around while putting his hand under the back of his aloha shirt. I knew what he was doing...trying to determine whether he should actually pull out his gun and shoot the woman. He gave a slight shake of his head to Keoni, who had also moved his hand behind his back.

A flush of anger spread across her face. Nearly screeching she said, "And now *she* brings them here to taunt me."

"Who is taunting you? Who is here?" called out Keoni in a tense but even tone.

"Bàozhǐ and Fù Hán. They are just beyond the woman with the cat on her shoulder," she said pointing with the pistol. "But they can't be here. I killed them both," she said.

"There is no one here but retired detective Keoni Hewitt and his girlfriend. And they are my witnesses that you have just confessed to two counts of murder," declared John Dias.

She pointed to my left. "He kept me from the Shēn family treasure. It isn't fair," she said whining.

She paused.

"As the wife of the eldest son, it is my right," she shouted.

Continuing to rant, she waved her pistol in the air for emphasis. John had already drawn his gun, but just then Toitoi stumbled again, her weapon flying from her hand into the water.

She looked downward for a moment. Then, in an instant, her behavior changed. Shaking her head from side to side, she began speaking in a garbled mix of languages. But even as she was melting down mentally, she seemed to have regained her previous physical elegance. With steps sure and shoulders erect, she turned and walked back toward the *Moku laki milimili*. At the moment, the yacht did not seem to be bringing her much luck.

John pulled out his phone and called the officers we knew were positioned along the pier, as we followed her at a slow but steady pace. Without her weapon of choice, she was now relatively harmless—at least to the trained professionals who would soon have her restrained.

"What will happen to her, John?" I asked, as we watched her progress toward the yacht.

"Well, I've alerted my team to take *her* into custody on murder charges and get someone down here to retrieve her weapon. Once I get that to the lab, I'm hoping we'll have some solid evidence. Speaking of which, the reason we're going so slowly is that I want her to go aboard Yamaguchi's boat. That's all I need to obtain a search warrant—and that should produce enough evidence to hold them both without any question of putting up a bond and skipping off to parts unknown.

"As Keoni can tell you, Toitoi may be mad as a hatter, and still be found guilty of murder. Clearly it was not an isolated incident of passion that led her to kill her husband. The woman is a danger to anyone who might interfere with her delusions. Too bad the Professor happened to look like the black widow's previous victim. As to what she claims to have seen...I get the images of the two guys in white, but what was that about the cat?"

"I've no idea, John. You don't see a cat anywhere around here, do you?"

"No. But you've got one at home, Natalie, don't you?"

"Yes. And that's where we left her this morning, isn't that true, Keoni?"

Looking down at me with his gentle smile and sparkling blue eyes, Keoni responded. "That's right, JD. We left her right there...on top of Bàozhǐ's old desk."

CHAPTER 22

I have found that hollow, which even I had relied on for solid.
Henry David Thoreau [1817 - 1862]

Our lives were muddled for nearly a week, as Keoni and I answered rounds of questions about what we observed on the day of Toitoi's arrest. On the day after the incident, we were interviewed about her breakdown and rambling confession of murdering her husband Bàozhǐ Shēn and Professor Fù Hán Zhāng. Since I only had to respond to the specific questions I was asked, I was able avoid giving evidence referencing my visions, which would be inadmissible at trial.

Another area of inquiry focused on what had happened at Brian Yamaguchi's yacht. Some of the activity had been a bit of a blur, so I was glad there was CCTV footage at the pier to confirm the sequence of events—even if it did not provide dialogue or subtle details. When Toitoi arrived at the *Moku laki milimili*, Yamaguchi was being taken into custody by a uniformed officer. The sight of her beloved being handcuffed must have proven too much for her fragile state of mind, because she tackled the officer aggressively and they both fell into the water.

By the time John Dias arrived at the yacht, Yamaguchi was secured to a piling and Toitoi was being pulled back onto the pier. Clearly, the water had cooled Toitoi's mental state, because, at least outwardly, she resumed her normal aloof demeanor while being arrested.

After our second session of making statements to detectives we did not know, John caught up with us in the parking lot.

"With Toitoi's confession, we can pursue the evidence

you've been holding. So, I'd like to send a CSI team over for that desk in your living room—and those little items you found in that hidden compartment."

"That's fine, John," I said, agreeing to a time for the pickup. "Has anything else emerged of particular note?"

"Not really. There was nothing remarkable at the Shēn's real estate offices, here or on Maui. We're waiting for reports on Toitoi's Maui home, as well as her cars on both islands. However, there has been one major breakthrough. When we accessed her cell phone, we found she'd made numerous calls to your hotel during the scavenger hunt. Best of all, there's a picture of her clinking champagne glasses with the Professor at that yacht club you frequent. We may never know how the two ended up there, but that photo certainly ties her to him physically."

On a subsequent trip to headquarters, we provided information about the acquisition of Bàozhǐ's desk. To avoid revealing my visions as a basis for our sleuthing, I then let Keoni take the lead. He gave a precise description of the discovery of the scrolls and Bàozhǐ's letter to his father. Keoni smoothly said that not knowing the value of the articles, he had placed them in plastic bags out of habit and replaced them in the desk—never mind the days they spent in his safe.

During each visit, we learned more about the cases on John's desk. Most important was the comprehensive toxicology report on Fù Hán Zhāng. Although the man died from a bullet fired from Toitoi's gun, the professor had been poisoned with aconite extracted from the *aconitum* plant. This accounted for his struggle to breathe, the nervous touching of his lips, and his inability to walk normally that I envisioned when he left the hotel suite where he had rendezvoused with Toitoi.

"Because of his age, and the symptoms you reported, I requested more than a basic tox screen," said John. "Soli told me the guy's cardiac muscular tone wasn't great and if he'd ingested enough aconite, he probably would've died of a heart attack."

"How was it administered?" asked Keoni.

"Looks like his tropical punch included a tincture of alcohol and powdered raw aconite root. An appetizer of rice crackers with curried tofu spread masked the acrid taste.

"Where would she get the poison?" I wondered.

"That's no biggy. It's common enough. It's often called the *Queen of Poisons*. You probably know it as monkshood. The flowers vary in color, but it's that helmet looking thing on top of the flower that distinguishes it."

I nodded my awareness of the plant.

"Evidently our perp is quite familiar with the plant. It's commonly prescribed as a sedative and is used in many homeopathic medicines. Especially interesting is that aconite poison is used on the arrowheads of the Ainu people when they hunt brown bears. It's also popular in Japanese flower arranging. You know, *ikebana*.

"And guess what? Toitoi does gardening and flower arranging. The CSIs just happened to find a lot of purple and blue aconitum flowers in her yard in 'Ulupalakua. It's a perennial, readily available for a quick flower arrangement—or murder. When I asked her about the plants, she didn't even blink. Told me she needed them for compounding traditional *kampō* medicine.

"When I asked Soli about the immediate effects of ingesting the poison, he said it stimulates several types of nerve endings. It causes pupil dilation and a tingling sensation on the lips and in the mouth, plus restlessness, dizziness, sweating, and weakness in the limbs. I'd say that corresponds to your vision.

"Yamaguchi may have sidestepped prosecution in the past, but it appears *his* luck's run out. Forensic investigation aboard the *Moku laki milimili* indicates the boat's been used for transporting a variety of controlled substances. And, we've got a lot more to link him to the Comacho cousins than that photo I saw during my visit to Bō Shēn's suite. As expected, the CSIs found the same dragon carvings on Yamaguchi's yacht as on the dinghy in which their bodies were found. Also, smears of their blood were discovered on the side of the yacht leading downward to the level at which the dinghy would have been moored.

"The big surprise was finding prints of both of the Comacho cousins in Toitoi's office. This makes her the centerpiece of all four cases, but given her fractured state of mind, several issues may never be resolved."

After that meeting with John, I realized that acquiring forensic evidence for the murder of Bàozhǐ would rest on the CSIs analysis of the Shēn Building...or Toitoi's Maui home. There was, of course, her public confession to two of the murders. But identifying her motives could be a gap in prosecuting her. If she could not, or would not, answer questions herself, the detectives were hoping to find proof of her criminal intentions in records like her correspondence or a diary. If so, where had she hidden such evidence? Perhaps in a bank safe deposit box or home safe...Or, had she created another hideaway in her home?

None of us could see an obvious reason for Toitoi to have killed her husband. There was no sign of spousal or other abuse. In fact, he and his family had cared for her very well since her arrival in the Islands. One issue that may have come between them was the possibility that she could not bear children. But the only supporting evidence I had was the conversation I overheard in my vision—to which I could never refer in public. Perhaps they got into an argument if Bàozhǐ caught her saying or doing something that could be injurious to his family.

For me, a hidden treasure still seemed the likely basis for the woman's felonious actions. But proof of Toitoi's treasure hunting rested on her having seen the riddle in Bàozhǐ's desk. Did the English language email of the riddle found on Professor Zhāng's computer present sufficient evidence of this? Even if that were true, her ability to understand written English, let alone Chinese may have been minimal during the time her husband was alive. Of course, she might have overheard conversations between her husband and father-in-law. While I was debating the details of her language skills, I realized the subject might never arise in court proceedings.

Determining her motive for the killing of Fù Hán Zhāng was even more perplexing. And then there were the technical questions about the crime itself. The first question was the possible use of the hotel's business center computer to email the false scavenger hunt clue to him. Then there was the hotel suite to which he was lured. Had a key card been cloned? Perhaps Toitoi or Yamaguchi had an inside person at the hotel. It seemed unlikely that anyone would be foolish enough to confess their compliance in such a muddled murder.

How could a shooting occur in a hotel without anyone witnessing something? But aside from my visions, no one reported seeing or hearing anything that could be connected to the professor's murder. And then there was the fact that so far there was no biological evidence connecting Toitoi to the crime.

Fortunately, some issues were resolved at lunch with John a couple of days later.

"When we examined the desk and its contents, we found Toitoi's fingerprints in the hidden compartment," announced John happily. "There's no doubt she knew about the riddle alluding to something being concealed in the Shēn Building. Speaking of things hidden, we found several interesting items in her home, beginning with books on jade, Kuan Yin artifacts, and poisonous plants.

"Evidently our Miss Toitoi didn't want anyone to know about her special references. Those books were hidden behind others in her office. Most of the rest of her library consisted of National Geographic magazines, Reader's Digest condensed books, and manuals for learning English and Chinese—all normal reading material for an immigrant from Japan married to a Chinese American."

The following night, John rang to tell us Bō had called him that morning to announce a surprising find. When the Shēn Building's elevator was being serviced, a wall panel behind the motor was discovered. Within a shallow space, was a brown leather strapped suitcase. Recognizing that it might relate to his granduncle's murder, Bō had the workmen halt their efforts.

"I made a beeline downtown. I rushed the suitcase to the lab and stayed while the techs processed it. Guess what we found? Brown and white spectator shoes, a white linen suit and a brown and ivory aloha shirt. We also found Bàozhǐ's wallet, a Timex watch with smashed crystal and a leather shaving kit. By the way, it appears that he died right after six o'clock. I don't know whether that was at night or in the morning."

All of that tallied with my visions. I may not have noticed the watch, but it could have been covered by his jacket sleeve. No sign of a hat, but I was the only person who knew the deceased had a straw hat with him on the day of his murder. While I might continue to wonder about the brands of Bàozhǐ's shirt and suit, most of my questions about his wardrobe and suitcase were now answered.

"Originally, there could've been fingerprints on the shell casing we found in the lining of the suitcase, but after a couple of years they'd have eroded. However, we did find three fingerprints—right thumb, index and middle finger—on the straight-edged razor. Evidently the polished metal prevented their deterioration. And guess who they belonged to? Toitoi.

"Bàozhǐ could have worn a wedding ring, but Toitoi might have been so money hungry that she sold it. Inside the wallet we found a scrap of stiff paper that may have been a boarding pass for the S.S. President Cleveland. But although that could've confirmed he was booked for a cruise, we don't know if he visited the ship and then left for some reason. We've been trying to find the records of the ship's trans-Pacific crossing from California to Hawai`i, but many of the records for the President Lines have been destroyed through the years."

"It sounds like you've got enough evidence for a conviction," observed Keoni.

"What will happen to her?" I wondered.

"Let's look at the two murders. I'd bet Bàozhǐ was killed in the morning. It takes a pretty cool killer to commit the first murder and immediately work a holiday sale without a hint of what she'd done. As to the professor, using poison as well as a gun, it's like she killed him twice. Nevertheless, if she has a decent attorney, she could get a plea agreement. But, even with mitigating circumstances for her mental state, I doubt that she'll ever breathe open air again."

"And her boyfriend?" I continued.

"Well, that's another case. I assure you, we're thoroughly investigating Yamaguchi. He's a clever fellow. Who knows what all he's connected to. Given his past ability to steer free of cells—padded or otherwise—maybe he'll land some deal with the Feds."

*　*　*　*　*

The next afternoon I received an invitation to the Grand Re-Opening of the Shēn Building. As I thought about past visits to Chinatown, I realized most had been celebratory. Often, they centered on the purchase of a *lei* or two on Maunakea Street— for parties or graduations, or for friends or family arriving or departing from Oʻahu. For the forthcoming occasion, I debated getting *leis* for Bō and his fiancée, but rejected the idea because of the mixed emotions they must have about recent events.

It was good that there was no need to stop for *leis*, because we were caught in traffic and arrived late. As we approached the building, I looked with appreciation at the refurbished façade. The washed bricks, freshly painted trim and stone pediment with a brass placard displaying the name Shēn in both English and Chinese over the door certainly declared the staying power of the small but righteous family. Inside, we were greeted by a poster of Jūnlì Shēn and his wife, smiling at us from the day the original Shēn dry goods store opened.

I squeezed Keoni's hand and thought about our many adventures during the last several weeks. It was true that we did not solve the riddle of the hidden artifact. But knowing that the woman responsible for the deaths of at least two men had been called to justice was a good thing. I was sure the man who erected this building would be proud of his family's continuing legacy.

"What do you think Natalie?" queried Keoni, as he turned to admire the architectural design and work of the contractors.

I was enjoying our tour of the building but could not get the lines of riddle out of my mind. *In the new town of our forbearers lies a building with a triad of windows topped by church-like arches.* Well, that's where we are.

"I think it's lovely. Look, they've restored the elevator to its original patinaed bronze," I said enthusiastically.

"Mmhm. It looks great," Keoni agreed. "I'm glad Bō didn't replace it with one of those refrigerator-looking elevators."

Sweeping his arm in front of me, Keoni slid the gate back and beckoned me to enter. I turned a couple of times to examine the refurbished elevator car.

*Traversing all floors...*Hmm. That's one way to describe how an elevator functions.

"Boy, you seem as excited as a kid on a merry-go-round for the first time."

I laughed. "I guess you're right. I think Bō has made some excellent choices for modernizing the building, without dishonoring its past."

Standing at the back of cage, I saw that a few floor tiles had been replaced and the center medallion shone like the day it was installed.

"You know that that character is the Shēn surname?"

Keoni nodded and hit number two. With a slight shimmy, the elevator rose to the second floor where we began our tour of the remodel. This level offered a reception area and bullpen for the real estate agents who stood ready to greet us with brochures. After another short ride, we arrived on the third floor, where we found a wide entry hall and two executive offices. There were so few guests remaining that we felt obliged to accept cups of punch made from passion fruit, orange juice, and lemon-lime sparkling water.

Back at the hallway, we hit the bell to call the elevator. After a couple of moments we heard the motor start. In a few seconds, the elevator passed us and continued down to the first floor. At the sound of a rattling thud, Keoni said, "Thank God there's a staircase. I hope anyone who's in the elevator is all right."

I followed him down the stairs, where we found the gate open and several people laughing as they exited.

"I guess the mechanism needs a little more TLC," said Bō Shēn. He turned to Keoni and asked "Care to see how this baby works?"

Keoni looked at me. I shrugged and he turned to join Bō to run up the stairs to the top floor where I knew the elevator equipment was located.

A couple of minutes later, I got a call from Keoni.

"Are you game to see if it's fixed?" asked Keoni. "Not much can go wrong. It'll either start or it won't."

"I guess so," I said hesitantly. "At least it's an open cage. If it stalls again, at least I can call out for help."

I entered the car again, ready to hit the button to take me up to the fourth floor. *A hidden door that needs no lock.* Another trick door. The elevator car was indeed mostly a cage. I didn't see where there could be a hidden panel.

I turned to hit the button for the fourth floor. After a slight rumble, I began moving upward. Feeling tired, I leaned against the back of the cage. *In the hub of the wheel, resides the Song Lady who hears the cries of the world. Like the Sage, be guided by what you feel...magnify the small...so that without substance can enter.*

Wait a minute. I was leaning against something pretty solid. As the elevator continued to jerkily rise, there was another rattle and everything came to a rocking stop that shook me. I tried to stabilize my stance but bounced off of the back of the cage. Momentarily, I felt something give behind my back.

At that point, Keoni opened the gate and waved me forward.

"Wait," I called out. "Something's got a grip on me."

Coming to my side, Keoni looked down as he carefully pulled my shoulder forward. "Is your skin caught, or just your shawl?" he asked.

"I'm fine, but I hate to tear one of Aunt Carrie's shawls."

"Okay, Natalie. Just step out of your shawl and I'll try to rescue it."

I stepped forward carefully and found that an edge of the metal Chinese character on the back wall was pinching a small amount of my shawl. As Keoni worked to free the heirloom fabric, I turned to stare at the metal medallion that was a near clone of the one set in the floor.

"I just realized that the pattern of the double circle framing the Chinese character is a classic Greek keystone pattern."

"Mmhm."

"The metal art on the back wall is sort of 3-D. In fact, the inner circle and character resemble a door."

With an "uh-huh," the man who has become my life partner

gently draped the shawl over my shoulder and joined me in contemplating the metal presentation of the Chinese character for the name Shēn. Convinced that I had discovered something, I began playing with the rim of the inner circle. After a few moments of prying at both sides, I became frustrated and expelled a heavy sigh. All of a sudden, the entire circle suddenly popped forward. Held in place by hinges on each side, I saw that the medallion served as some kind of cover.

"Wow. That's a surprise. It seems that your exhaling a heavy breath triggered a locking mechanism," said Keoni. He then rocked the medallion in different directions until it lifted up. Astonished, we stared silently at a dusty rosewood box sitting on a small shelf. Keoni lifted the ten-inch box out carefully and handed it to me.

"What's up guys?" said John, approaching from the penthouse. "You made it to the fourth floor, but we've been waiting for you to come in and be social."

His voice then trailed off. "Oh, my goodness, as little Shirley Temple would say. I think you've found what no one else could for the last half century or so."

I nodded, but was too worried about dropping the box to say anything.

"Let's have Bō do the final unveiling," suggested Keoni.

Within a minute we were inside the penthouse. For once I was pleased to have been late to an event. Except for an attractive woman looking out a window, Bō and Leah were alone. They were seated closely together on the leather sofa, opening a bottle of champagne.

As we approached a unique coffee table in bronzed metal and glass, John introduced the woman at the window.

"Natalie, Keoni, this is my friend Lori Mitchum. I think she'll enjoy this unveiling even more than her work at the ME's Office."

"What is that?" questioned Bō, as we set the rosewood box in front of him.

"That, my friend, is what an alleged predator has been seeking for about six decades," said John.

"I just thought it was a myth," Bō replied, "The story that

one of my forebears hid something in the walls of this building. When we found those niches in the walls of the third and fourth floor, I guessed the family altar had been moved a couple of times during the remodeling for the hotel."

I shook my head and brought out some tissues from my purse. Passing them to him, I said, "Whatever's in that box has been hiding in a niche at the back of your elevator cab."

"To think that this box and the suitcase were so close together for all this time is amazing," mused Bō.

"Well, they've both been found, and once the legal dust has settled, they should be yours," said John with the authority of his position.

Bō seemed in a daze as he gently dusted the box. Then, with shaking hands, he lifted the lid. He paused and stared at a red silk bag resting on a wadded piece of the same red silk. Tilting the bag forward with his left hand, Bō used his right to carefully loosen the ribbon at the top. As its silken sheathing dropped, an exquisite piece of pure white Hetian jade art was revealed.

The intricately carved statue of Kuan Yin stood about nine inches tall, resplendent with sugar-like crystals on the edges. Although more recent images of the Bodhisattva wear large crowns and elaborate dresses, this Lady, who is said to hear the voice of those who suffer, wore a simple flowing gown with hood from which a delicate crown of gold and assorted gems peeked.

Set within intricate details of carving within carving, were other small jewels: perfectly matched pearls in her necklace; rubies in her cross, sapphires for the eyes of a parrot on her right shoulder, and lapis lazuli on the surface of a vase balanced on her left hand. For all the opulence, it was the soft kindness of her face and the simple gesture of blessing by her raised right hand that captured one's attention.

In the midst of our wonderment, Lori said, "Look, there's a card at the back of the box."

She reached down and then set a piece of paper browned with age on the table for everyone to examine. It was a letter from Chāng Shēn to his grandson Bō:

Dear Bō. With this letter in your hands, you have already proven that as the son of my son you have accepted responsibility for the care of our family treasure. This venerable Lady of the Southern Song was given in honor of the support our Jūnlì provided Wong Hiram, a man of both Hawai`i and China. When war rained upon Shànghăi in 1932, Wong Hiram arranged for this representation of the Bodhisattva Kuan Yin to leave China with his daughters Jade and Pearl, under the care of his trusted friend Lee Chu-Hua.

This statue is one of a triad of statues shaped from a single piece of pure white jade from the White River region. While the sugar-like crystals are not unknown in jade, the adornments of gold and embedded jewels reflect the rare jade art of the Shēn-Yue Kingdom.

I am sad that I cannot join in the rest of your earthly journey, but I know you will find the answers you seek in times of need. As you know, white jade promotes wealth, as well as health and longevity. This Lady Who Hears the Cries of the World smiles upon all with a gentle countenance. You can turn to her courageous spirit with challenges large and small. Her vase represents the sacred nature of water to nourish your health and wakefulness. Her filial attendant, the parrot, will guide you in preserving the virtue, wisdom, and fruitfulness of our family through the years of your life and beyond.

Finally, should you ever meet her, please express our family's gratitude to Wong Jade for the generosity of her father. He truly reflected the spirit of the hui *which aids our people in times of challenging transition.*

At the bottom of the text was the mark of a stamp in Chinese that I assumed was Chāng Shēn's name. We all paused for a moment of reflection. As poet Richard Trench once noted, the treasures of one generation are conveyed to those that follow. I squeezed Keoni's hand and thought of the warmth of the peoples of Hawai`i, regardless of their generation or ethnicity.

EPILOGUE

My day is done, and I am like a boat drawn on the beach,
listening to the dance-music of the tide in the evening.
Rabindranath Tagore [1861 - 1941]

As John Dias predicted, the case of the State of Hawai`i versus Toitoi Shēn was concluded quietly with a plea agreement. She would never again wear red silk or high heels, but having committed her crimes in the Fiftieth State, she would not suffer death by governmental decree. Unlike the men she so callously murdered, she would simply pass whatever years remained of her life behind doors, corridors, and rooms separated by steel bars and locks until she drew her last breath. It was not an end I would desire.

After we gave all of our statements, it took a while for life to settle again into a pattern of normalcy. Keoni began organizing his expanded business with the help of Samantha Turner, who is happy to augment her financial wellbeing in the employ of a neighbor. I was pleased to dive into researching my next article for *Windward O`ahu Journeys*. Fortunately, all of the kittens that Miriam's Ladies and I rescued had survived. As they went to their appointed homes, Miss Una may have missed group play times; however, she has quickly adjusted to having little `Ilima all to herself.

John Dias has returned to handling varied and unrelated murder cases. When he is not on the golf course in his free time, we enjoy forays into antique auctions with him and Lori Mitchum, who has accepted a position with the Honolulu Department of the Medical Examiner. Sprinkled in his continuing banter are pleas for me to avoid unusual dreams, let alone visions.

There have been long spans of time in my life when I have had no sepia-toned images within jarring visions. And then they suddenly return. Of course, their absence has never guaranteed that my inner movie screen is playing innocent fiction, rather than poignant messages from another plane.

* * * * *

Slipping again into that state of seeing that which lies somewhere between waking and sleeping, I find myself looking through an antique maritime telescope. By an unseen hand, the image of a mauve toned world map refocuses, and I join the scene, at least in spirit.

I stand before the doors of a wooden gate which opens inward. I recognize where I am: a residential compound in the Shànghǎi of 1932. In full color, I now view a courtyard swept clean of the flowers of a large blooming plum tree. I hear the laughter of children. Soon a small girl and toddler round the corner of a building and dash into the courtyard. The older child chants a song of play. I may not know the words, but I recognize the universal pleasure of children enjoying a day out of doors.

The tinkling of a bamboo wind chime calls my attention to the crutch of the plum tree's trunk. From there, the yellow eyes of a white and orange cat peer into mine. With the flick of its tail, the feline crouches down. It seems ready to leap at me. Instead it drops onto the top of a sedan wedding chair and then races down one of its long handles to sit calmly on the ground staring at me. At that moment, the sun moves from behind a cloud and I close my eyes to its brightness. When I open them again, I see the girls shout with glee and run around the side of the building after the cat who is fleeing from them.

I follow the children to the last building within the walls of the compound. Piled to the right of a closed door is a stack of crates and cases reaching up to an open window. Pulling a few of the smaller cases from the side, the oldest child fashions a stairway to the window. Motioning her younger companion to remain silent and still, the elder clambers up until she can hold onto the window ledge and peer inside.

As the child shifts her weight, the boxes below her feet move against the crates below. The resulting scraping sound brings an immediate response. The door opens and a tall bronzed man showing both Chinese and Hawaiian features comes outside. Quickly the frown on his face softens into a smile when he identifies the prowler. Scooping the girl into his arms, he swirls her in a two-step before setting her back on the ground. He scans the courtyard and looks directly toward me for a moment. I recognize him from a family photo in the dining room of Pearl Wong. It is her father Hiram Wong.

He picks up the toddler, takes the hand of the girl and the trio enters the building. Although the door is shut, it offers no resistance when I move through it. The young man guides his daughters into the depths of a large room with few windows. Speaking words I recognize as the Yue dialect of Chinese, he directs the girls' attention to an event that is clearly remarkable to him. As they stand quietly to the side, he pulls a couple of chairs out from the back wall. On top of each he sets a box to boost each child, so she can fully view the endeavors of an old man bent over a workbench that shows much wear.

With focused lights on either side of him, the artisan looks to his left. He stares intently at three statues representing the Bodhisattva Kuan Yin. Placed closely together, it is clear that the three are fashioned from a single piece of jue suet Hetian jade. The lines of each piece are accented with sugar-like crystals on the outer edges. Two of the women are standing; one is seated. Each of them wears a flowing gown and a hood which frames her kind face and bejeweled crown of gold. Upon each of their chests rests a necklace of perfectly matched pearls with a cross of deep red rubies.

At the center of the triad of demi-goddesses is one seated on an open lotus leaf embedded with emeralds. Surrounding this expression of full enlightenment is a garden featuring flowers of multi-colored gems resting on gold stems. Upon a family altar I know, she will one day offer sweet incense in the bowl she holds in her lap.

The figurines on each side of the seated beauty stand in classic upright poses. On the left is a Kuan Yin standing on a globe studded with multi-colored gems. Wrapping her lower body and the globe is a dragon with gold accents who represents the masculine life force. It is conjoined with a silver accented phoenix that represts the feminine energy.

The statuette on the far right stands barefoot on a single lotus leaf covered in emeralds with a parrot with sapphires encircling black piercing eyes sitting on her right shoulder. Her right hand is raised in a gesture of blessing; a narrow vase sheathed in lapis lazuli sits on her left hand.

There are many tools on the shelves above the man. Beside the ones shaped of fine wood, are others embodying the leather of oxen, as well as the skins of dried gourds. There are also cylinders to hold the dust of the rubies that grind away unwanted portions of jade in the artisan's design. Next to these lay spindles and wheels for polishing. None of these tools show use on this day, for these treasures were fashioned long ago.

The aged man before us is the latest of many who have cared for these Ladies Who Hear the Cries of the World. He cleans them one by one with the reverence an artist pays the work of the master who has preceded him. A small smile pulls his lips upward with the discovery of each enchanting detail. His focused eyes direct the delicate probing and twisting of the brushes and pointed sticks he uses to penetrate the crevices of each design element.

After carefully sweeping the workbench thoroughly, he polishes each Kuan Yin with a succession of cloths and sets her to his right. When he is satisfied that all three are ready for their journeys, he turns to his audience. The eyes of the men meet for a moment and then, with a nearly imperceptible nod, the younger gives his assent.

From a shelf below his knees, the artisan brings up three boxes of highly polished rosewood. Each has been fashioned to a dimension that is one inch larger than the statuette it will cradle for many decades. After dusting, the man sets the boxes to the right of the figurines. From a drawer he brings out three red silk pouches with gold thread cordage and drawstrings. From left to right, he *places each representation of the goddess in a bag, draws it closed and lays it on a silken scarf within the box created especially for her. The three boxes sit like small coffins beside one another and I ponder the journeys of the two figurines I have not seen previously.*

Everything before my eyes freezes for a moment and then fades to the sepia of an early photograph. I inhale as though I have been without air for a very long time and smile with the pleasure I feel for having shared in this unique moment.

NOTES AND ACKNOWLEDGMENTS

In this third book of the continuing Natalie Seachrist series, I have drawn again on my years as a long-term resident of Hawai`i. As other authors have observed about their work, my characters have grown larger than the original conception. Wherever possible, I have presented factual information about the historical individuals and incidents described.

A Japanese submarine [a 78.5 foot-long two-man vessel named *A-19*] was captured at Waimānalo Beach on the island of O`ahu following the December 7, 1941, attack on Pearl Harbor. Ensign Kazuo Sakamaki of the Imperial Japanese Navy, became the first American prisoner of war in World War II, when he failed to detonate explosives he had rigged to sink his disabled craft. After losing consciousness, he washed up on the beach, where he was discovered by David Akui, a Hawaiian soldier. When his request to be allowed to commit suicide was denied, Sakamaki was denounced by Japan and spent the war in a succession of prisoner of war camps on the mainland of the United States.

By the time Sakamaki was repatriated to Japan, he had become an ardent pacifist. In 1949, he published a memoir titled *Four Years as a Prisoner-of-War, No. 1.* Successful in business, he seldom spoke about the war until 1991, when he was tearfully reunited with his submarine during a historical conference in the United States. The submarine had been captured intact and used as a promotional tool for selling war bonds throughout the war.

The SS President Cleveland was a trans-Pacific passenger ship owned and operated by the American President Lines. She and her sister ship, the SS President Wilson, sailed from California to Hawai`i and Asia from 1947 to 1973. The typical route of

279

these ships was from San Francisco to Los Angeles, across the Pacific Ocean to Honolulu and then on to Manila, Hong Kong, Shànghăi and Yokohama. The food items I have referenced were listed on the dinner menu for Sunday December 6, 1953, when the ship was *en route* to Honolulu.

Except for the insertion of a fictional couple, the details I have provided regarding Pan Am Flight 830 are accurate. On August 11, 1982, it departed from the Narita International Airport [serving the greater Tokyo area] with 270 passengers and 15 crew members aboard. Flying at an altitude of 36,000 feet, the Boeing 747-121 was approximately 225 kilometers northwest of Hawai'i when a bomb exploded. It had been placed under a seat cushion by a Jordanian Palestinian terrorist with ties to the 15 May Organization. As a direct result, Toru Ozawa, a Japanese teenager, died and sixteen other people, including the youth's parents were injured. I have amended my telling of this tragic story to account for the death of the parents of one of my characters.

It is largely due to the superb skills of the Captain, James E. O'Halloran III, and his crew that the plane was able to remain aloft long enough to reach Hawai'i. Later that year, Captain O'Halloran received a commendation for safely landing the plane in Honolulu. The plane was subsequently repaired and put back into service. In 1996, it was used as a prop in the film ***Executive Decision***.

Mohammed Rashed, who was responsible for placing the bomb aboard the plane, was eventually arrested and tried for murder. Due to a plea arrangement to secure information to aid anti-terrorist efforts, the man was released from prison in 2013, after serving about twenty-five years. The alleged instigator of this and other crimes, Husayn Muhammed al-Umari [also known as Abu Ibrahim], is one of the FBI's most wanted criminals. A reward of up to five million dollars for his capture is being offered by the U.S. State Department.

Although I have included a brief summary of aspects of the Hawaiian language, I have not attempted to draft one for Chinese, which has over 290 dialects. Because the Mandarin dialect is the official language of the People's Republic of China, the phonetic transcription system I have used for most Chinese words is Hanyu Pinyin Romanization. Occasionally, I have used Wade-Giles transliteration (dating to the mid- and late-nineteenth century) because of its familiarity to English speakers. This vocabulary includes words like *cheongsam*, the name Chiang Kai Shek, and the philosophical classic book the *Tao Te Ching* [rather than the *Dàodéjīng*] which are easily found in Internet search engines.

Where appropriate, I have used diacritical marks to indicate the tones in Chinese names, as the meaning of the name varies with the marks used. When no mark is used, the name may not vary in meaning, and/or the family with the surname may not know its origins. Today, many Chinese do not use diacritical marks at all, but I have included them to aid in the pronunciation of names for readers who know their significance. Again, note that speakers of the many dialects of Chinese will enunciate differently.

I should mention that Chinese (like Japanese and other Asian languages) places the surname (family name) before a person's given name. With the exception of Hungarian, this is the opposite of most European languages. As the Natalie Seachrist Hawaiian mystery series is written primarily for an English-speaking audience, most often I have followed the norms of English and placed the given names of characters prior to their surnames.

Many people have assisted with verifying information included in this work, as well as refining the storyline and text. Vital input in multiple areas of expertise has been provided by my editor, Viki Gillespie, bookworm and bookman. I also wish to acknowledge the late geologist Kevin C. Horstman, PhD, who guided many of my references to aspects of geological issues... especially jade in this book. I am grateful also for the specialized knowledge of unique reference holdings provided by Gina Vergara-Bautista, formerly an archivist at the Hawai'i State Archives.

For his continuing weekly commitment to listening to my oral reading of the manuscript, I wish to thank Tim Littlejohn, a State of Hawai'i library manager. Tim's input has been invaluable in encouraging my attention to cultural sensitivity and the harmonizing of myriad elements within my storylines. As always, I am pleased to acknowledge the support of authors by library staffs, including librarian Rona Rosenberg and library associate Sue Johnson of the Kirk-Bear Canyon branch of Pima County Library.

Fellow writers in a weekly literary salon have offered unending support and inspiration for several years. Bill Black, a writer of poetry and prose, has contributed vital input in several technical areas. Psychologist and mystery writer Dr. Kay Lesh has contributed keen observations of human nature. The perspectives of other participants have included: memoirist Margherita Gale Harris, MPH; the Reverend Patricia Noble, who was a resolute author, lecturer and philosopher; and the late Larry Sakin, a political writer and green energy entrepreneur.

Other early readers included Cotton Burlingame, clean energy consultant, and Nelda Garza, retired businesswoman.

Finally, I thank my husband John Burrows-Johnson for his patience and continuing support.

All errors, of course, remain my responsibility and I regret any you may uncover. Please contact me about any egregious flaws, as I would dislike repeating them. Also, I appreciate hearing your suggestions regarding historical or cultural themes that might be appropriate to this series.

You may contact me at JeanneBurrowsJohnson@gmail.com.

For sample Island recipes and information about other writing projects, I invite you to visit my author website: JeanneBurrows-Johnson.com.

.

A BRIEF OVERVIEW OF THE HAWAIIAN LANGUAGE

The Hawaiian language was unwritten until 1826, when Christian missionaries transcribed the sounds of the language into a thirteen-letter alphabet. Hawaiian consonants are pronounced as in standard American English. They include **H**, **K**, **L**, **M**, **N**, **P**, **W**, and the `okina [ `]. Often, the "W" is pronounced like an English "V." As there is no "S" in the Hawaiian language, plurals are determined by the preceding article. Each vowel is sounded in Hawaiian; they are similar in pronunciation to those in Spanish, and other Latin-based European languages:

A = *Ah*, as in above
E = *Eh*, as in let
I = *Ee*, as in eel
O = *Oh*, as in open
U = *Oo*, as in soon

Diphthongs are expressed as common English sounds. The "au" transliteration is pronounced as "ow" in "How." Diacritical marks indicate emphasis and syllable separation. A *kahakō* [-] placed over vowels, indicates a need to hold the vowel sound slightly longer, as seen in the "a" in the word "card." The `*okina*, [ `] is both a consonant and a diacritical mark; it indicates that the preceding vowel should be pronounced more loudly.

Please note, that in accordance with standard practices, foreign words included in this work are subject to the grammatical rules of English, including pluralization and possessives.

GLOSSARY OF NON-ENGLISH & SPECIALIZED VOCABULARY

The definitions within this glossary reflect the meanings used within the text of this book. Please note that many Hawaiian words have multiple spellings and (with or without diacritical marks) may have multiple meanings. Also, be aware that Hawaiian words, especially names, have ambiguous, layered, and sometimes hidden meanings. Use of the single word *Chinese* indicates the term is generally recognized in English as originating in China, sometimes being expressed with the same diacritical marks in both Hanyu Pinyin and Wade-Giles transliterations.

A

Adobo *Dressing, sauce.* [Spanish] A Filipino process of cooking, featuring protein or vegetables marinated in a vinegar-and-garlic based sauce, browned in oil, simmered in the marinade. The dish is often served with steamed white rice.

`Ahí *Tuna;* often yellow fin tuna. [Hawaiian] [Scientific name, *Hunnus albacares*]

Ainu Also Ainyu. *Human.* [Japanese] An indigenous people of northern Japan and eastern Russia. Today they inhabit the northern Japanese island of Hokkaido and formerly the northeastern Honshu. They also populate the Kamchatka Peninsula and the Sakhalin and Kuril Islands controlled by Russia since World War II.

Alahe`e [Hawaiian] Native Hawaiian shrub and tree that can grow to 20 to 30 feet in height. It features green glossy leaves and clusters of small, white, fragrant flowers. [*Psydrax odorata*]

Ala Wai *Freshwater way.* [Hawaiian] A boulevard, parkway, and canal in Honolulu. Built in 1928, the canal helped to drain the rice paddies and swamps of the emerging resort area of Waikīkī. It is crossed by two bridges before emptying into the Pacific Ocean.

Aloha   *Love, affection, compassion, loved one.* [Hawaiian] Traditional term for greeting and farewell, expressing love, friendship and mercy.

B

Basso   *Short, low.* [From Italian *bassus*] A deep, heavy, bass voice.

Boat Day   Between the 1920s and the late 1940s [except during World War II], the arrival of ocean liners at Aloha Tower was a major celebratory event in Honolulu. Luxury ocean liners were a major factor in the local economy. Passengers were greeted with **leis** and performances by **hula** dancers and the Royal Hawaiian Band. Boys and young men often dove into the waters of the harbor for coins thrown overboard by the tourists.

Bonhomie   *Good natured man.* [French] Buoyantly cheerful; good hearted.

C—D

Cheongsam   Also *Qípáo.* [Hanyu Pinyin Chinese transliteration] Tight-fitting Chinese dress with a slit skirt and mandarin collar. Originated in the Qing Dynasty [1644–1911]. A modern version emerged in Shànghǎi in the 1920s.

Cloisonné   *Partitioned; enclosed.* [French] Artistic work featuring enamel, glass, and/or gemstones within cellular frameworks of flattened gold, silver, brass, copper or other metal wire that has been soldered or welded.

Connoisseur   One who is an authority on issues of taste.

Coulis   *Strained liquid.* [French] A thick sauce made from puréed ingredients, usually of vegetables or fruit, often used as a base for other sauces.

Didión   *Desire, longing.* [from the Latin word *desider-*

atum] A diminutive form of the French name Didier.

Dim sum
Also *Diǎnxīn. Touch the heart.* [Hanyu Pinyin Chinese transliteration] Pastry, light refreshment, bite-sized foods. Often dumplings filled with vegetables, meat or seafood that is usually steamed or fried. Originating in **Guǎngdōng** province tea houses, it was traditionally served like appetizers, as a snack or before a larger meal; now served as a complete meal, especially as a brunch.

E

E komo mai
Welcome; enter and be refreshed. [Hawaiian] A traditional greeting.

En masse
In one group or body. [French]

En route
On the route. [French] Along the way, during a journey.

En suite
Immediately attached. [French]

Entrée
[French] A course preceding or between main courses. In the United States it is the main course of a meal.

G

Geisha
[Japanese] Artist or performing artist. Traditional female entertainer accomplished in dance, musical performance and poetry. Despite cultural misunderstandings, a **geisha** is a cultural icon, not a prostitute.

Gourmand
[French] One who enjoys good food excessively.

Gourmet
[French] A connoisseur of good food and wine, whose degree of knowledge often matches their refined palette.

Guǎngdōng
Expanse East. [Hanyu Pinyin Chinese transliteration] A province of the People's Republic of China [PRC] located on the South China Sea coast. Once known as *Canton* or *Kwangtung* in English.

H

Ha`ikū	*To speak abruptly; a sharp break.* [Hawaiian] A land section in **Kāne`ohe** containing a popular garden by that name.
Hale	*House.* [Hawaiian]
Hale`iwa	*House of the frigate bird.* [Hawaiian] Surfing beach and town on the north shore of **O`ahu.**
Haole	*Foreigner, of foreign origin.* [Hawaiian] Current usage, an *American, Englishman, and/or Caucasian.*
Hapa	*Part, mixed, portion, fragment, fraction, percentage.* [Hawaiian] A term frequently used to indicate someone of mixed heritage.
Haupia	[Hawaiian] Pudding made from the milk of the coconut palm.
Hawai`i	Fiftieth state of the United States of America. The name of the largest Hawaiian island. Between 1893 and 1894, the Kingdom of Hawai`i was established by **Kamehameha** the Great. The Kingdom was overthrown between 1893 and 1894, after which it was replaced by the short-lived Republic of Hawai`i. Established in 1898, the Territory of Hawai`i became a state in 1959.
Heiau	*Temple.* [Hawaiian]
Honolulu	*Protected Bay.* [Hawaiian] Located on the island of **O`ahu**, it is the largest city in and capital of the state of **Hawai`i**.
Hors d'oeuvres	*Outside of work.* [French] Originally referring to food partaken after working hours, it now refers to appetizers often served before meal, usually with wine or cocktails.
Huay	Also known as *kongsi* [Wade-Giles Chinese transliteration] and *gōngsī* [Hanyu Pinyin Chinese transliteration]. Social and economic support groups comprised of members from the same district, clan and/or language group. See also **hui**.
Hui	*Club, association or society.* [Hawaiian] Similar

Hula	lo Chinese **huay**. Traditional dance of **Hawai`i**.

I—J

Ikebana	*Living flowers.* [Japanese] The disciplined Japanese art of flower arranging noted for minimalistic design that features a scalene triangle [three unequal sides] and utilizes many plant parts.
`Ilima	See **Pua `Ilima**
Imu	[Hawaiian] Underground oven.
In situ	*In position.* [Latin]
Joss Stick	*Xiāng.* [Hanyu Pinyin Chinese transliteration]. A type of incense used in Asian temples.

K

Kahakō	*Macron.* [Hawaiian] A diacritical mark [a dash] placed over a vowel to extend pronunciation of the vowel's sound.
Kailua	*Two seas.* [Hawaiian] Bay, beach and town on the northeast end of the windward side of the island of **O`ahu**.
Kaimukī	*The oven of the kī.* [Hawaiian] A neighborhood in east **Honolulu**.
Kalāheo	*The proud day.* [Hawaiian] Name of land sections and features on the islands of Kauai and O`ahu. Windward O`ahu housing subdivision, school, avenue, and playground.
Kalaniana`ole	*The royal chief without measure.* [Hawaiian] Highway and beach park on east O`ahu, named for Hawaiian Prince Jonah Kūhiō Kalaniana`ole.
Kalbi	Also *galbi. Rib.* [Korean]. Grilled ribs of pork or beef marinated in a sauce of soy, garlic and sugar.
Kalo	*Taro* plant. [Hawaiian] A staple of the traditional Hawaiian diet used to make **poi**. [*Colocasia esculenta*]
Kālua	From *kā* [indicating a process] and lua [*pit*]. [Hawaiian] To bake in an **imu**.

**Kama`aina**  *Native-born.* [Hawaiian] Designation extended to non-Hawaiians who are long-time residents of Hawai`i.

Kamehameha *Hushed silence.* [Hawaiian] Dynasty of Hawaiian Kings, founded by King Kamehameha the First [1758-1819] of the island of Hawai`i who fully unified the kingdom by 1810.

Kampō *Method from the Han dynasty.* A Japanese practice of medicine [*Kanpō igaku*] based on traditional Chinese herbal medicine which is integrated into the modern Japanese national health system.

Kāne`ohe**  *Man of Bamboo.* [Hawaiian] Town in Windward **O`ahu, west of **Kailua**.

Kapa *Tapa.* [Hawaiian] Cloth made from the bark of **māmaki** or **wauke**.

Kaupō A native banana. [Hawaiian] Old fishing village in Windward O`ahu. Also, an old village in east Maui.

Kawai Nui *The big water.* [Hawaiian] Refers to a swamp, marsh, fishpond or canal. A large marsh and multi-part stream in Windward **O`ahu** that was once the island's largest inland pond.

Keiki *Child, offspring.* [Hawaiian]

Keoni Diminutive form of "John." [Hawaiian]

Ki *Ti plant.* [Hawaiian] [*Cordyline terminalis*] **Koa** Acacia tree [Hawaiian] An endangered species known for its fine grained wood. [*Acacia koa*]

Ko`olau**  *Windward.* [Hawaiian] One of two volcanic mountain ranges dividing the island of **O`ahu.

Kuahonu Also *Kūhonu.* [Hawaiian] One of three types of *crabs* found in Hawaiian waters. This variety is found on the muddy or sandy seafloors of the hotter areas of the Indian and Pacific oceans.

Kuan Yin Guānyīn [Hanyu Pinyin Chinese transliteration], also *Avalokiteśvara* [Sanskrit]. Originally Guan Shi Yin, a male *bodhisattva* [demi-god] in Indian Buddhism that was introduced to China via the Silk Road by Buddhist priests during the

Tang Dynasty [618-907 CE]. The deity was associated with feminine characteristics [**yin**] of compassion and kindness and by the time of the Song Dynasty [960 –1279] had become fully integrated into Chinese culture as *Kuan Shih Yin*, the female demi-god of mercy who hears all of humankind's sufferings. She is revered by both Buddhists and Taoists across Asia, especially women.

Kūlia *Stand upright or strive; lucky.* [Hawaiian]

L

Lānai *Porch, balcony.* [Hawaiian]

Lanikai [Hawaiian] Community on the southern edge of **Kailua** in Windward **O`ahu.**

Lau hala *Leaf of the hala tree.* [Hawaiian] Leaves of the screw pine tree are often used for weaving mats and baskets. [*Pandanus tectorius*].

Lau lau From *lau* for *leaf, frond* or *greens.* [Hawaiian] Packages of ti or banana leaves used to wrap pork, salted fish, and taro tops for baking in an ***imu.***

Lao-tsu Also Laozi. See **Tao Te Ching**.

Lehua Flower of the `Ōhi`a tree. [Hawaiian] The red variety is the official flower of the island of **Hawai`i.** [*Metrosideros polymorpha*]

Lei *Garland.* [Hawaiian] Usually made of flowers, leaves, shells, candy, or other decorations.

Liliko`i *Passion fruit.* [Hawaiian] [*Passiflora edulis*]

**Lili`uokalani,
Queen** *Scorching pain of the royal chiefess.* [Hawaiian] Last reigning monarch of the Hawaiian Kingdom; composer of many poems and lyrics, including the song ***Aloha `Oe*** [1838-1917].

Loke lani Common *red rose.* [Hawaiian] Now the official flower of the island of **Maui.**

Lū`au ***Kalo*** *[taro] tops.* [Hawaiian] Modern name for an Hawaiian feast.

M

Mahalo *Thank you.* [Hawaiian] Often printed on public garbage cans to encourage respect for keeping the environment clean.

Mahimahi *Dolphin.* [Hawaiian] Warm water game fish. [*Coryphaena hippurus*]

Maikoiko *Dance child.* [Japanese] Apprentice geisha.

Maile [Hawaiian] Flowering tree shrub in the dogbane family. Its fragrant leaves are used for making a long, open **lei**. [*Lyxia oliviformis*]

Makai *Toward the ocean; ocean side.* [Hawaiian]

Makiki *To peck.* [Hawaiian] Type of volcanic stone used as a fishing weight or adze. Neighborhood northeast of downtown **Honolulu**.

Makoa *Fearless, courageous, aggressive.* [Hawaiian]

Malia *Mary.* [Hawaiian]

Māmaki *Flowering nettle plant.* [Hawaiian] [*Pipturus albidus*]

Maneki Neko *Beckoning cat.* [Japanese] Called *zhāocái māo* in Chinese. These popular figurines are symbols of good luck, welcoming patrons to Asian restaurants and shops with a paw raised in welcome.

Mānoa *Thick, solid, vast, deep.* [Hawaiian] Valley and neighborhood that is northeast of downtown **Honolulu**. Location of the main campus of the University of **Hawai`i**.

Maui [Hawaiian] Second largest Hawaiian Island, named for the demi-god Māui.

Mauka *Inland, toward the mountain.* [Hawaiian]

Maunawili *Twisted mountain.* [Hawaiian] A stream, valley and ranch in **Kailua**.

Menehune [Hawaiian] A race of people (mythological or actual) said to have settled in Hawai`i prior to the Polynesians. Noted for their small stature and craftsmanship. Fishponds, temples and roadways across the Islands are credited to them.

Mokulua *Two adjacent islets.* [Hawaiian] Here referring to those off the **Lanikai** shoreline on the island of **O`ahu**.

Mu`umu`u   *Cut short, maimed, amputated.* [Hawaiian] Dress adapted from garb of nineteenth-century Protestant Christian missionary women, often featuring short sleeves and no yoke.

N

Niçoise   *In the style of Nice, France.* [French] Dressed with vinaigrette, this variety of salad includes mixed green lettuce, tomatoes and green beans, topped with anchovies and sometimes tuna.

Noir[e]   *Dark, black, gloomy, evil, a black person.* [French] A genre of novels and film in which the subject is usually crime and the protagonist displays self-destructive behavior. This genre is noted for amorality, ambiguity, cynicism, and dark undertones.

Nu`uanu   *Cool heights.* [Hawaiian] Valley, stream and neighborhood north of downtown **Honolulu**.

O

O`ahu   *The Gathering place.* [Hawaiian] The third largest Hawaiian island; location of **Honolulu**, the state capital.

`Ōhi`a   [Hawaiian] The red *`ōhi`a* is the official flower of the island of **Hawai`i**. Two varieties of trees, including evergreen myrtle that produces the *lehua* flower. [*Metrosideros polymorpha*]

**`Okina**   *Glottal stop.* [Hawaiian] A diacritical mark [`] used to indicate a break in sounding consonantal sounds, as that separating an interjection's syllables, like "oh-oh."

Olomana   *Forked hill.* [Hawaiian] A stream, peak and ridge in Windward O`ahu. The ridge is comprised of Mount Olomana and two lesser peaks: Pāku'i [*swift runner*] and Ahiki [named for an area overseer].

`Ōpakapaka   *Pink snapper.* [Hawaiian] [*Pristipomoides filamentosus*]

P

Paella
[Spanish; possibly coming from the Arabic word baqiyah, *left-overs*] Dish of rice, proteins and vegetables traditionally believed to originate in Valencia. Agricultural Laborers with limited resources often used snails as the featured protein. Through time variations developed, such as the mixed seafood varieties popular on the seacoasts of Spain and Portugal and points of emigration like **Hawai`i**.

Pali
Cliff or craggy hill. [Hawaiian]

Pāreau
Wrap around skirt. [Tahitian] Originally the term referred only to skirts worn by women. Today it is used more generally, meaning a piece of fabric wrapped around the body of any person.

Plate Lunch
Popular Island meal with an Asian style protein often served on a bed of shredded cabbage. Accompanied by two scoops of white steamed rice and one scoop of macaroni salad, and sometimes pickled vegetables.

Plumeria
Flowering and fragrant tropical tree including the frangipani, a genus of flowering tree in the dogbane family. [*Plumeria*]

Poi
Thinned paste made from pounded **kalo** [taro] root. [Hawaiian] It is the staple food of the traditional Hawaiian diet. [*Colocasia esculenta*]

Porte cochère
Door for Coaches. [French]. A roofed driveway at a building's entrance, intended to shield vehicular passengers from the weather.

Pouilly-Fuisse
A dry white wine from the Mâconnais sub-region of Burgundy, France.

Pua `ilima
Flower or blossom. [Hawaiian] The official flower of the island of O`ahu. A species of the hibiscus family native to some Pacific islands. The herbaceous shrub has blossoms with five petals, usually in colors ranging from yellow to orange. It grows upright or horizontally in sandy soil near the ocean. [*Sida fallax*]

Pūne`e
Sofa, couch, pew. [Hawaiian]

Pūpū	*Marine* or *land shell; circular motif; appetizer.* [Hawaiian]

S

Sashimi	*Pierced body.* [Japanese] Thinly sliced raw saltwater fish, served with varied garnishes and sauces.
Shànghǎi	City at the mouth of the Yangtze River in the center of the coast of the PRC. Having the largest population of any city in China, or the world, it is classified as a province.
Staccato	*Disjointed, clipped.* [From the Italian *staccare*, to detach]. Words or music presented in short, sharp bursts.
Status quo	*Existing state of affairs.* [Latin] Usually referring to social or political affairs.
Sucrosic	Sugar like.
Sushi	*Sour tasting.* [Japanese] Cylindrical dish made from hand-rolling-sheets of *nori* [edible seaweed] or sometimes a thin omellete, soy paper, cucumber, or perilla leaves, layered with rice that has been cooked with vinegar and a filling. *Kappa makisushi* is named for a Japanese monster that eats cucumber.

T

Taijitu	Also *Tai Chi. Great pole, highest point* or *goal.* [Chinese] Symbol for duality within the universal, indivisible wholeness. Meeting of *yin* and *yang*, dark and light, female and male, moon and sun.
Tángzhuāng	*Suit.* [Hanyu Pinyin Chinese transliteration] This distinctive Chinese jacket was adapted from a Manchu Dynasty article of clothing [the *magua*]. Now worn by women as well as men, it features a mandarin collar and open front with knotted buttons.
Tao Te Ching	Also *Dàodéjīng* [Hanyu Pinyin Chinese transliteration]. A book on Chinese philosophy. While

an early copy dating to the fourth century BCE has been discovered, its date and authorship by "The Old Master" continue to be debated. It is generally credited to Lao-Tzu [Lǎozǐ, Hanyu Pinyin], a legendary philosopher and poet believed to have been an official within the Zhou [Zhōu cháo, Hanyu Pinyin Chinese transliteration] Dynasty [1046-256 BCE].

Teriyaki *Teri, glaze* plus *yaki, to broil*. [Japanese] Cooking process featuring a soy-based marinade usually used for meat prior to broiling.

Touri [Hawaiian] Island slang term for tourist.

Tūtū *Grandfather or grandmother; aunt or uncle*. [Hawaiian] The term is used often as a title of respect for an older unrelated person.

U—V

`Ulupalakua *Breadfruit opening on back of carriers*. [Hawaiian] A community in the land section of Kula on the Leeward slopes of Mount **Haleakalā** on the island of Maui. Noted for a ranch and winery as well as other agricultural products such as sweet onions and strawberries.

Una *Tortoise shell*. [Hawaiian]

Voilà *There it is; there you are*. [French]. Contraction of the phrase *vois là, see there*.

W

Waikīkī *Spouting water*. [Hawaiian] The name of a chiefess; a famous beach on the island of O`ahu.

Waimānalo *Potable water*. [Hawaiian] Land division, bay, beach and other features on the island of O`ahu. **Waimea** *Reddish water*. [Hawaiian] Land divisions on the islands of Kauai and Hawai`i.

Waipahu *Bursting water*. [Hawaiian] Land division in central **O`ahu**. **Wauke** *Paper mulberry tree*. [Hawaiian] [*Broussonetia papyrifera*].

Wǔ lóng *Dragon dance*. [Hanyu Pinyin Chinese transliteration]

Y

Yakuza *Eight, nine and three*, in reference to a game of chance. [Japanese] Trans-national organized crime syndicates originating in Japan.

Yang *Masculine force in nature* [Chinese], expressed in sun, light white, gold, and strength. Chinese surname; clan and dynasty.

Yin *Feminine aspect of nature*, [Chinese] expressed in *moon, darkness* black, silver, and passivity. A Chinese surname and dynasty.

Questions for Book Club Discussion

1. How did the Prologue encourage you to read further?

2. Did you feel you were experiencing the settings within the story?

3. What aspects of life in Hawai`i did you find interesting and/or appealing?

4. Were all of your five senses (sight, hearing, smell, taste, and touch) stirred by this book?

5. Which of the places mentioned would you like to visit?

6. Did the characters seem believable to you? Did they remind you of anyone in your life...or in television or film?

7. Which characters are you looking forward to meeting in future books in the series?

8. Did anything in the plotline surprise you?

9. What historical event or aspect of Island culture would you like to explore further?

10. What did you learn from the Glossary of Non-English and Specialized Terms?

11. How well did this book relate aspects of history and multi-culturalism?

12. Was the book's cover appropriate to the story?